T0368773

THE NEW ROAD

L.J. HIPPLER

iUNIVERSE, INC.
NEW YORK BLOOMINGTON

The New Road

iUniverse books may be ordered through booksellers or by contacting:

iUniverse
1663 Liberty Drive
Bloomington, IN 47403
www.iuniverse.com
1-800-Authors (1-800-288-4677)

ISBN: 978-1-4502-3957-8 (sc)
ISBN: 978-1-4502-3955-4 (dj)
ISBN: 978-1-4502-3954-7 (ebk)

Library of Congress Control Number: 2010908933

Printed in the United States of America

iUniverse rev. date: 7/7/2010

AUTHOR'S NOTE

Novels are born in inscrutable ways. Even before my first one, *Cathedral Street,* was finished, I knew Michelle Miller, one of the less prominent characters in that book, had a story of her own to tell. I knew too that she wouldn't leave me alone until it was all down on paper.

The New Road is a work of fiction. It's set in a real place and time, Baltimore in 2009. But none of the characters or events depicted here ever existed outside my head. If any of them do resemble real people or actual events it is purely coincidental. As a novelist, I have taken the liberty to fabricate certain groups as well as characters and to rename some less important locations in this story.

The list of people I want to thank could go on for pages, but I'll keep it short. Thanks to Norma Boswell, Maxine Moore, Jean Pike, and Ellen Tomaszewski for their invaluable feedback on the completed manuscript. I can't say enough good things about the dedicated professionals at iUniverse Publishing who showed me no mercy until the final copy was as close to perfect as it could be. They turn dreams into reality for a living. Lastly, I'm not forgetting to acknowledge Pedro Claver Ibanez for the generous use of his last name.

This book is devoted to all the strong, loving women in the world who share Michelle's courage and heart.

L J Hippler
February 2010

Sometimes the biggest surprises are found in the things we learn about ourselves.
—Father Jerry Miller

CHAPTER 1

She already liked Vance Berg just a little less than when she'd first met him—twelve seconds earlier. Michelle Miller Ibanez put down the blue porcelain cup and eyed the short, fat man with the too big hair. "Yes, I guess I do have three names," she said. "Is that okay, Mr. Berg?"

"Whoa. Just makin' conversation." He pulled a brown file folder from a manila envelope, handed it to Michelle, and crumpled the envelope into a ball, which he dropped on the table as he sat down. "House bill 1664. We want to inform the neighborhood groups, and your name was given to me. It's an important piece of legislation, 1664."

"I'm sure it is. And thanks so much for bringing it down here."

Berg leaned back in one of the new chairs the Vitros had bought for their coffee shop and laid his index finger against his cheek. He saw himself as Michael Corleone, sizing her up. She was seeing Boss Hogg on meth. "You grow up in Canton?" he asked.

"No, I grew up in Catonsville. My husband and I moved here a year ago."

"I have to say this part of town never did much for me. They gentrified some of it. But it's still Canton."

1

"Gentrification's a part of it, sure. But Canton's about charm, recovering and honoring what came before. Maybe it's corny, but to me, it's all that."

"Charm? You're jokin', right?" The big man folded his hands on the table and leaned in. "These old factories need to go. They're like a hundred years old."

"Some are older than that. They go back to the Civil War. They made almost everything here, you know."

Vance Berg chuckled. "And those big guns on Federal Hill made sure that stuff got to the right army."

Michelle was sure she'd endured non sequiturs and conversations more irritating than this. But she couldn't remember where or when. "And you, Mr. Berg, where did you grow up?"

"Morrell Park. I never moved anywhere. Lived there all my life, in my Mom's house."

"Uh huh." She stuffed the folder into the side pocket of her bag. "I'll definitely be looking at this," Michelle said, glancing at her watch as she stood. "Thanks again for meeting me here." "Sixteen sixty-four. The bill's number 1664." The ombudsman stood up quickly but clumsily. "You want to look at it now so I can answer any questions?"

"I've got to be going. Thanks."

"You know, Jesus's wife had three names." He got it out quickly, like a car salesman whose customer was walking out of the showroom.

"Pardon me?"

"Yeah, Mary Magdalene Christ—according to Dan Brown." He held out his hand and smiled a big Morrell Park homeboy smile.

Michelle stepped back to the table, picked up the crumpled envelope, and slapped it into the man's thick hand. "We don't litter here in Canton," she said.

"Michelle," Mrs. Vitro called from behind the counter, "you want to take a couple sugar cookies home for little Carlos?"

Vance Berg pushed past her toward the door without a word.

"Thanks, Agnes, but I don't think so. He's four but just getting into those terrible twos you hear about. The last thing he needs is sugar."

"You look great in that blue suit, Hon."

"Oh, this is my old-maid suit," Michelle said, buttoning the coat over her white blouse before she went out.

"No, ma'am." Mr. Vitro didn't look up from the cardboard case he was cutting open. "That's no old-maid suit."

"Flirt," she quipped, squeezing the older man's shoulder as she left.

*

Walking home at that time of the morning was both a novelty and a treat. She walked fast. The long brown ponytail bounced on her back. It felt good, somehow cleansing after the meeting with Vance Berg. In Michelle's mind the ponytail was the last vestige of her youth. She was proud of it, and other lawyers had told her it was becoming her trademark in the courthouse.

That it was still warm enough not to wear a heavy coat was a treat too. The chimes of St. Casmir's tolled the hour as they had for a century. *Maybe it'll wear off*, she thought, *but this still feels like living in a movie set to me*. Wrens chirped with excitement as they vied for nest space on the ivy-covered wall of a little brick house on O'Donnell Street, two blocks away from her own. Michelle thought it looked a lot like the Betsy Ross flag house and wondered if it was from the same era. She made a mental note to look it up and find out, someday, when she had time.

She took that route on purpose. Coming straight down Boston Street would have been quicker. But she loved the thrill of turning the corner and suddenly seeing The Moorings and their new house. It was ten o'clock, but at least a sense of the morning freshness still remained on the harbor's surface. She stood on the top step and breathed it in for a few seconds before opening the door.

She dropped her brown leather bag on the dining room chair. The folder Berg had given her poked out of it, seeming to call her back. "Yes, yes, I know. House Bill number 1664. How could I forget?"

Neferkitty, her striped, shorthair cat, spotted Michelle and zoomed from the hall to the kitchen like a furry streak, delighted to see her human home at such an odd time. The coffeemaker was still on in the kitchen, and dirty dishes cluttered the sink. Michelle put her hands on the sink edge and sighed, closing her eyes and blowing out her breath. *I asked Carlos to not just leave dishes in the sink*, she thought. *And that's why he did it.* "There's a woman in every little girl and a little boy in every man," she recited as she washed the egg-encrusted plates. Sometimes she worried about her Carlos. Sometimes it seemed the little boy in him could be a petty, stubborn little boy.

Michelle put away the dishes and saw she had twenty-five minutes before she had to pick up her son. At the dining room table, she sighed again as she opened the folder. Her anniversary card from Carlos had fallen. She propped it up, carefully, lovingly, leaning it back against the white vase of roses that had come with it.

The House bill began as they all did, with several paragraphs of archaic legalese gibberish that meant nothing to her or to anyone she'd ever met. Michelle pictured a tiny man in short sleeves and a clip-on tie deep in the basement of the state house in Annapolis who typed the stuff up day after day. Her fingertip glided through the arcane mess of words and she made another mental note to get her nails done soon. "Blah, blah, blah. Blah, blah, blah," she murmured.

Neferkitty, thinking she was being sung to, jumped onto the other chair, lay on her back and looked up. "Are you gonna' stare at me upside down now?" Michelle laughed. "You little nut. Ah, here we go, $404 million dollars. Million? That can't be right." The next page began: TWO 4 LANE INTERCHANGE—THOROUGHFARE. She half stood and stretched to retrieve the brown folder with the red string. "Did that jerk even give me the right package?" Neighborhood Group Secretary: M Ibanez, 46th District, the white tag said. She went back to the sheaf of paper and continued to read. There were whole paragraphs about tonnage, steel. An entire page listed grades of cement. "Whatever all that means."

It went on like that. Michelle scanned and flipped through the rest of the pages, looking for something that made sense to her. But, it all looked the same. On the very last page was a map of Canton, her neighborhood, her home. It was an old map. The lines were wavy and blurred. It was one of those maps that looked like it had been run off on a ditto machine from the roaring twenties. But the two thick, black magic marker lines on it looked fresh, purposeful. The lines slithered obscenely across her neighborhood and ended in a hand-printed note: *Proposed Canton Thoroughfare Interchange.*

She kept looking through the pages, hoping to spot something she'd missed, something, anything that would explain it away, make it right. "No," she whispered, shaking her head in disbelief. Her eyes were still fixed on the piece of paper as if she were watching a car wreck and couldn't turn away.

"No," she said more strongly as she creased the paper and jammed it back into the brown folder. She stood up and was very still, silently holding it, staring at the white tag. M Ibanez, Neighborhood Association Secretary.

Neferkitty seemed to mimic her, on the chair, with one paw up. The cat stayed there, statue-like, frozen in mid-leap. "No." Michelle said it again, speaking to the paper inside the folder as if it was an alien being that had invaded her home and her life. "Oh, hell no!"

*

Opening the bright red front door, Michelle called back over her shoulder: "I told you it would be him!" She grabbed her Uncle Jerry's arm and hugged him even as she led him into her living room. "He's going to bless our house."

"I love it already," Jerry said. "It's so airy and light."

"You remember Christine." Michelle led him from the hall into an equally bright, modern living room.

"Of course, little Carlos's godmother."

"And this is my new neighbor, law partner, and best friend, Joanne," she said, physically turning him to face a dark-haired, tanned young woman who looked like she should have been on the cover of Vogue. "We run together every day," Michelle proclaimed. "Okay, we run some days."

"Hi." Jerry shook the woman's hand. "You're in great shape if you can keep up with this one. I've tried."

*

"So, you really like the house?" She led him though the rooms and up the stairs. Jerry enjoyed the attention, the joyous, freshly painted and decorated space, and the weight of his niece on his arm.

"I do. I love it. You've done a lot of work here already. You're just like your dad that way."

"I hope he likes it too."

"He's never seen it?" She didn't answer. "I thought he'd be here doing an inspection the day you found it."

"Um, we don't see each other as much as we used to. Seems like he's always busy. Anyway, are you ready for this?" Again, the light was the first thing to strike him when she opened the door. "Our prayer space."

Blue sky filled slanting, oversized windows. It matched the pale blue of the walls. A mahogany kneeler faced the window under a crucifix of mahogany and brass. Two simple but fine mahogany chairs made the room complete. It was simple, pleasant space; the light made it elegant.

"Oh, it is beautiful. You've made your own chapel."

"You know, I think it makes some people uncomfortable, though, when they visit."

"We live in a secular world." Jerry shrugged. "If that was an exercise bike instead of a kneeler you'd get all smiles." He went to the window to look down at the harbor and out at South Baltimore. "Why don't you go get your husband and we'll do the blessing." Michelle started down the stairs. "God bless you for doing this room, Hon," he called after her.

Two minutes passed, and she returned with a little entourage. Carlos carried the four-year-old who pushed, rolled, and contorted in his father's muscular arms like a fifty pound Gumby. "Hi, Jerry," Carlos said, awkwardly positioning his hand where it could be shaken.

Jerry made the sign of the cross. Michelle, Carlos, and Christine followed him. "Peace be with this house and with all who live here. Blessed be the name of the Lord." They all muttered a tentative Amen.

"When Christ took flesh through the Blessed Virgin Mary, he made his home with us. Let us now pray that he will enter this home and bless it with his presence." Out of the corner of his eye, Jerry saw Carlos shift his son to Michelle's arms. The boy rested happily there.

"May he always be here among you; may he nurture your love for each other, share in your joys, comfort you in your sorrows. Seek to make this home a dwelling place of love, diffusing far and wide the goodness of Christ."

Another ragged chorus of Amen.

"You say it too," Michelle told her son.

"Awen."

"Close enough," Jerry chuckled, touching the boy's feathery, brown hair.

Michelle put little Carlos down. He took a handful of her black slacks and held tight. "Thank you, Uncle Jerr," she said, giving him a hug as the others trailed down the stairs.

"My pleasure. I really thought your father would be here."

"Oh, he is. They're down on the deck still. They didn't want to come up."

"They?"

"Dad and his new girlfriend—Chlooooeeee."

Jerry had to laugh at the sight of a Maryland State officer of the court rolling her eyes like a twelve-year-old.

"You don't like her?"

"Oh, she's okay. She's just—I don't know."

"Well, it's a shame they wouldn't come up."

They started down the carpeted stairs. "Let me show you the kitchen. Then I have to get back to work."

"Yeah, I hope you can stop that road. I know what I-95 did to Arbutus."

"And this would be so much worse." Michelle moved slowly with little Carlos still attached to her leg. "There's lots of good, homemade food out on the deck."

"I heard that," Jerry said.

*

Outside, the boy squirmed and slid off Jerry's knee after a few uncomfortable seconds. He ran across the deck, took Chloe's hand, and led her to the edge of the pier where he wasn't allowed to go without an adult. "She really is good with kids," Buddy murmured. "When we met I thought she was just saying that."

"Nice girl." Carlos poured a Zima with surgical skill down the side of a glass and a shot of liquor into Buddy's empty one. "How did you meet her?"

Buddy retrieved his glass and dropped an extra shot of rum into it before adding the soda. "She answered my ad on Sugardaddie dot com," he said with a shrug.

The younger man snorted loudly into his beer, blowing it over the front of his tan shirt. "Buddy, you're hilarious," he laughed, wiping off

L.J. Hippler

his chin with a napkin. "Perfect delivery." He tried to dry his shirt with a second napkin. "No, seriously, how'd you guys meet?"

Buddy looked over his sunglasses at his son-in-law for a full two seconds before he pushed them back up on his nose and turned toward the table. "I should go talk to my brother," he said.

*

"Faaather Jerry," Buddy began, making his way just a little unsteadily across the new deck. He sat down with a thud. His fresh rum and Coke sloshed a spray of brown droplets onto the white tablecloth.

"So, what made you give Carlos that Jack Nicholson stare?" Jerry asked, smiling.

"You know, we haven't talked in eight years, and that's what you ask me?"

Jerry only looked at him and took another bite of peach cobbler.

"Hell, I don't know. I'm not feeling that good." Buddy sighed and rubbed the circular scar just below his collar on the back of his neck. "You're looking good. How'd you manage to hold on to all that hair?"

"I got mostly Mom's DNA."

"I think you did," Buddy said softly, without looking at him. "They're sending you away? After all those years at St. Mark's?"

"I'll have a parish in a place called Bentonville, on the eastern shore."

"But, you *have* to go? Aren't you like a cardinal or archbishop or something by now?"

"You're a funny guy, Buddy."

Buddy watched his son-in-law and Chloe lean over the rail and point to things on Carlos's sailboat like two teenagers on a field trip. "You're the second person to tell me that today." He sipped his drink and stared out at the harbor. "How's your life, Jerry?"

"Pretty good. Moving's kind of a pain ..."

"No. I mean overall, everything. What's it like?"

Jerry put down the fork and sat back in the chair. "It's a magnificent gift from God, the priesthood. I can't explain that to you. But there's no other life I'd trade it for." He braced himself for a string of expletives that never came.

"Well, I'm secure now. That's what money means to me. That's all it means."

8

"Where your treasure is, there your heart is also."

"Jesus. Don't you ever stop?"

"God's given you some wonderful gifts too, you know."

"Oh, I know," Buddy said, nodding and admiring the way the breeze made Chloe's yellow sun dress nestle into the curves of her body.

"I'm talking about your daughter. She's grown up and successful. But she idolizes you now just like she did when she was eleven. Buddy, don't cut her off."

A full minute went by, and Buddy was silent, staring at the water again, spinning the liquid around in his glass. "I gotta' go," he said at last. "Neck's killing me."

*

In the house, Buddy found his daughter. She was with Joanne, Christine, and two of the neighbor women at the big, glass dining-room table. Michelle was clicking a ballpoint pen next to her ear while the others scribbled furiously on note pads and day planners. He saw her at fourteen, on the carpet in his office, when the other girls would come over to do their homework. *You're still the queen, aren't you?* he thought, smiling.

She glanced up at him, and he pointed to himself and then to the door. "I'm going," he mouthed silently. She nodded, waved, and blew him a silent kiss in return.

Back on the deck, Buddy noticed how fast the sun was setting. He went to retrieve Chloe from her huddle with Carlos still hanging over the rail by the sailboat. "Let's go, Hon," he said, putting his left arm around her shoulders. "My neck's really hurting." He put his right hand out to his son-in-law. "Your wife's a very busy lady."

"Yeah, no kidding," Carlos said without smiling. "Welcome to my world." They turned and started for the stairs. "Great meeting you, Chloe," Carlos called over his shoulder.

Jerry was still at the table, starting on a second plate of the peach cobbler. "See you next time, Father Jerry," Buddy said as he ushered Chloe down the stairs. "Good luck in Bunghole, Maryland or wherever it is you're going."

"That's Bentonville," Jerry said as his brother walked off. "Thanks."

CHAPTER 2

SEPTEMBER 14–16, 2009
LIKE A YOUNG ARNOLD

When the loud rapping on the front door finally woke him, Buddy Miller was feeling less than amicable. The throbbing pain in his neck was exceptionally bad, and he needed that mid-afternoon nap. People normally came off the driveway to the side of the big white house. Only someone who'd never been there before would make the trek across the yard to the front door. "Please don't be another asshole selling magazines," he muttered, clumsily sliding back the chain.

A young man in a navy blue blazer, white shirt and a black tie that said RETRIEVERS in tiny yellow letters stood in the doorway. He filled the entire doorway. "Yessir." A surprisingly soft, timid voice emanated from the basketball-sized blond head. "Uh, Mike Drazinski—from the college. UMBC."

"And?" Buddy said, rubbing his eyes. "Oh, yeah, the intern program. They did say you'd be here today. Sorry, I was … busy upstairs. C'mon in." He tried to remember why he thought he needed an intern. He led the young man through the living room and the kitchen to the little office next to the bathroom. The room used to be his own office, before he'd had the house expanded. Opening the door, he remembered the things he couldn't bring himself to do any more: collect and file all of the tax information he'd been tossing into drawers for the last two years, and set up spreadsheets for that and for his two rental properties. "You good with spreadsheets, uh ..."

"Mike, sir. My friends call me Mike D or just D."

"Okay, Mike. So, are you good with spreadsheets?" Buddy rubbed his neck. "If not, let's not waste each other's time."

"I am good with them, sir. Getting better every day. It says that on my resume."

Buddy opened the door and waved his arm at the wide, wooden desk. "I'm afraid that lap-top's about had it. The battery's almost gone." He sighed as he shut down the screen. "My daughter's bringing over her spare PC. I thought I'd have it before you got here." He gestured at the wall of file cabinets. "There's lots of filing to do in the meantime. You up to that?" Buddy grinned at the younger man. "You look like that shouldn't be a problem. It looks like you could carry out my old refrigerator on your shoulder." The boy looked down at his hands in embarrassment. *He's just a shy kid*, Buddy thought, *just a kid in a big body. I need to remember that.* "Joke, man. Just a joke."

Mike D looked around the room. He put his hands into his pockets, at a loss as to what else to do with them. "I'm ready to get started, Mr. Miller."

"Let me get some of this stuff out of your way," Buddy said when the young man's eyes seemed to linger a little too long on the eight by ten of Chloe in her bikini on Maui. "Just get familiar with the stuff in that file cabinet. I'll be back later." He continued to collect pictures into a stack in his arms.

"Mr. Miller?"

"Uh huh."

"Do you mind if I pick your brain sometimes?"

"Pick my brain?"

"About how you made it. Mr. Peterson at school told me a little about you, that you were a self-made man and all."

"Yeah," Buddy chuckled softly. "That's me—self made." He picked up an old picture of his dogs, Bonzai and Strider, and put it on the top of the pile. He looked around for anything he'd missed and continued toward the door. "Yeah. Sure, why not?"

"Was it tech stocks?" Mike D called after him. "I know a lot of traders made money in tech stocks back in the day."

Back in the day? Buddy sighed as he turned around. "The key is, I knew when to get out of tech. 'Is your computer Y2K ready?'"

"Sir?"

"My God. You don't even know what I'm talking about, do you?" Buddy began to say something and then stopped himself. "I knew when to get out, that's all." He rubbed the back of his neck again. "Make yourself at home, Mike D."

*

She was late, and her father hated that; especially today he'd hate it. It had been an awkward morning, the start of what she knew would be an awkward day. Michelle's first mistake was to lay her old desktop computer on the play-school sized back seat of her aging, white Miata. She listened to it bounce and shuffle on the leather as she drove up the rough road on the last leg of the trip to her father's house. She turned and glared at it as if to scold the thing when she bounced over a particularly deep rut at the edge of the paved driveway.

Getting out of the car, she thought how very different the house looked to her now. It wasn't the big old sentinel of a house that, as a ten-year-old, she'd gleefully carried boxes into on that moving day. In the front yard, old Bonsai, the miniature shepherd, had run in circles until he nearly collapsed with joy over his newfound freedom and space. Now the yard seemed artificially green, manicured to the point where even the birds were afraid to disturb it. The house had become a pretty, plasticine, theme-park model of the one she'd played in, invited friends to, and come of age in.

She struggled with the clumsy metal box while trying not to wrinkle the lace on her black, summer dress as she opened the side sliding door. She made it into the dining room and nearly dropped the computer. "Dad?" she called, looking around at the new pictures and high-backed black chairs and table.

When the blond, young man appeared in the kitchen doorway, his sheer size almost made her yell out in fright. The forearms poking out of the rolled up sleeves of his white shirt were the size of her calves. She didn't scream because he looked more frightened than she was.

"Can I help you?" a surprisingly soft voice asked.

"Help me? Who the hell are you?" Michelle followed his eyes down and saw that in holding on to the CPU she'd hiked the dress up well above her knees.

"My name is Mike. I work for Mr. Miller."

A wardrobe malfunction too. Just what I need. "Where is my father?" Michelle was exasperated, both with the weight of the computer and her own embarrassment.

"Oh, you're Mr. Miller's daughter. I thought …"

"Uh huh. Please don't say it."

He didn't say he thought she was Chloe. "Let me help you with that," he said instead. He smiled a little boy smile as she let him take the CPU. Michelle was silently impressed with the way it rested in the crook of his arm like a box of chocolates.

"Michelle," her father's voice boomed from upstairs. "C'mon up, Hon." She went across the new maroon carpet to the polished wood stairway. Turning, she saw Mike D was still in the door, still looking at her, still with the smile.

"So don't you have work to do?" she asked.

"Yes."

She thought he looked like a giant four-year-old caught with his hand in the proverbial cookie jar. She saw Mike D actually pat the CPU as he turned back toward the office.

Buddy was in the bedroom tying a blue paisley tie. This room had always been his bedroom. The simple motion of his hands reminded her of how, as a little girl, she'd watch him put on his tie in the morning. It was a little thing, unspoken, but a morning ritual for them both. "Hi, Honey." He left the tie loose around his neck and went to hug her.

"Sorry I'm a little behind today," she said, sitting on the edge of the new king-sized bed. "I think we can still get there on time." The bed took up half the floor space in the modest room. "How are you doing?"

"I'm fine, Hon." He turned back toward the mirror. "I don't even know why we're going to this thing."

"You asked me to drive you."

"Sometimes I can't turn my neck very well and didn't want to chance driving." He finished with the tie, looked at himself in the mirror, and blew out a breath. "Maybe this will put closure on it. I guess I just want to get this over with."

"So, what's with Jessie the Body downstairs?" Michelle smiled, making a point of changing the subject.

"Mike. He's an intern from UMBC. I hired him to get my tax stuff filed over the summer. He's doing really well."

"He's kind of a shock if you're not ready for him."

"I guess he is," her father chuckled. "He's built like a young Arnold."

Michelle looked around the room while Buddy was in the closet. "I don't know about all that. But he's a big one."

"My ad said the assignment was *heavily weighted* with tax work," he called out to her. "Maybe they misunderstood."

Michelle took stock of the new things in the room, the things that weren't her father. The black and maroon silk pillowcases seemed out of place even on the new, oversized bed. She counted four new 8X10s of Chloe on the wall and the bureau, Chloe with her father in various locales. Her own pale visage in the hospital bed holding little Carlos on his birthday had been tucked behind them so that she had to search for it. "Chloe couldn't file that tax stuff for you?"

"Chloe sells real estate," Buddy said coming back out of the closet. "She's good at it. She's a very busy lady." He pulled on his navy blue suit coat and sat on the edge of the bed next to his daughter. "Don't get catty on me, Hon. Not today."

She took his hand but looked away from him at the pictures. "Ready?" she asked.

"Yeah. Let's go bury BJ."

*

Outside, Buddy turned away from the car and motioned her to follow him to the far side of the house. "We're going to be late," she said.

"It'll just take a second. I want to show you the wall I'm starting on."

"Wall?"

"Look," he said, pointing to a stone façade at least a foot taller than himself and the length of the house.

"My God, Dad," Michelle laughed. "You expecting an invasion by Mongol hordes? How far down will that go?"

"All the way to the water. Can you believe it?"

"No, I can't. Let's go."

*

Only in the car did they talk about her mother's uncle. To Michelle, BJ had always seemed to be an out of place person, a cosmic loose cannon that had come into their world by accident. Buddy felt bile rise in his throat each time he thought of BJ. "He took care of me for a long time, Dad." It was a careful opening, one that Buddy couldn't dispute. "True, he got weird as he got older, but he was part of our family." She looked over at him to see his reaction. "I remember him teaching me to sing Elvis songs."

"I loved your mother, but he was a leech from day one." Buddy relived the threatening conversations and how he was forced to pay for the old man's silence. *He's finally dead.* "You're right, Hon. Let's concentrate on the good times."

They did that. Or she did that and talked about them. Buddy listened with strained patience until they pulled into Glen Haven Memorial Gardens.

They parked on the road and walked to the graveside. BJ's coffin hung suspended over the grave, ready to be lowered down. For the first time in twenty years, Buddy saw his in-laws. They were old, shrunken caricatures of themselves, and he took some satisfaction in that. He watched as his daughter hugged them warmly and recognized the silent hate in their eyes when they saw him, the hate they had always shown him. The old man waddled toward him, eyes down but as pretentious as he could make himself. "The service is already done. But we appreciate you're here to show your respect."

Buddy almost laughed out loud. *The old dipshit sounds like Rip Torn on Quaaludes,* he thought. "Sure. BJ was part of our family, after all." As he started to walk away the older man grabbed his arm. "We could use some help with the funeral expenses," he said, looking down at his feet.

Buddy put his arm across the old man's shoulders and whispered in his ear. "Fuck … you." Elwood Monroe's eyes darted to his wife, to Michelle, and then back down to his own feet.

"You've got the money and we don't. You owe Brenda that. We're askin' half the gravestone."

Buddy saw his daughter watching the two of them, studying them from the other side of the grave. He reached for his wallet and pulled out a hundred dollar bill. "Stick this up your hillbilly ass," he whispered, smiling and stuffing the bill into the breast pocket of the man's old sports coat. "And stay the hell out of my life." He smiled over at Michelle and gave her a brief nod.

A shabby looking man in a baseball hat and T-shirt hit a button on the crane and started lowering the coffin into the grave. The coffin was gray. The blue canvas straps around it made Buddy picture the deep cuts BJ had dug into his wrists at the end. *A last grasp at pity, you pathetic bitch.* "Bye, bye, motherfucker," Buddy mouthed soundlessly to the coffin as the top of it disappeared below the red Anne-Arundel county dirt.

*

"Whew," Buddy sighed, closing the car door. "Let's go home." The Miata sped out of the front gate of the cemetery and onto Ritchie Highway after only a hint of a stop. A silent minute went by that made Buddy uneasy. "You okay, Hon?" There was no answer. His daughter kept her eyes locked on the back of the tractor trailer in front of them and downshifted into third with a ferocity that he thought might pull the gearshift out of its tan leather console.

"You can be so damned strange sometimes, Dad," she said at last. Buddy waited for her to follow up with something specific but nothing came.

"Strange?"

"Yes, strange." She still refused to look at him. "You had no feelings for BJ or for my grandparents, none at all. I could see that in your face."

"That's not true," he ventured back. "He did some good for us—for a while there. I went today out of respect for your mom. I guess."

"And why did you make it a point to have me take you there?" She looked at him at last, and Buddy saw his own eyes looking back at him, full of anger, frustration, and near tears. "Why didn't you have Chloe take you? She's your girlfriend or partner or whatever the hell she is."

"Oh, here we go. What is it really, Michelle? Is it so terrible that I found somebody young and pretty, not one of those frumpos you tried to fix me up with?"

"Diane was not a frumpo. She was a decent, sweet lady who was your own age."

"I pick her up for dinner and she's wearing socks and sandals, Michelle. Socks and sandals."

He saw his daughter's fingers dig into the steering wheel as she floored it and swerved around the truck without checking the other lane. He wished he could do a redo on the entire conversation.

"Well," he continued in what he thought was a lighter tone. "Why is it if Donald Trump marries a much younger lady, people think that's cool. If I do it, I'm Joey Buttafuoco." The sound of stones and gravel battering the underside of the tiny car was loud enough to make Buddy think for a second that they'd been hit. When he realized they'd only swerved onto the shoulder the relief was short-lived.

"Wait. Back up," Michelle ordered, turning off the engine and twisting her body to look at him directly. "Are you saying you're going to marry Chloe?"

"I was just trying to lighten things up a little. That's all." He turned and stared at the piney woods on the side of the road.

She turned to watch the midday traffic blur past on the highway.

*

Buddy got out of the Miata in the driveway at Nampara. She backed out and left without a word. "You'll be all right," he whispered to the red taillights as she crested the hill. "You're just like me. You'll shrug this thing off." He walked across the lawn, hands in his pockets, to look at the wall again. The stone structure seemed even higher in the fading light of the September evening, indestructible, formidable.

Buddy turned and hurried into the breezeway, checking the garage to see if Chloe's red BMW was there yet. It was, and he was glad. He didn't want to be alone.

*

She was in the kitchen, opening her mail. She had on the gray pinstriped pantsuit with the long jacket, and Buddy couldn't take his eyes from the curve of her neck above the white collar of her blouse. "Hey you," he said softly.

"Hey you," she answered, dropping the stack of mail on the counter. He kissed her for a long time and then kissed her again. "How was it today?"

"It was a funeral. Good as can be expected, I guess."

"How'd Michelle take it?"

"Ooh," he sighed, putting his hands on Chloe's waist, "she got kind of upset on the ride home."

"I should at least call her."

"You know, I think she just needs some time to herself. D'ju eat yet?"

"I just got home."

"Your little black dress handy?"

She smiled and put her hands on his shoulders. "What are you getting at now, Mr. M.?"

"Let's go out tonight. Someplace nice. I'm really up for some prime rib."

"Now that sounds wonderful," Chloe said, sliding easily out of his hands. "I did two closings today—two! And I'm going to tell you in excruciating detail about both of them."

Buddy closed his eyes and listened to her bare feet run up the stairs, and he then took a bottle of bourbon down from the cabinet. He hummed softly to himself as he poured a small shot into a glass. It was an old song from the eighties. He took a sip from the glass. The liquor tasted good, warm on his tongue. It warmed and comforted him as it went down his throat. He began to sing the song, softly, to himself. "Bmp, bmp, bmp, another one bites the dust. And another one gone, another one gone … another one bites the dust."

CHAPTER 3

Michelle spun her favorite University of Baltimore pen next to her right ear and tapped her left foot on the bottom drawer of the metal file cabinet. "Where do we even start, Joanne?"

"That's a hypothetical question, I hope." Joanne Wicks shook out her bobbed black hair and sighed as she leaned back on the wooden chair across from her law partner. "This new road thing is like a big snake. We haven't even been able to find the head of it yet."

"Oh, I know. Just thinking out loud. You know how I work."

After two years in the same office, Joanne did know how she worked. Since their partnership opened in '07 she'd seen the pen-twirling routine in conjunction with every complex case that had come through the black lacquered front door. Joanne knew the more insoluble the problem, the faster the pen would spin. Tonight it looked like the rotor blade of a tiny helicopter.

"Here I am, lowly secretary for the dinkiest neighborhood organization in Baltimore." Michelle began to recite her spiel for the third time that afternoon. "I get handed this stack of paper, and boom, it's a done deal?" She picked up House Bill 1664 and shook it to emphasize the point. "Did you try to call Fat Boy again?"

"Called him, texted him, faxed him. He's got the shields up, that's for sure." Joanne had dealt with Berg on other city issues, and she'd begun to visualize him as a Klingon. "Want to send him a real letter?"

"No. Let's save that till we can actually put some teeth in it." Michelle dropped the pen on her desk and rubbed the sides of her head, pulling her long, brown hair back into a ponytail. "I'm getting a runaround you wouldn't believe in Annapolis too." She looked up at the stained ceiling tiles as if beseeching their help, and she blew out a breath. "I'm the new kid. They all know it and they're going to try to ignore me." She continued staring at the ceiling. "Jo, I can't even tell you how much that pisses me off."

Joanne's cell rang in her pocket, an aborted ring, going silent before she could answer. She stared at the number and grimaced. "It's four o'clock."

"Mmmm," Michelle agreed, still holding back her hair, still looking up at the ceiling.

"Sooo, are we going to run or not?"

"Yes. Yes, yes. Let's do that."

*

They started slow, the two of them side by side on the sidewalk. That part was downhill but the cement sidewalks were cracked and lifted in spots by the roots of poplars. Kids were just out of school and peered out at them warily from under their hoodies and oversized baseball hats as they passed. Old women wearing scarves and black sweaters would stare and shake their heads, amazed, even a decade into the new millennium that grown women would run in public.

Once they made the left onto O'Donnell Street they could pick up the pace, moving into the wide road against the traffic. "A monument," Joanne huffed, running hard to keep up with her longer-legged partner. "If it's a historic site they can't touch it."

"Uh hmm," was all Michelle could answer. She looked straight ahead and toyed with the thought as her feet found a strong, steady rhythm. This had been part of Captain O'Donnell's estate, the same estate that gave Canton its name and where seventeen-year-old Betsy Patterson married Napoleon Bonaparte's younger brother on Christmas

Eve. *So, two hundred years later they can just run a highway through it,* she thought. *Like who the hell cares?*

They veered right, toward the harbor and Waterfront Park. It was the part Michelle hated, the uphill part. Now Joanne sprinted ahead, and she had to struggle to keep up. The hill seemed to stretch out forever, lined with what seemed like countless sets of white marble steps and orange brick row houses. Even as she fought for breath, Michelle thought how each house and set of steps that whizzed past represented a story, a history, a family. Then, down the hill to the wall at the water's edge they sprinted hard, their white shoes pounding like rubberized hooves on the black asphalt.

Michelle leaned against the wall, stretching, breathing hard, looking out over the water. The bay glinted, a brown green in the dying sun. On the other side ship cranes poked into the orange sky like giant working-class monuments. "Jo, you know what I think? I think this whole place is a monument. All of it." Her friend grabbed the green-painted rail and stretched her arms and shoulders.

As she breathed in the fall air, Michelle pictured the hundred generations of workers and dreamers, people who'd admired the same waterfront. "Hard working, decent people built this place one laborious day at a time. The faith and optimism of those families, their essence even, is in the bricks of their houses."

Joanne could sense the nearness of tears and put her arm around her friend's shoulders. "Damn, Chelly, you're getting downright poetic." There were catcalls coming from a trio of tween boys across the street behind them.

"This thing can't just happen," Michelle said, bouncing on her toes and shaking her hands as if they were wet. "Somehow—we've got to stop these bastards." Joanne gave her friend's shoulder a squeeze before they both turned and began a slow jog back toward the office.

A chorus of "Heeey, babeee" came from the three preteen boys. Joanne reached down to the curb as if she'd found something to throw at them and cocked her arm like a softball pitcher. The boys stumbled back in surprise. "Get a job, you little twerps," she yelled.

*

After ten years at Saint Mark's he felt he had enough memories to fill a fleet of tractor trailers. But four new, neatly taped boxes held all of his physical possessions. Jerry's things were packed. The four cardboard boxes were stacked outside his bedroom door. He kept wondering what it was he'd forgotten.

"Jerry." Father Tran's voice echoed in the empty hallway from downstairs. "You're gonna miss your own party."

"Be right there," Jerry called back as he pulled open each bureau drawer to make a final check. His friend was standing outside the open door before he got the last drawer closed. "Besides, they can't very well start without me, can they?"

"I'm not so sure." Father Tran bounced on his toes with impatience, his hands in his pockets. "Some of those big choir ladies looked pretty hungry." He looked down at the boxes and continued to rock forward and back. "Not much to move, huh?" Jerry continued to run his hands over the top shelves in his closet. "I had a parishioner once tell me about getting laid off after fifteen years. He said he carried out all of his stuff in a plastic bag."

Jerry looked back at him and raised his eyebrows. "And your point?"

"My point—sometimes it's like that. C'mon, let's go."

As they hurried across the parking lot in the drizzling rain the real rush of memories began. Jerry had to push himself to keep up with the shorter man. And the scenes in his head passed like guests in a greeting line at a wedding, just enough time to make eye contact and exchange a token handshake. On his watch a whole generation of kids had played in that lot. The first graders there when he arrived were in high school now. To him the kids were like a joyous stream that flowed continuously. Only the fashions changed. *The girls' screams, the boys' shouts and their laughter, it's always the same.*

They turned abruptly before they got to the front of the church hall. "In the side door," Father Tran murmured. Holding open the door, he put a hand on Jerry's shoulder and whispered, "You're supposed to be surprised."

Jerry could only think of Mrs. Prichard and the last time he'd helped her through that door, before she'd gotten her walker. "I love this parish," the old woman had said as he opened the same door onto a warm spring sun. "It just feels good. There's a patina of good all around it."

They were all there, his flock. And he did manage to look surprised when he came into the hall. He saw the McGinns, the Grozers, and the Klappenbergers that he'd married just the week before. His parish. Father Jerry's parish. He'd buried their parents, baptized their kids, and heard their confessions for half a generation. It seemed like they were all there. Jerry loved them all. He'd miss them all terribly and told them that.

Through dinner there were choruses of "We'll miss you, Father" and "Good luck out there," as if he were going to Antarctica.

"What kinda church building you got up there, Father?" Rob Hamden had managed to squeeze his lanky body in next to Jerry at the table. "I saw a picture of it on the net," the younger man said, the brim of his baseball cap a hair's breadth away from Jerry's forehead. "Looks like it needs some work."

"I'll have to have you and the other Knights come up and help me out."

Rob's dark brows nearly touched as he frowned in deep thought. "Make a list. And I'll work out what we need and how many guys. The roof first? You been on the roof yet?"

"No. I haven't been on the roof." *It was a joke, Rob,* Jerry thought. *God bless you, but it was just a joke.*

"How long's it take to get up there?"

"Oh, a couple of hours." Jerry looked to his left in search of an interruption. "It's a little further than Ocean City." Jerry didn't want to tell him that Mr. Thomason drove both ways the one time he'd been to nearby Saint Anselm's, that he'd been exhausted and slept most of the way.

"Try these," Father Tran barked, ladling some pot stickers onto his plate. Rob Hamden hustled away to other tables to set up a work team. "You won't get delicacies like this up there in the wild."

"You know, I'm not going to the Congo, it's only the eastern shore."

"Watch your back up there." Father Tran was stirring a cup of coffee, looking out at the crowd. His tone had turned serious.

"Watch my back?" Jerry turned to his friend, who continued to look straight ahead. "What is this, a gang fight? I'm just going to another parish."

"Just be careful. That's all. I've heard some things."

*

The church was empty and dark except for the single votive candle by the tabernacle. Rain pelted the stained-glass windows. The old wood creaked as Father Jerry knelt to give thanks for a decade of productivity and peace. A streaming collage of mental pictures filled his mind. The pictures of Masses and homilies, of weddings and first communions went on like the lines of people on Ash Wednesday, lines that seemed to stretch on forever but each individual precious.

He cut through the school building to avoid the rain and was surprised to see Father Richards in his office. The new priest looked up and smiled a smile tempered with vague annoyance at being interrupted. "Whoa, you're anxious to get to the nitty gritty," Jerry offered, a little territorial jealousy tinting his own tone.

"September," the younger man answered. "I want to get a handle on things before the school year really kicks in."

He's young, Jerry thought, heading out into the parking lot. *He's what the parish needs now.*

His van was on the opposite side of the lot. Jerry stuffed his hands into his jacket pockets and jogged across the asphalt in what was now a downpour. He saw Father Tran wrestling a wrought iron baptismal font into the back of the old vehicle. "Thought you could use this," Father Tran said in answer to his friend's confused expression. "We've got two of them at Our Lady of Victory." He slammed the door closed and flipped up the collar of his black raincoat. "Take care, Jerry."

Jerry wanted to follow the other priest and ask him what it was he meant in the hall. He opted instead to get into the van and out of the driving autumn rain. He took the stack of cards he'd just gotten from inside his jacket and stuffed them behind the passenger's seat. Water crashed down in a sudden torrent, battering and pinging off of the metal roof of the van. For an instant he was in the chopper again, in Vietnam. The chaos of broken bodies around him. Bullets smashing the ship's metal skin like hammer blows. Watching his friend drive off into the curtain of rain, he found his key and put it into the ignition. Then he sat and listened for a full minute to the storm, to the banging on the roof, letting it become rain again in his head. "A patina of good," Jerry said and smiled to himself, turning the key. "I did like that."

CHAPTER 4

SEPTEMBER 20, 2009
DOUBLES TOURNAMENT

"Doesn't that smell good?" Michelle smiled at her four-year-old as she wedged his ever-growing body into the car seat. The boxes of food from China East were steaming even on the exceptionally warm September day. The smells of egg roll, moo goo gai pan, and shrimp egg foo yung mingled and turned the inside of the little convertible into an exquisite bubble of security and cheer. But Little Carlos seemed more engrossed in the feel of the nylon straps across his chest and the click of the plastic snaps that held him snug and safe. As his mother came around to get into the driver's seat, she saw him staring up at her from the back seat with that mixture of awe and appreciation of the fun of it all. She savored the smell of the food as they drove down Boston Street, and her son's giggling when they went over the cobblestone section. She drank in the sensations, all of them. They were like a drug that induced a picture in her head of the previous May.

On the magical day they'd moved into the house, they'd eaten outside on the deck. Before she'd ever stepped inside that townhouse, Michelle had been swept away in a yearlong love affair with it.

Carlos had gone to get the food that time. She remembered how pumped she was, like a kid on Christmas, just deciding which box of dishes to unpack first. Her toddler and her cat both explored the kitchen floor around her feet, Little Carlos still experiencing the novelty of being mobile on his own and Nefferkitty, desperate to find something familiar in the awful mess the humans had made of her happy existence.

Michelle hummed to herself remembering how it had seemed like only moments before her husband was back. He'd called them from outside, "All hands on deck." He had the Chinese food already spread out on the table. She remembered how good his jet black hair had looked, how tanned his strong neck, the way the muscles on his bare arms seemed to constantly curve and remold themselves in the sun when he moved. Carlos just held her hand that day on the deck and looked deep into her eyes while their son rested in her lap. They saw their first big boat come by that day. The tour boat, City of Tolchester, was heading back to the inner harbor. They whooped and waved at the boat, the three of them. Some of the people on deck waved back.

She replayed that day in her head and watched through the window as her husband's sailboat eased up to the dock. Michelle smiled at the lithe way he hopped from the deck to the pier and tied the twenty-foot boat.

*

Now, Carlos came through the kitchen door wearing what she'd begun to call his puzzled look, where his dark eyebrows nearly touched, where his eyes darted around at everything as if he'd misplaced his keys and his life depended on finding them. He went to the hall and tossed his squall jacket onto the back of the couch, not hanging it in the garage as he usually did. "See what we brought home?" Michelle gestured like a game show model with her right hand at the still-hot boxes of Chinese food on the counter. She put her left arm around her husband's neck. "And, by the way, do I get a kiss or what?"

"Sure," Carlos said, not looking directly at her, and brushed his lips quickly over her waiting ones. "Was Little Carlos okay in the car?" he asked, stepping away from Michelle and toward the counter where he began to inspect the white boxes. "He acts like a little brat sometimes when I take him out."

"Um, he was great." She walked around to the other side of the island counter, putting it between them. "Everything all right on your sail?"

Carlos nodded with his eyes down and shrugged. "Maybe if you were home more he wouldn't act that way."

"What *way*? He's a little kid." She wiped imaginary crumbs from the countertop with the side of her hand. "And, come on, Honey. We talked about my career, even back in college. You know how much time it takes."

Carlos opened the box of egg foo yung and began to dig at it with a fork. "I thought we'd eat out on the deck," Michelle said, pulling her son away from the knife drawer that he was trying to open. "Remember that day we moved in? That was a fun day." Her husband readopted the puzzled look and kept eating. "We had Chinese food then too, on the deck." She got no response. "It looks nice out there," she added lamely.

"Too windy." Carlos dropped the fork with a clink on the marble countertop and turned away from her. "And I can see he's in one of his moods." The boy put his small fists to his face and sobbed for attention. "I'm gonna change clothes. We'll eat in the kitchen."

Michelle watched her husband disappear into the hall, walking a little more quickly than he needed to. Then she pulled Little Carlos to her and rocked him in her arms because she knew it would stop the crying. She stared out the window at the deck. The wooden table seemed forlorn and empty in the middle of it.

Only a minute passed before Carlos came back into the kitchen. "Okay," he said with a huff, "let's eat outside." Michelle let go of her son and walked around the counter.

"Good," she said and buried her face in his neck. "It makes me feel creepy when you act like that."

"Hmm. You don't have to work all the hours you do. We've got the money."

"We talked about this." She traced a line on his long neck with her finger. "It's not about money. I want to make my practice a success. It's important to me."

Carlos pulled her close and brushed his lips across her forehead. The feel of his arms around her made Michelle's day good again. "Hey," he called into the living room for his son, "all hands on deck."

*

The wall was almost finished. Buddy's contractors had worked on it all summer. It was a high, stone wall on three sides of what people had begun to call his estate. He looked down the length of the north section. It was perfect, straight and strong and a foot higher than his own six-foot frame. He hadn't planned on it, but he decided to walk it down that Sunday morning, through the trees, across the garden, and out to the beach where it ended. All the way down the hill Buddy pictured how, years ago, he'd put up the old fence. That summer had been a hot one as well. It was hard work, digging post holes in the rocky dirt and pulling the wire mesh tight by himself; working nights and weekends, it had taken the whole summer. But he was young then, and it didn't matter. The end of the wall jutted out across the beach and into the bay, the way he wanted it. *God*, he thought, *the schmoozing and promising I had to do to get that past the zoning board. It's worth it, though. No unwanted visitors now.* Bonzai was buried there, in the rocks above the beach. It was covered completely with ivy now, but Buddy knew where his favorite dog's grave was. He put one work boot on a hollow tree trunk and looked out at the morning sun sparkling on the Chesapeake. Buddy talked to the miniature shepherd, picturing him there on the rocks, ears up, listening. "It was us against the world that summer, wasn't it? Right after Brena died. Michelle was only nine years old." Putting his hands into his pockets, Buddy watched a small sailboat bounce on the whitecaps as it turned toward Tillman Island. "Just you, me, and Michelle in that old, drafty house. It's a different world now, boy. I'm paying more for this wall than we paid for the whole place back then." Buddy picked up a short stick and bounced it off the massive buttress to his left. "And the biggest worry I have now is that they get the color of the stones right." Chloe was just coming out onto the porch patio when he got back. She had on the peach-colored shorts that he loved. The shorts accentuated her long, tan legs, and they accentuated other things. "Hey, baby," he began, "you're up early."

"And where'd you go?" Chloe seemed to glide rather than walk to the breakfast table where she sat and began to peel an orange.

"Just checking out the wall. They're almost finished with it."

She put one foot up on the chair as she peeled the orange. She did it just the way his daughter did, and Buddy wished she hadn't. *She is older than my daughter,* he reasoned, *but not by much. It's awkward for Michelle. That's why she doesn't come around anymore. She didn't say that's why. But I know her.*

"Hey, I saw the neighbors Bill and Mary yesterday." Buddy pulled out the other chair and sat across from Chloe. They're back from Europe." He couldn't stop thinking about Michelle now and his grandson. He suddenly missed them both, a lot.

"Chlo, did you know there's a bike path now where the Berlin wall used to be? I had no idea."

She looked at him across the table and dropped an orange seed onto the bricks. "That's good, right?"

"Well, it's good. But the East and West Germans hated, really hated, each other for years. Now, it's like nobody remembers any of that, like it never happened."

"East and West Germans?"

"Yes."

"When was this again?"

"It went on for decades, the fifties, sixties, seventies—the whole cold war."

"I don't want to go to Europe anyway," Chloe said. "I want to go back to Hawaii." She put on her frowny face and peeked at him from under her blond curls. "Can we?" She stretched out her leg and began to rub his calf with her bare foot.

"We will. We'll do that. But, you see what I'm saying? About the importance of memories, about things, important things just going away?"

She moved her foot further up his leg. "Take me to Hawaii."

Her pink cell phone erupted in a line from a rap song. She grabbed it from the table and turned away from him in a single motion. She stood, leaning forward with her feet apart, as if facing into a hurricane. The shorts looked spectacular then. Buddy didn't care. "A lot of things happened in those years." He went on as she moved further away from him, talking as much to himself as to her.

Buddy could glimpse the wall beyond her. The morning light was glinting off the tan stone between the leaves of the oaks. He went on talking for lack of anything better to do, talking softly to the girl's back as she huddled over the cell phone. "Things seem to just go away," he said. "Important things that deserve remembering. And nobody cares ... nobody."

*

"God, how I despise Sundays." Sam Sampson made the statement to no one in particular. His wife sat across the table from him on the deck at the Chartwell Country Club, but he wasn't speaking to her. There was nothing to do on Sundays, nothing he enjoyed.

"Don't forget, dear, we have the doubles tournament tonight at 4:00," the wife said. "We should get down to the courts by 3:30 and warm up."

He watched as she put a hand up to her blond hair as she was speaking. She'd had her hair cut the day before. It was a new, short, trendy cut that she thought he'd like. And she was trying to make him notice. He did notice. *I don't give a shit—dear. After twenty-eight years of marriage you ought to know that.* His lips dropped into the sneer that signaled he pitied her for being such a simpleton. "I'll let you know when it's time to head down to the courts."

Her hand fluttered down from her hair and under the table like an injured bird. "It's the last doubles tournament of the season. I've been practicing a lot. I want us to do well."

"I may not feel like playing tennis this afternoon." Sampson frowned down at the fingernails of his left hand as if he'd never noticed them before. "Four o'clock you say?"

"Yes," she answered, showing a sudden interest in her own nails.

"I'll let you know."

He stood up then and went to the edge of the deck to flip open his cell phone. "Woolsey," he said into it. "Do you have the drawings in front of you? No. No! The ones for the interchange. I'll wait." Sampson didn't mind waiting, not today. He already knew everything he needed to know about the interchange, every dimension, every angle. In his mind he could picture how it would look with cars racing on and off of the cloverleaf when he had it completed in 2012. "What? I didn't call to ask you what goddamned day it is. I want you to look at those drawings." He could hear a rustling and thumping on the phone. Sampson knew his office manager was desperate to find what he wanted. *Must have caught him sleeping or playing with himself or whatever twenty-five-year-olds do on a Sunday afternoon.*

Sampson leaned over the rail and watched three golfers working their way up the fairway. "You got it? Zoom in on the cloverleaf section. The angle, is it twenty-seven or twenty-nine degrees?" He knew it was twenty-seven, but it felt good to make Woolsey sweat. One of the golfers hit a drive and the new, white ball plopped soundly onto the green beneath him. He watched, smiling as the ball rolled to within four feet of the cup and lay still, gleaming in the September sun. "Twenty-seven? Fine. I want you to stay where you are, Woolsey, with access to your computer and phone. I may need more information later."

Samuel Ripley Sampson snapped down the top of his cell and sauntered back to the table where his wife waited. "I'm excited again, you know, since 1664 passed in the House. I'm going to build another interchange." His wife winced as she tried to smile. She glanced down again at her watch. It was 3:35. But she knew she was going to listen to his story again, all of it.

"I was twenty-one when my father let me construct the big one outside of Norfolk." He plopped back down hard into the wicker chair. His wife tilted her head and blinked at this point because the ritual called for it. "It was summer. We were working on the beltway, up near Parkville." He took a long sip of wine and settled back. "I was standing in the piss hole when he told me. Can you believe that?" She smiled a wan smile and shook her head, as ritual dictated. "He said to me: 'We're about to pour concrete down Virginia. Go down there and honcho it for me.' That's just how he said it." Sampson's left hand slipped down between his legs and felt the old, familiar hardness returning. The memories, combined with an awareness that he was about to do it all again, were potent.

"Those senior engineers and managers were livid. The hate in their faces whenever they looked at me! Me, I was in my first year of college, had barely made it through high school. But the old man knew I could build a road. And I could make those lazy hillbillies work. He knew I could." Sam Sampson paused for a breath here, as he always did, and went on. "A month later, the rebar was down. We started pouring. Elkins it was who had the concrete trucks. Twenty-two hundred tons a day ... or maybe it was twenty-four hundred tons ..."

Sampson watched his wife begin to twist the skin on her wrist as if she were trying to unscrew her left hand. She knew the longest and most tedious part of the recital was coming. But she knew too that it was acceptable to look away at this point. She stared out, down the hill to the Severn. She watched as two powerboats went around a little sailboat that drifted down the current in the center of the river.

"And it rained that year. They tried to tell me not to pour the concrete—to wait. But I told them to kiss my ass ..." His words became a verbal blur to her at that point. She could listen and yet tune them out, like an old song on the radio when she was driving. "And now, ... I need to see Schnee. To see him this week."

"Schnee? The state senator, Schnee?"

"Yes," he said, looking past the tiresome old woman to the red and gold maple trees on the hill, and imagining I-82 beyond the hill, and the way it merged, dreamlike, with I-95. "Schnee owes me."

He let a few silent seconds pass before he looked down at his own Rolex. "Oh my, it's 4:02. We need to get down to the tennis court."

CHAPTER 5

Senator Schnee had his pants undone and was tucking in his shirt when Sam Sampson opened the office door. In Sampson's mind, that was strike one. "Hi, Sam," the Senator said, buckling his belt. Standish, the fortyish senatorial aide remained seated, looking bored and rolling his Maryland State flag tie around his index finger. Neither of them made an effort to shake Sam Sampson's hand or offer him a seat. *Strike two.*

"I'm trying out some new golf balls," Sampson said. "Spaulding XL3000s. See what you think." He handed the package to the aide, acknowledging the appropriate reverse pecking order.

"You know I can't accept gifts, Sam." Schnee said it with a tight-lipped half-smile.

"Oh, please. Three golf balls. What are they going to do, impeach you?"

None of Sampson's personal or corporate political contributions had been gifts either. Yet the 2006 election could well have gone the other way minus that last minute injection of cash. The three of them shared the same thought. "It's all right if I sit?"

"Sam. Sam. You're like family. No need to ask that."

"What brings you to Annapolis today, Sam?" It was the first time Standish had ever called him by his first name. *Strike three.*

Sampson dropped into the brown leather armchair across from the Senator's desk. "Now that 1664 has passed the House," he began, "you'll be glad to know CEPCO's ready to go with the prep work."

"Getting it through the House was a huge step, Sam, as you well know." Sampson stared only at Schnee as he spoke. "But Senate approval is required before construction can begin."

"Prep work." An exasperated whisper from Sampson.

"What exactly does that mean—prep work?"

Sampson stared at the younger aide as if he were the village idiot and had just pissed on his shoes. "Prep work is just that. Surveying, rerouting of utilities, some demolition. A lot has to happen before the concrete starts to pour."

The aide frowned, shaking his head. "Roads Commission is going to shit a brick."

"Fuck the Roads Commission!"

Schnee and Standish looked at each other like parents whose toddler has just ruined the dinner party. Schnee spoke first. "I think what Sam is saying is that, as state senator, I'm allowed a certain amount of discretion concerning construction spending."

"Uh—okay."

"Schedule a meeting with Sam's people and see what he needs."

Sampson stood up at that point. He was smiling for the first time that day. "I didn't mean to take up so much of your time. I'm going to let you gentlemen get back to running the state." He made a show of reaching across the desk and shaking Schnee's hand.

"I'm sure you know," the aide said, "there's a local group up there that could still oppose the bill if they get organized."

"What group is that?" Sampson sneered. "The fucking neighborhood watch?" Schnee let out a chuckle of appreciation. He examined the golf balls in their package.

"Don't forget 1968," the aide said, reminding them of Barbara Mikulski's entry into politics with SCAR. "If someone takes charge of this thing and they get rolling ... could be a problem."

Sampson came close to spitting. "We all know the Canton section of the interchange corridor is a shit hole. Those old factory buildings are death traps. Tearing them down will be doing a public service."

"If the need arises later on"—the Senator kept his voice low—"I'd suggest you pursue that line of argument." Schnee reached up with both hands and pushed the mane of gray-blond hair back on his head. "I can't say that kind of thing, but as a private citizen, you can." They were all silent. "And jobs, jobs, jobs," don't forget that," the senator added.

"Somebody might want to oppose me." Schnee raised his eyebrows and the aide winced openly at the grandiosity of *me*. "Well, if they do, Christ help 'em."

*

Michelle couldn't stop staring at the mirror behind the bar. The mirror was old. But then, everything in the Stricker Street VFW hall had long since blown past her criteria for being old. A white smear drifted down the center of the mirror. She had a mental picture of someone throwing a cup of laundry detergent on it about the time the Great Depression started. The fact that no one had bothered to move the paper HAPPY NEW YEAR! sign and wipe the smear away was making her crazy. Two large women danced in the closet sized square across the room while John Denver once again thanked God he was a country boy.

The flyer in the mailbox had said an emergency meeting of the neighborhood association, their first meeting in the better part of a year, would be held there at 7:00 pm. That it was 7:06 and she was the only one of the association members who showed up added to her sense of impending insanity.

The Vitros arrived and pulled up two wooden chairs next to her. It blunted some of the anxious edge. "Did Melvin Rank tell you about the I-95 interchange they want to build, right in the middle of Canton?" It was clear Mrs. Vitro had no idea what Michelle and Vance Berg had discussed that day in her bakery.

"I told Melvin about it, actually. I think the House in Annapolis is debating the bill right now. Berg, the ombudsman, contacted me and gave me the bill. I'm only the secretary-at-large. But for some reason he gave it to me. Melvin was in the hospital or something."

Sam Vitro and his wife both looked her as if she'd just made a speech in Uzbek.

Michelle watched the minutes tick by and the three of them turned to small talk. An intermittent stream of association members trickled in. They were mostly men, mostly old. She recognized their faces from other neighborhood meetings. They chatted and fell into comfortable cliques at tables around her. *This is a real meeting, not a bull roast,* she wanted to say. *At least they're here.*

It was close to 7:30 when the association president arrived. A bald man in his forties, who may have been Melvin Rank's son, opened the door and led him in. The people at the tables went silent as the old man shuffled with his walker and oxygen bottle past the long bar. No one stood to greet the man; only random whispers emanated from the semi-dark.

"Wow, he really is sick."

"He's barely makin' it."

"Poor old fart."

"He does very well for his age," Mrs. Vitro interjected in the man's defense. "I hear he still goes to his high school reunion every year."

"What do they do for entertainment, play Andrews Sisters records?"

"Andrews Sisters?" a fat man at Michelle's table chimed in. "They're still doing the Lucky Lindy."

The muffled laughter was barely fading when Mr. Caruthers took his shot. "Melvin's the only one in the neighborhood older than me." The tall black man said it with a certain combination of pride and awe. "He so old his pee comes out blue." Michelle didn't understand why that was funny. But she did note that it was a huge hit at the other tables.

The two wags next to her were not about to be outdone. They launched into a tag team series of quips about the age of their association president. "I hear Melvin still has a bumper sticker on his car that says *A chicken in every pot.*"

"I'm not sure just how old Melvin is, but I heard him say when New Year's Eve comes around he's going to party like it's 1899."

Michelle was determined not to react to any cracks about the man. But she'd just taken a sip of beer and found herself snorting it back into the glass. *Sorry, Melvin. That one really was funny.*

Still dabbing at her chin with a napkin, she got up and walked around the table to where the venerable association head was situated. She pulled up an empty chair and sat next to the old man. "I'm so glad you're here," she said, squeezing his shoulder. "We're already behind the eight-ball. The State's driving hard to start building this interchange, and we've got to push back immediately."

"I need to call Vance and have him squash this thing," the old man said, nodding.

Something like terror tickled Michelle's insides. "Uh, Berg is the one who told me about the bill. He gave me a copy of it."

"Vance knew about this? From the beginning?"

"Evidently. And evidently he never informed you until now."

"I've been sick."

"Melvin!" The fat one who had made the age quip took off his baseball cap to reveal a wide expanse of thinning red hair. "Just what is going on with this new road thing?"

Michelle got to her feet and took advantage of the moment. They all became quiet and focused on her. "The interchange Mr. Rank told you about is for real and it's on its way," she said. "This isn't a damned joke. And we're not here for a party." She didn't think she'd spoken that loudly, but she was suddenly aware she had the attention of everyone in the VFW hall, including the gray-haired man with the duck's ass haircut behind the bar and the two hefty ladies suddenly immobile on the dance floor. "I haven't lived here as long as some of you. But I love this community. And if this thing happens, your businesses and homes, if they don't take them directly, you'll lose them by losing the essence, the magic of what Canton is. We'll never recover from it."

"Help us then. Tell us what to do."

She didn't know who'd spoken. It might have been her own conscience. "This could turn into a pretty major undertaking—for all of us." In the space of a second, Michelle glanced down at her hands and saw her husband's pained frown as she told him of yet another obligation on her time. She pictured little Carlos's expectant eyes. She saw the eight new cases she had lined up on separate pages in her day planner. Looking up again, she found thirty-one pairs of eyes trained on her. "I mean, I'll certainly do what I can … but I have a very full plate right now." She turned back again to Melvin Rank, who had lost interest in her and was attempting to rebalance his oxygen bottle against the leg of his walker.

Mrs. Vitro spoke up. "Can't you find out what we need to do, Mrs. Ibanez? You're a lawyer. You know about that kind of stuff."

"Well, I'm pretty sure to have any effect at all we'll have to form a coalition. We're going to need a place, a headquarters of some kind." There was silence. But they all continued to watch her, waiting. "I'll do that much, okay? I'll rent a place. I'll get things started."

CHAPTER 6

SEPTEMBER 28–30, 2009
WELCOME TO CHARTWELL

Joanne parked in the alley on the side of what looked like the shabbiest building on Fleet Street. It was Monday night and nearly dark when they got there. Michelle said goodbye to her Uncle Jerry and flipped her cell phone closed. "It used to be—I don't know, a bakery or something." Mr. Caruthers and Mrs. Vitro were already waiting on the sidewalk in front of the door. The old black man looked somber. He wore the same oversized corduroy sports coat with an Oriole cap. Mrs. Vitro held a big, covered plastic tray in front of her.

The building looked old but solid. "It might have been that," Joanne said. "Or a cleaners, or a hardware store. Something from the 1930s." The peeling, pale green paint on the door frame and trim held no clues. No trace of a sign remained. Sturdy but bare, the old building stood like a court-marshaled soldier, stripped of his stripes. They all stared at Michelle's back as she tried to make the key work in the big, flat-faced door lock.

The inside was no more promising. Michelle found a light switch, but nothing happened when she flipped it. She heard her own breath rush out in a sigh that said more than a five hundred word essay on discouragement would. "Could just be the bulbs," Joanne said, dropping her keys and purse on the brittle linoleum floor. "I'll check the other rooms." The darkness and the futility of it all nearly overwhelmed

Michelle. And the overshadowing image of Carlos fuming alone with their son made her want to run home and say "the hell with all of it." Joanne came back, punching numbers into her cell as she walked.

"Everybody's gone home, Jo. We won't get a damned thing done tonight." Michelle put her fists to the side of her head and pushed as if trying to force away the doubt.

"This place works for me. Bunky's no-nonsense gym is two doors away. I want to check that out." Joanne's attempt at positive wasn't working. She snapped her cell phone down and stuffed it into her jacket pocket. "Look, why don't I go check on Carlos for you? You'll feel better if you know the home front's okay."

"Thanks. But they'll be fine. We just need to do this."

Mr. Caruthers wore a bright yellow tie that looked fluorescent against his denim work shirt. "Lights ain't working, missus? Where de box?" She tried again to place the man's accent. It could have been Jamaican but laced with black Baltimore.

Mrs. True poked her head in the door with an obscenely cheery, "Knock, knock!" The gray-haired woman stood awkwardly, holding a covered blue and white bowl and a bag of hot dog buns. Michelle thought she looked like some nineteenth-century urchin with a washtub. "I brought some sausage and sauerkraut. Where is everybody?"

"That sounds wonderful," Michelle said. "Put them ..." It was only then that she realized that there was no furniture—at all. The older woman smiled and carried the bowl into the other room to save her the embarrassment of answering. Michelle saw a phone on the floor then, the black plastic glinting in the growing dark. She almost ran to it, picked it up, and heard no dial tone. "It doesn't work either. Even the damned phone doesn't work."

It was then the two high school kids from the neighborhood meeting came through the front door. Both the girl and the boy looked wide-eyed and a little confused, instinctively hugging their laptops close to their chests. Seeing them, Michelle flashed back to her own teen years when she'd captained the basketball team. *Silly*, she thought, but the feelings were just the same: pre-game jitters when the other team looked like Amazons from a bad space movie. "Don't show them any fear," she whispered to herself.

"You say something, 'Chelle?" Joanne had come from the back room, her cell phone still at her ear.

"I said we've got two more great workers with us." She edged between the kids in the growing gloom and put her arms around their shoulders. "I apologize, guys. No place to work. But I am so glad you're here." The ceiling lights flashed, went off, and then came on again. They all stared at the ceiling as if they'd never seen electric lights before. The archaic fluorescent hum from the long, flickering dusty bulbs was the only sound.

"Finally found de damned box," Mr. Caruthers said, shuffling around the corner from the stairs. He carried a dirty brown rag the size of a pillowcase. "This was stuffed inside it. Lucky we didn't have a damned fire."

"We barely use the land line," Joanne said, tapping the cell phone next to her ear. "But I'm going to ream somebody's ass tonight anyway."

Her friend was well into the process of reaming someone at Verizon when Mrs. Vitro pushed one of her blueberry muffins into Michelle's hand. She saw that the boy and girl had mysteriously produced four brown metal folding chairs. They each sat on one and used the other as a desk. They were hunched over their fired-up laptops with the unassuming diligence of seventeen year olds. Only when she bit into the sugary top of the muffin did Michelle realize she hadn't eaten anything that day.

This was her team now. She had a good team. "We can beat this thing," she said to herself between bites. "God help me, we can beat it."

Mrs. True's face took on a look that was something like outrage as she watched Mr. Caruthers put a sausage into a bun and lace it with Tabasco sauce. "They're better with just the sauerkraut," she managed to get out through clenched teeth.

Caruthers straightened and bit off the end of the bun. "I cook a lot of sausage too," he said.

"The trick is to not overcook them."

Mr. Caruthers looked as if he'd just been slapped. "Well I cooks 'em till they bus'!"

*

Jerry had seen pictures of his new parish. Still, this wasn't what he expected. Twice he'd passed the driveway off the main road. *We need a sign. That goes right at the top of my list.* It was a long driveway, uphill and tree lined. Jerry was beginning to think he'd made a wrong turn after all when the flat-topped, cinderblock buildings appeared in front of him. Flat was the key word that popped into his head. The place was flat and somehow barren, a contrast to the lush farmland he'd just passed on the way. Only the yellow wooden cross by the front door let him know it was a church.

He parked the van next to the low building and tried the front door. It was locked. Jerry walked toward the box-like buildings on the far side of the parking lot, hoping to see someone, anyone. *Lots of parking for a little church*, he thought. *I guess that's good.* He looked out over the hills that surrounded the church grounds. The greenness of the trees and fields made the bare church seem like the shy girl left out at the party.

He was rapping on the door, more specifically, on a white, stenciled sign pasted in the window that said OFFICE, when he heard a small voice behind him. "You must be the new Father." He was glad to turn and see the short Hispanic woman in jeans and a flannel shirt, glad to see anyone. An aging brown Lab was wagging its tail. It seemed to be smiling at him from behind the woman.

"Yes. Hi, I'm Jerry Miller."

"I'm Carla," she said, extending a stubby hand. "I'm the parish secretary."

"Who's your friend?"

"That's Peaches." Jerry reached down to pat the dog's side. "Nobody knows where she came from or who gave her that name. She's just been here forever."

Carla and Peaches gave him a tour of the office with its well-used metal desk and file cabinets. An ancient desktop computer sat, dark and cold, on the desk. They walked him back over to the simple wooden church and sacristy. Jerry saw the brown water stains in the center and on one side of the ceiling and marveled that Rob Hamden had been able to spot that damage from just a picture on the Internet.

"Did you know there's no sign out on Route 50? I had trouble finding the turn."

"Oh." Carla looked up at him from under thick black bangs. "The sign got stolen—twice."

Peaches led the way back across the asphalt sea of a parking lot to the office building and beyond it. "That's her house," Carla said, motioning to a flat-roofed box with a square door cut in the front that looked barely wide enough for the dog's head. A chewed, red plastic water bowl lay near the front of it like a canine calling card. "The garage is ours too."

"Garage? I thought that was a barn." They stood in front of the only peaked roof building in sight as Carla undid the padlock and pulled open one of the massive tin-covered doors. Jerry stared into the darkness but couldn't see the back wall of it. "This thing is huge. What's it for?"

The little secretary shrugged as she snapped the padlock shut on the door. "I don't know. Storage?"

"Okay. Thanks, Carla."

They were back in the office. Jerry was fighting off a fast growing sense of exhaustion. "And where do I stay? The letter said the rectory was attached." She opened the rear door of the office to show a small bedroom with a cement floor. The twin bed in the center took up the majority of the floor space. The cinderblock walls had, in some bygone era, been painted a pale green. She led him to a tiny kitchenette beyond the bedroom and then to a bathroom with a shower that dripped. "I'm sorry. It's the best we can do, Father."

"No!" Jerry said, embarrassed that he was that transparent. "No, this is fine. I've been a little spoiled over the last few years." Carla said nothing. In the silence he heard only the insistent droplets on the shower stall floor. Thunk. Thunk. Thunk. "Really, I've had a lot worse accommodations."

By 6:00 pm Jerry had his things unpacked. He felt, in a way, liberated. He was feeling satisfaction and some pride in that he could make a move and a major life change that quickly. "A couple of hours," he whispered to himself. "Pretty amazing. But I am going to get that damned shower fixed, soon. And, old and beat up as it is, that bed looks very good to me right now."

He was propping up his crucifix on the top of the chest of drawers when his cell phone rang. He smiled, seeing Michelle's name. "I knew you'd call. How've you been, Hon?"

"Forget how I am. How about you?"

Jerry thought her voice somehow made the room brighter. "I'm fine. Just a long drive, you know."

"So . . .? What's your new parish like?"

"I can see some little challenges coming. It's not like St. Mark's." Peaches ambled over to put her chin on his knee.

"Wait till I tell you what I've gotten into. I think we're both looking at some challenges, uncle Jerr."

*

"That's him. That's the girl's father." Vance Berg squatted next to his boss's chair and whispered.

His boss stared at a man on the far side of the grand dining room, alone at a table by the windows. Squinting hard, he slicked back thick gray hair that appeared to be manicured rather than cut. His tan was dark next to the new, white silk golf shirt. "You sure?"

"I did my homework."

Samuel Ripley Sampson turned to Berg and tried to smile a beneficent smile. But the man next to him looked ridiculous, squatting next to him like some subservient member of a pack. "What's his name?"

"Buddy Miller."

"Buuuddyyyy Miller," Sampson drawled out the first name. He continued to study the man across the room as he took a long sip of his mimosa and a bite of coffee cake. "Buddy Miller, real salt of the earth name." He made a sniffing sound, blowing air out through his nose. "Tell him to come over here."

"Uh, why?"

He looked down in disbelief. "You're asking me why?"

"I mean why should I say he should come over?"

He bent low and spoke as if to a child. "Tell him it's a meet and greet for new members." He did the sniff again and shook his head as he watched Vance Berg huddle with the man across the room. "Hire the handicapped," Sampson mumbled to the other men at the table, "they're fun to watch—for a while." *Buddy Miller—Jesus.*

*

The heavyset man with the striped knit shirt and street slacks led Buddy through the open French doors to the VIP room. And Buddy visualized a picture he'd seen of the sun king holding court in the hall of mirrors. The morning light streaming through the ceiling high windows seemed to be channeled directly onto the big, middle aged man in the white golf shirt. "Buddy," the man gushed, "welcome to Chartwell." The sun king was suddenly on his feet with his hand out. "Sam Sampson. Join us, please."

"Do we know each other?" Buddy asked as he slowly eased into the empty chair. The chair was still warm from the little man with the big glasses who'd been vacated from it.

"I'm on the board of the country club." The big man said it as if he were apologizing. "I like to meet and get to know the new people."

"Actually, I joined last summer," Buddy said as he took off his Nike swoop hat and bent the brim of it. "So I'm not really new."

"I try to keep up," Sam Sampson sighed. "How about a mimosa? They don't get any better than the ones they make here."

"Kind of early for me. I'll have a little coff—"

"I'll have another one if you do. C'mon."

"Okay. What the hell."

Sampson nodded almost imperceptibly at a fortyish waitress and held up two thick fingers. Before Buddy could move his hat to the center of the table she was bringing the two drinks. He noticed the woman's hands were shaking as she put the glasses down.

The drink did taste surprisingly good. And it felt good to relax in the last of the September sun and let the sweet, potent champagne meander down his throat. The pain in the back of his neck lessened.

"How do you like Chartwell, Buddy?"

"I like it a lot. The doctor told me to take up golf, so I did that. But I just enjoy the greenness of the place, if that makes sense." Buddy glanced up to see Vance Berg staring across the table as if he'd found a new exhibit at the Druid Hill Park Zoo. The fat man had street shoes on and had propped them on the green felt chair seat next to him.

The sun king continued on with what Buddy thought was a semi-interesting monolog about the club and his relationship with it. "Live close by, do you?" Buddy wanted to laugh at the way the other men at the table perked up as if the oracle at Delphi was about to speak.

"I have a place on the shore, yeah."

Sampson held up the two fingers and did the nod again. "A place on the shore—there's a phrase you don't hear anymore." The big man turned his gaze, as if he'd just smelled shit, to Vance Berg. "Don't you have things to do downtown?"

"I was going to do that tomorrow," Berg said, blinking in confusion.

"Get it started now." Sampson leaned to his left and watched his employee slink away. "What do you think of a man who wears a hat in a nice restaurant?"

Buddy sighed and took a long pull on the new mimosa. "I'd try to give him the benefit of the doubt and assume he's an orthodox Jew. Otherwise he's from Appalachia." It seemed to him the laughter around the table was a bit much. A chuckle or a few sniggers would have worked. The sun king seemed to be convulsing with his hand over his mouth. He pointed appreciatively at Buddy with his index finger. "That's good. That's good."

"Nice to meet you all," Buddy said, sliding back the chair and grabbing his hat. "I was going to play a few holes, but it's kind of late."

"Let's hit some balls." Sam Sampson was suddenly sober.

"I don't know..."

"One bucket. Just to loosen up."

*

Buddy envied the green lawns of the country club and wondered how they kept them looking so dark and rich. New Titleists lay out on the driving range like tiny white droplets of paint on a kelly-green canvas. Hitting more of them out there was something pleasant to do while he admired the manicured grounds. "What do you do normally, Sam?"

"Construction." Sam Sampson looked out at the distance markers while swinging the club to loosen his shoulders. "I spend a lot of time in Annapolis."

"Yeah? My daughter just went down there."

The bigger man smacked a ball out past the sign that said 100 Yards. "No! Really? Politician is she?"

"She's a lawyer. Her name's Ibanez now. She represents some neighborhood association in Canton."

"Tell her to look me up next time she's down there, Buddy. I have an office."

With a swish that seemed to tear the air around them, Samuel Ripley Sampson hit a long, effortless drive. The ball landed past the 250 yard marker.

CHAPTER 7

OCTOBER 1–2, 2009
GROUND ZERO

Joanne found her partner wandering the hall on the second floor of City Hall. Michelle was wearing her less-than-happy face. "I thought we were going to do lunch."

"We still are," Michelle said with a sigh. "Two and a half hours I've been here and I've got nothing. The city Web site says to start here." She pointed to a yellow and black sign on the brick wall. "I started with that door and found out being a National Heritage Area is right up there with being proclaimed a national treasure. We need to establish a neighborhood coalition. Simple. But *nobody* from the mayor's staff to the janitorial staff seems to know how to do that."

Joanne looked again at the sign and peeped through the half-closed blinds into the office. "I want to talk to them."

"But that's not what we need."

"We know that, but they don't." She opened the door and swooped to the counter with Michelle in tow. "Hi." With a knowing smile, she captured the young black woman behind the desk. We represent North Canton and we're seeking National Heritage Area Status."

"That's a tall order," the woman chuckled. "You'd have to start by submitting a proposal, which will be evaluated by the board."

"So then what are the criteria for obtaining Heritage Area status?"

"Each area is examined on a case-by-case basis. Did you know Fell's Point is already a Heritage Area?"

"I'm not talking about Fell's Point." Joanne sighed and pulled a pen and notebook from her jacket pocket. "So let me understand." Her engaging smile had disappeared and her tone had turned like a faucet from warm to cold. "I'm supposed to submit some sort of complex request to you, but you don't know the criteria?"

"It's done case by case." The black woman stretched out the sentence, emphasizing each word.

"Can I have your name?"

"Hodges." In the space of sixty seconds, the mood had gone from light to sullen.

"First name?"

"… Lenora."

"Lenora, we're facing an urgent situation. The state is about to start construction on a massive interchange in the heart of a historic neighborhood. The National Heritage designation would allow us to stop that project in its tracks."

"Just a minute." Lenora Hodges turned and went through the closed door behind her as if she were fleeing a burning building. Ninety seconds later she reappeared with a short, middle-aged white man who was still shaking crumbs from the half-eaten doughnut in his left hand.

"I'm Ted Jamison." His short salt–and-pepper beard moved symbiotically with his lips as he said the words. "Weren't you here earlier with a different question?" He had to look around the woman in front of him to ask Michelle, who only raised her eyebrows and shrugged. "Now you're saying you have a city neighborhood problem that involves State Highway Administration?"

"Yes." Joanne's winning smile was again functioning. "Our coalition is fighting an existing State Highways project."

"What's the name of your organization?"

Joanne turned her head to look at her partner.

Michelle spat out the single line she'd been assigned in Joanne's one act play. "The Coalition to Stop 1664."

"I've never heard of that," Ted Jamison retorted.

"That's because we haven't officially registered our coalition yet," Joanne retorted back.

"Then you need to do that."

"We need the forms."

"See Ellen Fisher."

"Where's she?"

"Two doors down, this side of the hall."

A glance at her watch told Michelle that just eight minutes had passed before she was running her forefinger down the checklist on the front of the forms. "Summarization of purpose, list of current members—this is a piece of cake! I'll have it back to them in the morning."

*

A surprisingly warm afternoon sun painted an orange glow over the sidewalk restaurant and over the entire street. An October-in-Baltimore day, summer's parting gift. Michelle dropped into the second chair by the round table. "I didn't expect this to be easy, but damn." She picked up an empty water glass and clinked Joanne's. "You're pretty amazing, girl."

Her partner shrugged. "It's a game as old as time. Get in their face and be annoying and they'll tell you anything you want to know just to get you out of their office."

"I'd love a crab cake," Michelle said, pushing away the menu before she changed her mind and went for the rigatoni she really wanted. "Halloween's not far away, and I don't think I've had one all summer." Joanne ordered the soup and salad like Michelle knew she would.

Joanne looked good. She looked more than good, despite the day. Her long, chestnut hair fell onto the shoulders of her gray tweed jacket and caressed her beige wool scarf as if Vidal Sassoon had just arranged it for her. It made Michelle remember again why she'd chosen this woman as her partner in the firm, the second biggest adventure of her life.

Even back at the University of Baltimore she'd spotted those qualities, the ones she'd need to complement her own strengths. Joanne Wicks hadn't been the best student, but the determination, the aggressiveness, the focus—she'd seen those things under the surface. Michelle smiled again. She relished the satisfaction of knowing that one critical gut decision in her life was right on. "When we were clawing our way through law school, would you have guessed we'd be here, dong this?"

Joanne lit a second cigarette with an apologetic smile. "I know. I was quitting. Guess I fell off the wagon this week."

Michelle shrugged. "We're outside, right?"

"I'm not avoiding your question. Yes. Six years ago I could have pictured the two of us here. Doing this, specifically? Not at all."

"Well, it's the best possible PR for us," Michelle said, taking a sip of water. "And it's our neighborhood, Jo. If this interchange happens, the quality of life for all of us turns to crap."

Joanne took a long, final drag on the cigarette and crushed it out on the metal-topped table. "I realize this is important to you. But I think you know as well as I do that this—today—was just the beginning."

"Yeah. If today was an indication of what we're up against ... wow."

Joanne leaned her elegant head back and blew out a lung full of smoke into Fayette Street. "I'm not trying to rain on your parade, Michelle. I'm just saying."

And then there's the blunt honesty, she thought. *But the loyalty is there too. It's all part of the package.*

*

"Be careful what you ask for." Joanne was smiling and waving a sticky note as she sauntered into Michelle's office.

"And that means what?"

"It means I got you an appointment with our state senator's right-hand man." Joanne handed her partner the yellow piece of paper and plopped down in the guest chair.

"I know you're good at this stuff. But puh-leez, tell me the details."

"It wasn't that hard." Joanne waved a set of newly manicured nails. "I started with Roads Construction, and every time I mentioned 1664 they bumped me up a level till I was talking to this Standish guy."

"What's he going to want from us?"

"That—he was very vague about. But when you go over there ..."

"Yeah?"

"I kind of exaggerated about our group. I talked about massive grassroots anger—political leverage, you know what I mean?"

"Yes, I do."

"So, you probably don't want to bring up that neighborhood meeting in the VFW."

Michelle looked at the name and number on the paper and smiled. "Got it."

"And watch out for the ego on that one." She pointed to the sticky note in Michelle's hand. "Five minutes on the phone with him and I could tell he's living in some bizarro world where Schnee's Barack Obama and he's Rahm Emanuel."

*

"Hi. Mike Standish," he said, extending his hand to her as she stepped off the elevator on the sixth floor of the Maryland State office building. Michelle was surprised at how tall he was. She was pleasantly surprised that the senator's right-hand man was there in the hallway waiting for her, and not so pleasantly surprised when he suggested they have their discussion on the benches by the window.

"Wait. This is where you want to talk, right here in the hall?"

"Yeah." Mike Standish put his hands in his pockets and sighed. "I couldn't see making you drive all the way to Annapolis."

Michelle scanned the busy hallway. It was obvious that no one was coming to join them. And she was feeling the blood rise in her neck. "This is it, the two of us?"

"Yes."

"Uh huh. Look, I'm curious; shouldn't someone from the Roads Commission be involved in this meeting?"

Standish turned away to check the knot of his tie in the ceiling-high hallway mirror and then turned back to stare at Michelle. It was a type of stare she hadn't experienced in years: Harvard professor eyeing a sophomore who'd just questioned his credentials. "The Roads Commission is at the service of the senator in this case." He took in a quick breath through his nose and lowered his head so he was looking at her over the top of his glasses. "And, frankly, I'm a little concerned that a neighborhood group like yours is raising a stink about a bill that your own duly elected district rep has long since bought into."

Michelle took her hands out of her suit coat pockets and stood up straight so that she was nearly eye to eye with him. "*Long since* are certainly the key words in this case. Berg only made us aware of 1664 when he absolutely had to. And I'm still having trouble with this 'Roads Commission at the service of the senator' thing. The Roads Commission is an arm of the state government, as is the senator. Right? If I'm missing something here, enlighten me."

Standish rolled his cold green eyes and twisted his lips in disgust. "Do you have any idea how busy I am? I took the time to set up this meeting as a service to you. I don't have time to play word games with every hack lawyer from South Baltimore who thinks she has an issue."

Michelle tilted her head, smiled, batted her eyelashes at him. "Well, let's get to work then. I'm certainly not here to waste your time."

"First of all," Standish said even as he sat down on the banquette bench under the window that looked out Preston Street, "when there's a complaint about a project already in motion, we assume that you have an alternative plan. Do you?"

"Sure."

Almost imperceptibly the muscles in Standish's face tightened when he didn't see fear in hers. "So, you already have an alternative route?"

"We will, when you're ready for it."

"I'll need that. And I'll need a formal statement delineating why your group opposes this project. Can you do that too?"

"And I want a meeting with Senator Schnee." She reached over to touch the politician's forearm. "Not to minimize your importance in any way, Mr. Standish, but you've already said that the senator is the driving force here. And it only makes sense that we present directly to him."

He blinked, looked at his watch, and then looked out the window. "When will you have the alternate route, and the other?"

"When will I see the senator?"

"I'll let you know," Standish said as he was getting to his feet.

"I'll be waiting." Michelle grabbed her briefcase and stood to match him. As she extended her hand and smiled, she remembered the hack lawyer crack and longed to break the man's nose. "So nice of you to take the time to meet with me," she said.

*

Joanne had to adjust back the passenger seat of the Miata if Michelle drove, a task she equated with the building of Stonehenge. It had become an occasional ritual for them. "What year is this car?" Joanne asked when she could at last buckle the seatbelt around her. She tried to position her long legs so that her knees weren't bumping the dash.

"It's a '99."

"And what year are we in now? You know, you can afford a new car."

"I guess," Michelle said, power shifting into second gear as she catapulted the little car around a slow-moving garbage truck. "But this is my car. This car and I have a lot of history together."

Joanne was clutching the shoulder strap with both manicured hands. "There's not much room for your passenger."

"Little Carlos is fine with it, till I put him in the back," Michelle grinned.

*

It was nearly twenty minutes later when Michele managed to find an industrial side street close to the spot she wanted to find. She parked the car just under the highway. They both climbed out and Michelle pulled her clipboard with the map copies from the back seat. I-95 loomed like a behemoth above them. The traffic, even though it was three stories up, roared like an endless freight train. Innumerable tons of aged concrete and steel blocked the pale October sun. In that spot, it felt like late November.

Joanne was shouting over the din. "This is it? Ground zero?"

"As close as I can tell." Michelle alternately grimaced up at the overpass and down at the map in her hand. "The cloverleaf will come down here and take out everything, all the homes between here and Stricker Street."

The other woman thrust her hands into her coat pockets and started taking long strides toward the first block of row houses. "Couldn't we just mail them this info? We both have more productive things to do than this."

"Yeah," Michelle said, hurrying to catch up to her partner. "I guess I just wanted to see, up close and personal, what we're up against." She glanced back over her shoulder at the Miata. It looked vulnerable and small there, awkwardly jammed between the weeds and the endless concrete. Even as she walked away from it, she began to second guess leaving the car there.

Joanne stood at the bottom of the first set of concrete stairs and let Michelle go up and rap on the door. When no one answered, she rapped again. Her knocking reverberated back to her, hollow. The house, like the street, was empty and still. At the second house, they repeated the process. Michelle thought she heard a shuffling inside. She thought she saw the brown curtains move. But the door didn't open. "I guess you're right," she said coming down the steps. "This wasn't the best idea."

An older couple turned the corner and came toward them from up the street. The two people moved slowly, looking small and stooped in too-big winter coats.

Michelle and Joanne walked down to meet them.

"Hi," Michelle began, flashing her widest smile, "You guys live here?"

The man straightened and pointed to the next row house down. "We live at 1204. Why? You sellin' something?"

"No," Michelle said with a laugh, touching his arm as if he'd just told a joke. "I'm Mrs. Ibanez. This is my law partner, Ms. Wicks. We're with the coalition to stop the road." No response. "We just wanted to be sure we had your support as you'll be the most immediately affected."

"We just went to the drugstore," the old woman said, her gray head bobbing up and down.

"You've heard about 1664?" Joanne interjected. "It's the House bill authorizing construction of a new I-95 interchange right here." The couple looked at each other and then back at her.

Michelle held the clipboard with the maps out in front of her, pointing to it. "You see right here? That's where the clover leaf will be." The old couple pretended to study the map. "So, have you guys lived here long?" she asked, to break the silence.

"We moved here in '61." The man perked up with unmistakable pride. "I was making good money at Bethlehem Steel then, good money. And we could afford a house. Been here ever since." He reached out with his left hand, the fingers of his right still intertwined with those of his wife. "Can I have one of those maps? We didn't hear nothing about no interchange."

Michelle thought about the old man as she walked in silence with her partner back to the abandoned Miata. She pictured him unstooped and young, stoking the blast furnaces in the giant steel plant. *He must have been an impressive guy then.* With a quick flourish she opened the car door, fell into the familiar leather seat, and backed up the old car with a tenderness that had been lacking earlier. She'd just found her lost sheep.

Joanne wouldn't stop staring through the passenger window at the old couple as they made their shuffling way down the empty sidewalk, still holding on to each other's hands. "Isn't it something?" she said. "After all those years, they still love each other like that."

"Hmm. It's a beautiful thing."

"No one even told them. They're about to lose the house they've had all their life and they weren't even told. That pisses me off." Joanne rubbed the window with the back of her hand as if that would help her to see the couple as they grew smaller. "Really—that makes me angry." She rubbed her eyes. "Their world's going to be upside down soon. And they don't even fucking know it."

CHAPTER 8

OCTOBER 8–12, 2009
THE POE STATUE

If she was home, Michelle would have been putting little Carlos to bed, helping him say his prayers, and touching his silken hair one more time as he drifted off. Instead, she was waiting for another Vance Berg phone call that she knew would never come. Open in front of her was volume 16 of Assigns and Regulations: City of Baltimore. But the words on the pages had already melted into meaningless blocks of legal-speak. She spun her favorite pen by her ear and knew she had become far too good at spinning it.

She found herself staring again at her University of Baltimore painting. The watercolor was one of the few personal things she'd brought to the law office. The picture had always meant a lot to her. A bronze Edgar Allen Poe sat in the sun in front of the main library building. She liked that he wasn't sitting back in a majestic Abe Lincoln pose. He looked strangely lifelike, his head down and one hand up from the chair arm as if he'd just remembered something. Michelle had come of age intellectually in that library. She couldn't look out those windows at Charles Street and not think of the giants who had built her city. She wanted to be one of them, to stand on their shoulders and make it even better. Being ignored, marginalized, and set up to look like a fool was not part of her game plan.

When Joanne came through the door and leaned on it, Michelle knew her partner was tired too. She had been in court that morning, the morning that seemed so long ago. Michelle knew Joanne wore her tweed suit when she went to court. The skirt and jacket still looked fresh, smart, and perky. But Joanne leaned on the door frame like a scarecrow that had been propped there by a farmer who'd been in a rush.

"What?" Michelle threw out.

"Still nothing from Berg," she said with a sigh. "I say subpoena his fat ass despite the cost. It's the only thing he understands."

Michelle stared at the painting and spun the pen. "Technically, he is an ombudsman. Isn't there a rule that he has to spend a certain amount of time in his office?"

"The sign over on Montrose says he's there from 3:00 to 5:00 on Wednesdays and Fridays."

The pen stopped spinning. "I'll pay him a visit tomorrow. Face to face. He doesn't have the balls to return my calls."

"I'll go with you," she said. Michelle nodded. "Oh, and this young guy out here says he knows you."

Michelle went to the door to look into what had become the office bay. She saw the back of a big blond head that was unmistakable. From that angle she thought he looked like a lion in a sports coat. "He works for my dad."

"Shall I have him come in?" Joanne hadn't altered her scarecrow pose.

"No. I'll talk to him out there."

*

"Hi. Aren't you my dad's grad student?"

"Mike," he said turning toward her. "Mike Drazinski. We talked before."

He said it as if that were an explanation. In a second Michelle mentally went over the last time she'd been to her father's house. "We said hello to each other. Is that what you mean?"

"Uh, well, yeah."

"What can I do for you, Mike?"

"Your dad told me about the coalition. I want to volunteer, help however I can."

59

Something in the way he looked at her, the way his hand caressed the plastic tabletop, didn't seem right.

"Where are you going to find the time? You've got school. You work for my father." The boy smiled and made a big-shouldered shrug. "You probably have a girlfriend." He didn't answer. "What's your girlfriend's name?"

"Uh, Lisa. Look, I'll find the time," he said hurriedly. "I'll work it out." Michelle looked at her watch impatiently. He lowered his voice and asked, "So, what's it take to be a lawyer?"

"What?"

"It's something I've thought about ..."

She was passing Joanne on her way back into the office before he finished the sentence. "Let him fold some fliers or something," she said. "I really don't have time for this."

*

She sat back down at her desk and stared at Volume 16 of Assigns but the words seemed more meaningless than ever. Only a few seconds passed before she grabbed the phone and called her father's cell. The sound of Chloe's voice stunned her. "This is Michelle. My father, please."

"Hey," she heard her father's voice exclaim after a few seconds. "Nice surprise. What's up?"

"Why is she answering your phone?"

The sigh on the other end was almost palpable. "*She* has a name. And she lives with me, remember? You could be a little nicer to Chloe."

Don't talk to me like I'm nine! she thought but didn't say it. "Who sent Mike what's-his-face down here? Was it you?"

"Whoa. You lost me there, Hon."

"He showed up here today to volunteer. How'd he even know where this office was?"

A second of silence, and then: "I just mentioned to him ..."

Michelle slammed the phone down and was immediately stabbed with a pang of regret. Before even letting go of the receiver she knew she'd overreacted. Part of her wanted to call her father back. Part of her wanted to cry on his shoulder. Be a little girl again. She wanted to hear him tell her it was okay.

The uncompromising words of the road bill and mental pictures of dump trucks, like marauders in her neighborhood, flashed in her mind yet again. *And I should be home with my son and Carlos. Lots of other things I could be doing.*

She threw the heavy gold and maroon pen at the University of Baltimore painting. She threw it hard enough to break the glass.

*

Ombudsman Vance D. Berg looked out the rain-streaked window at Montrose Avenue and sipped a grape soda. To the left, he could see down the hill to the tar roofs and now bare treetops on Fleet Street. The buildings across the street were solid and well kept up. It was a wide street, newly paved. This was his street. He owned it. He owned his Ward. He felt more powerful in the old row house office than he ever did at the country club in Severna Park. Here he ruled. *Me,* he thought. *Not the Polacks and Greeks down the hill, not the Jew lawyers downtown. Me!*

He sniffed derisively when he saw Levi huffing up the hill under a black umbrella. The stocky lawyer wore the same plaid, short-sleeved shirts summer and winter. *I wonder if the asshole actually goes to court looking like that.* He continued to watch Levi as the man climbed the brick steps and rang the doorbell. He listened to it ring several times. It was a very old doorbell that sounded more like two pieces of pipe being banged together than a ring.

He enjoyed watching Levi's discomfort. Now he was banging on the door while trying to hang onto a fat, black brief case under one arm as well as his umbrella. Berg continued to stare through the window at Levi. He sneered at the gray-black beard and the loose skin that seemed to culminate in rolls on the man's forehead. *If the old fucker was a Dick Tracy character they'd have to call him Brow.* Only when the knocking became close to frantic did he saunter around the corner to the foyer and let Levi in.

"Didn't you see me on the steps?" Barry Levi's eyes bulged with indignation.

"I was takin' a shit." Vance Berg's voice rose with indignation. "Christ! Is that all right?"

Levi turned and shook his still-open umbrella on the brown linoleum.

"Hey, dickhead!" He loomed over the smaller man with sudden menace. "You live in a goddamn barn?"

"It's after 3:00. The Ibanez girl coming?" Without waiting for an answer, the lawyer tossed his umbrella into a corner, picked up his overstuffed briefcase, and straightened the dark blue yarmulke on the back of his head as he strode into the office.

Berg followed him and dropped heavily into his office chair. He stared at Levi and spun the chair left and right like a kid on a playground swing. "I've been ignoring the bitch for weeks. And we won't give her anything today. Got it?"

As if on cue, the doorbell clanked behind them. Vance Berg got up and took his time going around the corner to let Michelle and Joanne into the hallway. The two women walked in, wet and without speaking. They sat, along with Levi, in the threadbare orange chairs facing the gray metal desk. Levi allowed them a shadow of a nod while Berg put the tips of his fingers together in front of his face and resumed the left to right rotation of the chair.

"Nothing to say, Mr. Berg?" Michelle began after several seconds of silence. "You've been ducking us again." Berg only shrugged. "And who's this gentleman?"

Berg gestured broadly toward the round, bearded man in the short-sleeved shirt. "Why, Mr. Levi is my attorney." The tone of his voice had softened and taken on an oily, sarcastic quality. "So what?"

"Is he your personal attorney?" Joanne pulled out a leather covered notebook.

"No, I'm not." Barry Levi glared at her and snapped. "I represent all of CEPCO."

Vance Berg shot a blistering look at the lawyer even as he spoke to Michelle. "And how about you? Why'd you feel you had to bring your friend this time, Michelle?"

"Who's behind this project, Vance? Who's really pulling the strings? That's what I'm asking. You can't give me a straight answer, can you?"

"Why, the city of Baltimore, Ms. Ibanez." The oily tone was back. "The city of Baltimore."

"I don't need this shit." Michelle grabbed her bag and slung it over her shoulder though she wanted to slam it into the sneering faces in front of her. "You'll be hearing from us." She and Joanne waded out through a tense pool of silence.

Berg put his hands in his pockets and smiled as he stood at the window and watched the two women go down the steps and hunch over into the rain. "Well, damn!" he finally said. "Finest pair of asses that were ever in those chairs, I'll tell ya."

"That's not saying much, is it?" Barry Levi snapped the black briefcase shut and started out, dragging it behind him in the slipstream. "I'll let Mr. Sampson know about this meeting. I'll tell him tonight."

Vance Berg's large frame moved with startling quickness around the desk. He threw Levi against the door jamb, hard enough to shake the family pictures on the wall. "You ain't reporting shit, you dumb Jew cocksucker. Nothing happened here. You hear me? Nothing."

*

The two women ducked out of the downpour and into Joanne's black Lexus. Michelle stared at the rain on the windshield and blew out a long breath. "We still didn't get it," she said. "We're stuck. We still don't have the head of the snake." For several seconds neither of them said anything, staring ahead at the rain splashing in puddles on the shining asphalt. "It's not supposed to be like this, Jo." Michelle closed her eyes tight to contain the stinging tears.

"I'm sending those letters to Annapolis," Joanne said. "Next time they'll know we mean business."

"It's not just about meaning business." Michelle spoke while staring straight ahead. "He made us look like assholes, pure and simple. That won't happen again, not next time. There won't be a next time."

*

Michelle thought Monday might go on forever. She would have guessed it had already gone on for a week. Glimpses of the fiasco in Berg's office the Friday before regularly interrupted her reality like ugly commercial breaks. Words banged in her head like tuneless cymbals.

"The City of Baltimore, Ms. Ibanez. The City of Baltimore."
"And why'd you feel you had to bring your friend this time?"

"*My attorney.*"
"*All of CEPCO.*"

A week's worth of work lay in a pile on her desk, and she couldn't seem to focus on anything.

*

Around 4:00 the volunteers began to trickle in the front door and set up their improvised work stations on folding chairs, the corners of tables and desks, and in the hallway like administrative refugees. Michelle couldn't face them. They were doing their best. They were looking to her for leadership. She had nothing to tell them—nothing.

At 4:25 she had just opened one of the case folders in front of her when Mike Drazinski stuck his oversized head through her office door. She looked up to see him staring at her, smiling his little boy smile. She wondered how long he'd been in that position. She sighed and closed the folder. "Can I help you, Mike?"

"Just checkin' in, Michelle."

She cleared her throat, shoving the folder back into the overburdened inbox on her desk. "You can check in with Mr. Caruthers out there in the hall. And, Mike, most people here call me Mrs. Ibanez. Got it?" She saw his face fall and the smile evaporate.

"Sorry."

Oh damn, she thought, watching his wide back retreating into the hall. "Hey, Mike," she called after him. "You know, there is something I'd like you to do." The smile was back. He bounded, if a little sheepishly, back into her office. She scribbled on a yellow sticky note and handed it to him. "Just give me anything you can find on this."

"CEPCO? What is that?"

"That's what you're gonna' find out and tell me."

"Got it."

When he left she turned her chair around to face the wall shelves behind her and picked up a white cardboard box from the bottom one. Rereading the pages from the beat up white box had become a hobby for her, a stress reliever. She was keeping the box in the office now. Michelle had come to know most of her Uncle Tommy's poems by heart. She'd come to know the order of the pages in the box by heart, the order they were in when she got it. The diaries were on the top, battered, oil-stained spiral notebooks. The poems came next. She could tell they'd been worked on a lot. They were penned carefully on sheets of lined paper, each word written with care. Each of them mattered.

The pictures were next, and finally, that cryptic Reisterstown Road address scribbled on a napkin in a woman's handwriting. It was taped inside the cover of one of his journals. She looked again at the old piece of paper and lifted the lid of her laptop. But then she closed the journal and put it back in the box, in its place beneath all of the poems and pictures.

Michelle was about to slide the box, like a sacred icon, onto the shelf behind her office chair. She rubbed the bridge of her nose with her fingers. "You okay, 'Chelle?" Her partner was suddenly standing in the office doorway.

"Not great, but I'm okay." She raised the white box in front of her. "I started reading my uncle's poems again."

"The uncle who was murdered?"

"Uh huh. My Uncle Tommy. The diaries are kind of hard to decipher. Sometimes I can't figure out who he's talking about. But the poems always make me a little teary."

Joanne looked even taller than she usually did in her black pants suit. She perched on the edge of Michelle's desk. "You were close to him?"

"I never even knew him, actually. But I think he was a hell of a guy. He did a lot of things in his short life, you know."

"He had a hot girlfriend. I know that. You showed me the pictures."

"Yes, he did," Michelle laughed. "I'd love to know more about her, how they met, what became of her. But it's those poems that amaze me the most. He lived a tough life, never went to college." Her hand went over the top of the box as if she was dusting it. "He wrote some incredible stuff, full of optimism and tenderness in spite of it all."

Joanne's cell made a blooping noise. She looked at it and was on her way out the door in seconds. "Maybe you could get them published," she called over her shoulder. "It's worth a shot."

She sat up straight in the high-backed chair, took in a deep breath, and blew it out. She stared for nearly thirty seconds at the stack of manila case folders on the left side of her desk. Then she turned the chair around to put the old box back in its place.

"It is, you know." Michelle said it as if her friend was still there. "Maybe it is worth a shot. Someday." *Small bites of sorrow. Take it all in at the same time and your heart will burst. You'll go insane.* "I wouldn't let them print that one, Uncle Tommy—too personal—too deep."

CHAPTER 9

OCTOBER 13, 2009
NO MORE QUESTIONS

Inconvenienced is the word Buddy would have used to describe his morning, a morning spent waiting next to Mike Drazinski on a couch in the doctor's office. It had taken him twenty-five minutes to fill out the interminable medical form once again when they got there. In frustration he checked NO to everything and handed it back. The intermittent stabbing pains in his neck didn't make him feel horrible, or relieved, or afraid—just inconvenienced.

The waiting area felt cramped and dark; the couch was an ancient orange color from the 1960s. It felt to him more like they were in a low-rent apartment in Glen Burnie rather than an upscale doctor's office in Severna Park. Off and on, his neck ached like hell. Mike asked one vague, cryptic personal question after another until their trek up Richie Highway seemed like a cross-country saga. Buddy began to wonder why he'd asked the young man to drive him there. Inconvenience on steroids.

"How do you let another person know you care about them, Mr. Miller?" The young man's big, blond head hung down in front of him, and he rubbed his hands together awkwardly.

"You spend time with her," Buddy answered, staring at the clock on the wall. "I assume it is a her." Mike turned his head to give him an expression of equal parts hurt and disdain. "Show some interest in the girl, I guess. Hell, I don't know. Do I look like Oprah to you?"

Buddy had his own set of problems. The neck pain had become almost constant, debilitating sometimes. There were a hundred things he wanted to do around Nampara. And Chloe wanted him to do things. She had parties she needed him to go to with her. She'd planned another trip to Jamaica. *She wants ... a lot of things. Just fix this damned problem,* he complained silently to no one in particular. *I've got a life to live now, a good life.* Mike looked up and blinked as the nurse came out to usher the patient into the inner sanctum, a sign he was about to ask another question.

"Wait here," Buddy said, popping up from the couch faster than he thought he could. "This shouldn't take long."

*

Fifteen minutes later Doctor Silverberg walked into the room and around the metal table where Buddy sat. He hung an X-ray on the viewer, flipped the machine on, and stared at the black and white Rorschach-like image with both hands in the pockets of his lab coat. Long seconds ticked by. Buddy decided to play the waiting game too, making it a point not to speak first, not to move or even breathe heavily, thinking it would be construed as a blink on his part.

A full thirty seconds passed before the doctor spoke. "What happened, Mr. Miller?"

"What happened?" Buddy let himself exhale, thankful the game was over.

"With your neck. There was serious trauma at some point."

"Work accident. Long time ago." For the millionth time, Buddy replayed the mental footage of the fight in the Pigalle bar a decade before. He could still feel the weight on his back, the jolt like a cattle prod on his neck, and the exhilaration of finding the door handle and busting out into the cool night air. The whole detailed scene was condensed into the same two seconds. Sometimes he fixated on what would have happened had his hand not found the door handle. He didn't like to go there.

"Some sort of machinery involved? What happened?"

"It's not important. I didn't have any pain for a long time, years," Buddy said.

"Well, I hope you got a damned good settlement. The thing that went into your neck—nail, pencil, or whatever it was—did some massive nerve damage. You're lucky you weren't paralyzed."

"So, how do we fix it?"

Silverberg finally turned back to Buddy and seemed almost surprised to see him there half naked on the metal table. "I don't know that we can fix it. Like I said, you've been lucky. But an injury like this could deteriorate very quickly."

*

Back in the car, Buddy held his body at an angle with the back of his head between the window and the seat. In that unique position he felt almost comfortable. The doctor's words hung over him like a shroud. *This could deteriorate very quickly.* Part of him thought he should have pressed Silverberg on what that meant. Part of him didn't want to know. He held tight to the blue piece of paper with the painkiller prescription on it as if it was a winning Lotto ticket. Mike Drazinski flung himself into the driver's side and went through his entire seatbelt, wheel adjustment, and seat routine once again. The boy looked enormous in his old blue Volvo.

Once the car began to roll he went back into questioning mode. "Can I ask you another one, Mr. Miller? You did say once I could ask you questions. You won't think it's too personal?"

"Oh, Jesus." Buddy was beginning to picture himself as Shrek in the car with the Eddie Murphy donkey character. "Sure. Why not?"

"Okay. Relationships, like between older and younger people, what makes them work? What's the key?"

Buddy wanted to say that a big part of it for him was the pride he felt just being seen in public with a woman like Chloe. It was like a drug. He couldn't get enough of it. The admiration in the eyes of some young waiter when they were in a restaurant together or of a cop on a corner when they walked past him holding hands—each time it was like a fresh hit, a new high. It kept him going. He didn't just like the feeling; he thrived on it. *He won't understand that,* Buddy thought. *How could he?*

"Respect, Mike. It's all about respect, whatever your ages." Buddy suddenly felt like he hadn't slept in days. He closed his eyes and leaned back against the window, waiting for a response that didn't come. "Your girlfriend's older than you?" he prompted at last.

Buddy opened his eyes to see Mike staring ahead, bewilderment flashing like a neon sign on his face. "Well, Lisa, yeah, she's two years older than me. She's twenty-one."

"Oh, for God's sake."

"So ..."

"No more questions, Mike. Not now."

*

Even as Buddy Miller was feeling inconvenienced in the waiting room, his daughter was feeling stalled in Annapolis traffic. Before September, Michelle could have counted the times she'd been to the state capitol on one hand. The first was on Sister Stella Marie's fourth-grade field trip. It was an exciting place to her then, more so than Disneyland could ever hope to be. She remembered the Plebes marching in their perfect, white uniforms. She remembered the reverent way none of the kids spoke at the sarcophagus of John Paul Jones, and how they waited in line to peer into a lighted glass case at John Paul Jones's sword. It had been a warm day in May, the kind of day a ten-year-old would file away as a magic one.

Today, she'd be lucky to find a parking space, even in a pay lot. The spot she did find was in a lot almost at the river's edge. It was a twenty minute hike in uncomfortable shoes up to the State House and another ten minute hike to the annex. She did make it to the senator's office before 10:00. But she could sense already that there'd be no magic this day.

"Michelle Ibanez," she announced to Senator Schnee's receptionist, complementing the performance with her most upbeat smile. "I have an appointment with the senator this morning."

"You do." The black, middle-aged gatekeeper stared intently at the computer screen on her desk. Her eyes stayed there as she answered. "He's in a meeting right now. Why don't you go ahead and have a seat."

Michelle did that, taking comfort in the fact that her name was, at least, in the system and that there was no one else waiting on the worn wooden bench that took up the entire wall on the other side of the anteroom. She slid the alternate route proposal from her attaché case and skimmed the pages one more time, though she knew by heart now the words she was going to say.

By 11:00 she was sick of looking at the same words; and the hard bench was not nearly as comfortable as it had seemed an hour earlier. She waited until the receptionist was off the phone before making another foray to the desk. "So, he still in the meeting?"

"Meeting's over. But he's gone to lunch." The receptionist had revived her fascination with the computer screen.

"Will he be back soon?"

"Could be," the woman said after a few seconds of hesitation.

"So I guess I should stay here and wait. I'm still on his agenda, right?"

"Mmm."

The afternoon, minutes of it and then hours of it, inched by. Michelle leaned back on the bench with her arm draped over the back of it. A parade of paunchy, middle-aged women and men in business suits passed the counter with a muffled exchange or a "humph" on their way in or out of the inner sanctum. Watching them come and go, she began to think she truly was invisible. The receptionist never seemed to change her perplexed expression, focusing it alternatively on the computer screen or on a stack of envelopes and packages that she would sort into slots in a man-high gray rack next to her workstation. Roughly every hour the same young black man with a knit tie and his sleeves rolled up would push a chrome cart past the desk. He'd take the mail from the slots and put it into the top of the cart and hand over a stack of new mail from the bottom of it. Neither he nor anyone else acknowledged Michelle's presence.

It was 3:10 when she stepped to the desk for the last time and waited for the receptionist to get off the phone. She scanned the mail rack for the word: Road. That word and the name "Spanno" on a manila folder jumped out at her. She knew that Judge Trudy Spanno had been something of an institution in the Baltimore city court system for years. She didn't know the judge personally, but she did remember seeing her.

It was a little thing, but the name was the first familiar sight Michelle had seen since leaving the house that morning.

The woman put down the phone but refused to look up. Michelle leaned over the counter to put her face inches away from the receptionist's. "He never intended to see me, did he? But you still let me sit here like a simpleton all day." Michelle went back to grab her bag. She snatched the manila envelope that said Spanno from the rack as she passed it on her way to the door.

*

Mail Stop 216, she reasoned, must be on the second floor. She took the stairs. She adjusted her visitor's badge to make sure it was in plain sight and then took a deep breath and started down a hallway that looked to be longer than some of the runways at BWI. MS 216 ROADS COMMISSION—TRANSPORTATION and WORKS, the sign said. It was another office with a receptionist's desk in the front of it. The receptionist was not behind the desk, making Michelle almost whoop for joy.

In the inner office, a small woman with glasses and short curly hair sat behind a big desk. Michelle put on her most confident perky attitude as she went in. The woman looked up, startled. "Hi, Judge Spanno? Michelle Ibanez." She thrust the manila envelope across the desk as if she were awarding the judge a trophy. "You might remember me."

"Uh, no." The small woman straightened up in her chair, and Michelle remembered that some of the criminal lawyers would jokingly refer to her as Judge Judy.

"I came down from the city to see Senator Schnee about the new interchange in Canton. I have a proposal for an alternate route." She paused for a second, waiting for a response. None came. "So, on the way out, I decided I'd drop this copy off to you."

The judge stared at her cautiously. "How'd you make out with His Excellency, the senator?"

"It seems he was tied up all day."

An almost imperceptible smile flickered across Judge Spanno's lips. "And why did you bring this to my office?"

"I was on my way out. So I decided—"

"On your way out. So you decided to drop it off, yada, yada, yada … I know." Spanno tossed the manila folder to the far side of her desk. "Seriously, what do you think I can do for you?"

"You're someone familiar to me. You're behind the wall I've been trying to get over. And …" The phrase in Michelle's head was: *At least you're better than nothing.* What came out of her lips was: "You offer a strong possibility of hope to rectify this road project gone wrong."

"I do vaguely remember seeing you in the courthouse downtown." The judge's eyes went from Michelle to the envelope and back. "And I've heard your name. But you were never actually in my court."

"I have an extra copy of our alternative proposal. Can I leave it with you?"

"It can be pretty daunting down here," Trudy Spanno said, putting on her reading glasses. "I've found that out myself."

*

It wasn't the day she'd hoped for. But Michelle nurtured what feelings of relief she could glean from it as she made the long trek back to the parking lot. She dreaded talking to the neighborhood group on Monday. They'd want to know what happened. She knew they'd all be there at the meeting, Mrs. Vitro, Mr. Caruthers with his yellow tie and his Oriole cap, and the high school kids with their optimism, so vibrant but optimism so fragile. Even if they didn't ask, she'd see the questions on their faces, and she'd have to tell them something. But she couldn't tell them what happened today, not the way it really happened. She had a sudden, urgent need to be home with her own family.

She stepped faster and pulled her tweed jacket tight around her. It was after 4:00 and cold. A stiff wind blew in off the Severn River. The wind made it feel even colder.

CHAPTER 10

OCTOBER 15–16, 2009
NO LOOK-BACK. NO WAVE

There he was. Young Mike Drazinski was in her building, uninvited on a Thursday morning. Michelle didn't have a good feeling about it. She'd been coaxing a letter through the old and often maligned fax machine when she saw him. He bounced down the hall toward her office. He wore jeans and a bright Caterpillar yellow sweater that made his upper body look like part of an earth mover.

She came up behind him as he stood in the doorway of her empty office. "Mike, why are you here now?"

Whirling around, his face became red, flushed as if he'd been running. "Oh there you are," he almost gushed. He held a yellow, pocketed folder in front of him with both hands. She noticed that the folder came close to matching his sweater. "I found some stuff on CEPCO."

"That's great, Mike. But couldn't it wait till tomorrow night when you usually come in?" He extended the folder to her, still holding it with both hands. She took it. "And shouldn't you be at school?"

"I don't have a class until 3:00." He shot back the answer as if she'd asked an interview question he'd rehearsed for. "I got the impression this CEPCO thing was important, so I wanted to drop it by." Michelle walked around him with the folder and sat at her desk, leaving him standing in the doorway.

"Definitely some kind of construction company," she said, skimming the sheets of paper. All of this is kind of cryptic. Don't they have a Web site?"

"No. It wasn't easy. Even their address is just a post office box. I started looking and followed the string as far as I could." The young man put his hands in his pockets and leaned against the door jamb. He looked to her like he was not quite sure what was expected of him.

"Excavation and Procurement. We've got a start. And the name has to lead somewhere. Sounds like the Annapolis area. We've got that at least." She looked up for a second, smiled, and then stared down again at the pages. "Thanks, Mike. That's some good work."

Michelle was wondering what had become of Joanne. They had talked the day before about taking the petitions to the State House together. She wanted to introduce Joanne to the people she'd be interfacing with at the Bureau of Roads. They'd even joked about each of them carrying one of the cardboard boxes of signed petitions from the distant parking lot. She picked up her cell and called her partner's number again while she skimmed the CEPCO pages one more time. The call, like the others, went to Joanne's voicemail. She looked up after a minute to see Mike still in the same position by the door. "You know," she almost sighed, "I have to leave for a while. And I'm sure you have other things to do."

"Oh." Mike turned his head to look out into the hall, but his body stayed stationary. "I had a few extra hours. I thought I'd do some work here." Mike sniffed and shrugged. "This thing is important to me."

"You don't have homework? Not going to the gym? My father doesn't have work for you to do this morning?"

The young man shrugged.

Michelle wondered again about Joanne. She thought about the long drive to Annapolis. She looked down at the two heavy cardboard boxes of signed petitions next to her desk. She looked at him. She looked back at the boxes. "Let's go for a ride then. I'll get you back in time for school."

*

Well, I did carry some of them; Michelle reassured herself as Mike unloaded the two boxes from his shoulder and dropped them on the countertop in the Roads Bureau office. She had taken a stack of the forms from one of the boxes and carried it under her arm through the wintry cold. The two of them waited in front of the counter for someone to come over from the expanse of gray metal desks spread out in the room behind the counter.

Mike was watching a well-dressed older man in black slacks and a camel sports coat far in the back of the room. The man was sitting on the corner of one of the desks. He seemed out of place there, yet comfortable. His hands were down at his sides, and he swung his feet crossed at the ankles. From the intensity the man was eyeing them with, it seemed that he was somehow in charge and would soon be over to help them. None of the other men or women at their desks got up or even acknowledged them. Except for the man in the camel coat, no one seemed to know they were there. "Were we supposed to take a number or something, like at the DMV?" Mike asked.

Michelle smiled a wry smile and shook her head when she saw the boy actually look around for a ticket dispenser. "Hello," she called over the counter. "Little help here?" A large woman in a purple dress looked around at the others and then stood and shuffled toward the counter. The sound of her thighs rubbing together as she walked was the loudest sound in the room. "Hi. I've got signed petitions—for Canton, HB 1664." The woman said nothing. "Ibanez. Michelle Ibanez. I'm sure you know ..."

"Can you put them on the floor please?"

Mike D stepped forward and grabbed a box in each arm. He took them around the counter and through the swinging gate to drop them on the other side.

"You can't come in here!" The overweight woman could not have been more outraged if Mike had dropped his pants in front of her.

"Look, here's a copy of the original letter." Michelle slapped it down on the counter and turned to Mike. "Let's get you back so you can get to class," she said through clenched teeth.

Turning to go, Mike could see the well-dressed man still sitting on the corner of the desk, his Italian loafers tapping against the front of it. From the time they'd come through the door the man's eyes had never left them. He was sure of that.

*

Water rushed down the gutters on Fait Avenue like a mountain stream and rain continued to pelt the front window of their law office. At times it looked as if someone was squirting the window with a garden hose. "Two days now," Michelle mumbled to her partner. "Trudy Spanno, the one I told you about, the one with Roads. She's finally coming up to see what we've been doing. I was hoping the rain would at least slow down today."

"It sucks, no doubt. When's she supposed to be here?"

"Fifteen minutes ago." Michelle longed for some good news, something. She wanted, needed, this to work.

Joanne stared with her out the window. "Really sucks."

"Oooh, here she is." Michelle was surprised by the quickness of the little woman she saw bouncing into view on the corner under a pink umbrella. "Let's get away from the window so we don't look too desperate." Michelle let the bell ring twice before she opened the door. "Hi, judge. Come in out of the rain."

"I'm late," Trudy Spanno said, looking as if she'd just been shanghaied. "But there's no place to park—at all."

Michelle took the dripping umbrella and ushered the woman down the hall as she spoke. "Sounds like you don't get to town that often anymore." She was smiling. The judge was not. "I can get you one of those Canton T-shirts: Cold beer, hot women, no parking. Have you seen those?" The tightlipped half-smile she got in reply said more than words could. "Can I get you some coffee? Tea?"

"What have you got to show me, Michelle?"

"We'll start with the headquarters. Shall we go for a ride?"

*

Michelle made a wry mental note that Trudy Spanno was the only person other than her four-year-old who seemed to fit comfortably into the Miata. They took a long, circuitous route to the coalition headquarters building. She drove as slowly as she could manage down O'Donnell Street while she told about Captain O'Donnell and the clipper ship trade with Canton, China. Telling the story of the party at his estate where Betsy Patterson and Jerome Bonaparte had their first, fateful meeting, she hoped the judge hadn't heard it all a hundred times before.

"Looks like a lot of the old industrial base is still here too," Trudy Spanno said, visibly unimpressed and wiping the condensation from the side window with her hand. "My father used to tell me they called it Canton because they made so many cans here."

"Ah, that's good. I'll remember that one."

"These old factories will never produce anything again."

Michelle began to weave through blocks of well-kept row homes as they made their way south, toward the harbor. "You can see how much pride people take in their homes. And those factory buildings—you know, thirty years ago, the warehouses on the harbor side were eyesores. Now they're full of million dollar condos."

When they parked in front of coalition headquarters, four teen boys were on the corner. It looked like two of them would take turns fighting while the other two watched. "It's not much to look at," Michelle said, ignoring the show and pushing open the front door of the building with her shoulder. "But we're doing some good work here." The judge was still watching the group of boys on the corner. "Hmm, yes," she said, following the judge's eyes. "In the rain and slapping each other for fun. Too much free time and testosterone. It's a terrible combination."

"There are a couple of things I'd like you to see," Michelle continued. Outside, some distant thunder rumbled. Heavy rain began to pound the old storefront window, and she had to turn around and close the front door she'd left open. "These are full of signed petitions," she said, pulling open one of four cardboard boxes on a nearby table. "As you can see, we're doing this by the book. Each of those signatures represents a registered voter, by the way."

She pulled two manila envelopes from a file drawer and presented them to the judge. "The top one contains a second alternate route. The other is a list of assumptions. They're based on what I think the state's arguments will be and how we can counter them."

Trudy Spanno tucked the envelopes under her arm and peered silently into the box at the signed pieces of paper.

Michelle tried to fill the silence. "The gracious, hard working people, the charm, the commerce, the history. I love this place. It's like a diamond that just needs a little polishing."

Trudy Spanno closed the flaps on the top of the cardboard box and shoved it back across the shaky table. "Spare me the hyperbole,

Michelle. If I want smoke blown up my ass I'll go to a hot springs." She began to button her raincoat and look at her watch. "I need to get back to my van now."

Michelle turned out the lights and led her guest back through the battered front door. She continued to smile and tried to sound upbeat. *Loosen up, Trudy. We need this.*

The boys were still outside. They'd moved up from the corner and were directly in front of them. *Why, God, do they have to be right here, right now?* "Hey!" Michelle yelled with all the force she could muster. "Get away from here!"

"Fuck you!" came the reply in unison from three of the four boys.

"Why aren't you in school?" Judge Spanno chimed in.

"We been in school. Fuck you too, old bitch!"

The two of them moved up the hill to the safety of the little car, followed by a chorus of jeers and taunts. It was over in the space of two minutes, but the incident hung in the car with them like a foul smell. They drove back to the judge's van in silence.

*

"Thanks for the tour, Michelle," the judge said with one hand already on the door latch.

"Thank you for coming up. On a different day, you could have talked with some of our people. I hope you'll help us, Judge. We need your help."

"I wanted to see what you had ready for the Senate. And you showed me."

"Sorry about what happened back there."

"Not your fault. We'll be in touch." The off and on rain began to pour again. Michelle stayed in her car and watched the small woman climb into her van and drive off.

She didn't look back, she thought. *No look-back. No wave.* A cold emptiness filled Michelle from the inside out. She put both hands on the steering wheel and laid her forehead down on them. *I'd feel a lot better if she'd at least waved.*

*

79

Loneliness. It was a phenomenon Father Jerry Miller wasn't used to dealing with. In ten years at St. Mark's he'd dealt with every problem from anxiety to suicide prevention but never loneliness. There were times he'd wished for an occasional lonely day. Like most wishes, in reality, it didn't live up to expectations.

At 6:30 he'd found Peaches waiting for him outside the back door. The dog was a cheery sight, her eyes sparkling, her tail wagging, and her doggy breath visible in the fall morning chill. Three cans of Alpo remained under the sink in the kitchen. He emptied one of them into her bowl and made a lifelong friend by doing it.

After that, Jerry spent the remainder of his first Saturday at St. Joseph's going through all the records he could find in the office. The only ascertainable information he could glean was that more money seemed to go out each month than came in. He prepped his Sunday sermon and waited for the phone to ring. It didn't. More than a few times he was tempted to pick up his own cell and begin working his way down the contacts list. He didn't do that either. It felt like cheating. *This is a new situation. It's my new world. Making new friends is part of what I need to do.*

Confessions were scheduled from four to six o'clock. But he waited alone in the church until 5:25. Two older women appeared then, one of them with a black lace shawl over her head. He heard their confessions and was pleased to see that they stayed in church afterward to talk.

"My granddaughter drove us here," Mrs. Sanchez said, gesturing toward a black-haired teen in the back pew. The girl smiled and waved when she saw she was being pointed at. "We always try to get to confession on Saturdays."

"Well I'm glad you do. For a while I didn't think anyone was going to show up."

The woman looked at Jerry as if he were a visitor from outer space. "It's broccoli season, Father. Broccoli and pumpkins. That's where everybody is."

He nodded in agreement.

She nodded back. "We go out in the fields. We come back in to sleep. We go back out. That's what we do here."

Later, Jerry opened a can of soup and invited Peaches into the house to be his dinner companion. "Broccoli season, hmm?" The dog looked up at him and gave a contented swish of her tail on the yellow linoleum. "Who knew?"

*

The truck was coming far too fast into the parking lot. Jerry was outside after his first Sunday Mass at Saint Joseph's. He still had on his vestments. He'd been thinking about the little congregation, how they had a shyness about them. But he sensed a lot of warmth as well, in the touch of their hands and in their eyes. It was a maroon pickup truck, a wide one with wide tires. The big chrome grille looked dangerous in the midst of the people. The truck circled the parking lot in the space of a few seconds and screeched to a stop in front of the church door.

"Hey!" Jerry hurried around to the driver's side of the truck. "There are people coming out of church here. Slow that thing down!" A tall, lanky man in jeans and a white T-shirt got out of the truck. He made it a point to ignore Jerry as he walked around to the back of it.

"Vamanos," the man yelled, banging the inside of the truck bed with an open hand. Four Hispanic men jumped up onto the bed of the pickup. A fifth, with a white shirt and straw cowboy hat, handed a small child to his wife and then followed them.

"You can see these people out here." Jerry went on as if he had been acknowledged. "There are kids out here."

For the first time, the man looked at Jerry. Hate flashed from the eyes under the black baseball cap. "You're white, aren't you?"

"Last time I checked I was, yes," Jerry said. "I'd really appreciate it if you'd drive more carefully here."

"How's your Spanish?" The man strode back to the door of the pickup and got in as if the priest wasn't there. The truck pulled away with a force that made the five stooping men in the back of it lurch and grab on to the truck bed walls.

*

During Mass he'd thought the reticence of his flock to sing was due to a language problem. *They're used to singing in Spanish, not English. But that's not why they weren't singing,* Jerry thought as he removed his vestments in the closet-like sacristy. *It had nothing to do with language.* "These people are so beaten down they can't even sing."

CHAPTER 11

CAN I DO THIS?

"I'm so ready for a night out, Jo." Michelle was restacking the incoming case folders on her desk. Two meticulously neat stacks of folders, lined up one against the other, spoke of control and order. A helter-skelter pile in her inbox screamed chaos. "I don't care where we go or what we do. I just want some time with my own husband."

Joanne made a mental note that the National Boh clock on the wall said 5:45. "I want to try and get a run in before it gets dark," she said, frowning up at Mr. Boh's big, not at all businesslike eye.

"And next week I'll be back in Annapolis trying to figure out where we need to go from here. Ack! Enough! Let's get out of here."

*

The sense of anticipation Michelle felt as she walked the last block down the hill to the Chesapeake House surprised even her. Even after five and a half years of marriage she felt, at times, like a sixteen-year-old on a date. She knew enough not-so-happy couples to appreciate being one of the lucky ones.

"Hi. Just one?" The tall, young waitress wore a high waisted, mid-calf light blue skirt that made an almost inaudible swish as she walked.

"No. I'm meeting my husband here." *I'd be the world's worst waitress. But if I had to do it, I'd work here, just to wear one of those swishy skirts.*

The second time the waitress came back and found her waiting in the hall Michelle let herself be seated. She chose one of the comfortable old booths. It felt good to relax with the white wine she ordered and take her time reading each page of the menu, even though she'd been thinking all afternoon about what she wanted for dinner.

"You probably want to wait to order."

"Yeah," Michelle said, glancing at her watch and suppressing the tiny sense of unease that had begun to nag her like a throat tickle before a cold. "He should be here any minute."

"I'll look for him," the waitress said with a perky smile.

"He's tall, dark, and very handsome. You can't miss him."

Twenty-five minutes later her feeling of uneasiness had progressed beyond the tickly stage when Carlos finally appeared with the waitress close on his heels. He slid, without a word, into the opposite side of the booth. "There you are. Everything okay, Hon?" She said the words and suppressed the fact that her date had not bothered to kiss or even greet her.

"Some asshole wanted to test drive an SR250 right at the end of my shift. I couldn't say no."

"Oh. You could have given me a quick call and let me know you'd be late."

"Aw, Christ," Carlos growled, grabbing up one of the blue and white menus. "Can't we just eat?"

She let it go and drained the last of her first glass of white wine. She knew it wasn't going to be the fun night she'd hoped for. But it could turn around.

The patient waitress reappeared. "We ready?"

Carlos spoke without looking at her. "Bring me a Seven and Seven. And I'll have the steak, medium rare."

"You've got it."

"Maryland crab for me," Michelle added as the blue skirt hurried off with a series of quick swishes. "I haven't had a crab cake since that Thursday with Jo. Did I tell you about that half-day boondoggle at City Hall?"

"Yes, you did."

"And I still don't know exactly what the state needs. I'll have to drive to Annapolis again and try to get some answers."

Carlos turned his head and glared at what he thought was the kitchen. "Are they killing the damned cow back there or what?"

"Hey," she said, touching the back of his hand, "how about a little support?"

"I am so damned tired of hearing about the interchange, and the House bill, and your fucking neighborhood committee. It's all bullshit. You're not even getting paid for any of that."

"This is very important to me. And it's not going to last forever."

The young waitress showed up then with two platters as if on cue. "Here you go."

"Just a minute," Carlos said, cutting into the middle of the steak. He backed up and let his knife and fork drop onto the plate with a clatter. "This isn't what I ordered. Take it back."

Michelle watched the back of the waitress hurrying away from the booth and lowered her voice to an urgent whisper. "And you didn't have to be mean to that girl. For Christ's sake, it's not her fault you had a shitty day!"

They finished their meal in almost total silence. When the waitress brought the check, Carlos stared at it and charged his credit card for the exact amount.

"Was there a problem with the service?" The girl said it tentatively, as if she'd never had to recite those words before.

"The service sucked." Carlos spat out the words as if he'd been waiting for the opportunity to say them. "The steak was dry and the service was slow."

The girl's deflated look said more than words. Michelle almost moaned audibly for her. She took a twenty dollar bill from her purse and dropped it on the table, daring him to say something about it as she and her husband slid out of the booth.

*

She sat in the passenger seat of his new car, fumbling with the seatbelt as Carlos adjusted the mirrors. Her face was still red, stinging with embarrassment with the look the waitress gave them when they left. "What just happened in there? What's really going on, Carlos? Don't tell me it was just a rough day at work. You're acting like a total ass."

He frowned and said nothing, wielding the cold silence like a weapon. Michelle couldn't help contrasting her feelings with the anticipation she'd felt two hours before. It didn't help. It was that much harder to take.

*

It was 9:20 Sunday morning and Carlos still wasn't dressed. He sat sullen and silent at the kitchen table, still in boxer shorts and a T-shirt. "Don't you want to shave and get ready, Hon?" She tossed the question as if it were an incidental thought over her shoulder as she washed out the coffee pot. Her husband only scowled and reached for the sports section of the Sunday Sun. At 9:40 she asked him directly, "You don't want to go to church with us?"

"I thought I told you," Carlos said, not looking up from the magazine section. "There's a game I want to watch. It's raining. And I don't feel like it." He turned the page, still refusing to look up. "You go."

"You didn't tell me. And it wasn't that long ago that you said we'd always go to church as a family. What changed?"

"Give it a break, Michelle. When do we ever do anything as a family anymore?" His eyes went back to the newspaper.

She tried to convince herself it was a little thing, but it was one more psychological punch she had to roll with. Carlos's attitude on Friday night had been the worst. The hoops she had to jump through to keep the coalition alive seemed never-ending. And the Judge's long hoped for visit had turned out to be the biggest non-event since Y2K. In the grand scheme of things it was nothing. But it was something she didn't need today.

Michelle glanced around the corner to make sure their son hadn't yet come down the steps. "It's not for me. After nights like Friday, I'm getting to the point where I don't care what you do." With two fingers, she pulled the paper down from in front of him. "Little Carlos needs your example. He needs a father with a faith life."

Carlos looked up at her then. His eyes warned her not to push.

*

Outside, Michelle put up the yellow hood on her son's poncho. The late October rain was coming down again in a constant, sweeping sheet.

Now that she was outside, the rain was harder and colder than she'd expected. Even as they took their first steps, she regretted her decision not to drive. "Ooh, it's coming down hard," she said. "Good thing we don't have far to go." The five-year-old didn't speak but hunched his small shoulders into the rain and thrust up his hand for her to hold. The two of them ran across a semi-deserted Pratt Street, their boots splashing in the chilly, Sunday morning rain. "When we get back I'll make you waffles, okay? Just the way you like them."

"Uh huh."

It was one of those times when she envied the boy's innocence. She envied him the things he didn't have to deal with, like a career spinning out of control. *Thank God for Joanne. She's my rock right now.* She longed for a single day like one of his days, a day without a million problems flying at her like a swarm of locusts. A swarm of unanswerable questions was bearing down on her, and she had to handle them alone. *Can I even do all this?* she wondered as the twin spires of St. Casmir's came into view. *Can I hold it all together?* She squeezed the boy's hand a little tighter. *I have to, for him.*

"Crowded this morning," Michelle whispered as they slid into one of the wooden pews. In front of them was a family with two small boys. They stood on the bench and smiled at her over the back of it. *They've got to be twins.* An older woman with long white hair slipped in next to her as Mass started.

Michelle tried hard to tune out the unpleasant parade of problems marching through her consciousness. She couldn't. *Where is our marriage going? How the hell did it get like this? Dad—why won't you listen to me?* And her own words resounded like a mantra behind it all: *Can I do all this?*

The twins were taking turns sliding on and off the wooden seat. They'd look up to see if Michelle was watching. Little Carlos knelt with her and stayed still until they stood to say the Our Father. Even though his eyes could only see the back of the time-worn, wooden pew, he didn't fidget like the other boys. "Peace be with you," the older woman said. Nodding down at the boy she added, "He's like a little angel." Michelle allowed her fingertips to touch her son's small shoulders and to drift along the back of his white shirt. For five years he'd been part of her life, his presence as constant as breathing. But there were times, special moments when she thought her heart might burst with love for him. This was one of those moments. She'd remember this one.

CHAPTER 12

November 7–13, 2009
Fortune Cookies

On Saturday, Michelle wanted nothing more than to clean house. Since the ugly meeting with Vance Berg she'd been grasping in vain for things she could make sense of and control. Cleaning her house was a start.

She needed to clean. She would start upstairs and work her way down. She knew it would feel good to do it that way. She left her husband and son in the living room together. They were building a robot with Legos, and the TV wasn't on. They weren't watching football or watching the Shrek movie again for the two-hundredth time. They were doing something together. And that part of married life also made her feel very good.

Changing the sheets on the bed and vacuuming the bedroom, Michelle thought about them downstairs, about all of the good things in her life. *Why am I wasting so much time on this road thing?* In the bathroom, she moved all the jars and tubes and cups from around the sink. She cleaned the black granite countertop, polished it, rubbed it hard, made it shine. *I have what I really need right here,* she thought. *I can't mess it up.* She liked putting the things back on the gleaming surface, one by one, arranging them the way she liked them. It all looked new then. She could hear the murmur downstairs, Carlos chatting easily with their son. It was a sound that spoke to her soul. *Don't mess it up,* she thought. If life came down to picking battles, she wanted to pick the ones she could win. *Hold what you've got. That's what Dad would say. Don't mess it up.*

She could still hear the bits and pieces of Carlos's sentences over the sound of the vacuum. The sound of his voice echoed in the hallway above the stairs. She could hear them over the insistent hum of the machine. They were a little louder now. His voice had changed. She couldn't make out all the words, but his tone had changed. It wasn't the tone he used with her. And it wasn't his business voice, low and measured. She tried to catch the words. Scraps of half a conversation: "Mmm," he said. "I'm home ... all the time ..." She turned off the vacuum and sat down on the carpet, her back against the wall. She was suddenly uneasy. She wasn't sure why, but the beginning tickles of something like fear were climbing up her back.

She quietly scooted closer to the stairs, half of her hoping he would go on, half hoping he wouldn't. "You did your toenails too?" she heard him ask. The words went through her like an icicle in her chest. She put her elbows on her knees and her clenched fists on the sides of her head. "Yellow flowers? On each toe? Mmm, I want to see that up close and personal." She heard little Carlos tell his father to look at something. A murmur. The metallic snap of the cell phone cover. And the sound of her husband's voice again. His *at home* tone had come back.

Michelle left the cleaning and went down the stairs. Carlos was still sitting on the carpet with the boy. She stood behind them, next to the couch, and wished she hadn't heard the words. Then nothing would have changed. Carlos was spending time with their son at last, like she'd asked him to. The two of them were adding to the robot's head and arms with yellow Legos. A faint voice in the back of her mind repeated: *Let it go. Don't mess it up.*

"I heard you on the phone," she heard herself say. Carlos turned and looked up at her as if she'd poured scalding water on his back.

"What? Oh that. I had a call from work." He turned away from her and back to the yellow Legos.

"Were you talking to another woman?"

"Excuse me?" He looked up with a different expression, confrontational now. "It was one of the guys from work. What is this, Michelle?"

"Toes painted with yellow flowers? I heard you say that. Is there something going on, Carlos? Just tell me."

"No!" Carlos got to his feet as if the house were on fire. "I was talking to Mark from the office. It was a joke. Jesus, Michelle, you have to spy on me now in my own house?"

"I wasn't spying on you, dammit." She saw her son staring up at her and lowered her tone to a more conversational one. "I couldn't help hearing you."

"This is too stupid to even talk about," he said, squatting back down on the floor with his son.

*

Dinner out didn't override the phone call, but it helped dim the memory. That memory played continuously in the back of her mind like annoying white noise. But she willed it to stay in the back. She willed it to be paranoia on her part. For now, she was out with her three men. And that Carlos had initiated the idea of taking their son and her father out for Chinese food especially warmed her heart. It was the kind of Sunday evening Michelle cherished most.

"This one's the beef and broccoli." Buddy pointed to the platter on his right. "And that one's chicken. Which one do you want?" The five-year-old, uncharacteristically shy for once, pointed to the chicken. "Good choice," Buddy said, dishing some of the chow mien and noodles onto his grandson's plate. Michelle pretended not to notice, but she liked the way they interacted, her father and her son. She liked the way Buddy chatted and joked with the boy as the evening went on, not babying or talking down to him, treating him like a small adult.

They'd been hungry, all of them. And they talked easily of little things between delectable bites of rice and vegetables and sips of hot tea. They talked of things like the sudden fall chill, Michelle's old Miata, and Buddy's new wall.

"Where'd you say Chloe was today, Bud?" Carlos asked the question when he saw his wife wasn't going to.

"She's working. A real estate agent, especially down there in Severna Park, never stops."

"When do you guys get to do things together?"

"Do things?"

"I mean spend time together, do stuff together..."

Buddy reached down with a white napkin to wipe little Carlos's chin. "That's a good question. We need to take another trip."

Michelle put down her fork and gave him her *But Dad!* look. "Didn't you just go to Hawaii?"

"Well, not *just*." Little Carlos was reaching for the teacup with both hands and Buddy had to hand it to him. "That was months ago."

"Carlos and I haven't been on a real trip since our honeymoon."

"The two of them work hard together," Carlos interjected. Only Michelle recognized the tinge of harshness behind her husband's words. "They can afford it. They should go if they want to."

"I just don't want to see you taken advantage of, Dad." There was silence around the table. Only Little Carlos continued eating.

"You could afford a trip too, if you really wanted one," Buddy countered. More silence.

"Okay," Michelle said with a complete change of tone, "fortune cookie time!" Her father had to smile because he knew that had his daughter been nine years old she would have said the same words, in the same way. She broke open the brittle cookie and pulled out the sliver of white paper as if it were from the Oracle at Delphi. "Ready?" The three males nodded in unison. *"Your life will consist of many journeys.* Now that is funny."

The waiter brought back Buddy's Styrofoam container then. Buddy took it and put his arm around his grandson's shoulders to pull him close for a second. "Where you goin'?" the boy asked, looking up at him.

"Going home, young man. We'll talk later, okay?" Carlos stood and half-leaned over the table to shake Buddy's hand.

Michelle shuffled out of the booth and over to her father to hug him. "I'm so glad you're here," she whispered.

"Me too, Honey. We don't do this enough."

*

Fifteen minutes later the little family was back at The Outlook. Twenty-five minutes later Michelle was tucking in her sleepy son and kissing his forehead. She walked down the hall realizing she was just as exhausted as he was. She let herself bounce down on the corner of the bed and closed her eyes, savoring the good feelings of the night. Carlos was in the bathroom.

"Oh." She jumped up and picked her cell out of her purse. "Hey," she said softly when her father answered. "You never told us what your fortune cookie said."

"Michelle, you're killing me," Buddy laughed. "You called me for that?" The phone went silent for a second. "Just a minute." Thirty seconds passed before he came back. "Okay: *You will bring great joy to those around you.* Humph. I think we got each other's cookies."

"No, Dad. You got the right one."

"And you know, what we talked about ... about Chloe."

"I've gotta' be honest, Dad. Between you and me, okay? Don't you think she's pretty superficial?"

"No. She's not like that, really. Chloe's a more down-to-earth girl than you think she is." Michelle sighed into the phone, and her father cleared his throat as if he was about to make a speech. "I mean, she works hard. She's smart. And she's good at a lot of things."

"Hmm. No doubt."

"Be nice, Hon."

"You're telling me she doesn't have all your closets full of her clothes?"

"There, you see? She really doesn't have that many clothes, Michelle." He went silent for a second, and Michelle could almost see her father getting his thoughts in order. "She is serious about her nail art though. Gets those done every week religiously."

A cold spike of what she could only identify as fear passed through Michelle. "Really? She get her toenails done too?"

"Yes," her father laughed. "She does, actually. Can you believe it? Gets those little flowers on her toes. And it's winter. Nobody even sees them. But that's Chloe."

*

It wasn't easy for her. For days Michelle struggled with whether or not to tell her father at all. She struggled with how to tell him. *Excuse me, Dad. It seems your slut girlfriend has been screwing my husband.* It was hard to make the phone call, to be secretive yet upbeat enough to make him want to meet her for lunch at the Sulpher Spring Inn.

She'd even struggled with where to tell him. She couldn't put a finger on why it mattered or why she chose that place. He had grown up in Arbutus. *Maybe he'll be more comfortable there. Oh, come on. Just get it over with.*

She was ten or eleven when he'd taken her to the place for lunch, just once. She still remembered him ordering her a club sandwich and how exotic it had seemed, with different kinds of meats and pickles and onions and how toothpicks held the big sandwich together. The brick walls and knotty pine had looked ancient even then, not Fells Point renovations but relics from the days before exposed brick and old knotty pine were trendy. More important, she remembered her father sharing details about his own childhood. It was one of the few times he'd let down his guard and told about his own father's cruelty. Maybe that's why she chose the place.

"We just need to talk," she'd told him told him on the phone. She needed to sound serious enough that he would be there without question, but not to the point that he'd demand to know the problem right then. She'd gotten that right.

"Of all the places to have lunch on Friday the thirteenth," he laughed. "I'm sure you have a reason."

Now, looking at him across the table, she didn't know how to begin. She nibbled at her club sandwich and listened to him tell about his leaf mulcher, about how he only used it on the front yard. He laughed as he told about his trip to the doctor with Mike. He went on about the long stone wall, how the contractor was pushing hard right now because he'd have to slow down during the winter months. She knew it was her father's way of putting her at ease, telling her those things. "Carlos and I are having some problems," she heard herself blurt out. She watched his face fall. "It's serious."

"Oh God, Michelle, don't tell me that. Not you." She watched him put the palms of both hands to the sides of his face. Only two other times in her life had she seen him do that: when he talked about putting Bonzai down, and when he told her he had to leave Nampara. "Just the other night. You both seemed so ... together, content even." She looked at his face and felt sick for having started this. But she knew she couldn't stop now. "What happened, Hon?" He reached across the table and took her fingers in his hand. She wished he hadn't done that.

"It's been going on for a while," she said, searching for a starting point. "He's just kind of moving away from me. He's cold." She pulled her fingers from her father's hand and looked at him across the table. *Just say it*, she thought. *You can't leave here having not said it.* "Look. Here's why I'm telling you this." She sat up straight. "He's been seeing Chloe, Dad. I know it." Buddy snapped up straight in his chair as if he'd been slapped. She told him about the overheard phone call with Carlos. She reminded him of what he'd said about the painted nails. Buddy closed his eyes for a moment and looked down at the table. She could see his mind churning behind the closed eyes.

"No," he said at last, looking at her and shaking his head.

"No? What the hell do you mean—no?"

"You're way off base here. You've always had it in for Chloe because you can't stand me being with a younger woman." A stony anger suddenly shined in Buddy's eyes. "I'm not going to even say anything to her about this. I'm not because I know nothing happened."

"You know? How do you know that?"

"I just do."

"Do you think it was easy for me to tell you this, Dad? I'm not making this up. Jesus! The one response I wasn't expecting from you was denial."

"No," he said again, still shaking his head, still looking down. "You're wrong, Michelle. I don't know what's going on with you and your husband. But this is messed up. When you go home you're going to realize that and you're going to be embarrassed by this whole conversation."

"You just don't want to hear it." Michelle flung the words at him. But she herself didn't know where the words were coming from. "You don't want to hear it because it upsets your cozy little shacked up life, doesn't it?"

Oop, dere it is! He was right. She was embarrassed. She was embarrassed that she'd had to tell him. She was embarrassed by her father's total lack of sympathy, embarrassed that the words from that stupid early '90s song had popped unbidden into her head. She couldn't think straight. The embarrassment was turning to fury inside her. She could feel it coming to life, the fury, and she couldn't stop it.

Michelle stood up and fumbled for the wallet in her purse. She threw a ten dollar bill on the table and started to put on her suit jacket. She thought her father would say he was sorry and ask her to sit back down. He didn't. "While we're being honest," she said, jamming an arm into her jacket sleeve, "I want to know how your father died."

"What? Where'd that come from? What the hell are you talking about?"

"Come on. What really happened?" She grabbed her purse and stalked away from the table. After two steps she turned and came back like a tornado changing course. She leaned in close to her father. Sparks of anger seemed to fly from her eyes. "What happened, Dad?" she repeated in a husky whisper. "Just once come out and say it. What did you do to that old man?"

Chapter 13

November 18–20, 2009
Damn it's Cold

Sampson conceded to himself that he was pleased with the look of the new foyer. "It ought to be impressive," he said out loud. "She spent enough money on it to pay for a new Mercedes." He backed up to the front door and pretended to walk into the house, to see what his visitors would see. He had no doubt they'd know they were in the home of a man with taste.

Elaine Sampson came toward him carrying a silver tray of cookies. "Look at thiiiis," she sing-songed behind a cheery smile. "I thought we'd celebrate with your favorite cookies. Lemon parfaaaais." She sang the word parfait too. Her squeaky voice annoyed him, but he liked the way she looked. The black, below-the-knee skirt made her legs look even thinner. And her hair had been put back to the old way. She had it in the June Cleaver-like flip, the way it was supposed to be.

He could tell she'd spent time just arranging the perfect cookie squares. She'd stacked them in a seamless, cascading swirl around the tray. Sampson took the center one. He smiled as he took a large bite. The hallway phone rang. "Hmm hmm." He gestured at the phone with the cookie. She put down the tray and took a second to smooth the front of her skirt before picking up the phone.

"It's Vance," she said, handing it off to her husband. "Vance Berg."

"H'lo," Sampson said, still chewing. "Uh huh. Who? Ibanez? What is that, Mexican?" A malicious grin spread across his face. It was a wide enough grin that cookie crumbs began to fall from the corners of his mouth. "Of course I know who it is, idiot. What's she done now?"

Sampson held the half-chewed cookie in his mouth, forgetting to chew as he listened. "Well, why is *she* doing it?" The grin began to change shape like a smiley face on a slowly deflating balloon. "What happened to the old man?"

"Coalition—bullshit. That's meaningless. Any two patients in a mental institution can call themselves a coalition. It has to be approved, Vance." Sampson swallowed. He dropped the other half of the gooey cookie on the newly polished Chippendale table and used a finger to block sound from his left ear. "And how the hell did they pull that off? A better question might be how the hell did you let them pull it off?"

Elaine jumped when Sampson sent the offending phone flying across the entryway. It smashed against the blue-green wall and exploded in a shower of beige plastic pieces on the parquet oak floor. She was instantly torn between collecting the pieces of the shattered phone and picking up the dropped cookie from the new table. She went for the cookie. "What happened, dear?" Her question came out in a voice only a decibel above a whisper as she ushered the cookie and crumbs into her open left hand.

"Oh, some bitch lawyer downtown is making trouble about the interchange. Just trying to make a name for herself."

"That's awful." She pulled the sleeve of her yellow cashmere sweater down over her right hand and wiped the table top with it. "People should mind their own business."

Sampson's upper lip curled at the stupidity of the comment. *Fucking imbecile,* he thought. *I've got a real problem here, and she doesn't have a clue what I'm talking about.* "This bitch has made a major mistake." But his wife was already on her knees, gathering up the pieces of the broken phone. It was as if he'd said nothing. "That's it," Sampson shouted, "just worry about cleaning the damned floor!"

Elaine Sampson had to make her second instantaneous decision in ninety seconds. Continuing to look down would exacerbate the anger. But there was a good chance it would frustrate him, and he would walk

The New Road

away. Looking up, encountering his eyes, could make things much worse. She chose the first option. It nearly worked.

He began to stomp off but noticed the silver tray. *Ibanez. Coalition.* The words flashed off and on in Sampson's brain like infuriating neon lights. "You like to clean so much? Here's some more for you." He dumped the tray full of cookies on the floor in front of his wife. That she continued to look down even then fanned the flames. Sampson reached down to grab a handful of the doughy mess and flung it into her face. "There. Have fun."

She waited until his heavy footsteps faded around the corner before Elaine let the tears fall. One by one they eked out of the corners of her tightly shut eyes and drifted down to mix with the globs of lemon filling on her cheeks.

*

"So, we going to run or not?" Michelle went to her partner's office to ask the question. Joanne only tilted her head to look up from her desk. She ignored the hair hanging down into one of her eyes. The other eye was open wide. The eye spoke of confusion and silently screamed that its owner didn't want to run, or work, or even speak. But she did speak.

"We should talk."

Michelle turned and looked out into the hall. The two high school kids were still there, sitting next to each other on folding chairs with their laptops propped on their knees. They both had iPods plugged into their ears and appeared to be in their own high-school-kid world. Still, she closed the office door. She came back to sit down in the chair next to her partner and put out the palms of her hands in invitation.

Joanne let her own hands flutter up and fall back down into her lap in a gesture Michele had never seen her make before. "I don't know …" she began, shaking her head. "I don't know what's going on with you."

"What's going on with me?"

"This project, this whole road thing, it just continues to snowball and you're going right along with it." She waited for a reaction. Michelle only looked at her. "At first it was fine, good public service, good, visible pro bono, some good PR. Now it's becoming this thing that you can't seem to let go of, Michelle."

Now it was Michelle shaking her head in frustration. "I thought you understood. You're my partner." The word made Joanne flinch as if she'd been hit.

"It's taking over your life, 'Chelle, here in the office—and in your home too." Joanne looked down then and folded her hands on her desk. "I want out of this."

"The firm?"

"No," she said after a second of hesitation. "Just the road thing."

"I still don't understand why. I thought you were just as much on board with it as me."

"Why?" Her friend's body began to stiffen and her voice became just a little shrill. "Because we're supposed to be out finding clients and racking up billable hours. This isn't a damn charity; we're lawyers remember?"

"I'm blindsided here." Michelle could think of nothing else to say.

Joanne eventually moved as if to pat her partner's shoulder. She dropped her hand instead. "Let's go for that run," she said.

*

All the way down O'Donnell Street Joanne kept the lead this time. It was nearly dark. It had already turned cold, not chilly but cold, a deep, solid November-in-Baltimore cold. They started up the hill and Michelle tried hard to catch her. For Michelle the hill had always been the hardest part of their route. The windows of the seemingly endless row houses were mostly dark. The marble steps began to look like tombstones to her in the gloom. "Jo, wait," she gasped when she'd managed to get within a few feet of the other woman. Joanne turned around but her feet continued to pump up and down. She looked annoyed. It was their unspoken rule to never stop once they'd started running.

"What changed you?" Michelle could only gasp out the words. The hill and the sprint had exhausted her.

"Nothing changed. What I told you is how it's been."

"No, Joanne, you were different. You cared. Just weeks ago you cared. I saw you cry when we talked to that old couple."

Joanne only threw up her hands with a look of pain. She turned and charged as fast as she could down the hill toward the harbor. For the first time Michelle had to follow her partner in this part of the run, across Riverview Road and down to the wall at Waterfront Park. Joanne was already there when Michelle got to the wall, walking from the street to the brick wall and back with her hands on her hips. She looked more irritated than exhausted. She leaned with one arm on the bus stop sign and looked as if she were waiting for a bus that would never come.

Michelle thought of the families again, the ones she was fighting for. She thought again of the histories in each of those orange brick row houses they'd passed. She saw the combined history of it all. She saw clearly how much rested on her shoulders. She wanted to share it all with Joanne again. She wanted to make her see. She wanted to remind her just what they were up against.

They'd said enough for one night, maybe too much. Joanne eventually came back to the wall. She leaned against it and folded her arms across her chest. "Damn, it's cold," she said.

*

It was the shoes he saw first. Buddy was on one of Chartwell's new inside putting greens. He was concentrating, trying to figure out how he could make the white Titlest spin a little to the left when the scuffed, black brogues appeared in the grass next to it. The shoes were where they weren't supposed to be, and he looked up to see the overly round face of Vance Berg where it was not supposed to be, inches away from his own. "Nice in here, ain't it?" the face quipped.

"In here?" Buddy asked, noting that they'd forgone introductions.

"Yeah, here, inside. It's cold as a witch's tit outside."

"And you walked over here, on the grass in your street shoes, to tell me that?" Buddy knew Berg only from the awkward introduction to Sam Sampson in September. He was unimpressed with the man then as now. "So what's up? Sampson run out of friends again?"

"Naw, I don't even know if he's here today." Berg hadn't moved. He kept his face thrust out and his hands in the pockets of his rumpled black slacks. "Just wanted to say hi. You're Michelle Ibanez's father, right?"

In Buddy's mind the man had gone from irritating to annoying to threatening in less than a minute. Berg mentioning Michelle's name was like an actor violating the fourth wall with a filthy joke. "So?"

"So nothing. I'm just sayin'." Berg bounced on the balls of his feet, pulverizing the indoor grass. "I know Michelle. We've had coffee—city business." The look on Buddy's face said more than words. "Chill, Bud, I'm just talking here."

Buddy sighed and focused out at the stadium-like indoor driving range. "Really something, isn't it?" he said when he realized the other man wasn't leaving. Gray light illuminated the glass panels above them and made the massive building seem like a ballpark in summer for the small army of golfers slamming balls out into the measured off Astroturf. "It's winter but we can stand here in short-sleeved shirts in the middle of the day hitting drives out 200 yards. We're the lucky ones, huh?"

"Where you live at?" Berg came back after a pause.

"Rock Creek. Why?"

"Know where I grew up? Violetville—Morrel Park."

"Uh huh. I grew up in Arbutus. Similar thing. Same working class ethos."

"Same what?"

"Never mind." Buddy pulled another ball from his pocket and dropped it in the grass at his feet. "I've got another half hour to work on my putting."

Vance Berg stood behind him, hands still in his pockets, rocking forward and back in the black street shoes. "Michelle have kids? You a grandpa?"

With his head down, Buddy tried to concentrate on the way his fingers wrapped around the handle of the club. "Why would you ask that?"

"What's her husband do?"

Buddy whirled to face the other man, the golf club tight in his right fist. "What the hell is this?"

Berg widened his eyes in mock amazement. "Chill, big guy," he said. He stepped forward and put a wide palm on Buddy's shoulder. "Chill." Stepping away, the big man turned in a single motion and started up the wooden block path toward the restaurant. "You okay in my book, Buddy," he called back.

Buddy watched him go. He reached down to pick up both golf balls and drop them into his side pocket. "That is one creepy fuck," he said.

Chapter 14

November 23–26, 2009
Why Does She Hate Me?

It wasn't working for him tonight. It had almost always worked. Since Mike Drazinski was fifteen he'd thrived on those feelings of release he got when working out heavy. He went through the motions, but the psychic weight he carried remained unmoved. He had started like always, with some squats. It was legs and shoulders night. An hour in the UMBC weight room, time that normally to him seemed the length of a commercial, dragged on until he was sure the clock on the wall had stopped.

It seemed the other regulars came in, finished their workout, and left while he still struggled. It all added to the curious sensation he couldn't shake lately, that the world was passing him by.

Arnold curls. He saved them till last, like a treat. Normally, on legs and shoulder nights the explosive motion of blasting the sixty pounders above his head brought on that exquisite rush of endorphins he craved and thrived on. Tonight he only muddled through the exercise.

"What's up, big guy?" In the locker room, his friend Chip was stripping off a sweat-soaked gray T-shirt.

"Aw, I don't know. How about you? B-ball?"

"Oh yeah. It's constant till April, you know." Chip silently toweled himself down and pulled a white hoodie over his head. "Hey, you okay, my man? You don't seem like your usual self lately."

Mike wrapped a towel around his neck and zipped up his own sweatshirt. "Is it that obvious?" he asked. "Women—relationships. You know how that stuff goes."

"Hey, say no more," Chip laughed, putting up his big palms like a pair of stop signs. "I'm done here till after turkey day. You?"

"I'm gonna run the loop once."

It was totally dark when Mike began the two mile loop around the campus. It had gotten colder. Each time he passed under a streetlight he could see his breath stretch out in front of him like a long mini cloud. It was something a lot of people did before real winter came, run the loop. Shadowy shapes of other runners huffed and pounded past or toward him. Mike was glad it was dark. He didn't feel obligated to wave or smile.

An hour later, Lisa was waiting for him in the quadrangle. He saw her standing in a pool of light outside the book store. Her hands were buried deep in the pockets of her pea coat. He knew she'd be there, but part of him hoped she wouldn't be. Her dark blond hair was pulled back tight. He thought how it made her forehead look huge above her wire-rimmed glasses. "Hey," she bubbled. Lisa came out into the darkness of the quadrangle to meet him. "Where've you been?"

"I decided to run the loop after."

She pursed her lips and pointed them up to him. Mike dutifully bent down and gave her his cheek to be kissed. "Got a little cold," he said in explanation.

They went to the cafeteria and shared a quick, mostly silent dinner. "You're coming over, right?" She asked the question looking up at him over her glasses and popping a last bite of garlic bread into her mouth.

"I'm kind of beat—this cold. And I've got a lot on my plate tomorrow."

"Financial Management, I'll bet." Lisa continued to gaze up at him across the tiny table. She smiled, her eyes sparkling behind the glasses.

"Yeah, that. Plus, I have to work for Mr. Miller tomorrow. He always expects a lot from me."

They walked through the bookstore back out into the dark holding hands. She gave him another kiss on his turned cheek. For a moment, watching her walk away with her head down and her hands thrust back into her coat pockets, he felt sorry for Lisa. He felt sorry about what he was doing to her. She disappeared down the brick steps, and he turned away.

Mike turned in the other direction and took the concrete stairs two at a time, up into the starry night. Rounding the corner, he started down the hill to his dorm. As his feet pounded the sidewalk he groused to himself about Lisa, how she always wore the same baggy jeans, how, since he'd first met her he'd come to realize that he'd sold himself short. Just to start, she was too short and too stodgy for him. *What the hell was I thinking last year?*

*

In his room, Mike stretched out as best he could on the gray metal bed. The single bed barely accommodated his massive body. He curled up and put one forearm over his eyes. He'd worked hard all day, since early that morning. He'd lifted heavy. He'd run the loop. He should have been exhausted, but he wasn't. He got up and took the picture from his desk drawer again. From the gold frame Michelle smiled out at him, smiled his favorite Michelle Miller smile, her fun, mischievous, sexy smile. She was in her graduation robe, her arms around two of her friends. In the picture, her chestnut hair was down, cascading over her shoulders. She was taller than her friends, stately without trying to be. She was like no other woman he knew. She was a being from a different planet. Definitely a different planet than the one Lisa was from.

He touched the frame gently, drawing his fingers around the edge, staring at it for another minute before easing it into his backpack. He reminded himself that he had to get the picture back into the house tomorrow, before Mr. Miller realized it was missing.

*

The Dark Knight was Chloe's current favorite movie. But they'd watched the DVD three times now, and he could tell that even she was a little bored with those parts that didn't focus on the Joker. "She's under a lot of stress now. You know that, right?"

Buddy assumed she was talking about the movie. "Where'd that come from?" he asked before he realized her mind was racing down a different track. Buddy downed the last of his Seagrams and slid the glass onto the table next to him. He studied the way her blond hair fell over her shoulders and onto the white, flannel shirt she wore so well. He loved that. He even loved the way the sleeves of the shirt fell down below her wrists. He loved that she somehow managed to curl her lower body under the thick, orange and white blanket until she made herself look like a sort of elegant creamsicle. *You're spectacular,* Buddy thought. *You look better watching television on a Monday night than most women do on their wedding day.* Those were his thoughts. "Hmm, I guess I'm not sure what you mean, Hon," is what he said.

"I'm talking about Michelle. That's why she went off on you like she did." Chloe saying his daughter's name hit him like an electric shock. Over the past month he'd managed to keep his two women in separate spheres, both physically and in his head. "You said she got really angry and was saying all sorts of crazy stuff you couldn't even remember. That's stress. That's a typical reaction to high stress." Buddy nodded, wondering, dreading where she was heading next. "Let's invite them here for Thanksgiving." Her next sentence came out before he could mouth even the N of No. "Actually, you know what? I'll do it. I'll call."

Buddy's mind was a runaway train careening around a bend as he grasped for an answer. "Um, I'm not so sure. She was really mad at me, Hon. Still is." He was flailing for a way to stop the train when she grabbed his cell phone and flipped open the cover. Buddy's heart dropped like a rock into his stomach.

"It'll be fun. And a way to get you back together. I'll chat it up with Carlos while you two have a glass of wine and a chance to talk. That's all it will take. Don't you think so?"

Something like terror gripped him as she worked the phone. "Hey, Carlos," he watched her say. "Michelle around?" A long five seconds passed. "Hi, Michelle. Yes! I know, right?" He couldn't begin to guess what would come of this or how he'd deal with it. Buddy felt a pool of anxiety grow and bubble up in his gut. "We'd love it if you guys would come over here for Thanksgiving." The anxiety pool expanded as he watched that certain stiffness appear in the skin around her lips and in the corners of her eyes. He watched her as interminable seconds ticked off. There may have been ten. There may have been thirty. She flipped down the cover of the cell phone and stared at him. The look told Buddy more than he wanted to know. "Why does she hate me? Do you know?"

"Oh, boy," he sighed. "What did she say?" Buddy didn't want to betray the surge of relief that filled him because she still had to ask that question.

"She said no. She said she doesn't want to come here for Thanksgiving." Chloe threw the cell phone to the recliner on the other side of the room. It was only the second time he'd seen her close to tears—ever. "And she wasn't nice about it. Let me put it that way."

Whew. Just as well, Buddy thought. He tried to form a mental picture of Chloe stuffing and cooking a turkey while he peeled potatoes and set the table with fragile china. He tried hard. But unless he put it into the context of some alternative universe, he couldn't make the picture work. "I don't know, Chlo. It was a nice idea."

Buddy moved over to the couch and thought to put his arm around her. He did it to share his own feelings of relief as much as to comfort her. He knew how much worse this could have been. Her expression made him think again about touching her. "That call—it was a nice gesture, Honey. Thank you for doing that."

"You know, Buddy, a big part of your appeal to me was that you had no kids." It took a moment for him to comprehend that comment. *Your appeal to me....* The idea of Chloe evaluating and choosing him was from a mindset foreign to his own, an idea from yet another alternate universe. "Is it me? It's me, isn't it? She's not upset with you at all. You were just saying that. It's because of me she doesn't want to come here."

Buddy went with the first words that came to his mind. "Well, I don't know, Chlo." He made another attempt to touch her. The skin just below her neck was like ice. "Who knows? Maybe in Michelle's mind, you're like a stepmother or something. And she is still my little girl."

Chloe scooted further away from him on the couch and threw the blanket off her legs in a single movement. "A. We're not married." Her blue eyes bore into him. "And B. I'm nobody's mother."

"Oh, don't go there, Chloe. Not tonight."

She stood up then, a final escalation. "Don't go there, Chloe," she mimicked. "Not tonight. Not *ever* is what you mean! Do I want to have kids or not?" Buddy started to speak but thought better of it. "See? You don't even know. You've danced around that question since the night we met."

"Come on, Hon," he began lamely, handing her back the orange blanket.

She took the blanket, draped it over her shoulders, and pulled it tight around her. She started to stalk off and then turned to face him. "By the way, your *little girl* is thirty fucking years old. Why don't you start treating her that way?"

Alone, Buddy sank back on the couch. He tried to organize the words that came into his mind, deflated, and drained. "Trapped," he said out loud. And he was scared, something he didn't want to admit even to himself. *I haven't felt this miserable since Michelle's mother was alive,* he thought. He was scared of the thoughts about *his Chloe,* the unthinkable thoughts that he'd suppressed for weeks. Her words: *I'll chat it up with Carlos* clanged in his brain like a sour note in a symphony.

Buddy despised the feelings those thoughts brought on. The feelings welled up in his consciousness like a black tsunami. He tried to picture how it would feel to tell Chloe to leave, how it would be a relief, for maybe an hour. Then he pictured the terror of losing her. It annoyed him that fifteen minutes earlier his life had been quite good. *There are only two women on earth I care about. And now both of them hate my guts. How the hell did that happen?*

Buddy turned off the television, slumped back on the couch and put his hands over his face. "Aw, fuck me," he said.

*

Father Jerry was only a little disappointed when the Delmar family teenagers and their friends left the football field-sized Thanksgiving table. He thought they were great kids and had enjoyed their company for the last two hours, but he wanted to talk alone with their parents. He'd been thinking of John and Marie Delmar as the shy couple, the middle-aged white couple sitting in the back row on Sundays. They'd leave with just a word or two as they passed him at the church door. He was more than a little surprised when Marie had called to invite him for dinner.

"Great kids," Father Jerry began, sniffing as much as sipping from the crystal glass of sherry. "And I love your house. I have to confess, I could hear the theme from *Dallas* coming all the way up your driveway."

"You're too funny." Marie smiled. "Our farm is far from being the biggest around here."

The word *stately* kept popping into Jerry's mind whenever he looked at her. She was obviously the queen there in the solid, old white house. Her perfect blond hair was streaked with gray, but she sat up strong and tall. *Mistress of the manor,* he thought, *and she carries herself that way.* He thought it was beautiful the way John doted on her, just as he must have when they were dating in the '70s. "I get the impression that your place is one of the older ones, though."

"It is that." John Delmar jumped in with the statement. "Tobacco, that's how it started." The man was shorter than his wife, but muscular. He had a round, kind face. "Tobacco's what made Maryland rich when it was a colony, you know. Before Baltimore grew, before grain came in from the west for shipping, tobacco was king."

"How long have you guys been at Saint Joseph's?" Jerry asked the question to avoid the too long history lesson he foresaw heading down the track.

"Since it was built," Marie said. "Before that, we didn't have a church in this part of the diocese. We had to drive to Easton."

"Boy, that's what—forty-five minutes away?"

"You've got it," John said. "Do you speak any Spanish, Jerry?"

"You know, you're the second person to ask me that. And the answer is no, I'm afraid I don't."

"You won't get a lot of support from the other farmers around here," John went on. "They see the Mexican population more as a form of farm machinery than as neighbors. And they see you as a kind of outside agitator."

"I'm afraid John's right," Marie said, pouring Jerry a cup of coffee from a silver carafe. "I hate to say it, but I think you've landed in kind of a tough spot."

"So, how come you don't make that drive to Easton?"

"Because this is our parish. Rich or poor, we all share the same faith."

Jerry raised his coffee cup as if he were making a toast. "Good answer."

"Still," the tall woman smiled, "it won't be like your city parish."

"Father Dolan, he was the pastor of the little church I went to after Vietnam. 'Some days even the candles won't light,' he used to say. Sometimes it's just like that."

*

The dark little house at the end of the lane provided a stark contrast to the Delmar Estates. It was Jerry's last stop on the long holiday agenda. Even as he rapped on the door, he was again contemplating how good it would feel to climb into the rickety bed at Saint Joe's rectory. "How about some turkey, Father?" That was how old Mrs. Shoenmire greeted him when the door opened.

"That's the trouble with being a priest on Thanksgiving," Jerry said, patting his stomach. "I get twenty dinner invitations, but all on the same day."

"Then I'll pack some in a plastic bag for you."

"Wonderful," Jerry agreed, picturing how Peaches would be transported to dog heaven when he dropped it into her bowl back at the rectory.

The stooped little woman led him by the arm through what might at one time have been a living room. Stacks of old magazines and books covered the furniture and formed a maze that the old woman navigated like an expert scout on safari. "He's in the shop," she said, glancing back at him. Her blue eyes sparkled as if she was letting Jerry in on a secret. They passed through a second room with a similar décor, she hanging onto his forearm as if he'd be lost forever if she'd let it go.

When she flung open the door to what Jerry thought was a shed, the light startled him. It was a large shed. But, unlike the house, it was warm and well lit. What looked like a hundred hand tools, squares, tiny saws, and a variety of calipers gleamed on walls of white peg board. The room smelled of sawdust and oil paint, though Jerry couldn't see either. Franz Shoenmire was perched on his wheelchair in the center of it all. Jerry thought his long white hair and gold-framed glasses made the man look like Santa in his workshop. Franz could have been fifty years old or ninety; Jerry couldn't tell. But the man's eyes shined like those of a twenty-year-old. They matched his wife's. "You're bringing me communion yourself today, Father?"

"Yes," Jerry answered, still surprised by the aura of neatness and industry around him. "Man, what a shop you've got here. What are you working on?"

"Miniatures!" Franz and his wife said the word in unison.

"He makes little buildings," the wife said, reaching again for Jerry's forearm as if it was a handle. She led him to a wooden work bench that ran the length of the back wall. "See, houses, train stations, he does it all."

Jerry's eyes sped like a child's over a small sea of red, black and green roofs that covered the wide bench. His eyes fixed on what looked like a four-foot spike of concrete and glass. "And what is that? The Empire State Building?"

"It is!" the old couple shouted, again in unison from the center of the room.

"That's only the top ten floors of it," Franz added. "I did it to scale."

CHAPTER 15

DECEMBER 3–5, 2009
BARBARIANS AT THE GATE

It was one of those mornings when she couldn't stop looking at him. She loved the way he stood straight with little shoulders thrown back. She'd dressed him in his new blue pants and gray tweed coat. *My little man,* she thought with that sudden swell of love and pride in her heart. She loved that the preschool was close enough to be able to walk there with him. It was their adventure each morning. Michelle realized that it was becoming more of an adventure for her than it was for the boy.

They walked up Hudson Street in the cold but foggy morning. The few remaining leaves on the maple trees in the median hung drearily, brown and yellow. "See how the leaves fall off in the winter?" She walked slow, keeping pace with his short legs and holding his hand. Little Carlos only looked up at the leaves with wonder and kept walking, holding tight to his mother's hand as each tree appeared out of the mist.

Part of her longed for more time with him. Michelle wanted the time to explain how the trees prepare themselves for winter, how in the spring they would bud again and be green. She wanted to tell him how, when she was his age, her Uncle Jerry would walk her around the church grounds, how they'd stop and look at the different types of shrubs and trees. "There were a whole lot of trees where I grew up," she said, and settled for that.

"At Grampa's house?"

"Yes," she said, pleased that he remembered. "At Grandpa's house." Michelle longed to just talk with her *little man*, tell him about their neighborhood, their city, about her life, share it all with him. There were times she burned to do that. "Aren't they pretty," she said instead. She held his hand a little tighter and kept walking.

"Look both ways." She repeated it like a mantra whenever they came to a corner. Looking left on Melton she could hear distant engines and what sounded like the clacking of tracks on cement. Flashes of Caterpillar yellow appeared when there were breaks in the wall of fog. She told herself it was a road crew fixing potholes. Still, a sudden stab of coldness materialized in her gut and didn't go away. The sound of engines was becoming an ongoing rumble that rolled up the street toward them. "Let's go this way for a minute, honey." She and the boy turned toward the sound and picked up their pace. Crossing Fait, Michelle could see the alien yellow machines. They were a block away. She could see men driving pegs with orange ribbons on them along the curb. *This can't be happening*, she thought. *They can't do that. They can't!*

"Where are we going?" Little Carlos asked, not afraid but curious.

"I've got to see what they're doing down there. Just a little further, Hon."

"Nooo!" The boy turned back toward the hill and pulled at her hand.

She had to pull her son across the street like a wagon with a missing wheel. The closest worker was one of those driving stakes. "What are you doing here?" she asked, trying to ignore Little Carlos, who seemed to be intent on twisting off her right arm behind her back.

"Sorry?"

"What project are you working on here?"

"Oh, the new highway." The man grinned. "It's gonna' be a monster job. We're just doing the prep work."

"No you're not." Even as she said the words Michelle knew she was wasting her breath. "I'm head of the Community Coalition. That highway isn't going to be built here."

"Hey, Don," the laborer called across the street and began driving another of the stakes as if Michelle wasn't there. A bowlegged, fiftyish man in tan pants, a tan jacket, and a tan baseball hat ambled over to them. As he got closer the man pulled back his shoulders and stretched to his full height, throwing out his stomach and groin as if they were his credentials.

"You live here?" he began.

"I live in Canton, yes." Little Carlos had stopped saying words and lapsed into a chorus of "Uh, uh, uh!" as he tugged at her fingers behind her back. "There's no authorization to start this work."

"Yes, Ma'am. We have a work order. This is part of the new highway construction."

"My name is Michelle Ibanez. I lead the local community group, and I want to see your work order."

The man looked at her as if he'd just spotted Godzilla turning the corner from Fait Avenue. He whirled without a word, stomped across the street to a gray, Baltimore City car, and got in. She waited for him to come back with the work order. Her son had begun to alternate between tugging her arm and pounding her right leg with his fist. "Let's go!" *Let's go* became his new chant as the wait continued. Four minutes passed. Michelle watched the gray car pull away from the curb and disappear up Melton Street.

"You son of a ..." She stopped herself. The laborer next to her began to contemplate his navel as well as the wooden stake he'd just driven. She started back up the hill with little Carlos. The two of them walked in silence the rest of the way to the preschool. Her feelings of frustration, anger, and helplessness coalesced into a miserable stew. She had her son with her when she saw them. Somehow, that made it worse, made it harder. The road was no longer a House bill number and cryptic words on a piece of paper. The machines, the workers had made it all too real.

*

Ushering Little Carlos through the front door of the preschool, she bent down to kiss him. The boy looked up at her with his bottom lip protruding. "You mad at me?" He asked the question after she'd kissed his forehead.

"No, angel," she whispered. "I just ... No, I'm not mad at you. See you later, okay?"

"Kay," he said, bouncing down the hall toward the other kids in the big playroom as if nothing had happened. She smiled and waved. She thrust her hand into her jacket pocket when she realized it was shaking.

*

This shouldn't be a novelty, Michelle thought. Intellectually, she knew grocery shopping with her husband and son on a Saturday wasn't a big deal. But the actual doing of it had become a rare event. She didn't know when or how that happened. Carlos pushed the grocery cart the way he used to. And, like he used to, their son sat in the top of it with his legs dangling down, the backs of his small tennis shoes thumping the metal basket. "Looks like you've outgrown this," Carlos said as they reached the end of the produce aisle. Putting his hands under the startled five-year-old's arms, Carlos lifted him out of the cart and stood him on his feet. "You can walk with us now. You're big enough."

To his mother's amazement, the boy was fine with it. He ran to the rack at the aisle corner and did his best to touch each of the on-sale DVDs. *Okay,* Michelle thought, *now I remember why we need husbands.* "You know," she whispered into Carlo's ear, "if I had tried that he would have thrown a huge fit."

Standing in the checkout line, the two of them nodded at a young couple they recognized from two doors down. And Michelle waved to a woman she remembered from the car dealership. Carlos bagged the groceries as she paid the cashier. She felt oddly content, happy at the way they were doing those mundane things together. She felt a little silly at being happy for it. She smiled at her own silliness. For a few moments, the road, the yellow earth movers and the House bill seemed distant and less important.

*

Her contentment stayed on once they arrived home. Little Carlos found his coloring book and stretched out by the kitchen door. He worked at coloring the happy-looking duck on the page as if he were Beethoven composing the Moonlight Sonata. Michelle started dinner while her husband put away the groceries. When he'd put the last can in the cabinet she was feeling happy. She was inwardly ecstatic when she saw him sit at the table and open a jar of almonds, keeping her company. "Did you notice Margie Nestory in the store?" she asked. "She used to be the bookkeeper at your dealership. Doesn't she look good?"

"Too skinny," Carlos said, staring through the glass at the almonds as if he were searching for a special one. "She has a pretty face. But her body's like a stick. That's not attractive." Michelle was conscious of her still muscular legs and how her jeans seemed to be fitting tighter around them. She suddenly felt better.

They had a quiet dinner, the three of them. Little Carlos was engrossed in his plate of spaghetti. The boy was a neat eater except for spaghetti, and he ended up wearing much of it. Michelle had developed a pattern where she took three bites and then turned to her right to wipe off her son's face. The routine seemed to work for both of them.

Carlos took his time eating. He would place a bit of cheese on the fresh French bread and dip it lightly in oil before popping the bite-sized piece into his mouth. It was something she would never admit, but she loved to watch him eat and had since their first date. Something about the way he did it seemed incredibly sensuous to her. She'd never talked about it. She never told him.

They talked of little things, and of nothing, as they ate. "I can't tell you how much seeing that machinery bothered me," she said. "It was like barbarians at the city gate."

"Who knows what they were doing."

"Well, it's a good thing Joanne didn't see them. That day at the courthouse," Michelle said, laughing and wiping tomato sauce from her own mouth. "She had every person on that floor wrapped around her finger by the end of it."

"Why tell me that?" A black veil fell in front of her husband's dark, previously smiling, eyes. "You're never home long enough to make me a part of what you do. So, why even bring it up?" She dropped the story and turned again to wipe her son's face. It gave her a second to swallow the feelings of: *Where did that come from?*

*

Little Carlos was asleep almost before his head touched the pillow. She came back into their bedroom to find her husband on the bed in his boxers, thumbing through the latest *Car & Driver*. Michelle stretched out next to him and felt the silkiness of his thick, black hair. He kept reading.

She'd been thinking about it for weeks. She decided to say it. "We don't do anything anymore. Why don't we?" She let her fingertips glide over his bare shoulder. Carlos ignored her. He plumped the pillows, put his hand behind his head, and lay back on the bed. He clicked on the television.

"We just went shopping and had dinner. Of course we do things."

"You know what I'm talking about," she whispered. Her fingers continued down his muscular arm and then up his leg. Carlos tossed the magazine onto the nightstand just a little more forcefully than he needed to.

"I want to get some sleep, okay?" He grabbed the remote, switched the TV off again, and got under the covers in the space of seconds.

"Oh, okay." In the time it took to take a breath, she thought about it. "Okay," she said. "Sure."

CHAPTER 16

DECEMBER 11–12, 2009
THAT WAS AWKWARD

The instant city ombudsman Vance D. Berg stepped back into Shuffle's Saloon he could feel the transformation taking place. He felt himself lean a little forward as he walked, as if he were ducking through a doorway. His arms began to swing in time with James Brown's "Popcorn" blaring from the battered speakers over the bar. He edged onto the last empty stool and lit a cigarette. In seconds the bartender put a shot and a beer in front of him. "You okay in my book, Brewer," Berg said. It was his tag line. The words came without effort now that he was back. A man needed a regular line, something you say that's uniquely your own, something that let people know you were there and that you were still the same man. Vance Berg let his eyes roam around the dim, noisy room, taking it all in. Like a wolf back in his own lair, he was home again. It felt good.

On the other side of the horseshoe-shaped bar he could make out Gripper's hulking shape. Gripper—right where he was supposed to be. Berg took a long drag on the cigarette and nodded. The shape began a shifting, bobbing journey around the bar to him. He watched the shape as it moved and marveled at how it had never changed. The round, bearded face still sat, seemingly without a neck, on too wide shoulders. In the dark, it looked like an overripe melon on a stone wall. He thought how Gripper's bulging blue eyes still gave him that look of perpetual caught-in-the-wrong-place-with-his-pants-down surprise. *Same shape, same look. Same as all the way through Lansdowne High,* Vance Berg remembered. *Same big, dumb fucker.*

Gripper wore a white painter's hat with a big, upturned bill. He'd written RIPPER! on the underside of the hat bill in black magic marker. "Shit," Gripper laughed. "Look at you with a damn suit on. What, you been to a funeral?"

"I just came from work, dumb ass." He swirled the whiskey in his shot glass and blew a plume of smoke into his friend's face. "What's with that hat?"

"At's me now, man. At's what I call myself—Gripper the Ripper."

Berg wanted to press the other man as to why he'd written RIPPER on the hat. He felt a need to explain that *Gripper the Ripper* was an inherently stupid thing to say, that *Gripper* and *Ripper* just happened to be words that sounded similar, that together the words made no sense. He let it go. "So, how you been, Gripper?"

"See Kitty over there?" Berg could see there was only one female in the bar. She was a squat, middle-aged woman with short hair. If anything distinguished Kitty it was that she seemed more verbal and animated than most of the men, waving a lit cigarette like a conductor's baton as she spoke. She wore a gray sweatshirt with the sleeves pulled up on her forearms.

"Yeah, I see her."

"I pissed in her drink."

"You what, now?" Berg didn't bother turning toward Gripper. He only looked straight ahead at the woman across the bar and listened.

"She had her back turned, right? I had sweatpants on." Gripper began to laugh as he spoke. The laugh came out in ragged spasms between his words. "I just dropped it out and whizzed in her drink and put the glass back on the bar before she even knew it." Gripper's laughter accelerated into a high-pitched wheeze. He had to reach past Berg to hold onto the edge of the Formica bar top. "And get this, she says: 'Ooh, what's in this? I don't like this.'" The spastic laughter resumed and increased in intensity until Vance Berg had no choice but to turn and look at him. "I thought: Course you don't like it, bitch. I just peed in it!"

Berg, silent, stared for a few moments up at the black speakers on the ceiling. He took his time before he answered. He blew out a luxurious stream of tobacco smoke. "You workin', Gripper? You got a job?"

"No, no job. Got a new car though, Eclipse outside, you wanna see it?"

"That's good. But I thought you weren't working."

"No, I ain't. But I got to have a car. Right?" The blue eyes got even bigger and rounder. "Economic crisis, man. No jobs out there. Times are tight."

"Shit," Vance hissed. "The only thing tight in Violetville is your grandmother's asshole." He crushed out the cigarette in a black ash tray. "A real man can always find a way to make money." He folded his hands on the bar and leaned closer to Gripper like a lawyer at a senate hearing conferring with his client. "Move some blow over there till you get on your feet."

"Coke?" The word came out louder than he'd wanted it to and Gripper turned to look at the older man seated behind him. "I'm gonna try a rum and Coke, Mr. Patterson. Whadaya think?" Old man Patterson made a point of shifting his beer to the right and putting a wrinkled, liver-spotted hand up to the side of his face. Gripper turned back and lowered his voice a decibel. "You been in the city with them niggers too long, Vance."

"I'm just pointing out possibilities to you, moron."

"Yeah. But it's like nobody does blow in Violetville these days. They all into meth. And the hillbillies got that market tied up."

Vance Berg downed the shot and took a long pull on the beer. He stared straight ahead at Brewer's back. "Maybe I got something you can do." Gripper was silent. Berg shook another Marlboro out of the pack and lit it, relaxing, satisfied, knowing his fish had been hooked. "I know a man who needs some shit done, things a lot of citizens might not wanna do. You know what I'm sayin', Gripper? You up for that kinda' shit?"

"You tell me where and when, boss man."

Gripper was staring at him with those bulging, bloodshot eyes. "You not even gonna ask me what it is?" In the dim light, the cap bill with RIPPER! above the crazy eyes and Gripper's big round face formed a kind of bizarre Kabuki mask. "You a crazy motherfucker, Gripper."

Berg reached into his pocket and smacked two twenties down on the bar. "Here you go," he yelled.

"I'll get your change, Vance." The bartender said it without looking up.

"Keep it, Brewer," Vance Berg chuckled, sliding off the barstool. "You okay in my book."

*

The two of them trudged up the concrete steps to the parking lot. Berg pulled the keys from his pocket and started toward his black Town Car. "See my new Eclipse, Vance?" He turned and walked with Gripper to look at the little sports car parked behind his. "Cool, ain't it?" Vance Berg walked around the car, jangling his own keys and saying nothing. "It's a 2000, but it still looks cool. Don't it?"

"How much you pay for this?"

"Seventy-five-hundred, drive away."

He leaned close to Gripper and put a wide hand on the man's shoulder. "Did they at least kiss you first?" He gave the shoulder a playful shove, laughed, and walked to the Lincoln. "Gripper," he yelled back as he let himself fall into the tan leather driver's seat, "I'll be talking to ya. You okay in my book."

The engine of the big Town Car growled. The tires spun in the gravel, and Vance Berg screeched out onto Southwestern Boulevard. A rain of white stones and dust drifted down onto Gripper's Eclipse.

*

Early December was good. For Michelle, it was. Her husband seemed almost like the old Carlos. He was more loving. They could talk again without tension, if she avoided bringing up the phone call. He came home on time at night. She liked that he seemed to enjoy going with her to buy toys for their son and that both of them reveled in the game of hiding presents from their five-year-old. Christmas was two weeks away. It all felt good.

And her search for information on CEPCO was leading to names. Names would lead to histories and to who desperately wanted 1664 to pass. She could see glimmers of winning the thing, and she owed part of that to Mike Drazinski. "Let's take them out to dinner, Mike and his girlfriend." She suggested it over coffee on a Saturday morning. "Let's go someplace nice, like Sabatinos."

*

Carlos parked in the pay lot close to the harbor; and they walked up Fawn Street to the restaurant. The night was cold, but Michelle didn't mind the walk. Like she did as a little girl, she enjoyed peeking into the windows of the formidable old Little Italy row houses. Christmas lights blinked behind most of the curtains. She luxuriated in the novelty of a leisurely, stress-free walk holding onto her husband's arm. She felt she was in a scene from an old movie.

Mike and Lisa were waiting for them in the entryway at Sabatinos. "We parked on the street," Mike explained, sounding a little too serious, "right on High Street."

"Talk about luck." Carlos reached up and shook Mike's big shoulder. "This guy finds a free parking place in Little Italy on a Saturday night! Who does that?"

A small waitress with short black hair led them to a booth in the back. It was one of the large booths, with a tapestry on the wall and two candles on the table, more like a private room than just a table. She chalked it up to one more good thing to remember about the evening. They studied the thick menus in calculated silence like four bookies at the racetrack.

Michelle finally decided on the fettuccine Felicia while the two younger people scanned with their fingers down the menu to find lasagna. "The gravy is good tonight," Carlos intoned without smiling. Mike and Lisa replied with unsure, silent nods. "*The Sopranos*," Carlos had to explain. "That's what they always say."

"Oh. Okay."

"We always go for the lasagna," Lisa murmured to Michelle as if she were divulging a dark family secret.

"Me too. But I make that at home. So I try to look for something new."

"I like to cook too. Oh my god, when we get a house I'm going to cook something special every single night." They went on like that. Mostly Lisa and Michelle chatted, moving on to their childhoods and their pets, books they'd read, and their first dates. From the antipasto on, Michelle repeatedly looked up to find Mike silently staring at her. *Good kid*, she thought, *but he's a little intense. I'll bet he drives Dad up the wall.*

Michelle was as eager for dessert as either of the younger people. She pretended not to be. She and Carlos both ordered cannolis. She had coffee with hers. Carlos wanted a Sambuca with his. Lisa and Mike gave the desert menu their full attention for several minutes. After much debate they decided on caramel apple cheesecake. Michelle laughed when the small, dark-haired waitress put the plate between them and the two of them pounced on it.

Carlos ordered a Tom Collins after the Sambuca. "What sports are you playing, Mike?" He put his right arm on the back of Michelle's chair and jingled the ice in his glass with his left. "I went to Maryland in my undergrad years and played lacrosse."

"I'm not much into team sports," the younger man replied, moving his glass of Pepsi from the fingertips of one hand to the other. "I just lift."

"He lifts a lot," Lisa added, sliding her hand under Mike's heavy arm to emphasize the point.

"Terrapins were East Coast conference champs my senior year, Mike." Carlos made the statement raising his voice and clipping the words as if he were closing a deal. "Conference champs."

"That's great."

Michelle asked, "Sandra, what are you majoring in? I've been meaning to ask you that all night."

"Marine Biology. That's Lisa, actually."

"Oh, god, I am sorry, Lisa. Where'd I get Sandra?"

"It's okay. They kind of sound the same."

"Marine Biology, that's wonderful. He's in business. But you two complement each other so well!"

"Thanks." The girl smiled.

Michelle fished out her black purse from under the coat on the seat next to her. "I've gotta hit the lady's room before we leave."

"Me too."

Carlos Ibanez smiled and drained his glass as the two women got up from the table. "Funny isn't it, Mike, how women like to go to the bathroom in pairs? He raised his glass and clinked the ice in it.

"Another Tom Collins, Hon." The waitress smiled and took the glass from his hand to stop the clinking. "Now if two guys did that it would be creepy, huh?"

"Yeah ... creepy."

"How often are you at Buddy's house, Mike?" Carlos sipped from the fresh drink and leaned over the table.

"I work for Mr. Miller two days a week."

"Does he sleep a lot during the day?"

"What? No, not really."

"I just mean Buddy's an older guy—he's got a sweet young thing like Chloe—it must drain all of his energy just to take care of business." Mike looked down at the table and shrugged. "Tell me." Carlos took a long pull on the Tom Collins and leaned in heavily enough to push the wooden table forward. "Doesn't Chloe come home early some days? Maybe gives Mr. Buddy a little booty call?"

Mike put both hands on the edge of the table and shoved it, exploding it back under the elbows of the older man. "Maybe you better worry about taking care of business in your own house."

"What the hell's that supposed to mean?"

Lisa was suddenly steps away from the table, and Mike stood to meet her. Michelle was just behind Lisa. She sensed some tension, but Carlos was smiling at her and waving his glass like a cat with a mouse. "Had to get another one while you were gone," he said.

"Look at these two," Michelle said, putting a hand on the shoulders of each of the young people. She turned her head to look back at her husband. "Aren't they the cutest couple you've ever seen?"

Carlos was smiling a too broad smile at her as he awkwardly pushed the table away from his middle to get up. Michelle gave Mike a peck on the cheek. "Thanks again for CEPCO, sweetie," she said. "I owe you big time." Mike's face was a half-smiling mask. More light would have revealed it to be bright red.

*

Back on High Street, Mike was already in the driver's seat of his old Volvo with his hands gripping the wheel when Lisa got in. She was digesting the fact that this was the first time ever he hadn't opened the door for her. Mike didn't start the car. "We've got to talk," he said suddenly, not looking at her.

"About what?"

"About us."

*

Michelle and Carlos walked in silence back to the lot. She held his arm and sensed he was a little unsteady. "Sure you're okay to drive, Hon? I just had the one glass of wine."

"I'm fine," Carlos snapped, pulling the car keys from his pocket and shaking them as if to prove the point. By the time she'd gotten into the Lexus, Carlos had started the engine. She had to pull the door shut quickly as her husband took off toward the pay booth.

"That poor kid," Michelle said as she attempted to fasten the seatbelt over her long coat. "Her name's Lisa and I called her Sandra. Ugh, that was awkward."

Chapter 17

December 18–21, 2009
Meet Me in the Mall

The two of them battled for attention in Michelle's head: her work and personal lists. The little Judge was now insisting on more detailed notes to go along with the alternate routes. "Make them easily accessible and optically relevant," the E-mail said. *Whatever the hell that means.*

Little Carlos wants a hamster. She wasn't sure what that meant either. She knew that what he wanted wasn't a real hamster. *That would be too easy. And just as well. It would make Nefferkitty even more crazy than she is already.* From what she could glean from the boy's description, it was a mechanical or cyber hamster of some kind. No adult seemed to know. But they all knew that getting one would involve waiting in lines.

Then there was the formal statement of opposition to the new road. She'd hit another wall with it. *My list is fine: major neighborhood disruption, families uprooted, economic distress, quality of life issues.* It was a good list of reasons. *But I can't hand Standish a damned list. He'll laugh in my face.* Her words of summation kept coming out lame and amateurish.

Carlos wants a GPS. She'd tried to find out what kind of GPS he wanted. "I want a nice one," he said. "Don't get me one of those trashy ones." *Yes, that narrows it down, dear.*

Like 98 percent of the population, she was feeling overwhelmed by the sheer number of issues to be resolved in the remaining days before

Christmas. It was 8:45 and she was still standing in line at the Galleria Starbucks. *It's okay. I'm almost to the cashier, and I know what I want, a pumpkin spice latte.* The nervous little man in front of her kept turning and frowning as if she were crowding him. Her heart sank when he began to read off a list to the cashier. "Four Pikes Place coffees, one Cappuccino Americano …"

Joanne was already coming through the front door when Michelle grabbed the last remaining round table. "Good morning to you too, sunshine," her partner said when she saw Michelle's face.

"Ugh. Am I that obvious?"

"Mmm, yeah."

Michelle blew out a sigh. "I'm just going over all the things I have to do today. And of course I got in line behind some dickhead who ordered coffee for every human being on Pratt Street."

"Hmmm."

"Oh, I know you're right. I'm sure the guy's a fine gentleman. But why couldn't he have been standing behind instead of in front of me?" Michelle took her briefcase from the table and pushed it under the chair. "Little Carlos wants some kind of virtual hamster. Do you know what he's talking about?"

"No clue," Joanne said, taking a sip from the bottle of water that sometimes seemed like an extension of her left hand. "Why don't you get him a real one?"

"Don't even ask."

"Oddly enough, Mr. Hampstead." Joanne cracked her first smile of the morning at the similarity between the man's name and hamster. "Mr. Hampstead wants you to push for a trial date on those mattresses his ex-partner has in the warehouse."

"Oh, god, another letter I need to write." Michelle took a sip of her latte and stared out the window at the people, bobbing and hustling on their way to work. It was another gray, December morning. A few flakes of light snow were falling. The snow seemed to speed the people up, their movements becoming urgent and jerky, like actors in a silent movie. "And what does Joanne want from Santa this year?" Michelle asked with a sigh.

Her partner studied her for several seconds as if trying to decode what that meant. "If you're talking about buying me a gift, please don't. I'm telling people this year I just don't do gifts."

Michelle had already wrapped the funky purple newsboy hat she'd found in September. *Maybe not her day–to-day style. But that hat has Joanne Wicks written all over it. Very cute.*

*

As she watched Joanne leave for the courthouse, Michelle pulled a notepad from her briefcase. Minutes passed. Not a word materialized. Starbucks patrons came and went in a hurried, pre-workday parade. "I still have fifteen minutes before the stores even open," she mumbled to herself. She'd begun to doodle circles and stars in the margins of the legal pad.

Before she could stifle the thought, she wondered about what to buy her father this year. A feeling of depression swept though her like an icy draft. She forced herself to recite the list of clients she needed to talk to that afternoon.

She needed to pick up some tinsel and wrapping paper—soon—when? It wouldn't get done today. With another huge sigh, she thrust the pad back into the briefcase and buttoned her coat. "Sorry, guys," she whispered to all the men in her life. "I've got to go to the office. I've got to work late." In her mind, she saw Carlos's face, the angry eyes, his lips curled in that half hurt, half angry semblance of a smile. *I know you'll be angry, Hon. I can't help it.*

*

Vance Berg hustled across the frozen parking lot fantasizing about how he would have done it. In a perfect world he would have ripped the man a new asshole. He would have started slow with something innocuous like telling Sampson he was a pain. Then he'd accuse the older man of being a faggot and finish by defaming his mother.

From the initial hello he hadn't liked Sampson's tone on the phone that morning, sarcastic, clipped, and all too vague about what he wanted. The phone call had deteriorated into the kind of blustering, posturing performance that typified their relationship. *Just go to the mall. Meet me in the mall!* A man like Vance Berg had things to do on the last working

126

Friday before Christmas, a lot of things. *Now I'm supposed to sit in the food court at the Glen Burnie Mall. Just waiting, like some jerkoff.*

Berg didn't like being summoned, not at Christmas time. Sick, uncomfortable feelings from long ago resurrected themselves. The terror was still there, like a cold stone deep in his gut, like it was the day he was fired from Esskay. He was reliving that morning as he shouldered through the double doors of the mall and was hit with three different Christmas songs at one time. "It's beginning to feel a lot like bullshit," he sang under his breath. That was another December day. He was nineteen, waiting in that dank hallway before they called him into the office, afraid for what he'd done, sweating in the cold. If anxiety could kill he'd have been a dead man that morning. On days like this the old feelings came back—always.

He hurried past the storefronts with his head down, trying to remember which end of the mall held the food court. Shoppers darted around him in their *almost Christmas* rush. Passing Victoria's Secret, he reminded himself that he should pick up something for Diane, a little red teddy maybe. It would be a real present, one he could wrap and make a good show of. *I might get a blowjob behind that shit.*

In the food court. Under the Phillips sign. Where he was supposed to be. With seven minutes to spare. But there was no sign of Sampson. Chico's Tacos was the only kiosk without a line in front of it. He bought some nachos. Seconds after the shiny seat of Berg's black slacks hit the flimsy plastic chair Sampson came around the faux-brick wall. Samuel Ripley Sampson carried a tan cashmere overcoat in his right hand, and a large white shopping bag hung from the fingers of his left. A gaggle of teens bumped and giggled as they passed him, and the tall old man looked as if he'd just been transported into a stockyard where he couldn't get out without touching the cows or stepping in shit. He didn't speak when he sat down hard across from his underling, only let out a sigh of frustration.

Berg thought how sans golf cap, Sampson's thinning gray hair made him look even older and somehow more sinister. "Want some nachos?" he asked.

Sampson ignored him, propping up the shopping bag on a chair and folding his hands in his lap. "Ah, shit, Vance," he said at last. He shook his head and stared at the floor for effect. "We have a real problem with this Canton thing." Berg popped a nacho into his mouth. "And that's your area, Vance." He said it in a voice that sounded almost apologetic. A tentative nod from Berg. "Little miss super bitch just won't back off. And the city is refusing to tear any of those old shit buildings down before we get the bill passed in the Senate." Sampson seemed thoughtful for a moment. "Hell," he chuckled, "maybe she'll just go away somehow." A shrug and more nodding from Berg. "Bottom line, Vance, it started me thinking." Sampson shifted his weight in the chair in order to more directly face the other man. "What if an accident happened in one of those buildings? What if some kid got hurt or, god forbid, killed? What if some fires started?"

"Yeah. That might change some minds."

Sam Sampson looked away then, out at the holiday shoppers who continued to hustle with quick, cramped steps past the food court like stampeding cows. "I'm not sure you're hearing me," he said, still looking away. "Someone might arrange for those things to happen."

Berg popped more nachos into his mouth. "How?"

"Oh, who knows? In those old shitholes anything could happen. Maybe something's ready to fall or break. Who can help it if some retard brings it down on himself?" Sampson was still looking away. "You know what I mean, Vance?"

Vance Berg pushed the half-eaten nachos aside. "I guess so." His boss turned and glared as if Berg had just urinated on the floor. "Yeah, I'm hearing you," Berg corrected himself.

"And that's just if some kid got hurt. What do you think would happen if …" Sampson scooted his chair closer to the round table and leaned in. "I'm just talking hypothetically here … what if one of those bigger buildings like, I don't know, like the Koontz building went up in flames? What do you think, Vance?"

"Yeah. That would do it." Berg was already picturing pre-Christmas traffic on the Beltway, estimating how long it would take him to get up to Shuffle's. *Christ, I hope Gripper's there today.*

Sam Sampson suddenly looked at his watch. He stood and pulled on his overcoat. "Glad we got to talk, Vance. It was good." He picked up the white shopping bag and started back around the faux-brick wall. "I'm considering a nice holiday bonus this year for my people—the ones who show me they can pick up the ball and run with it." He stopped to nod his head just once as if to signal he'd done everything on his list and then braced himself to merge into the crowd. "Oh," he said, turning back, "Merry Christmas, Vance."

CHAPTER 18

DECEMBER 24, 2009
THE MAGIC

It was almost seven when Little Carlos ran into the living room, calling for her. "You had a good nap," Michelle said, hugging her sleepy five-year-old. "So you can stay up late with us."

"Till Santa comes?"

Michelle had the last of the plastic candles and two extension cords cradled in the crook of her left arm. Her son became a three-foot high shadow behind her. He waved his green Peter Pan doll in his left hand like a wand.

"No. You've got to be in bed when Santa comes or he won't stop here." The Grinch had just appeared on the big, flat-screen TV, and she was secretly pleased that the boy found her Christmas decorating skills more entertaining than any cartoon character.

She began to set up one of the candles in the entryway, in the tall, slender window by the door. Each Christmas her father would put out the same kind of electric candles. He'd put one in each window of the old house in Catonsville. The instant the orange light filled the hallway she was there with him again. She remembered the way he'd tape the candles to the sills, almost reverently. And, silently together, they'd appreciate how their light made the night magic. She liked that her son was with her in the same way. She hoped that he'd have similar memories about her some day.

"When's Daddy coming home?" the boy asked.

"Your Daddy should be here soon." The two of them started up the stairs. *He has been good about coming home—lately.*

Nefferkitty followed them into the front bedroom and jumped up onto the windowsill where Michelle was taping down the base of the candle. "Don't you even think about it, missy." The striped cat stayed on the sill, looking at her, wide-eyed and purring a loud, indignant purr. "There are lots of other places you can sit, you know." The cat purred even louder and then leapt down and marched off with her tail up like a flag of war.

There was the high window on the stairs to do before they got to the living room. It was higher than she thought. "Ugh!" Halfway up the stairs she stood on her tiptoes and stretched, balancing the plastic light on the tips of her fingers. Little Carlos stood behind her holding up his doll with both hands as if Peter Pan could somehow empower his mom. Nefferkitty perched on the step above and watched her human's antics with disbelieving eyes, the cat's tail swishing with rhythmic tension. Swish. Swish.

It was just as the candle tottered into place that her left foot slipped on the runner and she came down hard. Her right knee slammed into the oak stair. For several seconds Michelle saw the proverbial stars. She pulled her knee up to her chest and closed her eyes with the pain. It was a jarring fall. Her knee was already swollen and her back hurt. But she knew it could have been much worse. She limped down the stairs to the living room carrying the remaining lights, her little entourage close behind.

She sat on the floor by the tree rubbing her throbbing knee and unpacking the last of the ornaments. By now she'd lost track of how many times she had called Carlos's cell. And the office machine only repeated its "We open on Monday morning at blah, blah, blah..." message. Little Carlos sipped apple juice from his blue cup and watched the last of the Grinch. Nefferkitty was making it her duty to pounce on each empty box and loose piece of wrapping paper.

Michelle listened for the low hum of the garage door and for the click of the key in the front door. The last weeks had been good. It almost felt like the old Carlos was back. She didn't want that to change.

Her white Christmas ball, the one with the picture of Jesus surrounded by an alabaster shell, went in a special spot on the front of the tree. It was the ornament Carlos had given her on their first Christmas. She never told him it was that ornament that had won her heart. It was what signaled he was different. *That's when I knew. This one actually got it,* she thought.

A Christmas Carol, the old black and white version, was on the TV now. She thought she'd have to find something else for the boy to watch. But he seemed to like it. She got him some more apple juice and settled down next to him, putting her hand behind his back.

It was 9:45 when the front door opened. Michelle winced when she stood, reminded of the fall. But she was happy to throw her arms around her husband's neck. "Oh, thank god you're all right. I've been calling your cell for hours, but it was off."

"Really?" Carlos seemed confused and pulled the phone from his overcoat pocket to look at it. "I told you I'd be late."

"Well, yes. But it's almost 10:00." He shrugged and slipped out of his overcoat and scarf. The shrug told her not to press him on where he'd been. Carlos went to the recliner, and his son was straddling his knees before he'd gotten the chair fully tilted back.

"House looks nice," he mumbled without looking at her.

"It took a while, but I got all the lights up. Want some eggnog?"

"That's pure fat."

"Oh, I know. But I could drink a whole carton of it," she said. Carlos only grunted. "And fruitcake too. You know I love that stuff." Little Carlos climbed up to lie back on his father's stomach. "He had his nap and he's looking forward to going to midnight Mass with us."

"It'll be too crowded and I'm beat. You can go if you want." His words drained Michelle like nothing else had. The words surprised her. Her own reaction surprised her more. She looked at the Jesus ornament again and the disappointment became an iron weight in her stomach. She went upstairs without speaking and left them both watching the movie. She knelt in the prayer space but only looked out at the harbor. The lights on the boats and in the houses on Federal Hill seemed cold now, lifeless. Discouragement hung over her like a sullen blanket. "It's not that big a deal," she told herself out loud. Still, it hung there. She knew she had to get her son to bed and put out the presents, that she had to hold it together, whatever she felt. She was the one who had to make the magic happen, if only for her son. But part of her wanted to just stay there, looking out at the harbor, for a while.

When she finally did go downstairs Alastair Sim was throwing open the snowy window: "You there, boy! What day is it?" Little Carlos was asleep in his father's lap. They were both asleep, sprawled together in the big leather recliner. Nefferkitty lay on her back on the floor, paws up, exhausted under the piece of wrapping paper she'd been wrestling with.

Michelle lightly kissed her son and her husband. *It's all so fragile*, she thought. She could have fallen down the stairs instead of up them. She knew that. *I can't let a little thing bring me down like that.* She thought how Carlos could have been in an accident and not come home at all. *We think we're safe. But it's all so fragile.* She perched on the arm of the couch with her knees up to her chest and looked over at her son. *And, god, how he loves his father. Look at him.*

She slid the remote out of Carlos's hand, turned down the sound of the TV, and stared at the silent black and white images.

*

At the front door of the church Jerry turned and looked back across the parking lot. In the early evening winter dark, he could barely see the low, square building where he lived. It looked deserted. Only then did he realize there were no Christmas lights at all in the windows of that building. He carried a white surplice in his right arm, and the arctic wind slammed the battered door hard against his left shoulder. He sighed, bumping through the front door of the church. Once again, it annoyed him that the beige paint in the foyer was peeling as well as stained. "God's house with peeling paint," he mumbled. Because he saw it every day, that particular flaw bothered him most. It had become a symbol to him of all the problems in the parish.

Opening the inner door, he was glad to see the altar nearly hidden now behind a wall of red poinsettias. Mick had put some extra pine branches around the manger scene, hiding the broken two by fours and recycled paneling that formed the stable.

In the tiny sacristy, he hung up his vestments and took his chalice from the cabinet. It was a silver chalice with faded gold leaf around the base of it. The helicopter maintenance guys at Vung Tau had bought it for him somewhere in the village. *That's the kind of thing I need to remember,* he thought. *Our altar there was two fifty gallon drums with a sheet over them. It made this place look good.* The entire day had been that way for Jerry, another new problem in front of him, another Christmas memory conjured up. Christmas Eves in Vietnam, at St. John's, at St. Mark's—the Christmas Eve his father threw a butcher knife at his mother's back. He thumbed continuously through the memories like worn pages of a scrap book. "Whew, ghosts of Christmases past," he said out loud. He checked the place-mark ribbons in the sacramentary and shook his head. "Today. Now. Concentrate on today."

Hearing voices in the sanctuary, he went out into the church to see Julianne, the pianist, and some of the choir members huddled around her at the old upright. They started with "O Holy Night." To him it sounded as if they'd never heard the song before. But the choir was there. And it was one less thing he had to think about. "Mass is at six, Father?" Julianne asked, still pounding the piano keys.

"Six. Eight. And midnight Mass is at nine-thirty," he said with a grin.

"Oh." The woman continued to plug away at "O Holy Night." Jerry thought she looked a little deflated, but he didn't ask why. Instead, he just went back out the front door and across the parking lot to the office.

*

"Carla, I'm glad you're still here. Is that little store in town still open?" The church secretary looked frazzled. One side of her dark hair was pushed up like a windblown wig. "I think so." Carla's eyes reflected sudden panic, as if she'd just been asked a test question about the one thing she hadn't studied.

"Would you drive in for me and see if they have some of those electric candles that go in the windows?" He pulled out his wallet as he spoke and found a ten dollar bill.

"How many?"

"As many as this will buy," he said, handing her the money.

"Okay, Father. And Eddie won't be here."

"What? I don't have an altar server at all?"

"Little Wilfredo's coming. I called and his mother said he's on his way." Carla closed the door behind her.

*

The church was packed for the six o'clock Mass, and Jerry spent half an hour talking with people after. He took off his vestments and hurried back over to the office. The secretary had gone, but a brown paper bag was propped up in the middle of her desk. He opened it to find five of the plastic candles and a package of Twinkies. "I owe you, Carla." He carried the brown bag and the Twinkies back to his own bedroom.

Forty-five minutes later, when he looked back from the church door across the parking lot, he knew it had been a good idea. The orange glow in the windows was like a beacon of hope in the inky darkness. *Now it looks like Christmas.* He stuffed the last half of the second Twinkie into the full trash can as he went into the church.

By the end of the second Mass, Father Jerry was running on adrenalin alone. But he wasn't tired. Seeing the little church full of people energized him like a rock star at the MTV awards. People stood in line to receive the sacrament, a line that seemed to go on forever.

"So many people, Father!" Wilfredo was carrying the brass crucifix back into the sacristy. "Maybe some people don't know we have Mass every week." It was the sincerity of the boy that made it funny. He couldn't help but to start laughing. The boy wasn't laughing.

"Yes," Jerry said as solemnly as he could. "Maybe that's it."

Between Masses, Jerry had time for only a cup of coffee. He took it to the parking lot to look out at the windows again, wondering at himself for thinking the plastic candles that important. Leaning in the front door, munching on the cookie in the quiet cold, he began to realize how tired he was, not just from this night. It was a cumulative tiredness, built up over the past three months. He pulled in a long breath of the cold December air and walked back through the church to the sacristy. He found Wilfredo sitting on the counter, his worn-out tennis shoes swinging beneath the white altar server's alb.

"What are you still doing here?" The boy didn't answer. "You need to go home and get ready for Christmas."

"Clinton came to the door when you were out. He said he couldn't serve tonight."

135

Jerry sighed, blowing out the breath he'd taken outside. "Well, you've already done two Masses."

"I can do it." He had to admit the boy didn't look even a little tired.

"Does your Mom know where you are?"

"Yes, I called her."

"Okay then."

*

When the last hands had been shaken after the third Mass, it was all Jerry could do to take off the vestments and hang them up. The church was suddenly quiet again. Wilfredo came in, zipping up the too big, olive-colored ski jacket that made him look like an even tinier boy than he was. "Thank you, young man. I owe you big time."

The boy's eyes shined with a special brightness Jerry realized he hadn't seen for a very long time. "Tomorrow's Christmas, Father!"

"Yes. Yes, get yourself home now."

Jerry heard the front door close and allowed himself to lean against the wall and let himself slide down to the floor. One last picture of Christmas past. He was ten, like this boy. The cold, snow-muffled sounds in the early Christmas morning, distant lights in the windows of his church on the far side of the railroad tracks. All the feelings came back to him, a child's sense of wonder and hope. He felt it again. "Tomorrow's Christmas." *It's still there. In spite of everything the world throws at us, the magic's still there.*

*

Only a skinny string of lights around the palladium stage and the band's red Santa hats hinted that it was Christmas, or even December. The Jamaican sky outside the palladium matched the sparkling blue blackness of the ocean. Only the tiniest sliver of light separated the sky and sea. Buddy flipped the cell phone closed and felt regret coursing through him faster even than the rum. His daughter's phone was still tied up. He didn't want to leave a message. *I don't know what I'd say if she answered,* he thought. *What could I say in a phone message that wouldn't sound moronic?*

136

"'O Holy Night'?" Buddy looked quizzically at the waiter who set down their sushi appetizer platter. "I've never heard a reggae version of that one."

"Oh yah, mon," the tall black man's face split in a smile that displayed an extraordinary number of white teeth. "We playum all on Christmas Eve."

"Got another line for you," Buddy said, continuing the game they'd been playing off and on throughout the day.

"Let's hear it." Chloe sat up straight, folding her arms across her chest.

Buddy hunched his shoulders, put his palms out and made his voice raspy. "Just when I thought I was out … they pull me back in!"

"Oh my god. Too easy. *Godfather III.*" She smiled and took a sip of her drink. "Or were you talking about those people at the country club."

"Ugh. Let's not talk about them. But really, you are good. Is there any movie you haven't seen?"

"Lots of movies I haven't seen," Chloe chuckled, picking up a crab roll and popping it into her mouth. "But I was a film major for a whole semester, remember?" She lifted her glass and held it in front of her. "And by the way, I wanted Hawaii, but for a last minute idea, I'd say this vacation turned out quite well."

"It couldn't be better," Buddy touched his empty glass to hers. "Perfect way to spend Christmas. And since there's no driving home, I want another Singapore Sling."

"Me too," she snapped back, as if he'd issued a challenge. She touched the back of his left hand with her fingers. "And, know what else?" She leaned forward and whispered, "I think it can be even better. I think we can make it better."

*

As they left the pavilion, Buddy had to turn and run back to the dessert table to grab one of the miniature fruitcakes. It was Christmas Eve. He gobbled it down in two bites.

They took their time coming down the hill, their arms around each other's waists. The canopy of lights in the palm trees made a path that seemed to have no end. Buddy was appreciating the buzz he had going.

But the liquor left a heaviness in his legs. He took little steps, barely lifting the soles of his shoes above the grass. Chloe began to step out ahead of him, taking slow but long, casual strides.

As always, his doubts about her throbbed in the back of his mind like the pain in the back of his neck. And, like that pain, Buddy could will himself to suppress them. For the thousandth time he asked himself why he hadn't pushed Michelle for details. *What am I afraid of, really?* He watched the hem of the yellow sundress bounce like wavelets around her calves, and he knew what he was afraid of. The emptiness. The darkness of life without Chloe in it, *that* terrified Buddy Miller. As with the physical pain, he'd ignore the doubts for now and hope they'd go away. He could see that she was tilting now and again too, balancing on one foot. He stayed closer to her.

"I've got one for you." She turned toward him then with that mischievous, eyes-half-closed smile that, after a year, still gave him an internal chill. "Ready?"

"Mmm hmm."

"Okay: 'Is this it? Is this what it's all about, Manny? Eating, drinking, fucking, sucking, snorting? Then what? Tell me, then what?'"

He laughed hard at her mimicry, the heavy accent, and the deep voice. "Hmm," he said, "it's not Gandolph from the Ring trilogy?"

"Come on. You have to give a serious answer."

"Hmm." The slope got steeper and he gently put a hand on her shoulder. They both slowed, taking tiny steps in the grass. "*Zorba the Greek.*"

Chloe broke into a belly laugh like he'd never heard from her before. She laughed so hard she had to stop and lean against one of the trees. "You're serious, aren't you?" She got the question out between catching her breath and wiping a tear from one eye. "Really? That's your answer? *Zorba the Greek?*"

"Well, what was it?"

She shook her head, trying to stop laughing. "*Scarface.* You never saw *Scarface?*"

"Yeah, I saw it. But I don't remember that part." They stopped in the cool grass. She turned to him, and they kissed. "It sounded like you were describing the last two days." Christmas songs drifting down from the pavilion on the hill mingled with the sound of crickets. Even after a year of her, Buddy was still shaken by the thrill of those breasts against his chest. Her mouth tasted sweet, like rum and mangos.

The two of them fell as much as walked through the door of their room. He wanted her mouth, her tongue. He wanted her like a sixteen-year-old wanting his first kiss. He put his hand under her dress, and the silk of her thighs and buttocks drove him wild. Chloe ripped the white shirt out of the waistband of his slacks. She gripped the muscles of his lower back and pulled him to her, her nails digging deep into his skin. "God, Buddy," she gasped the moment she could pull her lips from his. "I want you so much."

"So, why don't you marry me?"

The girl backed away from him as if she'd been slapped. She pushed him away from her and walked to the couch. She sat on the arm of it and put her feet on the cushions. Her eyes never left Buddy, but her smile was gone. "You've never said that before."

Buddy was more surprised than she was at what his rebellious lips had come out with. But he couldn't tell her that. "I'm saying it now."

"You only said it because you're drunk."

"Well, yeah," Buddy answered, putting his hands deep into his pockets, trying to catch his breath. He rocked from side to side, a little from the alcohol, mostly from his own uncertainty. The bulge in his pants made him feel ridiculous. "You think I'd say that if I was sober?" he asked with a silly smile.

Her body stiffened until her back was like a stone pedestal. She pulled the white comforter from the back of the couch and draped it across her bare shoulders, her eyes never leaving his. "I didn't know how you'd take it, Chlo," Buddy heard his own lips mumble.

She continued to look at him for a long time without moving and then looked down. "Let's get some sleep, Buddy."

"O Holy Night," the reggae version. The music crept through the open window of their room like a now unwelcome guest. "Guess the band's been through their whole repertoire," he almost whispered. For a full minute the song and the crickets in the grass outside were the only sounds. Chloe pulled the comforter closer around her. She didn't answer him. "Well, I'm going to bed," he said, turning the corner toward the bedroom.

Chloe didn't move. He heard her voice, soft, hurt, coming out of the dark. "That was fucked up, Buddy ... saying that when you didn't mean it."

CHAPTER 19

DECEMBER 31, 2009
CLASS OF 99

"Gotta' love the little black dress," Michelle quipped to her image in the full length mirror. It was a remark she wouldn't share with anyone other than that tall, athletic woman she saw there. She looked good in that dress. And she knew it.

Earrings. When she was fifteen and buying her first pair it took her an hour to do it. Time had not simplified the process. Tonight she narrowed it down to two pairs, the diamond studs and the black onyx ovals. She glanced at the bedside clock and went over the pros and cons one last time. Carlos would like it if she chose the black ones he'd given her. And they did look more dramatic. She held them up to her ears. Something about the diamonds said new, simple, successful. The black ovals bounced back into their felt bottomed box.

"We're gonna' be late," her husband announced from the doorway, "and you still have to help me with these cufflinks." Michelle stood up and spread her arms for his approval. He smiled and came forward, handing her the cufflinks and his left wrist. "I can tie the best slip knot in Maryland in twenty seconds; but I can't figure these damned things out." His fingertips traced the line of her neck as Michelle fastened the cufflink. "You look pretty hot tonight, wife," he said softly.

She smiled at the way the crisp, white shirt fit him, at the heady scent of his cologne, at the fact that it was the nicest thing he'd said to

140

her since before Christmas. "You look pretty hot yourself, Mr. Ibanez." She fixed the other sleeve in seconds. "With your hair that short you've got kind of a Ricky Martin thing going on."

"Let's go." Carlos turned on his heel and grabbed the black top coat from the bed.

"Wait," she called after him. "You have to do something for me."

"What?" He tapped his watch in exasperation. "It'll be 2010 before we get there."

"Sing the first verse of 'La Vida Loca,'" she whispered.

*

Now this is the way New Year's Eve should be. Michelle felt like a kid passing the turnstiles at Disneyland as they stepped into the thirteenth-floor club in the Belvedere. Scanning the room, she marveled at her own luck, at being part of the miniscule percentage of people who could party in a place where Woodrow Wilson and JFK had spent time, where women wore dresses and jewelry they'd joyously agonized over since August, where men looked comfortable in the best tuxes the city had to offer, and where no one thought it ostentatious to be dancing to a band called Rolex.

It was more than a party. It was an entire milieu, one that Michelle Miller Ibanez thrived in. It was another thing she wouldn't admit to anyone other than herself. Some of the male and female alumni who greeted her she hadn't seen in a decade. But they all remembered her. The room was gorgeous. She felt gorgeous. The road thing, the office, Chloe, her father—they all existed outside now, in a different world. This world was friendly, fun. It was a world that loved her. And she swam in it like a goldfish tossed from a plastic bag into the warm Caribbean.

"How are you doing, Hon?" She prodded her increasingly silent husband. She ran her index finger up and down his muscular neck as she worked the room.

"I don't know that many people," he groused. "Guess all the jocks are home soaking their injured knees." She laughed and took his hand while she held court.

The real turning point came after the conversation with Arnie. She could only watch it happen, like a traffic accident in slow motion.

"Carlos, right?"

"Yeah."

"Arnie Zeigler. Long time. What are you doing these days?"

"I sell cars."

"Ooh, sorry. Hopefully, the economy will pick up next year."

In damage control mode, she was trying some jokes on the two men. But she spotted Mary Beth and Brenda. It had been nine years. She had to leave her silent husband on his own. "Oh man," Brenda said by way of a greeting. "Glad you didn't wear a red dress too—we'd all match and I'd have to go home." The three women laughed like giddy teenagers, as if the first decade of the new millennium had been just a long weekend. "I really wanted to dance tonight. But this band—ugh."

A short waiter carried a tray of Champagne glasses past her and Michelle plucked up one of them. "I guess they try to play something for everybody," she said. "The Alicia Keyes stuff is pretty good."

Brenda shrugged her bare shoulders and grimaced. "I guess I can buy that. But, please, Frank Sinatra? He's been dead for more years than I've been alive."

Michelle did a room scan for Carlos and saw him shuffling, alone, toward the bar. "Hang out here, will you? I'm going to check on my hubby." He was no longer wearing the mellow Carlos look he had when they walked in. She hoped to get that back. "Hey, big guy," she said. "Buy me a drink?"

He turned to her and leaned against the long, black leather bar, sipping the scotch he'd just been given. "You're as popular with the U of B crowd now as you were ten years ago."

"Isn't that great?" she almost giggled. "I love that." Behind her husband she saw a blond, curly head of hair that hadn't changed since Monica Lewinski was on the cover of *People* magazine. *Please tell me that's not Chad.*

"Oh my god! Chelly? Is that really you?" He had to go around Carlos to be facing her. The man was tall enough to easily reach out and cup both her bare shoulders in his hands. "And you finally lost that pony tail—unbelievable!"

"Chad?" she said. "Sure. I remember you too. The ponytail's just gone for tonight." She said it even as she ducked under the hands. "This is Carlos, my husband."

"Hi," the man said. "Chad Williams. Good to meet you."

"You're a lawyer too?" Carlos reached out as if he was suffering from exhaustion to shake Chad's hand.

"Yes. I do a lot of bankruptcy cases now—in northern Virginia, Crystal City—that sort of thing. Did you go to U of B, Carlos?"

"Yeah."

"Class of '99? I don't remember seeing you around."

Carlos drained his glass and put it down on the bar. "I don't remember you either." There was a long two seconds of silence.

"Is your wife here with you tonight, Chad?" Michelle hung a little more tightly onto Carlos's arm.

Chad Williams turned toward the bar and crooked his finger at the girl behind it. "Vodka and tonic." In the same breath, he answered Michelle with: "Divorced for a year now." Another silence. The man slid a twenty across the bar for the vodka and didn't look for change. "Carlos, how about you? You with a partner here in town? Got your own firm?"

"High end cars," Carlos said, staring at the man. "I sell cars."

"All right! You have a dealership? You online? What?"

"Let's get out of here," Carlos said. He'd already begun the weaving process through the crowd to the door.

"It's a half hour away from midnight," Chad called after the couple, looking confused.

"We've got another party," Michelle called back to him with what grace she could muster while being pulled by her hand. "It's in the neighborhood."

CHAPTER 20

"What the hell is this?" Trudy Spanno had pictured the meeting somewhere in the complex of office buildings further up Ritchie Highway. She guided her rolling Prius into an empty space at the far end of the parking lot and began to dig through the mélange of computer printouts, file folders, and weeks-old editions of the *Sun* to find the senator's E-mail. She knew she'd printed the directions out before leaving the house that morning. She found the folded piece of paper and put on her glasses to read it. "Seventy-seven oh two Ritchie Highway is what it says." She took off the glasses and squinted again at the number on the front door. "It's the damned Holiday Inn," she mumbled in disbelief.

Judge Spanno had an uneasy feeling growing in her gut as she fished her attaché case out of the red hatchback. The feeling got worse after the reception desk, when they directed her down a hall that smelled like a tractor trailer full of wet towels. *This better not be somebody's idea of a joke*, she thought. CF104 was the type of conference room she had hoped she'd never see again. Only one large woman with long brown hair and a brown dress seated halfway down a long table was there. The woman smiled but said nothing. Trudy could hear the fluorescent lights humming like stifled bees. The furniture and carpet might have been new sometime during Gerald Ford's presidency. "Am I in the right place?" a sheepish Judge Spanno asked the woman. "I got an E-mail this morning asking me to fill in for a Miriam Phizer... a meeting for potential contractors?"

"You're in the right place." The large woman smiled again and then didn't. The smile was like a light being flipped on and off. "Mr. Sampson's right down the hall."

"Okay, Sampson, I know him. Who else?"

"Umm, Randy, Al, Bill Mallory."

"Are they road contractors?"

The corners of the large woman's mouth turned down in discomfort. "Uh, they work for Mr. Sampson, yeah."

"I must be missing something," the judge said, rubbing her temples. "Who is Miriam Phizer? What does she do?"

"I know she works for SHA down in Annapolis." The woman seemed to be visibly relieved when the men came through the door. "She's a secre—I mean admin, like me."

Three men sat down almost in unison in the chairs across from Judy Spanno. She glanced at them just long enough to notice that the two younger ones had slicked-down hair ala 1989, and that the third one was older. He wore a dirty ball cap that he didn't take off. Sam Sampson marched to the head of the table and threw down a yellow pad on it as if he were auditioning for a play.

"Sam," Trudy said, trying to establish a link back to the real world, which seemed to be disintegrating around her. "Help me out here."

"Sorry?"

She shrugged. "What is this? Why am I here?"

Sampson took on a shocked expression and leaned forward with his elbows on the table. He pointed a little finger up to his lips, and for a second she thought he was mocking her with a Doctor Evil impersonation. "Senator Schnee was supposed to explain this to you. He told me personally that he would." Sam Sampson looked down at the table, shaking his head. "What we have here are our ATPs. That's Authorizations to Present Proposals."

"I know what ATPs are."

"Do you? Good, Trudy."

As the two of them spoke, one of the younger men brought a large cardboard box up from under the table. The admin woman stood and swished around to the other side of the table where she began reaching into the box and pulling out crisp, thick manila binders.

"You see," Sampson went on, "CEPCO is the only organization that's ready to utilize the stimulus dollars out there." Seven of the packets had been lined up with precision along the center of the table. The new covers made them shine like gold bars in the fluorescent glare. "The minute 1664 passes we're going to hit the ground running like you won't believe."

The second young man reached over to open one of the packets to a page marked with a small yellow sticky note. He slid the package reverently across the table toward her and smiled through thick, black-rimmed glasses.

Judge Spanno scanned the thick blocked paragraphs of legalese, slowly moving her fingertip down the page. She flipped to the previous page and did the same. Sampson leaned back in his chair and put one cowboy boot up on the edge of the table. The man in the dirty ball cap tapped the tips of his fingers together in front of his lips. The electronic hum of fluorescent bulbs above them was again the loudest sound in the room. She turned to the front page of the document, frowned, and shook her head. "This is an authorization to proceed," she almost gasped.

"Trudy," Sampson snapped, "there's been an obvious gap in communication somewhere along the chain of command. He leaned forward with his hands on the edge of the table, frowning. "Just sign these and we'll go back to the Statehouse and get things straight with the senator this afternoon."

"You're crazy as hell, aren't you? I'm not signing these."

Sampson's voice got louder, his tone sharper. "This isn't a game. Right now you've got a sweet job down there. But Schnee can see to it a month from now you're emptying parking meters in Pikesville."

"Screw you and screw Schnee," the judge managed to get out through clenched teeth. Trudy Spanno grabbed her briefcase and stormed around the table toward the door. She didn't look at them, only heard the words behind her.

"Screw you and screw Schnee? Isn't she a judge or something?"

"*Was.* She used to be a judge," she heard Sampson say. "Now she just works for the Highway Department." Trudy Spanno could feel her own cheeks burning with embarrassment and rage as she went through the conference room door and into the hallway. She could not remember that physical phenomenon ever happening before, not to her.

*

By January Annapolis had lost the last of its charm for Michelle. It wasn't spring or warm or magic as she remembered it on that fourth-grade fieldtrip. It wasn't fall with the bright October sun illuminating the yellows, oranges, and browns of the city's oaks and poplars into party-like flame. Christmas, the essence of it, with red and green, warm velvet, and candles in the windows of two-hundred-year-old storefronts, had come and gone. She had to dance around patches of ice and dirty snow on the cobblestones on the long walk to the State House annex. A cutting wind whipped down the street and stung her face. "It wasn't supposed to be like this," she muttered one more time. When this thing had begun she foresaw one trip, maybe two, to the state capitol. "Who knew I'd see all the damned seasons here."

The fact that she had a lunch date with her husband at 1:00 added a backbeat of tension to the jangled cacophony of thoughts playing in her head. The New Year's party on top of the last four months made her grateful for any chance to pull their floundering relationship together. "Nine-thirty now," she murmured, checking her Rolex as she maneuvered around a particularly ugly pile of iced-over snow. "See Judge Judy at 10:00. Out of there at 11:00. And I'll be at the Chesapeake House by 12:30, easy." It looked like a slam dunk. Still, she picked up her pace when the tan brick building came into view.

*

The hour with the gatekeeper outside Judge Trudy Spanno's office was like water torture. "My appointment was for 10:00," she told the big, white haired woman. "It's 10:45"

"Just have a seat," the woman cooed. "Her meeting with the senator sometimes goes a little long."

Her emphasis on the word *senator* was supposed to confirm to Michelle her relative level of importance. *Wonder where she got this one*, Michelle thought. *My life's going down the toilet and I'm having a conversation with George Washington's mom.*

When Judge Spanno did speed through the front door she didn't look happy. "Come in," she said without even a glance at Michelle. She dropped a yellow legal pad and black pen onto her enormous desk and sat down heavily. "His highness had much to speak of this morning," she said. "So I'm late. What can I do for you, Ms. Ibanez?"

"As I remember, you called me, Judge." Michelle swallowed the feelings of disappointment and anger that suddenly welled up in her throat. "What's going on with the interchange?"

"House bill 1664 has passed the House. It's on its way to the Senate."

"Well, I know that. What about the actual work that was started?"

"I pulled the plug on whatever was going on there."

Michelle waited a few seconds for more explanation. None came. "And what was going on there?"

"I'm looking into it."

"We're not talking theory here. I saw real workers on the street. Real trucks. Real earth movers."

"I'm. Looking. Into. It."

"Okay." Michelle nodded, thinking for a moment. She tore her eyes away from the desk clock that flashed an angry red 11:50 at her. She shook her head as if annoyed by a gnat and went on. "What exactly have I gotten into here, Judge? Is this thing a done deal or not?"

"What do you mean?"

"You know exactly what I mean. Be honest. Am I just some kind of straw man, set up to look like a loser? Am I the token opposition to make this thing look legitimate?" Judge Judy's silence said more than any affirmation could. "Then I want out. My whole life has gone to hell in the last four months for trying to stop this road. And all for nothing. It's like a bad joke—on me."

"I was up there," the judge said. "Remember?" She picked up the black pen again and tapped the same manila envelope Michelle had given her nine weeks before. "I saw the area. You showed me plans for an alternate route that looked pretty good."

"And?"

"And you followed it up with a bullet list of vague assumptions that wouldn't impress my ninety-three-year-old mother and a cardboard box of petitions that the House members apparently used for toilet paper." She stared for a moment at Michelle. Neither woman spoke. "The bill is in progress. Why do you think I'll support your cause?"

Michelle shrugged. "Maybe you know we're defending something decent and irreplaceable here." There was no response from across the big desk. "Maybe preserving the quality of life of thousands of good people means something. Maybe you want to help out another woman in a tough spot. Maybe it's part of some Byzantine scheme you have to stick it to Schnee. Really, I don't give a damn why you do it. I just need your help."

Judge Spanno got up from her desk and shut the office door. When she came back she sat down in the guest chair next to Michelle. "Here's how it works," she said. "Bill 1664 is scheduled to go to the Senate early in the Spring session. The interchange is a perfect candidate for stimulus dollars. The Senate will pass it, not in a week or a day but in minutes." Michelle listened as her heart went into freefall toward her stomach. "This will piss off a lot of people. But I can set up a Commission hearing to potentially table the bill."

Michelle looked up, hoping the judge wouldn't notice her fingers digging into the leather chair arm. "Go on."

"I'm depending on you to justify stopping this work." Michelle's heart began to beat again. "There are huge dollars riding on this. You're going to be up against some of the heaviest hitters in the state." Trudy Spanno stood up and straightened to her full five feet two inches. "Throw away that half-assed bullet list you had. You're going to need enough good words and numbers to fill a Jerry Lewis telethon. Can you do it or not?"

*

Stepping back out into the cold, Michelle adjusted the scarf around her neck and buttoned up her coat to the top. She took one more look at her watch. She didn't have to do the math again. She knew that even if she got back to the parking lot in less than ten minutes and made a flawless drive up Richie Highway she couldn't be at the Chesapeake House before 1:30. "Hi, Honey," she said into her cell as her heels clicked rhythmically on the frozen pavement. "Looks like I'm going to be a little late. Really sorry, Carlos. I should have known. Love you."

Leaving the message assuaged her guilt, at least a little. She told herself she'd really done her best. Still, she snapped the cell phone shut and walked a little faster.

Despite the regret about her husband, and lunch, and the uncertainty hanging over all she had to do in the coming thirty days, Michelle had a good feeling deep in her gut. The richness of the feeling surprised her. It was a warm, invigorating feeling that went all the way to her soul.

CHAPTER 21

JANUARY 19, 2010
JUST TO BE NORMAL

It was 11AM and she had three puny checkmarks on the packed page of her day planner. Michelle could only stare at the angry-looking list and wonder what to tackle next. She heard Joanne letting someone in the front door and was smiling to herself because if anything else came up she'd have to squeeze it into the margin. She looked up to see Mike Drazinski filling the doorway. He said nothing, just bobbed his head and gave her a broad smile. She smiled back because she thought his big blue pea coat made him look like a young Captain Kangaroo.

"Mike," she said, "why aren't you at my Dad's?"

"They're in Jamaica."

"In Jamaica? They went to Jamaica? At Christmas?"

"Umm, yeah." Mike Drazinski looked confused, as if that was information the world knew. "He said he'd call me when they got back."

"Well—good." She did see it as good, in a way. It had been the first Christmas in her life she hadn't at least talked to her father. She'd really expected him to call in spite of what she'd said that day in Arbutus. But knowing he was out of the country somehow made his not calling more tolerable. "Something you need from us?"

"Um, no."

She tossed her pen down on the desk in frustration. "It's January, Mike. Brand new year. Brand new semester. And you've got nothing else to do but drive into the city and hang out at a law office?"

He shrugged, put his hands in his pockets, and turned his head to look out into the hall as if a good reply might be on the wall. Apparently, there was not. "I'll just do whatever."

"Since you're here, Mike," she said. *And since you obviously aren't leaving.* "We have two new office chairs in those boxes over there. Would you want to put them together for us?" Without a yes or even a grunt of assent Mike pulled the two square boxes from against the wall to the center of the floor. He began to tear them open as if his survival depended on it. Michelle opened her middle drawer and rummaged through the Post-its and pens to find her Leatherman tool and toss it to him. "Here you go," she said. *He'll be tightening the nuts with his teeth otherwise.*

Forty-five minutes later Mike stood behind the two new office chairs, saying nothing and spinning them with his pan-sized hands. "Oh, look at you! Thanks, big guy." Joanne had walked in just in time to stop the gray one in mid-spin and take possession of it. "Now we can get rid of those ergonomic nightmares we've been using forever."

Michelle was equally relieved to get rid of the heavy green Naugahyde monstrosities they'd inherited when they took over the building. She guessed the old chairs had been in constant use since the Kennedy administration. The bright new ones made it obvious how bad the old ones were. She felt a sudden pang of guilt for taking advantage of the young man. "We're going to take you to lunch, Mike," she said. "Our treat."

"You two go." Joanne was already pushing her new chair toward her office. "I'm right in the middle of something."

*

They walked to the A Plus Deli in the cold. It was one of those January days when the deceptive brilliance of the Maryland sun made it seem warmer than it actually was. Together they walked down the hill to Broadway, Michelle setting the pace despite her heels. "Do you run, Mike?"

"Yeah. A couple of times a week. I do two miles."

"Two miles?" She smiled sideways at him as they walked. "I do two miles to loosen up."

"I can believe it," the young man laughed, taking bigger strides to keep up. They had to nearly run to get across Broadway before the light changed. He put an arm protectively across her shoulders as they jogged. An alarm jangled faintly in the back of her mind. *It wasn't wrong*, she thought as he held open the front door of the deli for her. *Not really inappropriate. But the arm was there a second or two longer than it had to be.*

"You know, Mike," she began while trying to squash her Reuben sandwich down to the point where she could take a bite of it, "we appreciate all you've done for us. Really, we do. But you can't just come to the office and hang out."

The boy put his hands up in mock agitation. "Dude, I'm trying to help. I'm trying to learn from you."

"You've got other obligations. What's Lisa think about your being here during the day?"

"Lisa's history."

Her mental alarm made a distant clang. "Oh. I'm sorry, Mike."

"Don't be." They were silent for a few moments. She could almost see the gears changing, thoughts forming in his head.

"This project, stopping this road, is something I'm passionate about. Be a part of something bigger than yourself, right?"

Michelle put down the sandwich and laced her fingers on the table in front of her. "I said we appreciate your help, Mike. But don't overdo it—dude."

On the way back, the light was red on Broadway. "Let's run," Michelle said. And she did, black heels popping like fire crackers on the asphalt, to the other side of the street, preventing a repeat of the arm-on-shoulders incident.

*

Back behind her desk and alone, Michelle spun the new chair like a top before she flopped down into it. "How was lunch?" she heard her partner ask from around the corner.

"Okay, I guess. Mike told me he broke up with his girlfriend. What a shame. I met her once. She seemed like a sweetheart."

"Awww."

"Well, it is sad. And call me crazy, but I'm starting to think the big goof has a little bit of a crush on me." Michelle waited for an answer. "Jo? You still there?"

"There could be worse things," the other voice finally replied. "He is kinda cute."

"Oh my god," Michelle laughed. "Be serious. I'm glad you feel that way. Next time you take him to lunch. He's all yours." Michelle leaned back in the chair, luxuriating in the novelty of back support. She stared at the new boxes of unsigned petition forms by her feet. She rotated the chair and saw the ever growing stack of State of Maryland Roads Commission binders on her book shelves. The chair kept turning and she took in the pile of new case folders. The folders seemed to be multiplying and encroaching on the last vestiges of open desk space. She put her hands up to her face. "Aggh!" she yelled out to her partner. "Oh, just to be normal again!" There was no response from the other office door.

"Really—sometimes I just want my old life back," she whispered.

*

If Buddy Miller was Superman, the Chartwell Country Club had become his Fortress of Solitude. He'd found a place of refuge that worked. *Living well is the best revenge* had become an article of faith for him. And he was determined to practice this new philosophy with rigor. Buddy's day started with breakfast at eight o'clock. With the first edition of the *Sun* he could make breakfast last until nine o'clock. When he got to the last sip of his Indonesian Civet he would envisage a collage of the people he hated. In seconds he could parade them through his brain. His father, wife, in-laws, the bevy of coworkers who'd tried to stab him in the back. *By the way, fuck you all,* he'd say to the entire entourage and then down the fine coffee.

On days when his neck pain was not a problem, he'd hit some balls, work out in the gym, and maybe spend half an hour in the hot tub before driving home to Nampara with a day's worth of wellbeing in his pocket. It was a good life. It was *the* good life.

But his neck was a problem. Pain perched on his shoulders and stayed there like a destructive monkey he couldn't shake off. He felt pain, too, from his fight with Michelle. And doubts about Chloe, no matter how he tried to reason them away, had begun to grow like a cancer in the recesses of his mind. Hope of enjoying that ever elusive sense of wellbeing anytime soon seemed dim. When Sam Sampson pulled up a chair and sat down at his table, the hope extinguished completely.

"Buddy! How's your day going, man?" The older man's tone annoyed Buddy. That Sampson leaned over the table and into his personal space annoyed Buddy. That Sampson hadn't bothered to take off his golf hat annoyed him a lot.

"It's going fine, Sam. What can I do for you?"

At that moment he saw Vance Berg appear from behind Sampson. In his black slacks and aged blue golf jacket the man looked like a rumpled storm cloud moving in. Berg also plopped himself down at the table. "You already know Mister Berg," Sam Sampson said. The ombudsman flashed Buddy a sarcastic smile.

Buddy relinquished the idea of enjoying the last sip of his coffee and pushed the cup away. He laced his fingers behind his head and waited.

"Buddy, Vance here has given me some—how shall I say it—disturbing news."

"Well, why don't you—how shall I say it—get to the point?"

Sampson let out a sigh and pursed his lips as another member of his round table showed up. It was the younger one with the thick, square glasses. He pulled up a chair next to Berg. "Woolsey, my office manager," Sampson said with an irritated nod. "Neither of us is the type to beat around the bush, right? I'll get to the point. It seems your daughter has been duped into heading up some ragtag neighborhood watch group. They're trying to stop a major highway project that's already in motion—can't be done, Buddy."

"Ahh, here we go." Buddy leaned back further in his chair. "Go on. Go on."

"I'm trying to help, Buddy." Sampson took on a more sincere tone. "As a father, you ought to talk to her. Let her know she can't win this."

"She's wasting her time," Berg chimed in from behind him. Sampson turned his head just long enough to give the man an instantaneous glare.

"She's being used," square glasses intoned, nodding as if he'd just endowed Buddy with a universal truth.

Buddy stood up then and grabbed his hat. "My daughter's a smart lady. She knows exactly what she's doing." He walked around to the far side of the table. "And the fact that you three clowns are here talking to me shows you're scared shitless of her."

"Hey, Buddy." Sam Sampson stood up as well. "That's uncalled for. You're crossing the line, my friend."

Buddy kept walking. With his hands in his pockets and his head down he hurried past both the driving range and the gym. He groped in his mind for a way to reach out to Michelle and let her know what she was up against. *I don't think she even knows.* The throbbing pain in his neck was becoming worse with every step. *Maybe they're right. Maybe she is defending a lost cause.* By the time he reached the front door of the club it felt like someone was driving a nail into the back of his neck. Buddy wanted nothing more than to find his car and get back home. He was feeling like anything but Superman.

CHAPTER 22

JANUARY 26–28, 2010
OH GODDAMN!

Gripper shined his flashlight on the tin-covered back door, dwelling on the massive padlock. He was thankful he had the key to it in his pants pocket. He switched off the light and jammed it into the back pocket of his baggy jeans. He'd traded the white painter's hat for a knit cap. Despite the cold, Gripper wore only the jeans and sweatshirt he always wore.

Turning the key in the padlock he felt a satisfying click. A sharp yip behind him startled the big man. He turned to see a small white dog in the dirt behind him. The dog barked a second time, and the sound seemed loud enough to wake up all of Canton. "Get outa' here you piece uh shit," Gripper hissed, kicking at it. The dog moved only two feet back, looked up at him, and moved his front paws up and down in a sort of dance.

Pulling the door open Gripper retrieved the flashlight and stepped into the utter darkness of the old factory building. When he managed to get the flashlight on the circle of light showed cracked cement floors and peeling paint. An occasional twisted sheet of tin lay amid small piles of dirt and battered cement columns. "Fuck," he said out loud. "Nothing here that'll burn." He shuffled forward, sweeping the beam of light in front of him. He'd been hoping for piles of newspaper, boxes, cans of paint, something flammable. "Fuck," he muttered again when there was nothing. "Fuck. Fuck. Fuck!"

He found a windowless stairwell and crept up. The second floor looked much the same. The third floor reeked with the stench of something long dead. Gripper didn't wear a watch. He'd begun to lose track of how long he had been in the darkness. It felt to him like he could have been in there for days. On the fourth floor were some windows, rust covered frames and glass brown with age. But the moon light was bright enough for him to make out shapes around him without the flashlight. The odor of death was even stronger on this floor. A smell like rotting meat, as all encompassing as the darkness, hung in the stagnant air.

A door that opened onto an iron fire escape had been nailed shut. There was a window next to it. Gripper found the latch on the ancient window frame. He managed to turn the latch and pushed. The window made a loud crack and swung open for the first time in a generation. A shower of dirt and rust rained down into the darkness below.

The row houses across the street were a floor below him and seemed to be empty. On the corner, what looked like several homeless men squatted or stood talking. There were no other signs of life on the street. For a minute, he listened to the rise and fall of the voices below him. Ideas staggered and floundered in his head. The flashlight beam showed only more bare concrete, a U shaped piece of tin and a painted piece of wood that might once have been a wall shelf. Gripper poked his bearded face out the window to stare up and down the street. The homeless men congregated on the wooden steps of one of the abandoned houses. For a minute Gripper was very still. He suddenly grabbed the wood and the piece of tin in his hands and propped them against the wall under the open window.

Back on the first floor, he inched open the door, making sure he was alone. He had to walk a few yards down the alley before he saw the white ball huddled in the darkness. "There you are," Gripper cooed. "Come here." The small dog started to run and then turned back. It took several minutes of coaxing before it would come close enough for him to grab it. "Yeah!"

Back in the building Gripper navigated the darkness and the stairs, quicker this time. With the flashlight in his right hand and the little dog cradled in his left, he was back at the open window in minutes. His breathing grew heavy, and his hands moved frantically. Stretching to his full length, Gripper shoved the dog through the window and out onto the fire escape. He reached down and grabbed the piece of tin and used it to block the animal from getting too close to the edge. With the piece of wood he nudged the tin back. He nudged it slowly, an inch at a time, so the metal and the dog behind it wouldn't fall. When he heard the dog whine in fear and frustration he knew it was stuck there.

*

Gripper flew down the stairs and across the street. As he got closer to the homeless men Gripper could see there were three of them now, and two of them were black men. They all were much older than him. One of them reached down and picked up a piece of pipe. The second eyed him warily and an old white man looked up as he stuffed a folded blanket into a lean-to next to the brick row house.

"Can one of you please help me?" Gripper was wringing his hands and had adapted a kind of pleading voice. "My dog got stuck on the window ledge up there," he said, pointing to the factory building across the street.

"What you was doin' up there?" The man with the piece of pipe swung it like a pendulum next to his leg as he spoke.

"I'm a building inspector."

"You a building inspector. In South Baltimore. At midnight." The man spit on the sidewalk as if to certify the point he'd made. "Faggot, get the fuck away from here 'fore I open your head up."

"Really, man. I got an emergency call about a potential fire hazard and I had to check it out."

The third homeless man backed away from the lean-to and stared at Gripper. He was smaller and older than the others. Small dark eyes shined in a leathery face framed by white whiskers and hair. Gripper pictured a white Uncle Ben who'd fallen on hard times. As if on cue, the animal let out a series of mournful howls and yelps from above them. "How'd your dog get up there?" the man asked.

"He just got away from me and jumped. And I can't reach him 'cause I'm really scared of heights." The old man looked at Gripper, then up to where the dog cried, and then back to Gripper. "Come on. Please! I'll give you a couple bucks."

*

The old man and Gripper tromped together up the stairs to the fourth floor of the factory building. "Where's your book at?" The homeless man spoke into the dark at the end of the flashlight beam.

"What book?"

"You're an inspector, right? I used to work down at Calvert Cliffs. If you're an inspector you got to have a book or a clipboard or somethin'."

"Oh, that, it's in my car."

"Goddamn, it stinks up here," the homeless man gasped. "No wonder you busted open that window." Moonlight streamed through the open window. On the iron grate the white fur ball huddled and began to howl. "How'd that dog get out there?"

"I don't even know. Just get him back in, will you," Gripper pleaded. "I'd do it but I'm scared shitless of heights." The old man leaned out of the open window, stretching to reach the piece of tin. "Here," Gripper huffed, lifting the older man by his belt. "I'll hold on to you." The man was able to put one knee on the ledge to get more distance. His fingers were inching toward the shaking dog when Gripper let the belt go and grabbed the painted piece of wood. Lightning quick hands rammed the board into the old man's hip. Gripper threw his full 230 pounds behind it.

When the man's slight body hit the concrete below it made a funny sound, like a cannonball made of wet rags. A wide smile cracked his bearded face, and a hysterical giggle bubbled unbidden up from his throat. He thought it was funny that the man hadn't yelled when he was hit, only let out an agonized "ugh" on his way down. For several seconds Gripper shook with convulsions of laughter. Then the laughter stopped. He shook his head to clear it and rubbed his hands on the front of his clothes as if they were wet. Finding the board at his feet, he threw it hard into the dark and heard it crash. Then grabbing the flashlight from his back pocket, he stumbled as fast as he could down the stairs.

*

Outside, the other two homeless men stood looking at the still one on the ground. Above them the little dog howled like a sorrowful Greek chorus of one. "Oh, goddamn!" Gripper said, appearing out of the darkness. "I'm so sorry!" Gripper pulled off his black knit cap and twisted it in his hands. "He fell. Is he okay?"

"Is he okay?" The first black man shook his head in disbelief. "That man dead."

"He dead or he fucked up real bad," the one with the pipe intoned.

"My cell's in the car. I'll go call 911," Gripper said while taking giant steps down the street toward Fait Avenue. "Oh, goddamn," he called back over his shoulder. "That poor guy!" Gripper saw one of the two black men swoop past him and the piece of pipe dropped to the sidewalk with a loud clank. He saw the man kneel down next to the dead man's lean-to and begin rummaging through it.

*

He was still in his silk pajamas and bathrobe when Samuel Ripley Sampson brought the site up on his laptop. He needed to read over the blog he'd written the previous Sunday and scan it one more time before posting it. He read it out loud, one sentence at a time, his lips moving silently as he concentrated on the essence of it. It said what he wanted to say. It sounded good to him, even better than he remembered. He read it out loud a second time:

"Once again the misguided members of this so-called Community Coalition have allowed their maudlin sentimentality to cause human suffering. Last Friday an elderly indigent man fell to his death as he tried to find shelter in one of the neighborhood's derelict facilities. It saddens me to see the suffering continue as these people in the association try to hold back the future of South Baltimore.

"People who truly care about others are asking important questions, questions like: How much more precious time must we waste before House Bill 1664 becomes a reality? How much longer must we delay the funding for much-needed jobs and prosperity?

"We want 1664 passed! The state wants it passed. The people want it. And most importantly, most urgently, we ask how many more of our good citizens must die before progress comes at last?

"Sam Sampson"

*

"I love it." It was ready to post. And Sampson felt he'd worked hard. He deserved a little pleasure. He deserved it now, not later. On the computer, he went to favorites folder and clicked on *Big Bore.* He brought up the kill-shot videos. The old man licked his lips in anticipation. There were two new ones this week.

The first one, the leopard clip, didn't work for him. The leopard was too far away. He didn't like the way it had simply fallen into the grass when hit. The hunter had to go to the animal, lift its head, and actually search for the entry wound so the camera could zoom in on it. Sampson backed out of the video and clicked on the second one as fast as his clumsy fingers would allow him.

"Now we've got something," he whispered when he saw the bull elephant charging the camera. The first shot hit the animal in the jaw. The air around the elephant's face turned pink with a fine shower of blood. The elephant kept coming forward, screaming in pain through a shattered mouth. The second bullet hit it between the eyes. A satisfying, audible whack, and the skull seemed to cave in on itself. Sam Sampson nearly laughed out loud in appreciation of the power demonstrated by the new .577 Nitro Express cartridge.

He could barely wait to click PLAY AGAIN. He watched the clip a second time and then a third. Sampson glared at the clock in the corner of the computer screen. His day was already behind schedule. He posted the blog, slammed down the lid of his laptop, and shuffled around the corner to the shower.

*

Gripper waited where he was told to, in the Westview Mall parking lot. A cold morning, the sky gun metal gray. He left the engine running and the heater on full while he waited. Gripper stared through the dirty windshield of his Eclipse at the Monday morning traffic flowing into town on Route 40 and sneered. "A real man always knows how to make money," he muttered. Fifteen minutes passed, and Gripper's body didn't move except for the heel of his hand pounding rhythmically on the steering wheel.

When the black Town Car pulled up next to his own car Gripper fixated on the fact that it was clean. Even in the morning gray the black fenders gleamed and seemed to sparkle. He wondered why Vance Berg didn't look happy as he got out of the car. "Fat bastard don't want to get up off that cash," Gripper chuckled to himself. He opened the car door and grinned with his hand out.

"Here, asshole," the big man in the gray checked suit said, slapping a plastic grocery bag into the open hand. Gripper at first thought the bag was empty. Then he shook it open and found five wrinkled twenties.

"A hundred dollars? That ain't what you told me, Vance." He was calling after the already retreating suit coat.

Vance Berg wheeled around and stomped back to the open car door. "And you didn't do what I told you to, simpleton." He put one hand on the door and one on the roof of the small car. "I told you I wanted to see stories on all the channels about flaming buildings. And what did I get? Two inches of shitty print in the *Sun* paper. All the way back on page four. Some bullshit about some old homeless fart falling out a window. The story about how Animal Control rescued his dog was longer. What the fuck was that?"

Berg had nearly made it back into the Lincoln when Gripper the Ripper found his tongue. "I'll do better, Vance," he yelled. "Next time I'll do better."

CHAPTER 23

He spent more on his annual membership at Chartwell than he used to make in a year. Now and then Buddy would remind himself of that. That morning the thought hit him. For a moment, he did feel uneasy about it. *Worst financial crisis since the great depression, people hurting all over the world, and look at me.* He took another fork full of the scrambled eggs with crab and leaned back in the leather chair to let the smiling young waitress pour him a second cup of coffee. He looked out the window at the sea of emerald green lawn that rolled down to the blue Severn. He sipped his coffee and counted the sailboats on the river. February and already there were five of them. He felt rested. He felt strong. His neck felt fine. Buddy Miller smiled.

The positive zeitgeist of Chartwell in the morning was tarnished the instant the man with scuffed black street shoes appeared in front of him. "Sam Sampson wants to see you," the man said.

"I'm sorry?"

"He wants you to come to our table."

Buddy remembered Vance Berg. He remembered their last conversation, and just looking at the man creeped him out. The smile looked crooked, almost disjointed on the big round face. The golf shirt and slacks were rumpled and ill-fitting. "You're who again?"

"Vance Berg, remember? I'm with Mr. Sampson."

It was the shoes, those beat up Navy surplus black brogues together with the golf clothes that clinched it for him. They were old man's shoes. *Some old fart counting widgets in the back of a warehouse would wear those shoes.* The shoes said all Buddy needed to know. The village idiot had come summoning him to an audience with the Sun King. Buddy felt like he was back in the finance department at Hunt Valley. "Tell him to come over here."

"What?"

"Did I stutter, Vance? Tell him if he wants to see me to come over here." Buddy turned back to his newspaper.

*

Blissfully alone, he'd finished with the lead stories and had moved on to the second page of the *Wall Street Journal* when Samuel Ripley Sampson rounded the corner and stood in front of him. "How about it, Bud?" Sampson smiled down at him just a little too broadly. "You wanna hit some balls today?"

Buddy lowered the paper and took off his reading glasses. "I'm really not in the mood this morning, Sam. Maybe another time." He did notice that Sampson's hat matched the black, silk golf jacket with the red and white Chartwell crest on each of them. He made a mental note that he might want to pick up a similar set for himself. "What's with your fat friend this morning?"

Sampson shook his head and gave a weary sigh. "What'd he say, Buddy? I just told him to ask you to come over."

"He seemed a little abrupt, that's all."

Sam Sampson pulled a chair from the next table and straddled it, his long forearms hanging over the back. "He's not my friend, Bud. Just an employee." He whispered the last phrase as though he was describing someone with colon cancer. "Construction guys. Little low on social skills, you know."

"Construction? That's what you do?"

"Sort of." The man's face was still smiling, but the muscles in his jaw turned suddenly hard and tight.

"Mmm," Buddy said. "Well, I'm *sort of* reading the paper here."

Sampson scooted the chair closer to Buddy's table. "Come on over and sit with the guys." Buddy sighed silently as he folded the paper and tucked it under his arm. He glanced back one more time at the sailboats as he followed the other man.

Buddy remembered them as the cast of characters at Sampson's round table. Vance Berg was at the right hand of the master. There were the young two younger bucks with moussed hair ala 1998 and predatory eyes. The little middle-aged man in the short sleeved shirt and big, square glasses apparently hadn't moved since the last time. "This some kind of business meeting then?" Buddy asked, sitting down at the table.

"That's right," the Sun King answered, "business meeting." The others smiled and bobbed their heads. "Get him a mimosa," Sampson barked at the waitress.

Hospitality aside, Buddy knew he couldn't deal with it. "Well, I can't help you guys." He turned and began the walk back around the corner. "I don't do work. Call me when you have a fun meeting."

"Stay, Buddy. We may be discussing things you know about." Short sleeves gave his boss a sidelong glance from behind the glasses. The young bucks showed their teeth and grinned at each other. "Michelle's name might come up. You can chime in then."

"What?" Buddy got no answer. "What's my daughter got to do with you people? What the hell is this?" They only looked at him and grinned. He turned again to go.

"Wait, Buddy. We have your drink."

He kept walking. "Stick it up your ass and you'll always have it."

*

Buddy couldn't remember how many times that night he'd woken up. Each time it seemed to take an hour to get back to sleep. He kept picturing Vance Berg and the clownish black street shoes. And he kept replaying the words, everything that had led up to the mention of his daughter's name at Chartwell. *Now I have to find out who these assholes are. Now it's important.*

In the morning he felt like a zombie, but he tried not to show it. He continued to analyze the conversations at the club while he smiled, kissed Chloe, and waved as she drove off to work. He kept seeing the strange dullness in the fat man's eyes and felt those intensely unpleasant feelings again as he sipped coffee and waited for Mike Drazinski to show up.

When Mike came into the office and saw Buddy waiting for him the young man's eyes widened in surprise. "Hey, Mr. Miller," he said dropping his backpack by the door. "Didn't expect to see you here."

"I do live here, Mike."

"Uh, yeah," Mike agreed with a nervous chuckle. "Wow, you got a tan!"

"Little bit of a tan, yeah. The beaches are great down there." Mike sat down in the office chair without taking off his coat. "So, how's the cataloging coming?"

"Real good. I'll show you." Mike began to boot up the desktop, still with his heavy coat on.

Buddy sipped his coffee and the two of them stared at the monitor as it came to life. "You were helping in my daughter's campaign to stop the interchange, right? You still doing that?"

"Absolutely." Mike pointed at the screen and began to rattle off an explanation of the columns and the figures on the spreadsheet in front of him.

Buddy listened for a minute and nodded with what he thought was the appropriate degree of gravity. "Um Hmm. That's great." The young man grinned with satisfaction. "You know what, Mike? I'd like you to start spending more time downtown, with her. Just tell me how many hours you're there and I'll pay you for it."

Mike stopped smiling and stared into the computer screen as if he was Mr. Sulu plotting a course for the starship Enterprise. "Um, did Michelle say anything to you?"

"Not lately."

"Well, the other day … she kinda told me not to come around so much."

"Ahh." Now both of them stared at the glowing spreadsheet as if cryptic answers to their unspoken questions lurked between the rows of numbers. "Do what you can. I want to ask you to keep an eye on her, you know? Make sure nobody like comes in and bothers her."

The boy seemed to relax, and he nodded. "When she knows you're paying me she'll see I have a reason for being there."

"You don't have to tell her that," Buddy snapped. "It's just—I'd rather you didn't tell her that part." Buddy's eyes swept one more time over the numbers at the bottom of the spreadsheet before he spoke. "Just tell her you're not that busy here. That I don't need you for very many hours."

*

The thought struck Michelle that she was at a place in her life where folding wash in the laundry room seemed like a delightful way to spend an evening. She'd given Little Carlos two of his father's undershirts to fold. The boy's tongue almost touched his chin as he concentrated on imitating his mother's motions. "That's good," she crooned. "Look how flat you made it."

Feelings of guilt lurking in the back of her mind spoiled her contentment. A legal pad in the bag upstairs held page after page of potential arguments her opponents could throw at her. She didn't need to see the pad any more. She knew them all by heart and added to them by the minute. When the time came, she'd have to come up with good, credible backup to refute each one of them. She had to know it all cold. *They're going to come at me hard. I have to be able to throw it back at them. No hesitation.* The pressure played on her mind, relentless, like an annoying song she couldn't get out of her head.

"Where's Daddy?" Little Carlos asked again, spreading out the second of his father's T-shirts on the tile floor.

I've wondered for months where your Daddy is, she thought. Another awful mind tune that refused to stop playing. "I'm not sure where he went today."

She put away the last of the laundry and was having heavenly visions of a twenty minute snooze when her son ran toward her waving his two favorite books. "You want to read?" she asked.

"Uh huh."

"Okay. But why don't we take a little nap first?"

"Noooo!"

When they were situated on the couch she began with *Bengi Engie*. She smiled at the boy's fascination with how the steam train left the round house and negotiated each turn and hill even though he was hearing the story for the hundredth time. She thought of similar books her father had read to her. Even there, then, in her own home she could still see the pictures and hear the words.

She knew the second book was his true favorite. She could feel him settle his small body in next to her when she picked it up. "Ducklings," she said, sliding her finger beneath the word on the front cover. "See how the little ones swim in a line behind their mother? They really do that."

"Where're they going?"

"Oh, probably to find food or make a nest."

"What do they do when she's gone—at work?"

She sighed and closed her eyes for a moment, then pulled him close and kissed the silken hair on the top of his head. "They just wait for Momma duck to come home. Then everything will be okay."

CHAPTER 24

TIME TO MAKE THE BREAK

Where the hell was she on Saturday? For the fourth morning in a row it was the thought Buddy opened his eyes to. "She said it was an open house," he mumbled into his pillow.

She hadn't called him that day, not once. And her cell number came back *out of service* time after time when he called Chloe. The thought had begun to nibble at his soul since Michelle had made her accusations. And since the day they'd returned from Jamaica, jealousy and doubt spread through Buddy Miller like a 2010 computer virus in a 1990s hard drive.

On Sunday he scanned the Internet to find an open house with her realtor, an open house in Severna Park, in Glen Bernie anywhere. There was nothing. On Monday he twice had the phone in his hand, ready to call Michelle and beg her for more details about what she knew. *He's with Chloe, Dad. I know it.* Pride, fear, and the ugly stew formed by the combination of the two wouldn't let him make the call.

Now he couldn't not think about Saturday. The sounds of morning TV commercials drifted up the stairs as he pulled on his jeans. The sounds were like fingernails on the proverbial chalkboard. He remembered how when she'd first moved in he'd loved those sounds. They were reminders that Chloe was there, that she was happy in his house, contented with living life as a couple, the two of them. Now the sounds made him want to scream.

Buddy glared at himself in the mirror as he shaved and thought again about Saturday. He began to dredge up all the other days when he didn't know where she was. The noise in his brain became deafening.

*

He found Chloe in the kitchen, nibbling on the last bite-sized piece of bagel and cream cheese, her eyes fixed on *Good Morning America*. She was wearing the turquoise dress, a knit dress that exquisitely fit all of her curves. Buddy thought how the dress went beautifully with her black boots. *She always looks fantastic*, he thought. *She looked fantastic on Saturday too.*

"Can you believe this guy?" She gestured toward the television with her bagel. "A striped tie and a white button down. He's hosting on national TV and thinks it's 1999."

"Where were you Saturday?" Buddy heard himself ask.

"Um, I was a lot of places." She didn't look up from the screen. "Why?"

"I tried to call you a lot of times. It said your phone was out of service."

"Hmm, yeah, sometimes it's like that." That she wouldn't look up at him was making him crazy. Chloe walked around the counter and dropped her plate noisily into the sink.

"What? Are you just going to leave that for me?"

She squinted up at him, mystified. "I rinse my own dishes. I'm smart enough to do that."

"Actually, you're not that smart," Buddy snapped. "You're about half as smart as you think you are. Just leave the dish. I'll clean your shit up like I always do."

The girl closed her eyes and shook her head. She began to close and open her fists. "A lot of other people think I'm smart."

"I'll bet."

"You see? That's you, Buddy." Chloe turned to face him. "What is it with you? More and more you're starting to fixate on stupid little crap like this and you won't let it go. You've become this sick person." Her eyes flashed with an intensity that said this wasn't about breakfast dishes any more. "You never want to meet anyone. You never want to go anywhere." The dress and boots suddenly seemed incongruous there in the kitchen. "Don't you see? You're shutting yourself off from everything—from your own daughter even." She threw the plate and it shattered on the wall next to the back door. She bit her lip and turned away from him to hide the tears overflowing her eyes. "And now you're doing the same thing with me." She grabbed her purse from the counter and took a step toward the door. "I'm the last thing you've got, Buddy. And if I'm dumb, you're a bitter old man. And I can do a lot better."

In a second she was gone. Buddy stayed where he was, facing the back window that looked over the veranda, his hands on the marble counter top. He heard the car start. He heard the garage door close. He didn't move. He listened to the engine of the car as Chloe backed down the drive and disappeared into Wednesday morning. In his mind Buddy saw the image of his own angry face in the upstairs mirror. He remembered the hate his father would routinely spew at his mother. When he did, the anger in his head turned to shame and then terror at the thought of being anything like that old man. But the feelings, his feelings were like the fear and tension he'd existed under with Michelle's mother. More thinking. Back to shame. "Sorry, Chlo," he whispered, "I know you're not dumb."

His eyes moved to the door and the broken plate on the floor beside it. *But I know I don't need this shit in my life either.* "She's not worth it. I can do better too."

*

For days the war of silence had gone on. Buddy and Chloe had made an art form of not speaking to each other if they could help it. He would venture downstairs only after she'd left for work. Living separate lives in the same house was a sure sign that life, as Buddy Miller knew it, was coming to an end.

Seeing the hawk that morning was one more step on the road to total chaos in his life. It perched on the rose trellis and looked through the window at him. "You son of a bitch!" Buddy yelled, yanking open the porch door. The predator was waiting for the smaller birds to come back to the feeders. It stared at him without fear, as if Buddy was a curiosity in a zoo. Only when he stepped toward the trellis did the hawk hop away to the hill. "That's it," Buddy said, grabbing up the only three stones he could find on the bricks, "stay right there, motherfucker." He threw two of them and the stones fell short. The third one missed the hawk by inches. Only then, with one last glare did it fly off, soaring up the contour of the hill and over the wall.

It's been like that lately, he thought. *All I've got left are the damned birds. And that piece of shit has to pounce on them.* In his mind, the event typified what his life had become. His was a life under siege. At least it felt that way. "My daughter's being threatened and she doesn't even know it," he muttered. Buddy grabbed the stiff straw broom from the corner on the porch and began to sweep the bricks. He swept with hard, quick strokes, even while a cold wind showered more leaves and twigs down around him. "Her husband's becoming a total asshole. Michelle hates me now. She hates … her." Carlos and Chloe … he refused to let himself go on with the train of thought. *How did it all get so hosed up? All of it.*

A gray dove suddenly burst out from a pile of leaves and tried to fly but couldn't. He saw that the feathers on her back were ruffled with a bloody hole in the middle of them. "Oh, you're what that hawk was after. You were supposed to be his breakfast, weren't you?" The orange cat made his morning appearance, this time easing out from under the rosebush. It eyed the dove and then turned around, its wide-eyed face toward Buddy. "You too? Haven't you been hit by a car yet? Get out!" Panicking, the dove tried again to take off but landed with a thud in the grass. "Easy, baby. You had a close call." After several minutes the dove made a third try. This time it darted off like a shot from a catapult.

Buddy tossed the broom back into the corner and went into the house. Through the house and back to his office he continued to mumble the litany of problems to himself. "I live with a woman who really doesn't know a thing about me and doesn't give a shit." Mike Drazinski had left three fat binders spread open on his desk. "Why am I not surprised?" He slammed them shut and threw them into the wall shelf. "He's supposed to be working for me. He started out great. Now the big doofus acts like he's on another planet."

The desk clock said 9:45. "Fuck it." He sat and rummaged in the left drawer of the desk until he found his old datebook. He looked up a number. It had been years. He wasn't sure the number was still good. "Hey, you," he said when she answered, "remember me?"

"Oh my god! Is this Buddy Miller? I still want to say Mr. Miller. You're retired now, right?"

"Mmm, just plain Buddy's good. But I prefer self employed."

She laughed. "You don't like the word retired?"

"Retired means sitting on a bench in the mall with my pants pulled up to my chest. I have a good six months left before that stage kicks in. How are you, Linda?"

They talked for twenty minutes about everything and about nothing. Buddy secretly reveled in the ease with which they'd slid back into their old friendship. Linda Okonski, the nervous schoolgirl. Linda Simkins, the young mom. Linda, his best friend. "You know, I still picture you as that perky new girl with the ponytail from Catonsville Community College."

"Oh, that is funny. And now my oldest is in college."

"Are you serious?"

"I am serious. Gunnar got a football scholarship from Penn State."

There was a short silence. "Hey," Buddy picked up, "you remember Jill? She still work there?"

"Uh, yes, she does. But she's not Jill Falzone anymore, Buddy. She's Jill Potter now, has been for quite a while."

"Oh." Buddy waited for his friend to go on, but she didn't. "I uh. I'd kind of lost touch with her and was just kind of wondering about her."

"Uh huh."

*

Once they'd said goodbye, Buddy stayed at his desk for a long time. He turned slowly, left and right, in the chair with his hands flat on the polished wood of the desktop. "Jill's married now," he said softly. "Has been for quite a while." The picture of Jill's smile stuck in his mind, the way she smiled at him that morning in the restaurant, the day he'd gotten home from Paris. A lot of Jill memory pictures played out in his mind. There were reasons they'd broken up, good reasons; but now he honestly couldn't remember what those reasons were. He reached out and rubbed the brass bull and bear she'd given him when he left Hunt Valley. "Well … good for her."

*

The Ibanez men had been sailors for generations. And Carlos felt as much as knew intellectually that the time had come. For the first Saturday in March, the weather was mild, warm enough, to even take out the sailboat. Michelle and his son were still asleep, so he made his movements quietly, easing on his squall jacket and tiptoeing out onto the pier. The relative emptiness of the harbor, the quiet, felt good to him. He could picture the open bay on the other side of the point, and the thought was exciting.

Carlos had filled the boat's motor with clean oil and replaced the sparkplugs the night before. He took satisfaction in knowing each part of his boat like a lover knows his woman. Still, he hesitated. *It is barely March after all*, he thought. *Hell, it's only been three weeks since the Snowpacolypse.* The Aztec had been a bobbing twenty-foot snowball beside the pier then. He stood by the wheel and took a deep breath before he turned the key for the first time that year. The motor came to life with a throaty roar in the early morning air, and his heart pumped hard in anticipation. His excitement intensified as he engaged the throttle and felt the hull of the sailboat jump away from the pier.

The boat's engine puttered unnoticed in the morning quiet as it moved out into deeper water. Carlos headed the boat straight out into the harbor, toward the old Domino Sugar factory, away from Canton, away from Michelle and their son. He knew that if it was April, even that early in the morning, he'd be dodging a flotilla of pleasure craft. Instead, he saw just a single sail and the white plume of one powerboat out beyond Fort McHenry. A single tattered blue freighter waited for a tug a half mile away in the shipping lane.

On the open water the harbor's breeze was replaced by a wilder wind. Carlos had to take care with his footing as he untied the canvas straps and checked the alignment of the rigging. The white capped wavelets were large enough to make the little craft bounce and heave. And the wind was strong enough that he knew he'd have to give the boat his full attention once he put up the canvas. He wanted to make the phone call before he got into that mode.

"Hi. Good morning!" He nearly yelled the words above the wind into the cell phone. "I'm coming." He laughed out loud at the response. "No, really, I'm just rounding Fort McHenry. Forty-five minutes to an hour, baby. Okay?" He put the phone in his pocket then and climbed to the top of the cabin to unleash the main sail. He turned it until it caught the wind like a giant pocket. The boat seemed to leap beneath him as if it too was thrilled to be free after a long winter. After only twenty-five minutes Carlos could see the low outline of Tillman Island in the distance. "Yes!" he shouted to the boat.

He remembered then that he'd be passing the buoy at Turner's station soon, that he'd have to keep a sharp eye out for the inlet after that point. With his left hand on the wheel, Carlos pulled out the plastic-covered map from under the seat and checked the depth numbers again. He remembered a large shelf running out from the shore somewhere near the buoy. The last thing he wanted that morning was to be stuck in the mud.

The cell phone vibrated in his pocket and his face broke into a grin when he saw the number. "Yesss," he crooned into the phone. "I am too. But couldn't you wait a few minutes to tell me that in person?" The wind howled and Carlos squeezed the phone hard against his ear. He could feel the boat moving on its own. His grin disappeared. The sailboat wasn't responding to the wheel as it should have. He had too much canvas up. He knew it. The sails banged and the ropes screamed with tension. But he didn't want to put down the phone or take his attention from it. "Yes, I agree, it is time. I feel like I'm wasting every minute I'm not with you. It's time to make the break."

Carlos had barely managed to get the sail furled when he noticed one of the Velcro wraps still waving in the wind. "Goddammit," he hissed through clenched teeth and began to climb back up onto the bouncing cabin. It felt as if a giant had pulled his feet out from under him. The deck, the water, the chrome guardrail spun together in front of him. He found himself face down beside the cabin, his hat gone and his right hand throbbing with searing pain. "Holy shit!" He cradled his right hand in his left and watched the cold, bottle-green water of the Chesapeake fly by below him, and knew how close he had come to being in it.

*

176

He steered clumsily into the inlet with his left hand and held his right hand up hoping to minimize the pain. He was overjoyed to see the big A-frame house on the hill that was his landmark. Five more minutes passed. Bare trees, shallow, brown water, and the putting of the boat's motor and then she was there, waiting on the pier like she said she'd be. Without speaking, he threw two bumpers over the side and tossed her a line to tie up the boat.

To Carlos she was like a goddess, up there on the pier in her short gray skirt and red jacket. She lithely got down into the sailboat despite her heels and the two bags she had slung over her shoulder. "What's all that?" he asked even as he put his left hand around her waist and pulled her close.

"Just some clothes and stuff. What's wrong with your hand, Honey?"

"I fell and bent my finger back." He reached over her with the hurt hand and grabbed the bags, a big straw one and a white canvas sack with black and red semaphore flags on it. He flung the bags back through the open cabin door. "I don't care about the hand. I don't care about this stuff. It's been too long. I just want you, now." Carlos crushed her to him. His mouth enveloped hers, and she couldn't answer.

CHAPTER 25

OUT HERE IN THE HALL

It started with a sketch, a rough drawing on the back of a piece of junk mail. It took him forty-five seconds to do it. Father Jerry had an idea for a new chapel at Saint Joseph's. It wasn't a practical thing to consider. He knew that. But, since Christmas, the idea wouldn't go away. His parish couldn't build a new church. *But to add on a chapel . . .*

The vision became just a little more real to him each time he redid the drawing. He pictured it round, like the base of a tower. And he mentally placed the chapel on the corner of the existing building, the building Jerry saw as an old, elongated barracks. Now, in the darkness of February, he found himself spending hours, rather than minutes, on his lap top studying pictures of country chapels. He liked the look of the smaller ones. *And we'll use form stone. Why not? If a little parish could build one of these in 610 AD why can't we do it now?*

Jerry couldn't help feeling proud of his latest version. He'd taken his time. He did it in ink on a piece of white poster board. "I have to say it. That's not bad." He said it to Peaches, and she shuffled her red-brown tail in mild approval.

Jerry eased the newest drawing into his black briefcase and ushered the dog out the back door. "Get in your house and stay warm," he told her. "I'll be back soon." He wanted to let Carla know he was leaving, but he found the parish office empty. With a sigh, he pulled his cell phone

178

and called the woman's saved number. Four rings went by, then five rings, and then six before he got her voicemail. "Carla, its Father Miller. It's 9:45 Wednesday morning. I'm pretty sure you were scheduled to be here today. Give me a call."

Hoping to find an explanatory note, he stepped behind Carla's desk. His foot kicked a cardboard box that said Clorox-Ultra and it jingled. He opened the top flaps to find what looked like Sunday's collection: church envelopes mixed with ones and fives and pockets of loose change. "Damn," he said, squeezing the box into one of the lockable file cabinets. "She should have gotten that into the bank. Damn!"

Jerry actually made the old tires of the van squeal as he exited the parking lot. He was still shaking his head in frustration when he got to Route 50 and saw the Saint Joseph's Parish sign on the ground—again. He pulled the van onto the shoulder of the busy road and closed his eyes, holding the wheel with both hands. "Call the cops one more time," he told himself. "Try the state police 'cause it's on State Route 50." He took a deep breath, let it out, and jammed the van back into drive.

*

Mrs. Shoenmire looked surprisingly unsurprised when she opened the door. "Come in, Father. You want to see my husband?"

"I do."

She led him again by the forearm through the first book-filled room and then pointed to an empty chair in the second room. Franz Shoenmire was asleep in his wheelchair by an ivy-covered window. "Oh, I'm sorry," Jerry said, "I'll come back."

"Nooo," she whispered, her hand still clamped onto his jacketed arm. "He'll be awake soon." She let go and hustled back the way she'd come. Jerry sighed, put a hand over his eyes, and sat down in the tattered, pink overstuffed chair. From somewhere in the house he heard a clock tick. That and the old man's breathing were the only sounds. After several minutes, the two sounds were joined by a third, a china tea cup rattling on a saucer as Franz's wife returned. "Thanks," Jerry said, and balanced the cup of tea on the worn arm of the chair. The old man's head jerked and his eyes opened, looking at Jerry with a filmy disbelief.

"Did all that racket wake you up, Franz?"

"Father?" The man blinked, and the film in his eyes began to dissipate.

"Are you okay, Franz? I have a favor to ask of you."

Shoenmire repositioned himself on the wheelchair with his arms. Jerry saw a young man's sharpness gradually return to the blue eyes. "What can I do you for, Father?"

"If I gave you a picture of something," Jerry asked, fumbling for his briefcase, "do you think you could build me a model?"

*

She was on her home turf. Michelle felt the some of the old self-confidence return as she and Mike ducked out of the rain and into the City Hall building. Despite the morning's tension, she was surprised at herself for taking a kind of giddy pride in showing Mike around. She felt like a tween sharing her favorite rock star's web site.

Lawyers, state politicians, business owners, and hangers on, they buzzed through the upstairs hallway like angry bees. All of her adult life, Michelle had recognized the hallways for what they were: backstage before the play. Step into the courtroom itself and you're on stage. Defendant, victim, spectator, relative, prosecutor, perp, everyone has a role. Before the first word is spoken, clothes, demeanor, and body language define who you are and the part you'll play.

But before and after the play the same characters are waiting or passing each other in the hall. There the masks are off. Pretense is gone. She'd always seen the hall for what it was, a controlled space where the players spoke and negotiated unencumbered by convention. *This is where it really happens,* she thought. *Here's where secrets are learned and deals are made—out here in the hall.* "Looks like you'll have to stay here, Mike. The E-mail said only key players at this thing. No telling how long it'll take." She saw a look of disappointment flash on his face and then dissolve.

"That's fine," he said, taking a giant step past her to grab a newly open bench space by the wall. He seemed oblivious to the players around him. "That's why I brought my laptop. I've got a ton of homework to do."

You may be a smart guy, Mike, she thought. *But you don't have a clue what goes on here.* "Okay, good."

Two steps. Two steps and Michelle was through the door of the conference room. She'd left the bustle of the hall and gone on stage. It was one of those rooms where tension substituted for air. It was difficult to breathe if you let it be. The only sound in the room was the labored inhalation of the fat, sixtyish man at the end of the long table. The man leaned back in the chair with his legs spread. A wrinkled tie draped his ballooning belly. *There has to be at least one like him at every meeting. Must be a rule somewhere.*

No one spoke or made eye contact with her. She took a chair at the far end of the table, far away from the fat man, dropped her notepad on the table, and owned the space. She could play the posturing game too. She was aware of the stares of the tall gray-haired man and his cronies across from her. She sat up straight in the oppressive silence and made her face an expressionless mask. She stared away at nothing. She waited.

When Trudy Spanno breezed through the door Michelle half expected to hear a bailiff say: "All rise." The small woman took the chair at the head of the table and jumped in. "This will be short and sweet," she began. "Two points." No one except the judge breathed. "Advanced funding to CEPCO for preparatory work on the interchange has gone away."

"What?" Sampson sneered with the word rather than asked a question. "What the hell, Trudy? Senator Schnee himself approved that funding." He pointed his long index finger up the table like a pistol.

"I've spoken at length with the senator," Trudy Spanno countered without changing her tone. "And he now understands that release of that funding was, uh, premature."

Sampson put one hand on the table and pushed himself away from it. His gray head had begun to bob as if he'd grabbed a high voltage wire. "We'll see."

"We won't *see* anything. It's done." The two younger men with Sampson looked down and scribbled furiously in their day planners.

"And here's point two. On the ninth of April this year," the judge intoned, "there will be a hearing in Annapolis." Sampson groaned audibly and shook his head. She went on reading in the same monotone, but now the tiniest hint of a smile creased the corners of her mouth. "To reassess the feasibility of the Canton interchange as put forward in House Bill 1664." Samuel Ripley Sampson was out of his chair and on his way to the door as if the room was on fire. "A letter detailing specific requirements for this hearing will be mailed to all appropriate parties …"

*

It was when the gray-haired man burst through the doors that Mike recognized him. It was the same man he'd seen in the back of the Roads Commission office bay last fall. The man's face was as close to purple as any human face he'd ever seen. Mike ached to know what had happened in the room. That the older man and the two younger ones, seeming to literally ride his coattails, crossed the hall and positioned themselves in front of Mike seemed to him too good to be true.

"Motherfuckers!" The man was pacing back and forth in front of Mike. His hands were deep enough in his pants pockets to make his suit coat stick out behind him like a tailfin on a rocket. "Motherfuckers!"

"How'd they do it, Sam?" The younger man with the black-framed glasses had begun to imitate his boss's pacing. "I don't get how they stopped our funding. I mean we *had* that!"

"I don't know." Sampson stopped the pacing and suddenly pointed with one finger into the air as if signaling a revelation from God. "Somehow they back-doored Schnee. But this isn't over. Oh, I guarantee that." Mike sensed their eyes on him, but he kept his head down, staring at the computer. He didn't want to break the spell and stop the words coming. "I'm gonna break that bitch's back." The words chilled Mike like ice water in his veins. "Nobody fucks me like this. Especially not that cunt."

Michelle came through the wooden double doors and crossed the hall to the bench where Mike Drazinski sat. The three men didn't move. "You're gonna' get your ass kicked," Sampson hissed when she came close. He loomed over Michelle, and his finger came close to her face. Mike was instantly on his feet, and the others realized that his shoulders were as wide as the two younger men's together.

"Are you threatening me, Mr. Sampson?" Michelle asked. "That sounded like a threat." Sampson continued to glare, his eyes locked on hers.

"Of course not, I was speaking metaphorically."

"Be there on the ninth. We'll see who gets his ass kicked, metaphorically that is."

"You're damn right I'll be there."

Michelle watched the backs of the three men bounce and melt into the crowded hall. "They say anything to you before I came over?"

"Not directly to me," Mike said, thrusting his laptop into its case. He bit his lip and watched with her down the hall. "I wanted to be in there. I wanted to learn something."

"I think you learned things today," she said as the suits and coifed hair swirled by them like a fast running stream. "You learned a lot."

*

This is how it started. Buddy thought he might be able to reverse some of the damage in the same way he'd begun it. *Here we go. Round two.* He thought morning would be the best time, but when he came into the kitchen she didn't look up from the TV. Neither of them spoke, but the way the muscles in her face tightened told him more than he needed to know. "You know," he said softly as he poured a cup of coffee, "we can't just not talk forever."

Seconds passed before she answered. "You're the one not talking." She still didn't look at him.

"I'm talking now," he offered, knowing it was a lame thing to say, knowing too that he didn't have anything else.

"How do I know you're not going to just go off on me again? You said some ugly things for no reason, Buddy."

"But it's been almost a week."

Chloe was suddenly on her feet and facing him. "So, because a week has passed, that makes it all right? And what was all that about, Saturday, Saturday, Saturday?" Part of Buddy was wondering how she was managing to make him feel small while he was looking down at her. "Where the hell do you think I was on Saturday?"

Buddy licked his lips and thought hard before he answered. "I couldn't reach you and it was the first time you didn't call me. I kept thinking about that."

She sighed and grabbed up her coat and purse from the counter. "I don't need jealousy, Buddy. You told me you'd never do that." He started to speak and then just shrugged and looked at her. "I'm beginning to think it's better if I just leave."

"No!" Buddy was surprised by the urgency in his own voice. "No, really, don't do that." But she did leave, at least for work.

He found himself once again by the window as she drove off. *That didn't go well.* He was tired of staring out the back window, tired of feeling like the bitter old man she'd characterized him as. As if on cue, the big orange neighborhood cat appeared again, slinking out from under the bushes. Buddy rapped hard on the window. "Get out of here, you son of a bitch!"

He tore his eyes away from the window in embarrassment and went back to pour a second cup of coffee, not wanting to dwell on what he'd become. He heard another car and went to the front door. When he saw Mike Drazinski's old Volvo come up the drive he felt a surge of relief. He was suddenly sick of being alone.

*

"Heey, there he is—Iron Mike."

"Hi." The younger man looked up from the office chair with an awkward grin. "What's this Iron Mike?"

"I don't know. I think my brother, the boxer, fought somebody with that name." Buddy shuffled toward the window with his coffee cup. "So, how've you been? How's school this semester?"

"School's brutal, Mr. Miller. But I'm on top of it."

"Good. Well good, that you're on top of it, not good that it's brutal."

Mike leaned back in the office chair and put his hands behind his head. "And I have been doing what you told me, spending time with Michelle. Uh, your daughter."

"Yeah? Everything okay with her lately?"

"I guess. I know she was really kind of mad at her husband."

"How do you know that?"

"I heard her telling Joanne that he was out on his sailboat last Saturday and broke his finger."

"Last Saturday?"

"Yeah. She said he hadn't called her all day, and by the time he got home his hand was all swollen and blue. She had to take him to the emergency room at Bon Secours." Buddy didn't say anything, and the young man put his hands down into his lap. "I don't mean to be talking behind her back. I'm just saying."

"No, that's fine, Mike. I asked you the question, remember? What else?"

"Well, like yesterday, she took me with her to that meeting at City Hall. Man, that was kind of intense. She's probably told you about all of that already."

Buddy put his cup down on the window sill and turned away from it. "No, she didn't. We uh—haven't had a chance to talk for a while."

"Well, we were there because the little judge held a meeting. And she told all the contractors the interchange is not a done deal after all."

"Seriously? That's great."

"But one of them, Sampson, was really pissed."

At the name Buddy felt anger and fear collide in his gut. His doubts about Chloe and the previous Saturday were shunted to the back bench of his mind. All the scenes at Chartwell replayed for him again. But he was seeing them in a new light. The pieces fit now. Sampson singling him out. The prying for information. Later, the slurs about Michelle. His feelings of anger and humiliation mingled to form a volatile cocktail.

"Sampson comes out into the hall when it was over, right? He had two other guys with him. They came right over by me. It was like he wanted me to hear."

"This is Sam Sampson?"

"I guess. I just know his last name's Sampson."

Buddy walked over and sat on the corner of the desk, listening with his arms folded across his chest. "I'd like you to dig around a little more when you're with Michelle. Ask questions. Now, about yesterday, tell me what Sampson said. I want to know exactly what he said."

CHAPTER 26

MARCH 14–15, 2010
THIS IS ALL BOGUS

"Six-fifteen." Michelle's red and white Natty Boh clock, the clock Joanne had lately been begging her to take off the wall because it seemed unprofessional, said 6:15. It irritated Michelle that the thing continued to just tick on, Mr. Boh's big, jolly eye looking down at her, oblivious to all she had to get finished that night. The clock said 6:30 when Joanne walked past the open door with her long coat on. "Where are you going?" Michelle was embarrassed at how shrill her words sounded when they came out.

"I've got a date for dinner," her partner said, stopping in midstride and backing up to the doorway.

"I thought you were going to help me with these budget statistics."

"I've been here for ten hours, Michelle." Joanne's tone had changed, as if she were now reading from a script. "And I told you before; I'm just not as invested in the coalition as you are. I'm just not. Besides, we don't really know what the Roads department has set aside this year. All we have are the numbers from '08. The stimulus package makes this a whole new world. Classic apples and oranges. The money argument's not going to fly."

"Okay, go."

Joanne's tall, tweed-clad form disappeared in a huff and then reformed in the doorway seconds later. "I work here, Michelle. I don't live here. You ought to be spending more time at home yourself."

"Okay. Okay. Have a nice evening." She listened to the front door close and Michelle couldn't decide which annoying fact stabbed her more deeply, that her best friend was abandoning her in the face of a major crisis or that her best friend was right.

The hands on Mr. Boh pointed to 7:35 when she began to seriously question why she'd spent so much time on the spreadsheet in front of her. *The most powerful people in the state will be there. And there I'll be, pointing to a spreadsheet with a pointer. Can I possibly look any dorkier than that?* Michelle stared out into the darkness of the hall and listened for sounds, though she didn't expect to hear any. She hated being alone, there, in the office. It gave her a feeling of being buried alive, that the world had moved on and forgotten her. *Maybe she's right. Maybe this is all bogus. Not only will I be pointing at a boring spreadsheet, but one full of bogus numbers.*

Michelle closed the laptop and was considering leaving when she decided to run down her list of open issues. She drew a black star next to the budget issue and put a check next to an issue she felt confident about. It was a list of worst-case scenarios, of questions that could stop her cold. The list had been growing each day, like a monster, like a cancer. "Four weeks," she said out loud. "Dear god, I've got four weeks to do this."

*

It was 8:45 when she rang their neighbor's doorbell. The glossy black door opened to reveal Mr. Stillwell already standing behind her son. Little Carlos was smothering Peter Pan to his chest with both arms. "Oh, thank you so much," she gushed. "I really didn't know I'd be this late. Hope he wasn't a bother." Mr. Stillwell smiled a tight-lipped smile. And the two sets of eyes in front of her told her all she needed to know about the details of her son's evening.

It wasn't until she sat on the edge of her son's bed, waiting for him to finish in the bathroom that the tiredness hit her. It drained her as if she'd taken a bite of Snow White's poisoned apple.

That Carlos wasn't home had long since ceased to be a novelty. What bothered her was that she'd become accustomed to his not being there. Good or bad, she was learning to refuse her mind permission to dwell on where he might be. *I thought he'd be home for the game at least,* she thought. A year before, in March, they had been laughing together, watching the Trailblazers and Knicks. *That was just a year ago?* She would tell friends that they were best friends as well as husband and wife. The Knicks game—she was sitting on his lap, drinking a beer, his strong arms around her. And now they—weren't.

Little Carlos looked tired too. In his new flannel pajamas, his long brown hair tousled and in his face, he looked especially small to her. When he came close, Michelle put her hands on his sides. Her long fingers fit almost completely around his waist. "Were you a good boy tonight with the Stillwells?"

The boy pushed out his lower lip and looked down. "They didn't have anything for me to do."

"Oh," she said, stroking strands of his silken hair out of his eyes. "Sometimes when people get old they forget that little boys need to be doing things. But they were very nice to take care of you for me while I was working. So, you be nice to them too, okay?"

"Where's Daddy?"

Her watch said 9:30. Michelle bit her lip and continued to smooth out the boy's hair. "He's late tonight, isn't he? And it's real late for you not to be in bed." She turned down the covers and sat next to her son as he knelt to say his prayers. Seeing his little hands folded, his lips moving with earnest but silent words made her long to just hold him. She tucked him in and lay down on top of the cover, still dressed, beside him. She could feel the boy's heart beating, like a bird trying to escape, from the hot little body next to her arm.

In seconds little Carlos was asleep, and she began to succumb to the cloud-like softness of his pillow. She closed her eyes, but a parade of thoughts continued to march through her brain.

Where is his daddy?

Do I even want to know where he is? It can't just go on like this.

How much in stimulus dollars does the state have? Who's getting them? Who'd tell me?

What the hell's going on with Jo?

I wonder where my Brown's Treatise went to.
Just where is his daddy ...?

*

Jerry still had thirty minutes before the 8:00 AM Mass. He carried the wood and glass model like the work of art it was, holding it in front of him, taking small, careful steps. There was a bath towel over it. He wanted some time to arrange the model on the side table in the church foyer. Holding down the towel with his left hand, he protected the miniature building from the vicious March wind that whipped twigs and leaves across the parking lot like flotsam on a stormy ocean. After both the 8:00 and 10:30 Mass, Jerry was pleased to see that almost everyone stopped to take a look at the miniature chapel. Children of all ages were the most taken by it. A little girl of about six grabbed the edge of the table to hold her place. She tried hard to peek into the tiny glass windows. "Does it light up, Mamma?" she kept asking. Other kids crowded behind her and bobbed around each other to get a look.

Mrs. Schulz was the one adult who returned to stare at the 12" high model more than once. Jerry watched from the corner of his eye as he shook hands by the door. He watched her repeatedly position her large frame in front of the table, moving occasionally to allow the growing tide of kids to come back. "Love that little church, Father," she said, finally leaving it. "Do you have any more? I'd like to buy one from you."

"That's the only one," Jerry stammered, "but I wish I had about a thousand more people who felt that way."

"Then you could build a real one." It was a simple parting quip the woman made on her way out. But the words went through him like an electric shock. To Jerry, it was a first, shaky confirmation of what could be. He rode that breath of new hope into the afternoon. His good mood lasted through lunch at the local IHOP, but not long after.

He was searching the office for the parish phone list but couldn't find it in, on, or around Carla's cluttered desk. The good mood faded with each recipe and expired coupon he had to shuffle aside. What remained of it popped like a bubble when he found three pieces of mail from 2008. Jerry was still holding those unopened envelopes in his hand when he saw a white truck roar like an aggressive cloud across the front window. He heard it go around the building and stop in the back.

Running out the back door, he found the oversized truck had filled the backyard of the rectory. The wide front tires were up on the grass. The rear bumper was inches from the dog house. The tall, thin driver stood outside the truck. Hands on his hips, the man stared up at the high garage door.

"Hey," Jerry began, "this is private property. Get that thing out of here." It was the same man he'd confronted in the parking lot months before.

The tall man glared at him but didn't make a move to get back into the truck. "It's Sunday ain't it? Where's your dress at?"

"Why are you here?" Jerry asked the question while making a point of looking at the vehicle's rear license plate.

"Some of my laborers didn't show up. I'm looking for 'em."

Peaches trotted around the corner of the building then and began sniffing at each tire of the truck. Jerry reached down to her collar and pulled the dog close to him. "If I ever see you around here again I'm calling the police. You don't belong here."

"No," the man growled as he opened the door of the truck, "*you* don't belong here."

Jerry continued to hold on to Peaches until the truck backed out of the yard and roared across the front parking lot. "Come on, girl," he said with a gentle tug of the dog's red leather collar. "You can stay inside with me for a while."

*

She still couldn't find it. "Come on," Michelle chided herself, "I really need that book." She'd looked in the junk drawer, the tool drawer, and all the kitchen drawers. She'd scoured the kitchen cabinets, even looked behind those glassware cooking pots from her mother-in-law that she'd never used or intended to use. There was no reason her copy of *Brown's Treatise of Debate* should be in with the pots and pans. There was no reason it should be in the kitchen at all. But she'd run out of places to look.

Michelle strained to remember where she'd had it last. She could picture herself looking up something for the Koppers Brass case. She even remembered the words. She remembered turning down the corner of the page... *It's on the boat!* The previous July she'd gone with Carlos on an overnighter to Talchester. *I know that's where it is.*

She pulled on her heavy gray sweater and searched out the long flashlight from the hall closet. A peek into the living room confirmed that Little Carlos was halfway into *Shrek 2* and totally engrossed. *He'll be okay for two minutes.*

In the garage, she was surprised to see that the boat keys were not on their hook by the electrical box. She'd received more than a few husbandly lectures about always putting them *back where they belong*. And it was only by accident that she spotted them on the work bench, behind the grinder. "Humph."

Outside on the pier, the March wind bit through her bulky knit sweater as if it wasn't there. She pulled it tight around her and braced the butt of the flashlight against her stomach with both hands. It felt odd and awkward hopping down onto the deck of the sailboat at that time of the year, in the cold and the early evening dark. Michelle tucked the heavy flashlight under her left arm while she fumbled to find the key to the cabin door. She thought about how good it would feel to be back inside, snuggling on the couch with her son and a cup of green tea.

Almost no light came in through the small, oblong windows at the top of the cabin. She left the child-sized cabin door open and the bitter wind whistled in behind her. She scanned with the flashlight across the floor. She felt along the cabin wall with her hand for the inset handle; and eventually she found the storage compartment. Pulling on the handle, Michelle blew out a sigh of relief. The flashlight beam illuminated the tattered brown cover of *Brown's Treatise* just where she'd left it.

Carlos was adamant about leaving objects of any kind loose on the boat. Before and after each voyage he would religiously check to insure that even the smallest item was *stowed*. That's why it stunned her when the light flashed across a white canvas strap on the cabin floor. A nodule of dread formed in her gut. The nodule grew as she lifted the strap and the white, red, and black bag it was attached to. Inside the bag she found a comb, deodorant, shampoo, everyday things, things you'd need for a day trip or a week end. They were a woman's things. They weren't her things.

*

When the front door opened at 9:15 Michelle was in the hallway holding the bag in front of her. "What's this?" she asked simply. Carlos brushed by her and his son as if they weren't there and went through the living room to the kitchen. She followed him and threw the bag on the wooden table where it landed with a bang. "Tell me about it."

"Fuck you."

"Tell me!" Michelle hadn't meant to scream and the sounds coming from her own throat surprised her. Little Carlos started to cry. She saw a look on the five-year-old's face that she'd never seen before. Tears rolled down his cheeks and his eyes called out to her with a questioning look of confusion and fright. In the same single moment she thought how this ugly picture might live in her son's memory. She wondered if the damned purse had damaged her tabletop. She felt embarrassed that her septuagenarian neighbors might be telling other people how the upscale lawyer next door went all Jerry Springer.

Without a word she took the boy by the hand and carried more than led him up the stairs to his bedroom. He started to cry in earnest then, thinking he'd done something wrong but not knowing what it was. She took his small shoulders in her hands and lightly kissed his forehead. "I want you to do me a favor, okay?" Her son looked down, pouting but not crying now. "Build me a house out of Legos." The boy's eyes drifted to the closet where his toys were and then back to his Mom.

"What kind of house?"

"A big, tall house like ours, okay?" To her relief, he ran to the closet door and began to drag out the yellow box of Lego pieces.

The anger inside her reasserted itself as she hurried down the stairs and into the kitchen. She pictured again the pain she'd seen on her son's face, and the anger coalesced into an icy rage in her chest. Carlos was sitting down with his feet up on the table, the colorful purse next to them. He had opened some salted almonds and was shaking them around in the can.

"Tell me about the bag, Carlos."

"Why were you on my boat?"

"Wait," Michelle said, looking up at the ceiling and pushing long strands of hair out of her eyes. "Let me get this straight. You go out for a day in the boat. Then I find another woman's bag of stuff on the boat. And that's your response? That's what you say to me? 'Why were you on my boat?'"

Carlos didn't budge or blink. "That looks like your bag anyway."

"It's not my bag!" That he wouldn't respond, that his eyes showed no emotion infuriated her. "Just once in your life, why won't you admit it? Come on. Say it. Say it out loud!" He continued to look at her. One by one he picked almonds from the can and popped them into his mouth. Michelle grabbed the bag from the kitchen table and shook it. "I know who owns this," she said. Her husband didn't answer. But for the first time she saw a glint of fear and hesitation in his eyes. "And I'm going to personally give it back to the little bitch!"

CHAPTER 27

MARCH 17–19, 2010
I CAN'T EVEN TALK TO YOU

Pressure, prolonged, day-to-day pressure, is an unpredictable thing. Michelle reminded herself of that. At times her own actions had begun, not to just surprise but to blindside her. One example was the sheer relief she felt watching Mr. Rideout's wide back hulk out of her office. The client wouldn't be back. She knew it and was glad.

For the previous forty-five minutes she'd listened to details about the startup of long-term care facilities. It was more detail than she would have imagined possible. Three quarters of an hour. The man's body never moved in that time. He stayed stationary like Jabba the Hut, and she watched the man's mouth move like a miniature threshing machine topped by dead eyes. In her head she computed the research and hours involved in doing the contracts he wanted written. The hours. A year before, she and Joanne had been hungry for billable hours. Now the thought of taking on more terrified her.

Joanne seemed to be lost behind one of their massive law books when Michelle stepped into her office. Five manicured fingernails on each cover and a wisp of brown hair above the book were the only signs of her presence. "Whatcha doin'?" Michelle began.

"Working on the Homewood case." The book eased down, and Joanne stared up at her through the reading glasses, looking like one of

194

Harry Potter's schoolmates at Hogwarts. "Wow. You look kind of beat already today."

"I guess I am. I'm exhausted and depressed."

"That doesn't sound like you, 'Chelle. Normally, you're the one who thrives on pressure." Her partner slid her reading glasses down on her nose and looked over them.

"Yeah. But when things aren't so good on the home front... it's just tough when you're not getting that support. You know?"

Joanne pushed the reading glasses back up on her nose and stared down again at the law book. "Problems at home?"

"Oh, it's no big deal." She stood up then and straightened her jacket. "Keep researching the Homewood thing, and after lunch we'll talk about how to attack it."

Michelle shuffled back into her own office feeling older than Barbara Bush. *Things aren't so good on the home front.* It was the first time she'd made that admission to anyone other than her father. Doing it hadn't given her the relief she'd expected. It didn't feel good at all. *This must be how a junky feels at her first twelve step meeting,* she thought. *Hi, my name's Michelle. My husband's having an affair and I'm a loser.*

Hi, Michelle!

In the midst of that reverie she heard the doorbell ring again.

"I got it," Joanne said. Her heels clicked on the tiled entryway.

She heard a man's voice mingle with Joanne's and found herself hoping fervently that it wasn't a new client. Michelle put her head down and tried to put that anxiety as well as the others back into their respective compartments. She'd deal with them later.

"He's baaaack," Joanne mimicked, leading Mike Drazinski through her open office door. "He tells me he has a proposal for us." Michelle stared at the young man for a second and then gestured to the guest chair. She vacillated between vague feelings of irritation at seeing him there again and relief that she wasn't facing another demanding client like Mr. Rideout. Mike had on black slacks and a black knit tie that went well with his herringbone sports coat. She considered commenting on this new *young-guy-with-a-purpose* ensemble but thought better of it.

"We're more than a little busy here this morning, Mike. What can we do for you?"

"I've been a volunteer on STOP 1664 for a while now. I want to offer my services a little more formally."

Michelle scowled and sat back in her chair, shaking her head. *Whew. Who's been coaching you?* She thought. *Whoever it was, I think they've got you actually believing your own bullshit.* "Didn't we talk about this a while ago? Or did I dream that?"

"Two things." Mike went on undeterred. "One. Your dad said he doesn't need me at his home that often anymore."

Dad. Okay, the coaching question answered. "Why is that, Mike?"

"I've pretty much got all of his tax information cataloged. And the second thing, I'm thinking about law school in about two years. Being with you is a great opportunity for me to learn. I'll be your apprentice now."

"We can't pay you," Michelle said.

"I'm not expecting you to."

Michelle looked over at her law partner, who gave a shrug and then a head bob toward the next door office. Once there, Joanne closed the door behind them. She turned and cracked the door open again, peeking out into the hall to be doubly sure Mike wasn't listening. "We ought to take him on," she whispered.

Michelle closed her eyes and sighed. "We're fighting for our lives here. We don't need to be babysitting a nineteen-year-old on top of everything else."

"What can it hurt? He'll be like a mascot." She stopped talking again and listened against the closed door. "Just take him around with you, like when you go to Annapolis and City Hall."

"I don't know, Jo. I'm not seeing it."

"You're the boss." Joanne shrugged and put her hands up. "I'm saying put him to use. He's doing it for free. If he gets bored and leaves, what have we lost?"

They walked together back into Michelle's office. The new Mike Drazinski hadn't moved. He sat up straight in the chair, self assured, his fingers laced in front of his knee. Michelle walked around her desk and sat down behind it.

"We've had this conversation before," Michelle began. "You're a fulltime student. You have other obligations. I really don't understand where you're finding the time to work here. And, by the way, *thinking about* law school is very different from being in law school."

"I know my responsibilities," Mike retorted, his blue eyes boring into hers. "When I can't keep up with school I'll quit here. And I think I've already shown I can be an asset to this office."

Michelle had to admit, despite the coaching, she didn't know where the newfound confidence was coming from. She'd not seen it before, but she liked it. Young Mike Drazinski had a captivating set of dimples when he smiled up at her. She'd never noticed that before either. She glanced up at Joanne who stood by the open door and gave a tiny nod. "Do you have class tomorrow?"

"Not until 2:00 in the afternoon."

"See you here at 8:00 AM? Looking correct like you are now?"

"You've got it." The dimples flashed at her like lights on a marquee.

*

It wasn't there. The woman's bag Michelle had found on the boat was not in the kitchen cabinet where she'd put it. She slammed the cabinet door shut and then opened it again to make sure she hadn't missed it. She checked all the other cabinets. The bag was gone. Anger. The word didn't come near to describing what she felt. She couldn't come up with a word that described what she felt. Anger was part of it. So was shock. So was disappointment and it was all wrapped in a sense of *how could this happen?* so intense it made her want to scream.

Thirty minutes later in the car, her hands were barely controllable enough to click her son into the car seat in the back of the Miata.

"Where we going?" The boy looked mystified, as much by the aura of tension emanating from his mother as by the change in their routine.

"I'm driving you to pre-school today."

"But we always walk."

"There's no time to walk today. We have to drive."

Once she'd rushed little Carlos into the preschool and kissed him, Michelle ran back to her car and began punching numbers into her cell phone. "Hi, Judge. Boy, you've been busy," she said when Trudy Spanno picked up. She got no answer. "I tried four times to call you yesterday. Looks like I have better luck when I call on my cell."

"What is it, Michelle?"

She was surprised by the judge's tone and resolved to make the conversation a quick one. The judge was a busy woman. "I need to ask about stimulus dollars. How many are already available for roads this year?"

"I can't tell you that."

"Not counting the Canton interchange, how many roads projects are shovel ready?"

"I can't answer you, Michelle."

"If not you, who can, Trudy? This is public information, right? You're a public servant, right?"

A monstrous sigh came back at her from the phone. "Even the appearance of collusion, Michelle. The hearing date is set. You need to distance from me now."

"Wow. Okay, fine."

"It's not a personal thing. You know as well as I do how these things work." Michelle flipped closed the cell phone, and with it that compartment of her life. She had another compartment to deal with.

The decade-old Miata screeched to a stop in front of the Mercedes dealership where Carlos worked, stopping traffic on Ostend Street. But she'd already been around the block two times, looking in vain for a parking spot. This one came open and she was taking it.

Carlos was with clients. The couple had their backs to the glass door but her husband saw her coming and his eyes were open wider than she'd ever seen them. Michelle threw back the glass door. "What the hell, Carlos?" The middle-aged couple looked up at her like Kansas farmers staring at a funnel cloud. To Michelle they didn't exist.

Carlos was already on his feet. She heard him mumble something reassuring to the couple even as he grabbed her arm and wrestled as much as guided her into the hallway. "I was making my first sale in two weeks," he got out between clenched teeth.

"Fuck your sale. The bag, Carlos, what did you do with it?"

He bit his upper lip and shot a glance into the office. What he saw shattered what flimsy hope remained that his clients weren't hearing them. "I trashed it. I threw the bag away. All right?"

"Have you lost your goddamned mind?" Her question was not a rhetorical one. "Do you think that solves anything? Just what are you thinking?" He didn't speak. "Carlos, tell me. I need to know. What the hell kind of game are you playing with our lives?"

"I threw it away to keep you from making a fool of yourself."

"Oh, that makes sense. Now that the bag's gone, I'll just forget you're screwing that bitch and everything will be fine."

"It's not just that damned bag." Carlos was looking at her with something like pity now and shaking his head. "The road, this hearing, it's got you so stressed you don't know what you're doing. I'm worried about you, Michelle."

She could only stare at him. She wondered what she could possibly say to him after that. She wondered if her head was actually going to explode or whether it only felt that way. "I need to get away from you now," she managed to whisper. "I can't even talk to you."

*

By 9:15 she was in her office. Everything seemed to be where she'd left it, a lifetime ago. Her notebook lay in the center of the desk pad, open to the current day. The same two gray folders topped her inbox. Mr. Boh looked down from his clock, which continued to tick off the minutes as if nothing out of the ordinary had happened. She could hear Joanne's telephone voice performing in the office next door. *Sweet normalcy.* She sat at her desk, closed her eyes and rubbed her temples. For the moment, it seemed she'd pulled her life out of its nosedive toward hell.

When she heard Joanne go silent she got up and went in. "Jo, I have the names of three people in Annapolis who may be able to help us with some budget numbers. Will you call them, please?" Joanne gave her the expression normally reserved for new clients who were short on communication skills.

"That would be a good job for Mike," she snapped.

"Is he scheduled to come in today?"

"I think tomorrow."

"Oh, Jo, I really need this today. Plus, I need your tenacity. These people will just blow Mike off. And can you believe Trudy won't help me? She didn't even want to talk to me this morning."

199

"That kind of makes sense, appearance of collusion and all that, you know."

"Yeah. So, would you do this?"

"Sure," Joanne sighed. "I'll do what I can."

Back in her chair, Michelle tried hard to put her life back in order, assigning the disparate parts of it to their compartments. Usually, she could do that. Today it was like sifting through the rubble of a bombed out city. For a full five minutes she stared at the inbox on her desk and listened to the sounds, Joanne being Joanne on the phone, the fax machine humming to life and pushing out sheets of paper in its stolid, late-twentieth century way. She heard the muffled sounds of trucks on the street, the drivers intent on delivering packages and food and gasoline. The world around kept moving while her life was dead in the water.

Instinctively, she punched in the number of Jerry's Eastern Shore parish on her phone. "Father's not here now," the Hispanic woman's voice told her. "He's at the hospital. Shall I have him call you?"

"Yes. Please do that." Michelle knew her Uncle Jerry couldn't make everything all right. She hadn't truly believed he could do that that since she was eight. But her Uncle Jerry was still her rock. He always knew the right things to say.

She forced herself to pick up one of those new gray folders and open it. A Mr. Lane wanted to pursue zoning changes and a business license to open a neighborhood grocery store. She heard the doorbell clank and knew Joanne was still on the phone. She found Mr. Caruthers standing on the front step. He drew himself up to his full height as she opened the door. "Hi. What brings you here, Mr. Caruthers?"

"You haven't been down to the headquarters for a while." The tall black man stuffed his hands into the pockets of his tan corduroy jacket. Michelle was pleased to see he still wore the yellow tie. It stood out like a badge of honor. "Next month's the big one for us down Annapolis. Just wanted to make sure everything's okay." He reached a hand up then to take off his Oriole cap and hold it at his side. "Sorry. I had my hat on inside." It occurred to her that she'd never seen the man take off his hat before—for anything. Michelle felt a single hot tear glide down her left cheek, and she reached up to swipe it away as if it was an annoying fly.

"Yes," she said. "And we're ready too. I hope you can be there at the hearing." She smiled confidently at him because that's what the man needed.

"Well, thank you. I'll be going then." Mr. Caruthers put the cap back on his head. "It's gonna' be all right, Miss Michelle," she heard him say as he went back out the door and down the stone steps. "Whatever happens, it's gonna' be all right."

Michelle went back to her chair but didn't sit. She picked up the gray folder, closed it, and dropped it back into the box. She walked into the other office and let herself fall into the chair opposite Joanne's desk. "My husband's having an affair," she said simply. The words hung in the air like a surreal cloud, but she'd put them out there.

Joanne only stared and put one hand up next to her lips. "You know that?"

"Yes. I know it for sure now, and he doesn't deny it."

Joanne carefully put down her pen and lowered her eyes. "Oh god, Michelle, I am sorry."

"And I know who it is—the bitch my own father lives with." Her partner looked up as if she'd just been poked with a cattle prod. "Bizarre, huh? I know where she works too. I was ready to go down there this morning."

Joanne took a breath and lowered her eyes again. "Don't do that, Michelle. Not smart. Not smart."

"I know. I got as far as the beltway and turned around. But you can imagine how I feel, Jo. I feel like I'm losing my damned mind. You're the first person outside my family who knows about this."

Joanne brought her eyes down again and shook her head. "I ... I honestly don't know what to say."

CHAPTER 28

MARCH 22, 2010
IT'S LIKE A GIFT

Before he even knew where he was, Buddy's eyes were open, staring into the predawn dark. He'd had the dream again, the one where he saw his dead father's face laughing at him. He threw off the covers and sat up like a shot, trying to escape the image. Chloe rolled over and looked at him with eyes that were barely open slits. He wanted to tell her about the dream. He wanted to explain how it always came back at times like this, when he found himself up against problems that seemed unsolvable. He wanted her to know how it felt to be him, that he was going to lose his mind if he didn't tell her, tell someone. But Chloe constituted one of those problems. "I've gotta get up," was his best effort. "Gotta get out of here."

He threw on some clothes and went downstairs in the dark. Even as he burst through the back door and into the yard, he was draping his red plaid hunting jacket around him. He followed the brick path that meandered through the center of Nampara, all the way down to the beach. It surprised him how easily he was able to follow it without light. His body wasn't terribly stiff. His neck didn't ache. It all surprised him.

At the end of the path he stood still, hands in his pockets. The tiniest hints of light tinged the sky on the horizon out over the bay. He stayed there, not moving, waiting for the dawn, listening to the black wavelets smack the sand. In what seemed like minutes the dawn broke over him. Another gray, dew drenched morning had materialized out of the dark.

Buddy took slow, measured steps back up the brick path, toward the house. The anemic light revealed what looked like two black carpets lying by the new gate in the wall. Foreign bodies in his otherwise well organized domain. He went off the path to investigate. The two new wooden doors in black, plastic covers had been laid down flat on top of newly planted arborvitaes. "Sonofabitch! How could anyone be so fucking stupid?" He tried to lift one, but couldn't budge it alone.

Back in the kitchen he found cold coffee. Chloe had already gone to work. He refused his mind permission to think about how much he missed her being there, even when they didn't speak. He poured a cup and heated it in the microwave. "Shit." The coffee was weak and stale and as unsatisfying as the morning.

When he went to the office, Mike Drazinski bopped through the front door even as he came through the back. "Hey, Mr. Miller."

"Umph."

"What am I supposed to do today?" Buddy gave him a look that would freeze fish and turned to stare out the back window. He continued to fume about the doors while Mike booted up the desk top. "Mr. Miller, what segment of the market's going to come out of this recession first? I'm thinking Tech."

"You're thinking Tech." Buddy started slow and quiet while the anger in him rose like flood waters behind a dam. "You should be thinking about what you're doing here. Try thinking about what you're supposed to be doing for me today." Buddy started for the back door and then whirled around. "And for Christ's sake, pick stuff up and put it away. For the last month you've been going away, leaving this office looking like a shithole!"

Bursting through the back door for the second time that morning, Buddy picked up speed as he hurtled down the hill toward the two laborers who now stood by the midsection of the wall. Coming closer, he could see they were leaning against the wall, peering out at him from under their hat brims as they sipped Dunkin Donuts coffee. They looked like they could have been father and son. "Which of you assholes laid those doors down on my new trees?"

"Sir?" The older one put his cup down on top of a metal tool box.
"I asked who laid those doors down on top of my trees."

"It was almost dark when we got them last night. We didn't think ..."

"Exactly. That's the fucking problem. You didn't think. Well, get them up!" The two men were instantly by one of the massive plank doors, lifting it. "Why the fuck does God let assholes like you reproduce?" Buddy left that parting shot and started back up the hill to the house.

In the guest bathroom he tore off his jacket and began washing his hands. He bent over the sink and waited, letting his heart stop pounding before splashing water on his face. An angry old man stared back at him from the mirror. Rage continued to bubble and gurgle inside him, desperate for a place to go. It clogged his chest, the rage, forcing his breath out in short, staccato gasps. His impulse was to run, but he continued to look into the mirror. The image was foreign to him. Yet he was drawn to it, like seeing himself in a coffin. "That's not me," he whispered, staring into the tortured eyes. "No. I don't want to be you."

*

It was an hour later when Buddy went back into the office. He was careful to softly pull the door closed behind him. The younger man didn't look up but peered deep into the computer screen as if his future were written in code between the rows of numbers. "Sorry, Mike." There was no answer. "By the way, it'll be growth stocks that'll lead the way out. Tech will come along later. You heard it here first." Still no response. "You know," Buddy continued, "how you ask my advice sometimes?" Mike pulled his eyes from the monitor and waited for more. "You ask me business questions, where's the market headed? Blah, blah ... all that. You're a smart guy, Mike. You'll be fine in that arena. But don't forget about your personal life. Things can happen in life that make you kind of ..."

"Bitter?"

"Uh, yeah, I guess you could put it that way. Sometimes, you try to do the right things, but people persist in fucking with you. And when you don't know how to hit back, the frustration just builds. I'm saying you can't let that frustration control you. It makes you want to avoid … hell, I don't know what I'm trying to say here." Buddy pulled the armchair away from the wall and sat down next to the young man. "Sorry I jumped in your shit earlier, all right?"

Mike closed his eyes and nodded. He put his knuckles out for a fist bump. "We cool."

Buddy chuckled as he put his considerably smaller fist next to Mike's. "Look, I'll be honest, my daughter and I—we haven't spoken for months. I've got a bad feeling about this stuff going on behind the scenes. I'm really afraid for her right now." He lowered his voice, though there were only the two of them. "When you're downtown with her, work even more questions into the conversation. I've got to know how she's doing. I'm asking this as a friend, Mike."

*

It was close to midnight when Vance Berg pulled into the gravel parking lot at Shuffles Saloon. That he didn't see Gripper's Eclipse made his already churning stomach contract into a giant knot. He had backed the Lincoln up against the weeds and was waiting, sweeping the lot with his eyes and deciding what to do next when he saw the hulking form emerge from the cinderblock stairwell. "Gripper!" Berg turned off the engine, flung open the car door and called out, all in the same instant.

The form turned and lumbered toward him. The bushy beard and turned up hat brim were unmistakable even in the near total dark. A rusted white pickup pulled into the lot from Southwestern Boulevard, the headlights illuminating Gripper. Even Berg was surprised by the fish- belly white skin and glazed, angry eyes. "Damn, I'm glad you're here, Gripper. I didn't see your car."

"At's cause I got a new car, Vance." Gripper motioned toward a bright yellow Camaro convertible on the far end of the lot.

"You shittin' me? That's yours? It looks brand new."

"It is new, motherfucker. It's a 2009." Gripper's speech was slurred and halting, but the smoldering eyes had come to life under the upturned hat brim that still shouted RIPPER! in black magic marker. "Like you told me, a real man can always make money. Ain't no recession in Violetville. The blow business is doin' just fine."

An odd half smile flitted over Vance Berg's face, reflecting the mixture of disappointment and grudging admiration going through his head. "I need your help tonight, Gripper." Berg put a hand on the other man's big shoulder. "You know where the old Koontz building is? It's in Canton. I'll give you the key."

Gripper's eyes flashed in the dark, and he slapped the hand away as if it were a rabid squirrel that had just landed on him. "What are you gonna' give me, twenty dollars? I don't need your little shit money now."

Vance Berg stood his ground. His voice became an urgent, growling whisper. "Look, I know we fucked you that other time. But this is easy money, Gripper." He pulled a wad of cash from his pants pocket and jammed it into Gripper's empty hand. "Here. Five hundred dollars, up front. It's all set up for you this time." Gripper stared at the money, rubbing the crisp new bills together with his fingers. "Get in, start the fire, and get out. It'll take you an hour, for Christ's sake. Do it and I'll give you another two thousand when it's done. It's like a gift. I'm giving you a fucking gift, Gripper!"

*

Aw sonafabitch. Gripper was mystified when he stepped out of the pristine Camaro and found the right front wheel on top of the curb. He'd parked only about two feet from a yellow fire plug rather than the car length he'd estimated it to be from the driver's seat. *How'd that happen? I must be way more fucked up than I thought. Concentrate.* Still, when Gripper took some steps his legs moved with a natural buoyancy he hadn't experienced in recent memory. The bulky roll of cash felt good bouncing in his pocket. Vance had told him the door on the unlit side of the building would be easy to find. In and out. A $2,500 payday out of nowhere. *Gripper the Ripper is back and better than ever, motherfuckers!*

A white light like a flash bulb from the far corner of the building blinded him for an instant. Gripper assumed he'd somehow missed the door and was turning to retrace his steps when he had a sudden need to empty his bladder. He was leaning against the rough brick of the building with one hand and listening to the satisfying patter of urine on the sidewalk when the bright light reappeared, flashed in his face, and stayed there.

"Sir, please zip up and place both hands on the wall. Spread your feet." A stocky city cop materialized out of the darkness and came toward him. Light from a nearby flashlight reflected off the man's wide, shaved black head. A smaller, younger white cop held the flashlight.

Gripper heard the younger cop speak into the mouthpiece of his radio, something about public urination. He wanted to make it clear to the officers that it was a known fact public urination was to be considered a non-event if no members of the public were there to witness it. He had no doubt they'd let him go with a "Sorry we bothered you, sir." In Gripper's mind the argument spelled itself out flawlessly. What actually came out of his mouth was something like: "Imshna uh urinash."

The first cop stood behind him and kicked his feet out even wider. He began patting down the sides of Gripper's legs. The second cop lifted the flashlight and shined it down on them. The sensation of strong hands touching him caused the drug induced haze in his head to vanish like a whiff of smoke. "What's your name?" the black cop asked.

"Gripper."

"What?"

"My name's Norman."

"If I look in your pockets am I going to find any weapons, Norman?"

"No."

"Where'd this money come from, Norman?"

"Payday. I just got paid."

The hatless cop took the cash and walked to the police car at the corner. There he laid it out on the hood along with Gripper's wallet, keys, and cell phone. Gripper couldn't take his eyes from the key to the Koontz building. It lay obvious and loose, away from the other things on the hood of the car. It was the one thing he couldn't explain. They'd notice that key. He knew how cops did things. They'd be asking him about it, again and again.

The realization shot through Gripper's mind that they hadn't cuffed him, that for the moment he was free. It wasn't a conscious decision. His legs had decided unilaterally to run, and Gripper watched himself as if watching a movie as he took the first two long strides. His own speed surprised him. "Hey!" The bald cop had turned and grabbed Gripper's left arm with both his hands. But the hands couldn't hold him or even slow him down. Gripper felt himself pull free and take a full third stride. Beginnings of elation. For the better part of a second, Gripper felt like he could actually make it to freedom.

The sound of the heavy metal flashlight hitting the concrete. And an overwhelming wave of force hit his lower back like a cannonball. A glimpse of a white shirt sleeve told him it was the second cop. Gripper watched the sidewalk rise up and slam into his chest, depriving him of air. Several grunts and he was immobile. The legs that had begun this misadventure now abandoned him. Gripper felt himself being dragged, like a bag of rocks, to the back of the police car.

Within seconds, the three of them were in the cruiser and breathing hard. The bald one started the car engine and said some words into the police radio. The younger cop in the passenger seat tried with wet fingers to wipe the dirt from his blue hat. He turned and glared at the prisoner through the black, steel grate. "Why's your hat say RIPPER, asshole?"

Gripper didn't answer.

CHAPTER 29

MARCH 23–24, 2010
YOU LITTLE BASTARD!

Michelle had taken Mike to the A Plus Deli. She did it mainly to get out of the office. Lately, Joanne's moods vacillated between morbidly quiet and blatantly snarky. She knew she couldn't talk to Joanne anymore; and that knowledge, along with all the rest of it, was driving her into a world-class funk.

The same dreams dogged her every night now, long, never-fulfilled searching dreams. The setting changed, but the dream was always the same, her running down hallways and through tunnels, chasing some elusive something. Whatever it was stayed one maddening step ahead of her.

Maybe Carlos was right. Okay—a little right. Maybe I am kind of losing it. Each day Michelle was finding it harder to concentrate. Innumerable times each day she tried to envision the upcoming hearing. She'd try to picture the personalities she'd be up against, to imagine what they might throw at her and what she could throw back. But inevitably, the pictures in her head would deteriorate into scenes from the horror movie that was substituting itself for her life. Carlos's dead eyes when she confronted him with the bag. The way he ate almonds at the kitchen table that night, and ignored her. The canvas bag when she found it in the flashlight beam on the boat. The hate in Sampson's face in the courthouse hallway. And, above it all played an awful Greek chorus of "How could that happen?' And the white, canvas bag.

"When are you going to Annapolis again?" And there was this, the drone of Mike Drazinski's voice asking incessant questions. Just his tone was annoying.

"Are you going down there any time this week? How do you keep up with your regular cases? Are you getting paid at all by the Coalition?"

She'd begun to look right past Mike and ignore the questions. *He'll get the message and shut up soon—I hope.*

"How late do you work at night, in the office?"

The sound of Mike's voice was flirting with the *infuriating* mark on her annoyance scale as she tried to think. The questions kept coming. They were like wind chimes in a hurricane. *And I cry at every little thing now. That stupid commercial about dogs in the pound with the Willie Nelson song playing, and I was bawling like a baby.*

"Who watches your son while you're working at night? Carlos? Where is Carlos now?"

"Shut up!" Shut up!" Something snapped the instant he said her husband's name. It came together for her then, sick and sinister. "Why do you want to know about Carlos?"

"Just askin'," Mike shrugged, visibly taken aback.

"Now it's time for you to answer some questions."

"Um, okay."

"Who's paying you? Who's paying you to keep asking these damn questions?"

Mike held his water glass in both hands and looked down at it. "I can't tell you that."

"You're in on it too. You're helping them." The pained look of confusion on Mike's face only stoked her anger. It was the look of someone who'd been found out. "That's what you've been doing all along isn't it? You little bastard!" For the first time in the establishment's existence, the A Plus Deli went silent during a lunch hour.

He stared at her, stunned. That she stared back at him and said nothing made it worse. "Okay. Okay! I don't know what you're talking about. But it's your father that's paying me, all right?" She kept staring at him and said nothing. "Please. Please don't tell him I told you this. He made me promise I wouldn't."

She thought he was lying. She'd know soon if he was. If he kept on talking she'd know. "He's worried about you. He doesn't like that Sampson guy. He thinks they might try to do something to hurt you. And he doesn't trust your husband. I think he's right both times."

"You're a liar. Chloe's been screwing my husband. Chloe and Carlos, the two of them are paying you, aren't they? That's why you're always prying, always watching to see where I am—so you can report back to them."

"No!" The boy's face was a snapshot of pure bewilderment. "None of that's true." Mike was shaking his head with his mouth open, his brain grasping for a place to begin.

"Convince me none of that's true."

"Because your Dad even had me follow her for a while. And he hired a private detective to track her pretty much 24/7 for all of the last three weeks."

"Are you saying she's never met with Carlos? Not any night? Never on any weekends? How can you know that?"

"Nooo." Mike sighed in frustration like an overgrown child. "Maybe you assume she screws around because she's hot and young and all that. But just two days ago I saw the detective's report. There was nothing. Like on Wednesday nights, the detective said she has a class on the history of film at UMBC. She works like six days a week. Sometimes she visits her sister over in Highlandtown. Sometimes she goes to the mall, gets an Orange Julius and sees a movie—by herself."

Mike leaned forward. His words were slow and distinct; as if he wasn't sure she could hear him across the table. "Honestly, my sixty-six-year-old grandmother lives a wilder life than Miss Lagrange does."

It was the way he'd used Chloe's last name that did it. Michelle started to laugh. She burst out laughing, hard enough to attract more stares from the other customers, some of them as far away as the counter. She grabbed a napkin and held it to her face to blot the warm tears of relief suddenly flooding down her cheeks.

"What's so funny?" Mike was more confused than ever before in his life.

"You are," Michelle got out between alternating spasms of laughter and tears. "You're just funny." She tried to clear her eyes with her left hand. With her right, she reached over and patted Mike's forearm like a concerned mom. "Finish your sandwich," she said.

*

It was a warm enough morning to walk around the whole of Nampara without a jacket, the kind of morning that soothed Buddy Miller's soul. He was happy to see the gates the county codes insisted on were installed, one at either end of the west wall. He walked over to the first gate and put his hands on the heavy wood and the bars and swallowed feelings of acute embarrassment for the way he'd spoken to the laborers that day. He swung open the gate, taking pleasure in the weight and newness of it. He made a mental note to have the contractor add a bonus to the workmen's paychecks.

Birds chirped. Green buds at the end of the oak branches seemed to shoot out like time-lapse photography in front of him. It was early enough in the day that pockets of mist still hung in the valleys and low spots of his land. Climbing the hill to the house, he kept turning around to take it all in. Each time he turned, he'd stand still for a few seconds, looking.

*

Into the house and through the kitchen. A glance out the front window showed him that Mike's car was already in the drive. He felt good about that as well. He wanted to make sure Mike knew about the first quarter dividends and capital gains. He wanted them gathered up and posted before they got out of hand.

Turning the corner, he saw the black pants suit and white blouse, brown hair pulled back tight into her signature ponytail. She was sitting on the edge of the desk and smiling at him when he opened the office door. "Hi, Dad," she said simply. All he wanted was to hold his little girl. He pulled her close for a few moments before he spoke. "I'm not here to cry on your shoulder," he heard his daughter say. Even as she spoke, she was doing just that. But he didn't bring it up.

"Are you doing okay?" he said at last, letting her go.

"Um hmm. I just realized some things and ..." Behind Buddy's back, she saw Mike's wide-eyed stare and she hesitated. "And I wanted to talk to you."

"Let's go for a walk," The sentence gushed out of Buddy as if no one had said those words before, ever. "I've got some things to show you. And Mike ..." He grabbed a six inch stack of envelopes from the table by the door. "Dividends, Mike, for the first quarter. Total these and get them into the spreadsheet for me. Okay?"

"Sure," Mike answered frowning at the realization that he was not to be a part of the morning expedition.

"Well, aren't you the slave-driver?" Michelle chuckled at her father.

"That's right. Usually I stick a broom up his butt so he can sweep the floor while he works."

"All right! I knew Mike was capable of multitasking."

Mike looked down at the envelopes. Buddy could sense his silent discomfort at suddenly playing straight man for the two of them. But he noticed too that a touch of Michelle's hand on the young man's shoulder as she passed seemed to put him at ease again.

*

He started with his daughter down the brick path that he'd just climbed. Buddy's mind was flooded by scenes of Michelle as a little girl. The day they'd found the old place and how she'd loved it. He saw her ten-year-old self running like a banshee up those same bricks along with the two dogs.

"I'm sorry, Dad," she said, bringing him back to the present. "But this big stone wall is just kind of funny. You can't wall out the whole world."

He kept walking, the mental pictures still coming.

"But then," she added gesturing with her arm at the nine foot high fortress-like structure that stretched all the way down the hill to the water's edge, "maybe you can." They both laughed. "Don't do that, Dad. Don't wall yourself up. That's not you."

Silence, but a not uncomfortable silence, as they made their way down the hill. Close to the beach, they turned off the path to stand by Bonsai's ivy covered grave and look out at the bay. "I have a lot of questions," Buddy said.

"Me too. You go first."

"How'd we let this happen, Michelle? You and me—it was like I had lost a part of myself."

"I thought it was Chloe who was having the affair with Carlos. I told you that and you wouldn't back me up." She waited to see if he'd answer. He didn't. "I'm so sorry, Dad. I owe you both a huge apology."

"Who is it then?"

"I only know it's not Chloe." Michelle shrugged. "My turn—how's your life going?"

"My life sucks right now. Chloe has one foot out the door. We barely talk any more." Buddy took in a full breath of morning air and let it out. "Worst part is—I did it. I pretty much destroyed the good thing we had with my stupid jealousy. Now I don't know if we can ever get it back."

Michelle nodded and put her shoe on the mossy log that lay over the dog's grave. "Carlos and I are together in name only. It's been like that for months now. I told him to make a choice, her or me." She watched the morning sun glint on the lively blue-green wavelets of the Chesapeake as it had for eons. "And, you want to know something? I hope he chooses me. After all that. All that pain and deception, and I still don't want him to go." Her father only sighed and shook his head. "What a pair we are—huh, Dad?"

"And the other thing?" Buddy asked the question but continued to look out across the beach. He reached over to caress her neck and shoulder. "What happens if you can't manage to pull it out of the fire?"

"Which thing?"

"The road thing. The senate hearing coming up. What if you lose?"

For several seconds she only looked straight ahead, surprised, saying nothing. "You know, it's funny, in that arena losing never occurred to me."

Chapter 30

MARCH 26, 2010

THE IMMENSITY OF THE UNIVERSE

It started that Friday night. Vance Berg was in his office late. It started with the phone call from Levi. That the lawyer didn't say hello infuriated him. When Levi started in and kept on about the Koontz building it made the fury worse. "You need to get in there tonight," Levi snapped in a clipped, demanding tone. "You've had a week and done nothing. So get on it chop-chop."

"Fuck you."

"What did you say?"

"Go fuck yourself, you ugly little kike. You work for me, remember?" Berg leaned back in his office chair and put a shoe up on the edge of his desk. Rage rushed through his bulky body like a drug. He wished desperately he could strangle the man on the other end of the phone.

"You're not going to do it then?"

He didn't want to tell Levi about Gripper, about how his primary tool for torching the Koontz building seemed to have vanished from planet earth along with the key to the building. *Where the hell is Gripper? Maybe they put him in rehab forever this time. Wouldn't surprise me to hear the idiot was picked up in the middle of Southwestern Boulevard with a load of shit in his pants.* Levi didn't need to know any of that. "You listening, you Jew bitch…? This is the sound of me hangin' up." He slammed down the phone, stood, grabbed his coat with a shaking

215

hand, and kicked the chair from in front of him. He'd only gotten one arm into the coat sleeve when the phone rang again. "Yeah." His voice was hoarse, choked, and barely audible with anger.

"Vance, am I misunderstanding something? You are *not* going to the Koontz building tonight?" Berg was trying his best to speak but no words came out.

"I didn't say that." He finally did get the words out. But, on the other end of the phone, Sam Sampson was silent. There were only two seconds of silence.

"I want that done tonight. Do what we talked about. Just do it." There was a click. His boss had hung up without another word. The big man stood, seething, motionless, still holding the receiver in his hand, his coat half on. *This must be what it feels like when you get fucked in the ass in prison,* he thought. Levi would pay, he swore that. *If it takes ten years, that little bitch will pay.*

It was after nine. He'd do it. But he had been planning to see Diane. *What the hell? She's no beauty queen. Older than George Burns and bent over like a witch in a cartoon. No great loss.* Still, he contemplated calling her. He reached to pick up the phone, then drew back from the desk and shrugged the rest of the way into his winter coat. *If I don't call I won't have to hear her shit.* "Fuck it."

*

He couldn't find a parking space anywhere close to Hudson Street. He began to speed recklessly up and down the side streets, making the tires of the black Chrysler spin and smoke with each start and the brakes squeal with each stop. Kids on the street had begun to turn their heads to look. Someone would notice the car and remember. At one dark corner a young teen slinger sidled up to the driver's side and jiggled a plastic bag of yellow and black capsules at him in the window. *This has to stop.*

Virtually jamming the vehicle into a loading zone, his mouth went dry when he saw the big, tin sign that said: Cars towed at owner's expense to the Green Street garage. *Shit! Make it quick. Get in, get out.* Even from there, it took seven minutes to get to Sampson's vacant building, the one next to the Koontz. He counted the minutes, one by one as they passed. Fumbling in the dark with the lock, he listened to his own raspy breath rushing in and out of his open mouth. *I had the one good key and gave it to that fucking idiot.*

He could go in through the roof. He'd get up there and climb to the roof from the building next door. Once on the roof, he struggled to make his eyes adjust to the thick darkness. He inched toward the edge of it with his hands outstretched in front of him. Bending down to see the crinkled tar roof of the adjacent building below, he banged his forehead on a black painted iron rail. "Ahh! Sonofabitch!" Through the pain he registered horror, realizing the other roof was at least eight feet down. It looked to him like eight stories.

In a rush of desperation he pushed his bulk over the brick wall and hung by his fingers until he dropped. He landed on his feet and fell to his side with a jarring thud. Even as his feet had hit the roof, he realized the wall was too high for him to climb back up.

Had Vance Berg been a man who shed tears he might have cried at the perfect shit storm of events that seemed to dog him that night. "Fuck me." Squatting against the brick wall, he put his head between his knees and sighed. He tried to convince himself that he would be able to get down the steep, ladder-like stairs to the first floor and, somehow, out the front door of the building before the fire started in earnest.

This roof felt spongy beneath his feet. Pebbles and old tar crunched and crumbled beneath his black street shoes. And the noise stoked the fire of his anger even higher. The cold night air seemed to magnify the sound. It sounded to him like fireworks, that all of south Baltimore was hearing him. "Fuckin' shit!" The black shape of the skylight box was five steps away, maybe four steps if he took longer ones.

Vance Berg found himself looking up then, amazed by the stars in the night sky, amazed at the bright clarity of them against the inky blackness. He was mesmerized by the variety of the stars, their different sizes, and at the immensity of the universe that held them and him.

Only in the instant his bulky upper body slid past the jagged tar paper, past the black painted beam that cracked his skull did he grasp what was happening. His mind screamed at him to reach out for something. But his arms and shoulders were as stiff and unresponsive as the rotting wooden joists that flew past his eyes in the time it took to blink.

*

It was early on Sunday morning when a newsboy, stuffing early edition papers through the windows of cars on Hudson Street, saw the hand. The fingers were spread wide as if grasping for something. It was a big, thick, white hand. Rays of early spring sunlight illuminated the hand in a window on the second story of the Koontz building.

CHAPTER 31

MARCH 29–30, 2010
THINK ABOUT IT

It was morning, and Buddy Miller had not yet tasted coffee. When he found the restaurant at the country club still closed he considered calling 9-1-1. But his rational side convinced him the authorities wouldn't understand. Tucking the Monday morning paper under his arm, he bounced on his toes and stared into the window of the Chartwell golf shop. For Buddy, the morning paper was made to be read *with* breakfast. The newspaper with breakfast was the only aspect of the morning he still enjoyed since he and Chloe had taken on their mutual code of silence.

A young black man in a pristine white dress coat hurried down the hall toward the closed kitchen. "Excuse me," Buddy said, "do you know what's going on? The restaurant usually opens at eight o'clock."

The young man made a jolting stop in mid-stride and gave Buddy a toothy grin. "It looks like 8:30 today, sir. Big party in the club last night and we're a little behind." He started toward the kitchen and then turned and flashed the grin again. "Maybe we'll be able to open earlier," the young man added. "Just hang on."

"Maybe we'll open earlier," Buddy mimicked under his breath as the waiter hustled away and the caffeine jones grabbed his nerves and jangled them like an out-of-tune piano. "Yeah. And maybe bin Laden will shave."

He went back to his study of the two mannequins in the shop window. The man was in mid-swing with a 4 iron while the woman watched from behind him, her thin mannequin hands on bony mannequin hips. Both sported expensive sunglasses with the price tags still on them. The arms of their matching white sweaters were tied artfully around their necks.

Buddy saw, too, the reflection in the window glass of a woman behind him. She was a small woman, in her sixties, with short, blond hair. He thought she looked painfully thin, standing there, straight, as if at attention, with her back against the wall. She held a shiny gold purse in front of her. Buddy mused how she must have thought it went well with her pale blue pants suit, but how it didn't. *At least I won't be the only one in the restaurant having breakfast. That's always a little awkward.*

The woman took two steps forward and stood next to him. Buddy shuffled a step to the right to get out of her way. She followed him. In the glass, he saw her turn her head and look up at him with a nervous smile. *Oh, please,* he thought. *I'm used to filet mignon these days. You're a can of clam chowder that's past its expiration date.* He ignored her.

"Hi," the woman said, "do you know me?" She reached up and patted her hair with her left hand.

Buddy shrugged and shook his head. "If we've met before I guess I forgot."

"I know you. You're Mr. Miller. I've seen you around here a few times."

"Okay."

"My name's Elaine. I'm Sam Sampson's wife. You know him, right? I've been married to him for twenty-nine years."

"Oh, come on!" Buddy would have walked away if there were somewhere else to go. "I've listened to shit from him and from his flunkies for the last six months. Now he's sending his family. Just turn around and get the hell away from me before you get your feelings hurt."

"No!" She reached out to touch his arm but changed her mind and let her hand drop to her side. "It's not like that." Hands shaking, she opened the gold purse and took out a thick, unsealed envelope. "Take this, please. Give it to your daughter."

Buddy opened it and looked at the contents. He saw a list of names and addresses, some checks. "What the hell is this?"

"Just tell her to do background checks on those people." She closed the purse and clutched it in both hands, held it close to her chest like a talisman for protection. "Do it before next week. Otherwise it won't help you."

Something in the woman's voice made Buddy take her seriously. "Why are you doing this?"

Elaine Sampson made her eyes barely open slits and gave her head a tiny shake. "It's because of what happened—to Vance. I just can't stay silent any more."

"Because of what happened to Vance … I don't know what you mean."

"Please," she whispered, "just do it."

"Okay." Buddy was afraid she was going to cry. "I will. I'll do it." He folded the envelope in half and slid it into his back pocket. "Married for twenty-nine years, huh? And to the same person. That's pretty amazing. I envy you."

The pale, blue eyes turned cold with an anger that transformed the woman's face. "Don't envy me," she said.

*

Like O J in his prime running downfield, Buddy negotiated the tables in the Chartwell dining room. He carried a bottle of Dom Pérignon champagne in his right hand and Monday's morning paper under his arm. The Sun King and his entourage had congregated at a round table near the side door. As he got closer, he saw Sampson put on a broad smile and speak to the skinny one with the square glasses. The entire table laughed. Sampson quipped: "Expect to do some celebrating, Buddy?" They laughed a little harder.

When he tossed the newspaper on top of Sampson's plate the laughter was replaced by an audible group intake of breath. Sampson was no longer smiling. "Your fat fucking friend made the front page," Buddy said. Sampson stared up at him, ignoring the newspaper as it congealed into the gooey cinnamon role beneath it. "Well, he's lower right corner, but it's still the front page."

"Ombudsman Berg and I were personal friends, if that's what you're talking about."

"You told me he was your employee."

"I misspoke then, if I said that." The tall man's voice was coming out in something close to an angry squeak. The young man with the fresh mousse looked down at his coffee cup and frowned. Square Glasses rolled his eyes. Sampson straightened suddenly as if remembering something important. "How dare you come in here and defame a man who died in an accident."

"The piece of shit died doing sabotage in Canton—for you."

Sampson threw back his chair and was on his feet. The others stared as if he was an apparition that had suddenly manifested itself in front of them. "Come outside," he said. The tall man crossed the dining room with giant steps and flung open the door to the outside dining area. Buddy followed, still carrying the bottle.

Once on the expansive deck Sampson walked to the aluminum rail and grabbed it with both hands. Like toys below them, three middle-aged men in orange knit shirts were putting on the fourth hole green. A muffled "Whoohoo!" drifted up to the deck and broke the silence. "See that?" Sampson pointed down at the men. "Must have been a thirty footer." Buddy only stared at him and let the bottle of Champagne swing gently next to his leg. Sampson turned his gaze back down at the men, saying nothing, the muscles in his long neck visibly twitching. Buddy caressed the bottle with both hands and waited.

"You won't find any connection between Berg and my company," Sampson said at last, staring out at the now empty green. "I have no idea what he was doing in that building."

"That's not what the other psycho said, the one they caught on Friday night."

At that, the tan drained out of Sampson's face until it nearly matched his white golf shirt with the Chartwell crest on it. The older man's hands clenched into grapefruit sized fists around the rail. "There's nothing about that in the *Sun* story."

"True dat, as they say. And yet, you know what I'm talking about, don't you?" No response. "The police blotter for that night tells me they arrested a certain Norman Fishback, AKA Gripper. Lives with his mother in Morrell Park. They picked him up outside the Koontz building."

"What the hell are you even talking about?"

"Funny, that's what he said—at first, according to the police. Then they found something like a quarter pound of cocaine strapped around his belly and the conversation gets real confusing. He talks about 'Vance wanting it done.' He talks about setting fires in various buildings around Canton. The report's hard to follow because the poor bastard alternates between talking, crying, and begging them not to send him back to Jessup."

"You don't have a damned thing. Talk, that's all you've got."

Buddy shrugged. "Berg worked for you, and this moron worked for Berg. I have hard evidence of that. Trust me." Sampson's smile became a tight-lipped sneer. He shook his head. "You're fucked, Sampson. You try to use those fire incidents at the Senate hearing and I'll make sure all of this shit goes public. I'll make sure you never even smell another government contract."

Sampson let out a bitter laugh and leaned in, putting his face close to Buddy's. "You're a joke. You don't even know how to start slandering me."

"You would never have guessed I'd find out about Berg and his halfwit friend either. Yet here we are talking about them."

"You think you can threaten me? You—threatening me? Next week I'm gonna crush your daughter in Annapolis. And I can crush you." Sampson didn't back away. He stood up straight. His eyes came to focus on the Champagne bottle Buddy now gripped tight by its neck. "My ancestors were landowners in Anne Arundel County for a hundred years before yours got off the fucking potato boat."

Trying to make sense of the non sequitur made Buddy's mind momentarily blank. "… What now?"

"Look at me. I'm Sam Sampson. You're nothing. You can't threaten me."

For a second, a fleeting instant, Buddy actually felt sorry for the old man. He shifted the bottle in his fist and turned to go back into the dining room. "Think about it, asshole. Think real hard."

*

223

"I owe you one," Michelle said, taking the legal binder from Jeri Fairfield. The white-haired woman looked at her with blue eyes as centered and stable as the room they were in. "I'll be praying you won't need it." For a decade Michelle had admired her first mentor's office. The extra tall windows and polished teak gave it a feel of old-world stability that she had never quite been able to duplicate. Jeri Fairfield kept an ornate, cut glass decanter of Port wine and two glasses on a small round table at the side of her desk. *We'll win this thing*, the glasses seemed to say. *We'll win it and when it's over we'll have a drink and smile and talk about it.* Michelle didn't know if the glasses were ever really used, if the wine in the decanter was the same wine she saw there in 2003. But she took comfort in it. She allowed the feel of stability in the place to ease her own feelings of doubt, fear and regret.

"Forget it. Believe me, I never want you doing one of these for me."

Michelle laughed in spite of herself. "That's not what I meant but—you know what I'm saying."

"Sure."

"You've done a fantastic job on this, just like you did on the original stuff. But I'm praying, too, that I won't need it."

*

She sat and waited in the kitchen for Carlos, looking through the window at the pier. The pier, the water, the sky were all empty, gray, and forlorn. She watched the sailboat bounce and rock in the choppy water. It used to mean adventure to her, the sailboat. Now it was a symbol of different things.

Odd, she thought, *how we always talk here.* Now that she thought about it, they'd shared their first kiss in the little kitchen of her old apartment. A year later they'd planned their wedding there, making notes on a tiny, rickety kitchen table. A quick mental collage, seven years of kitchen related memories, of good meals, of laughter, of discussions, of decisions made, of tears. Seven years of life with Carlos. *Now this.*

When her husband came through the back door at 6:20 the whole scene seemed surreal to her: same husband, same kitchen, but it wasn't the same at all. She felt like an actor in a play she despised.

If she didn't know Carlos as well as she did, she might have believed he was drunk. He affected an awkward semi-swagger to cover his insecurity with her in times like these. "What are you doing home so early?" he opened. "You're usually not here till around eight."

"Oh, cut it out, Carlos. We need to talk."

"Where's my son?"

"Our son is with the neighbors next door." *Where was this concern for your son when you were doing that bitch?* That was what she wanted to ask. She didn't let herself fall into that trap. "Please talk to me. It's sick to go on like this, trying to pretend nothing happened."

Carlos dropped into the wooden kitchen chair and hung a long arm over the back of it. "So talk."

"Bottom line, I still do love you. I want our life back, the life we had." She put her hand across the table toward him. After a moment, he took it in his. "But we're going to have to work hard together to get it back."

"I love you too, very much. You're my wife, the mother of my son. I tried to show you I loved you."

She searched his eyes for some sign of what was transpiring in his head, a glimmer, a blink, a tear. She found nothing. "Tried to show me? How have you showed me that? By ignoring us? By sleeping around with her? What you showed is that you don't love me; you don't love your son. You don't even love yourself."

He pulled his hand from hers and rubbed the back of his neck with it. "It's all about me, isn't it? You forget how it used to be, how you used to make me the center of your time and attention. If you'd just show me the same care you give to your career and this fanatical fucking cause of yours."

It was time to say it. She couldn't dance around it any longer. "I've had separation papers drawn up. I got them today."

Carlos leaned back then and waved his hands in the air. "Oh, I want to get our life back, Carlos. I still love you, Carlos." His voice and his eyes both swam in sarcasm. "And, by the way, here are the fucking divorce papers."

"It's an option, dammit! You told me you loved her too, didn't you? You can't have it both ways. Don't you see that?"

"What a conniving bitch you are."

225

"You can say that to me? After what you did?" Pages of appropriate responses flooded her mind while anger flooded her being. *It won't do any good. This is going nowhere.* She closed her eyes and clenched her fists. She let the anger pool in her gut untapped. "We could start over, Carlos. I'm willing to try." She picked up the long yellow envelope that held the separation agreement and put it in the center of the table. "But I'm not going to play the begging wife. I'm leaving this right here. If you decide you want to go, if she's what you really want, just sign it and leave it." He was like a statue staring at her. "Please, Carlos. Please think about this."

Chapter 32

April 2–9, 2010
Good Friday

Jerry told himself he could still run every day if he wanted to, that his knees and ankles were just as strong as they ever were. He told himself that he and Peaches preferred to walk in the afternoons. It would be a shame, with the way the spring sun illuminated the strawberry fields and made the bay inlets into post cards, to waste those views by running past them. There was something different about the sunlight in spring. The light itself seemed fresh and reborn after a long winter. Jerry didn't talk about it because he didn't really understand it. But he could see it.

And Peaches would rather walk. All the men's health articles talk about walking as the best source of cardio. Who runs anymore anyway?

Arturo, who did the landscaping, and Carla were both in the parish office when he got there. "Hey, Father." Arturo smiled a toothy, mustached smile and lifted a paper cup in salute. "Happy Good Friday, if you can say that."

"Ignore him, Father. My little brother says some silly things."

Jerry pulled off his black sweatshirt and poured himself a cup of the freshly brewed coffee. "Why do we call it that anyway, Father Jerry?" He could already see Arturo was in one of his chatty moods, and Jerry was planning/hoping to relax for fifteen minutes and then firm up his homily for the evening.

"That's not a silly question at all. Our Lord had to die for us in order to redeem us from sin. Without that awful Friday, there'd be no Easter Sunday. That's why we call it *good*."

The parish secretary hopped into her chair and maneuvered it behind her desk. He always thought it cute that she had to put her toes down to make her feet touch the floor. "Maybe all the things we've had happen here, you know, maybe that's been our Good Friday. Don't you think so, Father?"

"Hmm," Jerry said as he watched the yellow sun bathe the new tract houses across the road.

"So, our Easter's coming," she said. As if it were an afterthought, Carla handed him a white pad as he went toward his office. "Here's some phone calls for you, Father."

When he saw Mrs. Willis's name he knew the list was an old one. "I talked to her yesterday." *Oh, Carla, you're killing me here.*

He saw his niece's name and his dull sense of annoyance became a lot sharper. *Dammit,* he thought even as he punched in the numbers on his own phone. *Carla and I need to have a long talk.* Michelle answered and relief flooded him. She sounded strong and well. "I know I'm late getting back to you," he began, tossing the pad across his cluttered desk. "I just got your message."

"Uncle Jerr, I hardly know where to start." He heard the strength ebb out of her along with the simple sentence.

"Tell me."

"The good news is I made up with my Dad. The whole thing with Chloe I told you about—it wasn't like I thought it was."

"Ah, that is great news." He could picture Buddy's reaction, picture the two of them. He could piece together every word of their conversation.

Then she went on. "Oh," he said at intervals. "Oh no... oh, boy." Jerry hated listening to himself repeat the same inane phrases again and again. He wished he could think of something else to say, something at least a little more profound. He had nothing.

"I've got to go, Uncle Jerr. Pray for us, okay?"

"You know I will, for you and your dad too. After Easter I'll take a couple of days and come up there to see you." Jerry put down the phone and opened the note book to a blank page. He stared at the page in silence as minutes ticked by. He waited for the words to come. They didn't.

"I'm going out," he said, grabbing his sweater with one hand while he opened the front door with the other.

"Shall I say you'll be back soon?" He'd caught the secretary off-guard. She'd nearly slipped off the unstable office chair.

"Sure, I guess. I need to walk a little more."

*

That evening, Jerry glanced out over his flock and began like he always did, as he had for a lifetime of Good Fridays. And they all had come again, as they had come for millennia, the old, the young, the sure and strong and the not so sure or strong. They waited to hear the message again. *Like we all do.*

"The journey of this Good Friday is not some sentimental journey that we relive once a year as we follow Jesus to the cross of Calvary. The journey of the cross is a real live journey. I believe that all of us at one time or another have journeyed to our Jerusalem where we've encountered the cross; it could be the cross of separation from God, or the cross of separation from the human race. The journey we travel this evening is a journey into the reality of life."

"'What is truth?'" The Good Friday truth is that life hurts. All of us here have experienced that truth. We, like Jesus, know how it feels to have someone we love disappoint us, perhaps even betray us."

Bring her home, Lord. Bring her through all of this.

"We celebrate the mystery of the love of God today: that 'God so loved the world, that he gave his only Begotten Son.' Love unthinkable, beyond all possible expectation. That's the mystery of this day, and that's why we call this Friday *Good*."

*

When Jerry at last pulled the church door closed behind him and started across the near empty parking lot he realized that he could hear crickets for the first time that spring. Behind him in the church, some of his parishioners were still singing at adoration. The two sounds seemed to merge and complement each other. After every few steps he stopped, just to listen. The last of the day's sun was glowing orange behind the stand of maple trees on the big hill. It had gone down below the hill before he finally made it across the lot.

*

Chloe came home when she usually did, at 5:25 within a minute or two either way. She went upstairs without speaking like she did now, in what Buddy had come to think of as the new normal. But his heart dropped into his stomach when she came back down the stairs carrying her travel bag. "Where are you going?" She gave him the *have you lost your mind* look, but this time there was no good humored smile to follow it up.

"I'm going to my mother's for a while, maybe for good."

"Oh no, Chlo, we've got so much going for us …"

"We *had* so much. Now we don't even talk." She opened the door to the garage.

"But you'll have to drive all the way down from Towson just to go to work." *How lame was that?* he thought. She didn't bother answering. He watched her car back out in the drive way; and his mind went blank. He had nothing to say. But he had to try again—to say something. With desperation in his gut but no plan in his head, Buddy jumped into the SUV and followed her. Down the drive and the windy, wooded road in the evening dusk, he was feeling more ridiculous by the second but didn't stop. At the stop sign on Fort Smallwood, she pulled over and got out of the car.

"What do you want, Buddy?" She was screaming over the roar of the traffic on the busy road. "Do you have something intelligent to say or not?" It was then he saw the orange cat slinking out of the bushes, coming down the hill from Nampara. The big cat jumped a muddy ditch and gave the two out of place humans an undisguised look of disdain before darting across the darkness of the busy road. Buddy and Chloe saw the maroon Buick spring around the curve. Both of them watched the slow-motion horror of the vain scurrying and the wide front tire rolling over the animal. The bulky car sped up and disappeared into the dark while the animal screamed and rolled, a ball of pain, off the asphalt and back into the muddy ditch. Chloe screamed even louder than the cat and ran to the ditch, leaving her still running car.

"Oh, Jesus," Buddy muttered as he reached in to turn off the car's engine. He followed her. "Is it still alive?"

"Yes," she yelled. "He's hurt bad, Buddy!"

She held the cat in her arms, and Buddy lifted as much as guided the shaking woman back to his own vehicle. "Let's get him to the vet, Honey."

The animal hospital on Ritchie highway was a fifteen minute drive away. But it seemed they were going there by way of Pennsylvania. Every light shined red in the rush hour dark. They'd caught the traffic at its peak. A river of red taillights stretched out in front of Buddy as far as he could see. The orange cat seemed even bigger in the car and enormous on Chloe's lap. She had done her best to wrap him in her jacket, but the cat would periodically claw and bite in an insane rampage to be free. Its mournful, guttural howl/cry seemed to make the heavy vehicle shake. Buddy watched helplessly as she struggled to hold the animal down and keep the claws away from her face.

Their ecstasy at seeing the lighted sign that said Animal Hospital dissipated when they realized how tightly packed the lot was with cars. "Let me have him," Buddy said, grabbing the barely wrapped ten pound package of terrified feline. It was all he could do to hold the jacket tight with both hands and run for the door while Chloe parked the SUV. He marveled as he ran that she had managed to hold on to the cat through the whole trip.

Buddy pushed through the door and kept going up the hallway, running a gauntlet of outraged stares from a hodgepodge of people, each waiting for attention to be given to their own Fluffy, Rex or Snowball. The teen aged girl acting as receptionist gave him a look of equal parts horror and disgust as he rushed past the counter and up to a short, blond woman in scrubs that he assumed to be the vet. "Can you take this cat in, please? It was hit by a car and hurt bad."

"Is the cat a regular patient here?"

Buddy almost thought she was joking. *No he just comes here on special occasions.* "It's not even our cat. We saw him get hit by a car and rushed him in."

"You'll have to take him to your regular vet."

"Oh, come on! There is no regular vet. The poor thing's dying. Give me a break here." The doctor looked out at the rapt expressions in the hall full of faces. She looked at the desperation in Buddy's eyes and chose to take the cat rather than risk a scene. She disappeared with it through a green painted wooden door and Buddy blew out a massive sigh of relief.

A long five minutes later the small woman came back though the door and around the counter. Strands of graying, blond hair now hung in her eyes; and Buddy could see spatters of dark red blood on the front of her green scrubs. He'd managed to intercept her before she got to Chloe. "How's he look? Will he make it?"

"It's hard to say. I don't know." She let both sentences ride out on a single breath. "The back leg's been fractured in at least two places. And I'm sure there were internal injuries. Hard to tell just how much damage was done." Buddy heard a low, quiet moan come from Chloe. "Honestly, the cat's chances aren't good."

Chloe was bent over in the plastic waiting-room chair, holding her head in her hands. Her tan knit dress and her hose had been shredded on the front and side by the cat's claws. And, caked-on mud made obscene stains on her dark blue hose and shoes. "Do what you can," Buddy told the vet.

"I'll say it again, it doesn't look good. This could be expensive. And you said it's not even your cat."

"Forget the money—whatever it takes." The woman sighed and frowned. She looked at her watch and at the other people lined up in the hallway. "Do you need me to sign something? What?"

"No." She glanced at Chloe and back to him. "I'll do what I can."

*

They drove home mostly in silence and to a dark house. Chloe stood in the center of the living room and waited for him to lock the door. There was only a dim light from the kitchen. The semi-dark made her look small there, like a little girl, her dress torn in several places and her dark stockings smeared with brown mud. "I'll walk down and get your car," Buddy said.

"I hope he's okay," she said, finally breaking the silence.

Buddy put his arms around her. "I hope so too." He whispered it into her ear. "We'll find out in the morning." They stayed like that for a long time, their touch speaking more eloquently than words. He held her tight but gently, as if she was a precious find that he didn't want to lose. After a minute, she let herself rest on him, her cheek on his chest.

More minutes passed. "We did everything we could. Actually, you did it. You really care about that old cat, don't you?"

She pulled herself a little tighter to him. "We are good when we work together, Buddy. We used to have something incredibly good. Magnificently good. Where'd that go?"

"Please don't leave, Chloe."

"Keep holding me like this and I won't go anywhere—ever."

The two of them put their lips together. It was the tenderest kiss either of them had known. For a while, they rocked together, slow dancing without music.

*

The red numbers on the bedroom clock flashed 2:44. Michelle stared at them, willing them to change to at least 4:44 so she could get up and make the day start. Once she'd begun it, the day would be closer to over, and with the day, the Senate hearing would be over. Then she could stop. How good it would feel to stop preparing, stop anticipating new threats—to stop studying. The hearing felt to her like another law school exam. And, like them, once it was completed, she could enjoy that sweet sensation of relief, of having turned in the paper, having done her best. But this was the mother of all exams. With it behind her she could focus on saving her own life. She could drag it all back from the brink.

Michelle slid soundlessly out from under the sheet. She went to her son's room and looked in. He was sleeping, a deep sleep, smiling even then, his hands stretched out above his head. She closed the door and continued down the hall to the prayer space and knelt before the brass crucifix on the wall. Out the window, the harbor seemed unnaturally still and soundless. Only an occasional house light blinked on Federal Hill across the water. For several minutes her eyes went from the crucifix to the harbor and back. "Help me," she whispered in prayer. "I've done all I can do—with all of it. You know I have. It's in your hands now."

Back in their bedroom she saw Carlos hadn't moved. He slept face down on the sheets, one long arm hanging off the bed, his fingertips touching the carpet. She stared down at her husband's bare back. *I used to dream about that body*, she thought. She wouldn't admit, even to herself, that occasionally she still did. Michelle pushed on his bare shoulder and then pushed it again, harder.

Carlos turned his head and grimaced up at her. "What's this? You can't sleep, so I can't either?" He said it without rancor, almost lightly. "How are you getting there tomorrow?"

"Dad's coming to pick me up."

"Mmm. Okay."

"I almost made a terrible mistake, Carlos." He blinked and sat up in the bed. She could see his eyes, suddenly awake, glowing in the dark. "I thought I knew who the woman was. But it wasn't her at all."

Carlos looked down and shook his head. "Does it matter, who she is?"

"What about us? What about your son? He'll have only a mother during the week. And on weekends—what? You'll take him to the zoo? What kind of bullshit life is that? Is she really that important to you?"

He didn't move. "I still love you, Michelle," he whispered after seconds had passed. "And I love our son. You know that. I just don't know. I don't know what's going on in my head anymore. I just don't know." With eyes closed, he brought up his hands and rubbed the back of his neck. "I have to decide what I want."

"That's just it." She continued to whisper, but her voice had become urgent and raspy. "You have to decide. We can't go on like this. Make a choice, Carlos."

He turned his body and let himself fall face down. "You need to try and get some sleep," she heard him say into the pillow.

*

"It's 6:30 now. We'll get there long before 8:00."

"Yeah, Dad. But I have to get the rest of my notes at the headquarters."

In the chilly morning dark, everything felt alien to her, being ensconced in the back of her father's big SUV with Mike Drazinski driving and her father riding shotgun in the front. Even the neighborhood seemed an alien place at that time of the morning. Only the vaguest hints of light brightened the edge of the April sky. Delivery truck drivers and empty cabs scooted by as if embarrassed to be caught at their pre-dawn chores.

Carlos would be up soon. She could hear him muttering about how she'd walked out when their marriage teetered on a precipice. Little Carlos would be wondering where his mom was, why she wasn't going to walk him to preschool like she always did.

"We'll park here and you run in, okay?" Her father's voice drifted back from the front seat as if he were miles away.

"Sure."

*

Coming out of the old store front, Michelle pulled the heavy door closed behind her. She was surprised to see some of her people already huddled on the dark corner outside. A couple of tepid claps and a "Good luck" emanated from the group of shadows. She waved at them and climbed back into the white SUV. The wide tires had just begun to roll when Joanne, in plain gray, Rocky-like sweats was suddenly rapping on her window.

"Oh my god," Michelle gasped and lowered the window, pleased to see her friend's familiar face. "What are you doing here?"

"Had to pick up some notes," Michelle said. "I could ask you the same question."

"I'm going to work out. Bunky's Gym, remember?" Joanne shrugged her left shoulder with the bag slung over it. "Look, good luck, 'Chelle. Hope the political gods are with you today."

"Thanks. I'll need them." Mike gunned the engine, shooting the vehicle into the left lane when he saw an opening. Michelle leaned back and raised the window. She watched Joanne walking off in the dark toward Bunky's Gym, a canvas bag bouncing on her back. It was a big bag, white, with black and red semaphore flags on it.

CHAPTER 33

APRIL 9, 2010
THE VOICE OF GOD

Opera house, Buddy thought when he saw the white marble columns and balconies. One of the *sixty-year-old scafoozas,* as he liked to call them, a lady his daughter had set him up with, had insisted they see La Traviata. The Senate chamber looked amazingly like the opera's set, all too appropriate for the drama about to be acted out below. He bounded down the carpeted balcony stairs two at a time, determined to get a seat in the front row. In the time it took him to sit and turn around, the balcony seats were almost filled. He recognized some of the Coalition people from the corner packed into the seats to his left, the large woman with the blue, flowered dress and the small active one with the curly, gray hair. The tall black man with the yellow tie was between them.

Buddy found himself next to a round, middle-aged man in a plaid suit and open collared shirt. He took him for a professional spectator, the kind who goes to divorce court on his days off rather than watch TV. "'Bout time they got started," the round man quipped. "This one was supposed to start at 8:00 this morning. Now it's 10:00." Buddy nodded, wondering if Mike had been able to get into the chamber when the door finally opened.

Someone on the floor below coughed into a microphone and the entire chamber snapped to attention. "Ouch!" The round man laughed. "I'd say they did a good job with that new system." Buddy remembered

236

then the recent news story about the electronics in the State capitol building being updated for the first time since 1905.

"Can you heah me, Senetah?" A deep, Eastern shorey kind of voice bounced off the white marble.

"Sounds like the voice of God, don't it?" Buddy's seatmate asked. While *Voice of God* may have been a little over the top, there was no doubt that even in the nether reaches of the balcony not a word would be missed.

Buddy recognized Michelle's ponytail and saw her put down her briefcase on one of the newly finished upper desks. He felt the old pride again. He'd worried about how distraught she'd seemed on the drive down, silent, her eyes closed, curled up against the car window. *Look at you now—totally in charge like always.* The same pride had bubbled up inside him as he watched her on the softball field when she was twelve, or when she captained the basketball team at sixteen. Then as now, it was all he could do not to yell like the world's biggest doting dad that this was his daughter. *Give it the best you've got, honey.* He told her silently now what he'd told her then. *Just do your best and it'll be fine.*

With a pop, the sound system went dead. He watched the players take their places on the stage below him in the anonymity of indistinct murmurs. The speaker, with white hair, round glasses and a rumpled, blue suit, looked like the speaker in a Senate hearing should look. In another blue suit, a middle aged, curly haired woman staked out the desk next to the speaker, her movements quick and self assured. An aide handed over a thick notebook from behind her. Buddy watched the woman adjust the chair up and the mic down. *Must be the little judge Mike talks about.*

The polished desks and tables filled quickly now. Black suits, red ties and coifed hair. Tall, serious looking women postured in gray or brown tweed. He recognized cliques of those quintessential political war horses Michelle told him about. Balding heads and checkered sports coats, 20-year-old ties draped over round bellies and rumpled, white shirts, they were scattered around the Senate floor. *They look like William F Buckley near the end*, Buddy thought.

"Can you heah me?" The loud snap of a wooden gavel and it was on.

With the rest of the packed balcony, Buddy leaned forward to catch the opening arguments. He noticed how Schnee made it a point to describe the interchange as if it already existed. Buddy tried to pick out the buzz words and count the number of times the Senator used them. Traffic flow. Jobs. Stagnant area. Deteriorating neighborhood. Renewal. Renewal seemed to top the count.

And when her turn came, he smiled at the way his daughter managed to counter them with words of her own. Community. Historic. Solid. Bedrock. And anointed by history. *Anointed by history—Honey, you are good!*

Specifics then, a litany of specifics that seemed to go on for days. One by one, contractors were called up, uneasy in their bad suits and clip-on ties, reciting canned spiels about pouring concrete, timetables and rebar. Buddy kept picturing a string of bad acts on American Idol and no Simon Cowell to shut them down.

Michelle responded with a litany of her own. In business since 1960. Lived there for four generations. Since the nineteenth century. But the more she spoke, the more alone and isolated his daughter seemed. Buddy ached to help her. He just wanted it all to end.

He saw the senator give a distinct nod to the thin man with thick glasses who had covered the table next to Michelle with a varied assortment of paper. "Mr. Phillips has headed up the feasibility study for this interchange over the past year," Schnee said.

The thin man had his jacket off by this point. He stretched his long upper body over the table and looked up at Schnee then down at his spreadsheets like a man bobbing for apples. "Madame, being with State Highways, you know that there are $375 million dollars already appropriated to new highway construction. This project is considered shovel ready. So DC has stimulus money to give us."

"And $150 million of that has clamps on it," Michelle shot back instantly.

"You're out of turn, Ms. Ibanez," Schnee broke in loudly, emphasizing each syllable of her last name.

"She may go on," the speaker remarked, not even looking up from the figures in front of him. "The state has such a great advantage in numbers here. We'll grant her that benefit."

Only in that moment did Buddy realize just how tall Sampson was. The long body draped over the back of the chair while the legs poked out in front of the table. The U-shaped configuration put him directly opposite Michelle. Sampson passed a legal pad back and forth to the stodgy, bearded man with the short sleeves and yarmulke. Whenever Michelle spoke the pad seemed to move with more urgency. It looked now like a ball in a handball tournament.

Michelle continued as if the interruption had never happened. "As much as $75 million of that will go for improvements to the existing I-95 corridor. If that happens, the State will face the ugly specter of a half done project running out of funds." She took a breath, a short one. "And we all know 'Shovel Ready' is a political term of art. There is no guarantee of Federal dollars. If the dollars *are* approved it could take another year to get them."

The thin man deflated, cartoon-like, down to his normal height and glared alternatively at her and at his spreadsheets.

"Yeah," Buddy mumbled, "eat that you fucking clown." The professional spectator giggled.

Buddy saw Schnee lean forward, hunching his shoulders and looking down at Michelle as if she were a roach he was about to crush. "What do we know so far then?" The senator laced his fingers on top of the open notebook in front of him. "We know there are already dollars allocated to be spent on this project. We know the need for and the practicality of this interchange. It has been studied exhaustively. We know the interchange will go through an area that is—how shall I say it?—marginal. Notice too that Ms. Ibanez's disadvantage in numbers stems from the fact that few neighborhood residents came here to support her."

As if she welcomed that barrage, Buddy saw his daughter stand up and drop her pen on the table. "It says a lot," she began, "that this project's most numerous and vociferous supporters are contractors hungry for a piece of the pie." A muffled ahh sound drifted down from the balcony. "Our neighborhood residents are predominantly blue collar people who—how shall I say it?—actually work during the day. They may not be the same high profile constituents you have. However, they do vote." The way she paced told her father she was far from finished. "And let's revisit those feasibility studies. Most commute times around cities similar to Baltimore are much worse than our own twenty-one minutes. Did you know in Philadelphia the average driving commute is thirty-nine minutes, in Newark forty-seven, in Atlanta thirty-three? Can it be the State of Maryland has spent years evaluating a project we don't even need?"

The Speaker raised his head then as if waking from a nap. "You're drifting off subject, Ms. Ibanez. Don't abuse the privilege." The floor was silent. "Summations then," the Speaker half asked, half announced.

Schnee watched Michelle take a new page from the back of her folder at the word summation. "Mr. Speaker," he said, "I suggest we dispense with summations in this instance. The meager issues we have here are being beat to death as it is." The Senator shook his head, took off his glasses and sat up straight, the lion-like mane of once blond hair sparkling like a banner in the ceiling lights. "However, I would like to say that CEPCO will be our primary construction contractor in this instance. And, Mr. Sampson, you've talked about what you call 'unrelenting degradation of the neighborhood that lies in the path of this interchange.' Can you expand on that for us? Give us some specific examples?"

Buddy watched the stocky lawyer scribble furiously on the legal pad and thrust it under Sampson's nose. Even from the balcony he could see Samuel Ripley Sampson's tanned face turning a Bond paper white. The lengthy body stiffened. "I only know what I read in the papers," Sampson managed to croak into the microphone.

Schnee cleared his throat and glared across the floor. An awkward silence hung for several seconds in the air. "I'd anticipated a little more from Mr. Sampson. Uh, Mr. Speaker, why don't we break for lunch and resume this at, say, two o'clock?"

The white-haired Speaker pushed his glasses up on his nose and stared down at his watch. He weighed the fact that it was already 12:30, that the Senate still had to tackle a hellish State income tax add-on for health care, that the Severna Park Marina dredging hearing was scheduled for 3:00, that Spring recess was still a week away, that there were two fried soft crabs waiting for him at the Sly Fox Pub. "Senatah, if we break now we ah not comin' back," he said. "I'd like to take a vote."

Judging from their effect, the simple words had seemed to come from on high. Schnee, the spectators, the bailiff, all seemed frozen in time. "Well then," the Speaker intoned. "All in favah of immediate implementation of bill 1664, Canton I-95 interchange, please raise your hands."

In the upper section of the Senate seats four arms shot up. Then another, and another. Buddy could hear his own heart thumping against the inside of his chest as he counted the hands in the air. Including Schnee, there were nine.

"All in favah of tabling discussion on the 1664 interchange at this time please raise your hands."

Four hands. Two dead, awful seconds ticked by. Buddy watched as one of the war horses eased up a hand, then let it fall, and then raised it again. One of the black suits sent a hand into the air. A second war horse raised his hand, index finger pointing heavenward. A flurry of hands then in the back row of senators. An "Ah" and a muted whoop from the balcony. Buddy held his breath as he counted—thirteen hands in the air.

The sound system went dead again. Schnee, the Senate speaker, and the little judge stood and leaned in to put their heads together. Buddy could see the senator's big hand go down flat on the sheets of paper in front of him; and the judge's tight curls vibrated as she shook her head in an emphatic NO. He could see the Speaker's face swiveling between the two of them, the expression on it screamed: colonoscopy sans anesthetic.

The sound popped back on with the noise of the Speaker clearing his throat. "We have reached a consensus," the voice of God said. "Furthah discussion on the Canton leg of the I-95 interchange is heah-by tabled for the foreseeable future."

*

The speaker's gavel came down in the space of a second. Michelle watched it fall in slow motion. The simple wooden hammer landed with a crack, and her life would never be the same. She knew that.

It was a gesture, a formality. But it was also the referee signaling the goal was good. And it was Donald Trump saying, "You're hired." It was all that and more. She was startled by a tsunami of crinkled smiles and what seemed like a hundred extended hands reaching for hers in the pink marbled hall. She looked for Trudy Spanno, but hers was not one of the faces in front of her. Outside the chamber, Mike and her father raced to be the first to hug her. Her father won. She marveled at how wonderful it felt to have his arms around her again, as strong and comforting and as magic as when she was five.

The sensations of comfort extended to the plush, tan leather seat in the back of her father's SUV. Buddy and Mike hustled her across the parking lot and settled her into the vehicle as if she were a long lost Rembrandt painting. "How do you feel?" Mike kept asking, the soft voice drifting back to her from the massive head and shoulders in the front seat. She smiled at how, even in the big Explorer, Mike looked like an adult driving a child's toy car.

"I'm fine," she replied more than once. "Really, I'm great right now. But please don't make me talk. I've been talking for hours."

"She did good, didn't she?" Mike Drazinski went on undeterred, just redirecting the questions to Buddy.

"She did good? Are you kidding? She ate their damn lunch." They went on like that, adulating her as if she wasn't there. Her father and Mike more than once rehashed the morning blow by blow. Michelle let them do that. She leaned her head on the window and watched the farms and yards and houses glide by her like a green tapestry she'd never seen before. *The men in my life*, she thought. *God bless 'em. Where would I be without them?*

She prayed that the central man in her life was waiting for her. It was over now, the road, Sampson, Joanne too; they would soon all be gone like an interminable bad dream. The two of them could start over now. *He never stopped loving me. He said that.* In what seemed like five minutes, they were passing Camden Yards. Harbor Place was just around the corner. *We can start over now. In a year we'll be even stronger than we were.*

Catching sight of the harbor, Michelle burned to be home. Each second was like an eternity. "Thank you, guys," she said, grabbing her briefcase and opening the door when the vehicle had barely stopped in front of The Moorings.

"Want me to come in with you, Honey?" Buddy whispered as he jumped out to hug her a final time.

"No, Dad, I'll be fine."

"Call me. Okay?"

"I will," she said, waving to Mike through the windshield and stepping fast up the driveway toward her house. Good karma, positive thinking, good luck, whatever people chose to call it, Michelle knew in her heart that those feelings fed on themselves. Those feelings could transform reality. Thinking back to those basketball games when her team had come from behind, she could still remember the thrill. A single basket at a crucial time was a spark. The spark would turn to a blaze and lead to those turnaround wins. She'd seen it happen too many times not to believe. It could happen now too. He'd be there, waiting for her. "How could he not be?" What happened that morning in the State House was too good not to bring more good karma with it.

His car wasn't in the garage. Still, she ran up the stairs to the kitchen. More accurately, she unleashed her feet and let them pound up the stairs. She let them ride the giant wave of adrenalin that was rushing through her. Bursting through the door, she found only Nefferkitty staring at her, wide eyed. The cat's tail swished with enough force that she could hear it. It was the only sound in the house. It was an instant in time that would stay like a brand on her memory. In that instant she knew. The man she loved was gone. Her child's father was gone. The dream was gone.

"Oh, Carlos," she heard herself say. She walked to the foyer, to the antique table by the front door. The whisper of her shoes on the carpet seemed like thunder. The envelope was there, lying bent and askew on the polished mahogany. Michelle's heart sank to the depths of her being because she could picture the scene like a hologram. Carlos jamming the separation agreement back into the envelope. Carlos throwing it on the table on his way out. "He really did it."

She didn't want to pick it up, but she had to. She had to finish the scene, complete the awful ritual. He'd signed it. *Carlos T. Ibanez.* Cold, black ink. Written with a force that nearly tore the paper. That was all she had left. His goodbye to her.

CHAPTER 34

ON TUESDAY

Buddy stared down at the phone number his daughter had given him. He wondered what it was about making the call that seemed so traumatic. Through the window he could see the branches of the oak trees closest to the house. *Budding early.* The branches swayed in the spring breeze as if calling him to come out, to celebrate the end of a ferocious winter. It was what he liked to call a moment of clarity, one of those all too rare, shining minutes when it all made sense. *Yet here I sit, afraid to call my own brother.*

"Hi, Jerry," he said into the phone at last.

"Buddy? Well hi. Everything okay?"

"Yeah, everything's good. Look, I'm calling with a question about wedding vows." The phone was silent. "Chloe and I are getting married and she wants me to come up with some vows."

"Um, okay. You do like dropping these bomb shells every decade or so, don't you?"

Buddy went on as if his brother hadn't said it. "I'm coming up with nothing here, Jerry. I called because you do this sort of thing all the time. Any ideas?" Buddy heard his brother sigh, then nothing. "You still there?" he asked after seconds passed.

"Sure, I'm here. What do you want to say—in your vows?"

No idea, he thought. "I want to make them about trust," Buddy heard himself saying, "respect and trust."

"Good. Respect is good. I've got something for you to think about." Buddy listened in silence while his brother went on to tell him about wedding ceremonies in ancient Rome, about how he'd e-mail some thoughts and ideas. "Are you sure?" Jerry asked before they hung up. "I have to ask the question."

"Sure? Who's ever *sure*? I do know this time's not like the first. And it's not about me. It's about a partnership, the two of us making a life going forward."

Another two seconds of Jerry silence. "If that's what's in your heart, Buddy, and you both feel that way, you'll be fine."

*

He poured himself a rum and Coke in celebration. Buddy stirred it with his finger and took it with him out into the spring evening. He propped the back door open and left it that way for the first time since the fall. She wouldn't be home for another hour. At the table on the brick patio he watched the birds on the feeders and drank in the sensations of early dusk. He relived the talk he'd had with Chloe at that same table in September, the talk about Hawaii and the Berlin Wall. "It's all so different now," he exclaimed to himself and to the patio table.

He tried, one more time, to piece together the events that had brought him to this place over the course of one winter. He'd nearly lost both Michelle and Chloe, the two women he loved, and he wasn't sure how. Now, he'd won them both back. He wasn't sure how he'd done that either.

With a muffled clumping sound, the orange cat dragged its broken back legs across the threshold and out onto the patio bricks. "Look at you." Buddy turned his chair to watch. He smiled at the animal's resilience. Just then, the cat noticed Buddy, and it became like a staring statue. The cat's head looked huge, attached as it was to a thin, broken, and bandaged body. "You're getting better every day. Just respect the birds when you're all healed, okay?"

The animal dragged itself forward into the last remaining patch of sunlight and plopped down. The wide green eyes stared up at Buddy as if this human had been the cause of a major inconvenience. "You're still pretty beat up. But, considering, you look almost healthy." Buddy put his feet up on the table and took a long pull on his drink. The two of them were quiet and still for several minutes, both taking the time to breathe and heal.

"Chloe and I are getting married," Buddy said into the trees. "One week from today. You believe that?" The cat began moving its tail in slow, tentative swishes. The intensity in its eyes hadn't changed. "Maybe you're right." He returned the cat's stare. "Maybe I am crazy. Only time will tell." Buddy swallowed the last of the rum and Coke and took a long, deep breath. "Today, I told Father Jerry about it too. Glad he didn't ask a lot of embarrassing questions. I think he's happy for me. I think he's pulling for Chloe and me."

Buddy pushed away from the table. "Sometimes you have to make a choice and just go with it. You know?" With a single motion, he stood and sent the empty glass soaring over the dogwoods. He heard it smash against the new, stone wall.

"Look at you, beat up but still full of life." He walked slowly over to the cat. "Do you want to live here with us now?" He stooped and rubbed under the cat's chin with a single finger. "I think you do." A race-car like purr filled the whole patio. Taking his time, he eased both hands under the broken animal. The cat let him. He took small, careful steps as he carried it into the kitchen. "Come on; let's get you something to eat."

*

That morning Michelle walked with Little Carlos to daycare, but she changed their route. They walked, without talking, up Lakewood to Foster, the five-year-old taking quick steps and holding on to his mother's hand. When they turned the corner onto Melton much of the tension in her chest dissipated like a puff of noxious smoke. The wide street was empty except for a single yellow bulldozer being rolled up onto the back of a massive flatbed truck. She didn't stop but slowed her pace. Her son made his steps slower too and made them a little solemn. She needed to watch as the driver secured the earth mover. She needed to see the chains tighten and to see the thing driven away, harmless.

The truck finally lumbered down the street and little Carlos sensed his mother's relief. "We drew yesterday," he said suddenly. "I drawed a big house."

"What color?" she asked squeezing his little hand a bit tighter as the oversized trailer lurched around the corner.

"Purple."

"Purple's good."

It was the Tuesday after. It had been less than a week. She realized she was still perched on an emotional tightrope. The elation of winning in the Senate still hung like a pleasant dream on one side of her consciousness while the realization that she was alone now gaped like a black hole on the other side of it. *So this is what it's like,* she thought. *From here on.*

She remembered that day the previous fall when she found the trucks and City workers on the street, starting on the interchange. She remembered the way her son acted then, writhing and crying and pulling her arm. "You're such a big boy now," she said as they topped the hill and the door of the daycare came into sight. "You're getting bigger and stronger all the time."

*

Even as she turned the key in the front door of her building, Michelle heard the sounds. They were angry sounds, metal file cabinet drawers slamming, books and folders being thrown into cardboard boxes. Joanne wasn't supposed to be there. When she looked into the office of her ex-partner, Joanne stared up at her, silent but defiant. "You were supposed to be out of here by now," Michelle said.

"I'm almost through."

Michelle continued down the hall to her own office. She'd barely sat down behind the desk before Joanne was leaning in the open door as she had so many times before. But now Joanne in her doorway was like a filthy joke that didn't work. It was a sick parody of what had been.

"I'm not the heartless bitch you think I am," Joanne began after a few silent seconds. "I have regrets about this."

Michelle slammed shut the middle drawer of her own desk. "Regrets? Why would you have regrets? He's yours." She'd never seen Joanne Wicks in that position, wanting to speak but lacking the words. She could tell Joanne's mind was racing for those words. She could see in Joanne's eyes the frustration of not catching them. Michelle wasn't about to help her. She said nothing.

"I tried to tell you—that last time we were running I tried. I couldn't."

"When did it start? You owe me that much."

Joanne opened her mouth to say something, but she gave her head a shake and didn't. "It doesn't matter. But I will say he came on to me. He offered it all to me, Michelle, not just sex, the whole package. And I took it."

"Umph." Michelle folded her hands and looked down at the desk. She tried to come to terms with what she was hearing, with the fact that this conversation was even taking place.

"I took it because I started out with nothing." Michelle didn't answer; so she kept talking. "Remember how I waitressed through all those years at U of B? You were going to so many parties you couldn't keep track of them all while I worked like a damned slave. That's why your grades were always better than mine."

"Am I really hearing this? You expect me to feel sorry for you?"

"You had it all given to you. I had nothing. Do you understand that? Nothing!" Joanne was close to tears. They could have been tears of sorrow or tears of rage, Michelle couldn't tell which. "So, when he offered, I took it."

"I have nothing else to say to you."

Joanne turned back toward the hall. "Congrats on last week."

"Just get the hell out," Michelle said.

CHAPTER 35

APRIL 14–16, 2010
GREAT SKIN

"It is wonderful to see you all again," Jerry said at the start of Saturday evening Mass at Saint Mark's. The words were coming straight from his heart. "I was invited back to do a baptism and I decided to stay over. I haven't done many baptisms in my new parish. And you'll be glad to know I didn't drop the baby."

In the sacristy, the hall and even the parking lot, Jerry could hear the whispers. The words were almost always the same.

"Father Jerry's back."

"To stay?"

"No. Just to visit. It's good to see him, though."

He didn't mention it, but Jerry thrived on the validation he heard in those words. He thrived, too, on reconnecting with his friends.

For some reason, Father Tran's house always seemed more like a home to Jerry than did his own. When he was living at Saint Mark's, he was in the same duplex. The two apartments were identical. Yet, Tran's always seemed homier, warmer somehow, more inviting. *Got to be the lighting,* he thought as he took off his jacket and settled into one of the plush arm chairs. *Something about the lights.*

"Feel good to be back, Jerry?"

"It does. It's great to have people to talk with too. I share space with an old Lab named Peaches. Did I tell you? Great company, but she doesn't talk much." Tran laughed for close to a minute. *I should do standup comedy in South East Asia*, Jerry thought. *I'd kill every night.*

"That's good. When she starts talking it's time for you to get out of there."

The doorbell rang. Rob Hamden stood in the doorway with two steaming pizza boxes in his hands and a dark, quart bottle in a bag under his arm. "Two meat-lovers with everything," the man almost sang, "hot from Zella's."

"Comfort food—the epitome of it," Jerry laughed. And as they opened the boxes he thought about how the pizza was just that. Thick gobs of mozzarella melded with sausage and pepperoni, tying them happily to the thin, chewy crust. Jerry did take comfort, in all of it. Three hungry men sharing excellent food, and things to talk and laugh about. It made for a sense of comfort as old as time.

"Let me show you guys something," Jerry said, grabbing two napkins to wipe his lips. He hurried out to the old van in the driveway and opened the back. He'd positioned one of the models of the new chapel between some books and towels to keep it stable. Carefully, he lifted it out. He held the miniature chest-high coming through the front door. "What do you think?"

Both men at the table stood and came over to see it. Jerry could see that Tran was impressed. But Rob Hamden was entranced. His eyes both widened and softened in a way that Jerry had never seen before in the decade he'd known the man. "That's gorgeous," Rob breathed, squinting through his glasses at the chapel's glass windows as if he were trying to see inside. "Where'd you get this?"

Jerry placed the model in the center of a side table so they could all see it. "One of my parishioners made it."

"No shi . . that's amazing." Rob Hamden's eyes stayed glued to the tiny windows. "I've been into model railroading since I was about eight. I know about scale buildings. And this is primo."

"What church is that?" Father Tran asked the question as he grabbed the last slice of pizza and enfolded it in a napkin.

"That's our new chapel at Saint Joseph's," Jerry said. "That's what we're going to build." He'd never said it before, not out loud, not to other people. "Ballpark, Rob, what would you pay for a miniature like that?"

Rob Hamden shrugged and picked up the miniature chapel again. He turned it from side to side in front of his eyes. "A hundred bucks, give or take."

"You're serious?"

"Oh, yeah. This is perfect 1/16 scale. That's what all the collectors want."

*

Once Rob had left, Tran took the wine bottle that he'd been given from the paper bag and showed it to Jerry. A white label read HAMDEN ESTATES—WHITE. The words had been written in a steady hand with a blue Magic Marker. "Hamden Estates?" Jerry asked. "What's that mean?"

"That's Rob's backyard." Tran was already twisting a corkscrew into the top of the bottle. "That guy must have twenty different hobbies, and he's good at most of them. Let's give this a try."

"You know, when I drove up here yesterday morning I felt like I was getting away from something. I saw coming back here as a kind of R and R."

"Makes sense," Tran said. "You were here for ten years. All your friends are here." He tasted the white wine and put down the glass with a grimace.

"And, believe me, I love that. But now, I can't wait to get back. Crazy, isn't it?"

"It's not crazy," Father Tran said stuffing the cork back into the bottle and sliding it into the dark nether regions of the kitchen cabinet. "That's where God wants you. And you know it now. That's all."

*

Her father was already there, waiting for her. He was standing on the corner of Light and Fayette with his hands in the pockets of a new black Pierre Cardin suit. Michelle saw him smile at her like the iconic Cheshire cat as she pulled the Miata into the pay lot. "Look at this handsome guy!" she joked, happy to drop her keys into her purse now that she'd parked and picked up her ticket.

"I've got a lunch date with a high powered lawyer," Buddy said. "How are you, Hon?"

"I'm okay."

As they started together down the hill Buddy looked over his shoulder at the decade old sports car at the edge of the lot. "Do you ever think about replacing your Miata?"

"No, I don't," she answered, poking a finger into her father's stomach. "You're not the first to ask that. My little car still looks good and she's doing just fine."

Michelle was thrilled to see her father, more thrilled than she expected to be. *Maybe because we had been apart so long.* She knew it was the kind of April morning they both adored. The sun shone in that spring-in-Baltimore way that made all of downtown look new, and clean, and, somehow, magical. *Maybe it's because the sun's been gone so long.* "You're looking amazingly happy, Daddy dearest. Things better at home?"

"Um, yes. Things are much better at home." Buddy looked at her sideways as, without trying, they marched, in perfect step down Light Street. "You haven't talked with your uncle lately?"

"I talked to him yesterday."

"And?"

They stopped for the DON'T WALK at Baltimore Street and were engulfed in the instantly formed, silent crowd waiting to cross. She respected the communal silence until they reached the other curb. "We talked for quite a while—mostly about Carlos and all that." At the same moment they both saw the sign for Burke's and picked up their pace. "He's excited about those miniature church buildings. If he can sell them he can build the new chapel."

"That's it?" Buddy held open the brass-handled door for her.

"That's it."

The two of them slid into one of the dark wood booths and grabbed menus. "Tell me about this again, Buddy said. "He's selling miniature buildings to raise money?"

"Uh huh.

He was running his fingertip down the list of lunch specials as he asked the question. "Whatever happened to Bingo?"

Michelle heaved a sigh of mock frustration as she scanned the same list. "You two are supposed to be brothers," she said. "Will I always have to be your go-between?"

They ordered and Buddy took off his reading glasses to fidget with them on the table. "You really want a cheese omelet? It's kind of late for breakfast."

"I'm in a breakfast mood. What's with all these questions? And what's going on with you and Chloe? Tell all. I want to hear about somebody else's troubles for a change."

Buddy studied the glasses in his fingers as if they were from outer space. "I'm really surprised Jerry didn't tell you," he said.

Michelle knew then why she was there, why her father had called. "What?" she asked, suddenly conscious of a tightness in her facial muscles that she hoped she was hiding. "You're getting married?"

"Yes, we are."

Michelle forced her lips to smile.

"It'll be a minimal ceremony, just us and a judge."

She nodded.

"Be happy for us, Honey. Please. She's a good woman. You'll see that."

"Oh, I am happy for you, Dad. You know what you're doing. And it's not a surprise, really. I guess I always knew you would."

Silence came and swept over their table. The clinks and clatters of silverware on china and snatches of other conversations around them became enormous. When the silence receded, it carried with it their threads of conversation, carried them out into a sea of distance. "So, what's next for you?" Buddy asked, tucking the glasses into his shirt pocket. "Not long-term. I mean like day to day."

"Well, nothing special, Dad. We're having a party—a little party tomorrow night. Just celebrating shutting down the coalition headquarters …" Michelle listened to her own voice trail off. And she watched his expression turn into the Daddy-wants-to-help look that she'd recognized a thousand times since that day when she was five and fell off the front porch into his tomato plants.

"You've been through a car wreck," Buddy said, putting his hand across the table to touch hers, "an emotional car wreck. I know—this on top of everything else. But I had to tell you."

"I'm fine." She pulled her hand back to stir the cold coffee in her cup. Michelle wanted to explain to her father that she wasn't weak, that she was still the strong, competent woman that made him proud.

She wanted to explain to him that lately, at the most unexpected times, an invisible fist seemed to slam into her stomach; and she just couldn't be strong, or smart. That sometimes she couldn't even speak until she caught her breath again. She took a tiny bite of the omelet and looked away. She told him nothing.

"You need to heal, Hon," she heard him say. "Take some time off. You have that option, you know." She looked at him, a blank look. Buddy smiled and shook the ice in his rum and Coke. "If nothing else, have a couple drinks and relax." He put the glass aside, still smiling. "I never thought I'd tell my little girl that. But you know what I'm saying."

"I do," she answered, smiling back. "I'm hearing you, Dad."

*

It was 7:10 when Michelle walked into the Coalition Headquarters for the shut-down party. She couldn't resist mentally comparing it to the first time there, when there was no furniture, no lights or phone, and no encouragement to be found. Tonight she found three long folding tables filled with food and drinks. Someone had finally found a use for the old **STOP 1664** signs, building teepees with them at random around the floor. Red and blue balloons bounced or rolled on the floor around the signs or bobbled in the air at the ends of red ribbons. *And 1664 is just a number again.*

She had on a suit that she hadn't worn since the previous spring. The skirt felt a lot shorter now than she remembered it. Michelle found herself trying to scoot behind one of the 1664 sign structures when Mr. Caruthers ambled up to greet her. Mike Drazinski was already there, in the back office. She saw him bringing out the last of the folding chairs and thought he looked exceptionally businesslike in a new white shirt and well fitting black slacks. "Look at you," she said, putting a hand on his back. "You're here early. You've got everything under control. You're a good man, Mike D."

"Not a problem."

Michelle went with him into the office and glanced back at the open door before pulling a bottle of Seagrams7 from her bag. She put it in the lower right drawer of the gray metal desk. "No, this isn't something I do every day," she said in reply to the young man's questioning look.

"It's a tradition I picked up from my dad. For any life-changing event that comes along he has a shot of whiskey and a piece of fruitcake—always."

"That sounds like something he'd do."

"It's April. I'm pretty sure there's no fruitcake out there. But would you get me a cup of soda?" Mike disappeared and was back in what seemed like seconds with two cups of Coke. "Okaaaay," Michelle said, still looking warily toward the door. She poured a long shot into her cup and touched her Styrofoam to his. "Let's get this party started." She took a long sip of the drink and enjoyed the delicious sense of warmth as the liquor went down her throat. "Oh. That's been a long time coming." Mike continued to hold his cup out to her. "No way. How old are you now?"

"Almost 20."

"Almost 20. Do you have any idea what the penalty is for serving liquor to a minor?"

"You're not really serving it to me. We're just friends, sharing it."

"Well, silly me. I'm sure the judge will understand that." She took a second sip and watched a look of disappointment drift over Mike's face. With a sigh that lasted several seconds she uncapped the bottle again. "This never happened—got it?" She poured a little of the whiskey into his Coke.

"What never happened?"

"Good answer. Now let's go say some goodbyes."

*

"Speech! Speech! Speech!" They all started yelling it when she stepped out of the back office. Mike dragged over one of the ancient wooden chairs for her to stand on. "Um, no. Between that chair and these heels I'll end up in the emergency room." He went to find her a more stable stage. But she remembered too the tightness of her suit. Michelle Miller Ibanez standing on a chair in a short skirt and heels was not an image she wanted to leave in the minds of these people.

"Thanks anyway, Mike," she said, waving off the newer, old chair he'd found. "Standing right here's fine." She looked around and was amazed at how the room full of people became utterly silent. "I feel like we've been through a war together," she began, "all of us." That brought

255

whoops, claps and about three times as much sound as she would have thought possible. "Now the war's over. And we won!" More cheering. *I could get used to this part,* she thought. "This Coalition Headquarters is shutting down tomorrow. And we're here to celebrate that. We can go back to our lives and … pick up where we left off. Just know you've done a wonderful thing, keeping this neighborhood alive and vibrant. And I'm going to miss seeing every one of you."

"You did it," a man shouted.

"No, *we* did it. Have some of this good food and enjoy yourselves." The good karma around her was almost palpable. Michelle drank it in like sweet wine and let it warm her. She felt like she had shaken more hands that night than she had in her lifetime. She found herself craving more.

A stocky, middle aged woman with dark-framed glasses ran up to Michelle waving a small hand in front of her like a fan. "Ms. Ibanez, I finally get to meet you. Doug and Jennifer talk about you so much."

"Doug and Jennifer?"

"Yes." The woman pulled the two high school students in close to her. Michelle saw the curly haired resemblance in the three of them.

"Oh my god, you're brother and sister," she laughed. "I never knew that. Did you, Mike?" *Doug and Jennifer, they have names. For eight months they've been the high school kids. Of course they have names.*

"No," Mike laughed. "Never had a clue."

She saw Mrs. Vitro looking ecstatic as she gave out muffins with both hands. Mr. Caruthers and Mrs. True leaned against a wall and chatted like senior diplomats at the UN. *And the lion will lie down with the lamb. What a wonderful way to end all this.* As the evening went on, Michelle had the feeling she was coming out of an emotional coma and looking around at a new, vivid world. Positive vibes filled her like a wonder drug.

*

It was after 10:00, and most of them had gone home. Once it started, the exodus accelerated as if the entire Coalition suddenly remembered they had families, homes and lives to live in the morning. She could count the people remaining on her fingers with two thumbs and a forefinger left over. Michelle fairly skipped back to the room with the old desk in it.

Mike followed her and she pointed to the door with one hand while she opened the bottom drawer with the other. "Now I can have a drink for real," she grinned. Mike Drazinski leaned his massive shoulders into the doorway, looking out into the bigger room, just once glancing back over his shoulder. She chuckled realizing that he had the same expression on his face that little Carlos had when she'd caught him raiding the Whitman Sampler box. Michelle retrieved the bottle of Seagram's from the drawer and waved it under her chin. He turned his eyes back to the hall as she poured a long shot of it into her Coke and propped herself on the corner of the gray metal desk.

He looked back a second time. She did the bottle wave again, and motioned him over with a crooked index finger. "Give me your cup." Mike made himself a cover between her and the door, his leg touching hers. She took his nearly empty Styrofoam cup and filled it half full with the whiskey.

"Hey," the young man laughed, "I don't want that much." He grabbed her left arm and she laughingly took the cup in her right hand, holding it away from him.

"So, you don't want it?"

"Yes, I want it. Just not that much." He put his left hand on her leg and leaned forward with his right to try and retrieve his drink. His large hand felt surprisingly good on her thigh, and Michelle decided in an instant not to remove it.

"You've got great skin."

Michelle laughed out loud, almost spitting out the mouthful of Coke and whiskey. "I have great skin? Did you really just say that?" She handed him the cup, but Mike didn't back away. His leg still touched her calf, and the hand had begun to massage her thigh. "Where'd that come from—great skin?"

"I don't know," the boy said softly, his face close to hers, "you just do."

"Great skin for an older lady, huh?"

His body leaned in even closer. His blue eyes looked deep into hers. "Oh, it's not that ..."

Then, his lips were on hers. A part of Michelle wondered why they were there. She wondered how that could have possibly happened. Another part of her wondered at the fact that his lips were so soft. And warm, warmer than she'd ever imagined they'd be.

CHAPTER 36

APRIL 19, 2010
JUST THIS DAY

A large, middle-aged black woman manned the reception desk outside the office of Barry A. Levine, Justice of the Peace, Anne Arundel County. The purple suit jacket she wore had padded shoulders that made her body seem as wide as the expansive, shiny circular desk in front of her.

"Hi. Buddy Miller," he said. "We're scheduled to be married this morning."

The woman looked up at them, owl-like, through large, square glasses. She pulled open a tome of a ledger and scanned wordlessly down the page, the quintessential gatekeeper. "Miller–Lagrange," she said at last. "You're on for 10:30."

"Great," Buddy answered with a smile. The knot of tension that had existed in his chest since his eyes first opened at 4:00 am partially untied itself. The gatekeeper looked at him, then at Chloe, and then back at him, unspoken questions shouting from her eyes.

Oh, it's not smart, lady, I know that. Yes, she's half my age. But it's not like the first time. You think I don't remember that? I remember all of it. Here I am years, lifetimes, eons, later, and I remember every word, every feeling, every nuance of that day.

Watershed days are like that, good or bad; they're etched on your brain in excruciating detail. That cheap brown suit from Sears. Those new brown shoes pinching my feet.

Funny, if I met that young version of myself today I wouldn't know what to say to him. We wouldn't know what to say to each other. The real mystery—in many ways, I still am that man.

"I'm gonna' need your blood test paperwork."

The knot in Buddy's chest snapped tight again. He watched the smile on Chloe's face droop into a frown. "We don't have it," the prospective bride said. "The people at the clinic told me we don't get that. They said they'd send it directly to you."

The big woman stared at them, shook her head, and frowned. *Here we go,* Buddy thought. She clicked her tongue, turned, and rolled her chair toward the file cabinets behind the desk like a destroyer steaming into harbor. "Have a seat over there," she called back to them.

Different courthouse, different era, but it feels so much the same. I can still see Brena with that old green dress and that yellow flowered wreath in her hair. If not for that day there'd be no Michelle. I don't want to think about how empty life would be without her. Hell, I wouldn't have even found Bonsai, the most faithful dog known to man.

Who else was there? Oh, Christ, yes. Her asshole parents. They were probably younger then than I am now. Tommy was there, tall and strong and young—and alive. And Jerry always being Jerry. I think that guy was born a priest.

We must have looked like idiots to other people. How young and hopeful we must have looked too. Too dumb to know better.

He and Chloe were halfway across the carpeted floor to the bench when the big woman called over her shoulder again. "Ms. Lagrange, where are your flowers?"

"We don't have any," Chloe called back. "We're keeping things simple. Very simple."

The gatekeeper sighed and turned, mumbling to the file cabinets. "Usually there are some flowers."

Another bench to wait on. I remember that big wooden bench in the Towson courthouse. Waiting on that bench with Cliff from American Galvanizing. Back then we wondered if the bride would even show. Cliff. Thin hair in a ponytail. And those gold disco chains dangling around his neck like a shaman's talismans. Wonder what became of that poor bastard.

He glanced over at the woman he loved. She perched, straight and prim, on the green Velour bench.

Look at her, like a blond Jackie Kennedy. Perfect white jacket and shoes. Some things are nothing like back in the day.

First time for Chloe, though. God, I want to make this day good for her. The idea of forever, a lifetime, even a year is too overwhelming. Isolating the day helps. Just this day! I want to make her happy. I want to make her feel secure. Right now, more than anything, I want that. Just making her day is a place to start.

At 10:20 their neighbors, Bill and Mary arrived in the hallway. Mary hugged the almost bride and gushed about how gorgeous she looked. Bill wouldn't stop pumping Buddy's hand. He went on with what seemed like the world's longest run-on sentence about traffic and the lack of parking. "Sorry we cut it so close."

"Hey, I'm just glad you're here, man."

"So," Mary began like a second grade teacher with a new class, "I want to hear your vows; you were going to make up your own vows."

"We decided not to," Chloe said, dropping her hand onto the back of Buddy's. "We're keeping it real simple."

"I guess I decided not to," Buddy added. "Couldn't come up with anything."

I should tell them I even called my brother about it. I did like what he told me, about weddings in ancient Rome. They called each other Gaius, the equivalent of Mr., and Gaia, Mrs. I don't know why, but something about that epitomizes respect—it's timeless. It's simple and fundamental and authentic. At the same time, kind of mysterious. But I wasn't able to turn it into a vow.

"Your brother had some ideas," Chloe said, as if reading his thoughts.

"Yeah, Jerry's the best at what he does."

She smiled and squeezed his hand. "Sometimes I think you actually like your brother. Wouldn't it be silly to wait ten years before you call him again?"

"Funny," Buddy chuckled, "coming from you that makes sense."

With an ominous "Humph!" the big receptionist edged out from behind the desk and banged through the double doors at the end of the hall. It was 10:25. Buddy felt the knot in his chest grow and get even tighter. When the office door of Barry A Levine failed to open at 10:30 the knot grew even more. The receptionist hadn't reappeared. All four sets of eyes were fixed on the door. By 10:32 the knot had become a large, hairy fist gripping his heart.

A diminutive man with thick, gray hair, a large nose and a bow tie opened the door at 10:33. "C'mon in," he said simply. Once the four had trooped through the door the small man closed it behind them. "Buddy and Chloe?" he asked, taking their arms and guiding them to the center of the room. "Good. I have my bride and groom." He glanced at the other couple. "And I have my witnesses?" Bill and Mary nodded dutifully and folded their hands in front of themselves. "Let me grab my book and we'll get started."

Buddy glanced sidelong at Chloe but for once couldn't read her expression. "How're you feeling?"

"I feel like Julia Roberts," she whispered.

"*Pretty Woman?*"

"*Runaway Bride.*"

Buddy heard the office door open and close noisily behind him. Out of the corner of his eye he saw the purple bulk of the receptionist's jacket. He saw what looked like a sheaf of paper waving in her thick right hand. The black receptionist rushed up next to them as they waited. In her left hand she carried six perfect long stemmed pink roses. Gently, she bent Chloe's arm and cradled the roses in the crook of it. "A bride got to have some flowers," she muttered. Buddy saw Chloe blink. He saw the tiniest of tears form in the corners of them. "Thank you," he whispered to the gatekeeper and meant it with all his heart.

*

"Do you, Buddy Miller ..."

Where and when I am Gaius ...

"Take this woman, Chloe Lagrange ..."

There and then you are Gaia.

CHAPTER 37

April 20–21, 2010

Fellow Travelers

She didn't have to do it that day. Michelle visited the coalition headquarters one final time. She went there to make a last walkthrough and return the keys to the owner. She didn't have to walk there either. But it killed some time. On the way, she took a few extra minutes to appreciate the morning sun on the harbor and the sweet feel of April after the worst winter in a century. To her, April had always been synonymous with new beginnings. She made it a point to walk slowly, to make this task last. She made it a point not to look at Bunky's Gym when she passed it.

Michelle had turned out the lights and was starting back toward the front of the headquarters when she heard a tapping on the door. Mrs. True stood in the open doorway. She had on a new flowered dress, a pink one. Mr. Caruthers was with her, looking dapper with his hands behind his back.

"Hi," Mrs. True bubbled.

"Well, hi! Are you guys following me?"

"No. We were going to the bakery and saw the door open."

"I'm just closing up, giving back the keys, all that, you know."

"We're going to miss you so much, Michelle. Come around sometimes."

She thought about the irony of those two together, and how pleasant it was to see them. "I'll miss you too. We were all like fellow travelers on a long journey. But now the journey's over."

*

The walk back to the law office, up Elliot Street to Smallwood and over, it was uphill, all of it. On a cool April morning she figured the walk should take her forty-five minutes. She made it take an hour. Still, he was there. Mike Drazinski sat on the stone steps waiting for her. His eyes were fixed on the street, waiting to spot her Miata. He didn't see her walking until she was only a few feet away.

Oh, please, she thought. *Please tell me that's not what it looks like.* But it was. He held a long-stemmed red rose in the big fingers of his left hand. "C'mon in," she said, ignoring his smile and the outstretched rose as she walked around him to open the door. She went through the office suite, turning on the lights with Mike close behind her. She went into her own office, heavily dropping her briefcase on her desk as if she was alone.

Mike opened with, "I was wondering why no one answered the door. Where's Joanne today?"

"She's gone."

"Gone?"

"Did I stutter? She won't be coming back here again."

The young man took several seconds to digest it. "Oh my god. It was her? It was Joanne all along?"

"Is that for Lisa?" she asked, acknowledging the rose in his hand for the first time.

"Lisa? I haven't even seen Lisa for a month. It's for you. I just wanted to brighten your day a little."

"Lisa's smart and sweet. She's a very nice young woman, Mike."

He laid the rose on the desk then, carefully, placing it diagonally across a blank pad of legal paper. "I know about your husband and about the things that happened." Michelle didn't answer. "There are things I wanted to say before but couldn't. Now I can." She stared at the boy, saying nothing. "I've been in love with you since the first time I saw you. You were carrying that old computer into your dad's house. Do you remember that day?"

"I'm trying not to hurt your feelings here, Mike."

"Didn't you hear what I just said?" He put an open hand across her desk. Michelle leaned back in her chair and refused to look at the open hand. "You were a friend to me in a difficult time. I'm grateful for that. We were fellow travelers for a while. And it was a hell of a trip we were on, Mike." She came around the desk and put her hands on her hips, the principal sending him back to class. "But the trip's over." She was tempted to shake his hand, but thought better of it. She maintained her physical distance from him. He took the hint.

"When we kissed, it was a different story." His voice came out in a rough whisper. She saw the intensity in his eyes but heard too the desperation. "You can't deny there's something special with us."

"I don't know what you *think* happened the other night. A kiss, yeah. But the truth is, nothing happened."

"Something happened for me."

Michelle shook her head. "No it didn't, not really. And there is no *us*, Mike. Never was. It's that simple."

He turned without a word; and she watched him go. She thought how Mike Drazinski looked even taller than he had that day in her father's dining room the previous fall. The back of his wide, white shirt seemed to stretch across the entire hallway. She'd miss that back. His steps quickened as he traversed the hall and turned the corner. She listened to the front door open, buzz, and then close. A cold silence settled like fog over the law office.

"Fellow travelers ... the trip's over," she murmured. "Where do I even get this stuff from?"

*

If Buddy had tried to verbalize just how his world had changed, he couldn't do it. But the difference was undeniable. Chloe had hurried off to work with a quick kiss, as always. The cold April rain continued off and on in waves as it had all morning. He stared out the window at the rain as he stood by the kitchen counter and swiveled his head, just to savor the miracle of his neck being pain free. *Pain free* had been his watch words for a week; and yet the novelty of it was still there. Physically, the world around him looked much like the old one. But the new world was like a diamond in a new setting, same planet in a brand new universe. Hope and potential seemed to light up the air around him. He smiled and poured another cup of coffee.

Buddy wasn't dancing as he carried his coffee to the office, but his movements were something close to it. Mike Drazinski wasn't in his chair, hunched over his laptop as he habitually was at that time of the morning. The normally cluttered desk and work table were almost bare. And the cardboard boxes Mike kept under the table were missing. "Humph," Buddy sniffed, turning over a picture that lay face down on one of the white book shelves. Michelle smiled at him from under her graduation cap. "Hey—I've been looking all over for this picture." He propped it up on the shelf the way it should have been.

Going to the window, he lifted the Venetian blind with his finger to see Mike packing something into the back of his old, blue Volvo. "What the hell?" he mumbled. Grabbing a jacket from the back of a chair, he went out to the driveway. "Hey, Iron Mike, what's going on?"

"I'm moving out, Mr. Miller." The young man shoved a pile of text books to the side in the small trunk of his car. "It's amazing how much of my own stuff I accumulated here in a couple of months."

"Sooo, you're quitting? I thought you had another month of school."

"I do."

"Well, I guess you just want to concentrate on finals now."

"Yeah. Yeah, that's it." Mike continued rearranging the fat text books in the back of the car. Buddy began to help him.

"That's good. That's smart. I understand, but damn, Mike, I hate to see you go."

The rain had been ebbing but started again in earnest.

"I know you've paid me for one more day. I'll do that," Mike said. "And I wanted to say congrats to you on your wedding too."

Buddy nodded and wedged the last of the cardboard boxes into the car's tiny trunk. "Thanks, Mike."

"I always knew you and Ms. Lagrange belonged together, even when you were pissed at each other."

Buddy had to laugh. He laughed more at the boy's simple sincerity than at what he'd said. "I think you're right, Iron Mike. What's Michelle got you doing now?" Mike was silent, looking out into the trees as

The New Road

the rain drops pelted his hair flat onto his head. "Or are you finished downtown?"

"Oh, I'm finished. She doesn't want to see me again. She made that real clear."

In the second it took him to close the car's trunk, Buddy realized what had happened. He felt foolish for not seeing it earlier. "There was something going on—you and Michelle?"

"I loved her. Still do, I guess." Mike wiped the rain from his face with a wide hand.

"Oh boy." Buddy breathed more than spoke the words. They both stared out at the dripping oak trees and were silent. "I'm going to say something that will sound stupid to you right now," Buddy began. "Sometimes we have to be cruel to be kind."

Mike Drazinski sighed and thrust his hands into the pockets of his jeans, looking like a giant ten-year-old who'd just been told to give up his Xbox.

"You're not going to understand right away," Buddy said. "And I don't even know exactly what happened. But I know my daughter, and she was very kind to you."

"I've got some things to wrap up." Mike's voice had dropped an octave, down into his business tone. "I'll back up all your files, get everything in order before I leave—I'll give you one more day of work."

"Uh—yeah. I do need you for that day. But forget all that backup stuff, okay?" Buddy pulled up the hood of his jacket over his head and imitated the younger man's posture, with his hands thrust deep into his pockets. "Look, can you drive a truck? A big truck?"

267

CHAPTER 38

APRIL 22, 2010

YOUNG MAN WITH CASH

Michelle decided it was fun to feel like a Harbor Place tourist for a little while. It was a game to play while she waited for her Uncle Jerry. She liked the funky hats at Hatsinthebelfry. And she'd just decided she liked the scarves too. The Klimt pattern didn't work for her at all—too patchwork and hippie looking. She picked up a William Morris floral and draped it over her shoulder. The pattern screamed *old lady*. She pulled it off in an instant. A bright yellow scarf drew her like a magnet to the opposite side of the shop. She pictured herself wearing it with her blue dress and with her blue suit. She knew she wanted it. "Uncle Jerr!" she yelled when she saw him flit by in the hall.

Jerry turned and smiled but had to dance around an obstacle course of racks and shoppers to get to her. "There you are," he said, taking his niece's arms. "I thought you said we'd meet on the corner."

"I did, but I got distracted." She led him by his arms over to the yellow scarf. "Is this cool or what?"

"That's you," he smiled, looking at the label, "Manhattan Deco." Michelle grabbed up an orange one in the same pattern and held it in front of her as she looked in the mirror. "How are you doing, Michelle?" Jerry asked the question as if they were alone in the store.

She exhaled, an elongated breath, and still holding the scarves, dropped her hands to her sides. "I'm fine."

"Where's Little Carlos today?"

"He's with his granddad ... and Chloe, his new grandma." Jerry started to laugh. Then they both laughed. Michelle wiped her eye with her right sleeve. She took her uncle's hand and held on tight to it. "I have to admit, it is kind of funny. Six months ago I would have sooner handed my kid off to Charles Manson." Jerry nodded and waited, giving her a chance to talk. "Dad says I should take some time off."

"That's your call."

"Honestly, Uncle Jerr, most of the time I really am fine. But every now and then ... I look around and ask: 'What the hell just happened here?'"

Jerry rubbed the silken yellow scarf between the thumb and forefinger of his left hand. "Remember, things that happen to us are just that, things that happen. Don't let them change who you are." He took the edge of the yellow scarf and draped it over her shoulder. "Get this one," he said. She backed up from the mirror while holding up both scarves in front of her. "It's a complicated process, Michelle, living a full life."

"Now there's the understatement of the century."

"Friends become enemies. Enemies become friends. Sometimes the biggest surprises are found in the things we learn about ourselves."

"You wanna' get some lunch?"

"Why do you think I drove over from the eastern shore?"

Michelle spun around to the sales woman behind her. "I'll take both of these," she said.

*

The trip back, the hypnotic, mechanical process of driving, it gave Jerry a chance to think. He weighed the pros and cons of the last eight months and contemplated how far he'd come at St. Joe's Parish. One of the biggest pros was the warm feeling he got when he pictured the rows of gleaming new miniature church buildings that filled all the hanging wall shelves in the church's barn-like garage. He thought about how Franz's industry and perseverance alone constituted a miracle. The old man had managed to crank out a nonstop stream of new and more intricate models faster than Jerry could get the materials to him. Both of the Shoenmires beamed with the joy of being needed. The process was as beautiful to watch as the result.

If he could manage to sell those little buildings, the dream of a new chapel could become a reality. "If it's too good to be true...." He cautioned himself not to invest too heavily in a dream. *But it's been done before*, he argued back to his negative side. *Regular people building cathedrals—tossing bricks from hand to hand while they sang hymns. And what is a church building but a solid expression of faith?* "Don't underestimate what the Holy Spirit can do."

Approaching the bridge, Jerry started repeating a phrase he'd heard years before. "Crossing the Bay Bridge—like going from one world to another." He couldn't remember who'd said it or the context of the conversation; but the words rang true for him on a couple of levels that April afternoon. The eastern shore of the Chesapeake was historically considered rural, and the other urban. That hadn't changed since the 1600s. He knew that even the mindset of the people changed once your tires touched asphalt on the eastern side. As often as he'd seen it, Jerry's heart jumped as he rounded the curve on Ritchie Highway and saw the four mile long span over the sparkling bay. The other end of the bridge was too far away to make out.

*

Even before Jerry turned the van into the church parking lot he saw the top of the truck. It was a big, box-like truck, the size of a small moving van. The truck was pulling away from the side door of the garage by the time he neared the church. He could see the hands of the driver flashing around the steering wheel as the big vehicle was maneuvered out of the narrow spot. Jerry had to pull the old, gray van as close as possible to the side of the gravel drive to keep from being sideswiped.

He hadn't been able to see the driver's face for the glare of the sun on the windshield. The truck looked new. It was when he realized there were no signs or markings of any kind on it that a wave of panic made his blood freeze. He stopped the van, threw open the door and ran after the white truck. It was already making the turn, out onto Route 50. Jerry could just make out the license plate numbers. "Damn," he yelled, running back up the drive, breathing heavily, mostly from fear.

It looked like 779JHV. He repeated the plate number to himself. *Maybe it was JHG.* "Damn! Damn!"

He ran back, past the van with its door still open and the keys still in it, up the drive and to the office door. "Carla, what the hell happened?" The stodgy secretary stood next to her desk decorously holding a large black gym bag in front of her as if it were a monstrous purse.

"He took all the little houses, Father."

"Who, Carla? Who? What do you mean, took them?"

"He didn't say his name."

Jerry turned and bolted back out the door in a single motion. He ran, panic clutching at his heart, to the barn-like garage beside the church. He threw open the tin-covered door. In the dark interior, he could see only empty shelves, bare concrete and some scraps of white paper on the floor. Emptiness hit him like a wave. He turned to see Carla standing behind him, still clutching the ridiculous gym bag. He had to consciously restrain himself from grabbing and shaking her. "Why did you let him take them, Carla? What happened here?"

"I gave them to him, Father."

"What?"

Carla dropped the gym bag in the dust and clumsily pulled at the zipper. It opened to reveal thick stacks of what looked like $100 dollar bills. "The big young man had cash. He bought all the houses." She straightened to her full five feet. She looked indignant. "I'm not dumb. I counted the money, Father. He had more than enough. He donated it for the models, all of them."

Chapter 39

April 23, 2010
Anywhere You Want

She had an hour to kill before meeting Trudy Spanno. Michelle convinced herself that going into the townhouse was a practical thing to do, that she needed to take one last walk around to make sure all of her things had been moved out.

It was only when she closed the front door behind her that it all hit home. That echo reverberating through the empty rooms and up the stairs, made the leaving of it all too immediate and real. Intellectually, she she'd known she would have to take her son and move on. But it was in that moment she knew it in her gut. She'd never be back in that house again. The feelings boomed over her like a rogue wave. In that instant she felt the loss, not just of a house but of a way of life, and of her most precious dreams. For a minute she couldn't speak. "Too much sadness at once," she whispered into the silence of the empty house. *Small bites of sorrow. Take it all in at the same time and your heart will burst. You'll go insane.*

She was drawn upstairs to what had been the prayer space, barren now without the kneeler or the crucifix. Her eyes went to the jagged section of the carpet beneath the window. She remembered how angry she'd been with Nefferkitty the day the cat had done that. Today, both her cat and her son were staying with *Grampa* and *Miss Chloe* and loving it.

She went to the window and stared out at the harbor. The joyful April sun played on the wavelets, mocking her feelings. "Gotta get out of here," she said, as if explaining her actions to herself. "Judge Judy's probably already waiting."

*

Even as Michelle left to meet with Judge Spanno, Joanne Wicks was making the longest journey ever down Lombard Street. She punched off the car radio and fumed. It seemed every light was turning red to spite her. It was a sunny Friday afternoon, warm for April. At every corner a motley stream of pedestrians surged before the hood of her car, flooding across the crosswalk in both directions. She banged her fists on the steering wheel as if trying to scare them away. "It's the middle of the afternoon! Don't you assholes work?" Periodically, she would glance over at the long yellow envelope that sat next to her on the leather seat like an unwelcome passenger.

When the tower of her condos came into sight her level of frustration jumped exponentially. "I need to talk to him," she said to the envelope. "It can't be. He'll be able to explain it to me." After what seemed like hours, she screeched into her parking spot, slammed the car door behind her and was halfway to the elevator when she remembered the envelope. She ran back to get it and began again toward the elevator. She was clenching the envelope tight enough to make her hand ache.

She burst through the door of the condo, dropping her purse to the floor as she walked. She ripped the sheaf of paper from the envelope while taking long, powerful steps toward the bedroom. "Carlos," she began, "this separation agreement, I read it once and then read it again and again. Please tell me what this is about."

Carlos leaned back in the king-sized bed, naked except for his red striped boxer shorts. "You're the lawyer. You tell me. What's it say?" Mechanically, he popped salted almonds into his mouth at regular intervals. His eyes stayed fixed on Boston and Miami. It was late April and the playoffs were nearly over.

"You and Michelle had a prenup, Carlos. You never told me that. It says you signed this prenup."

"Yeah." He said it with a *tell me something I don't know* tone. "Before we got married, I signed it. But since we were married in the State of Maryland, I get half."

For a moment Joanne suspected that he was joking with her. She almost told him to be serious, that this was important—to both of them. Then the moment passed. Her heart began to waft down into her stomach. She laid the dog-eared sheets of paper on the dresser and took a step closer to the bed. "Umm, no. It says, very clearly, that you're entitled to only half of the assets acquired since your marriage."

When a beer commercial filled the flat screen he looked up at her. His fingers continued to fish for the last of the almonds in the can. "No, you're wrong. She's got something like four and a half million dollars. I've told you that. Not to worry. I get half."

"Correct me if I'm mistaken," Joanne went on. The sound of her lawyer voice kicking in helped her keep the fear in check. "The townhouse in The Moorings makes up the bulk of what the two of you have acquired together over the last five plus years. That house, right now, is worth about half of what you paid for it."

Carlos put down the empty can of nuts then and stared up at her. His deep brown eyes seemed to be searching hers. She thought he had begun to comprehend. In an instant, she mentally recapped the passionate plans they'd made together, their plans of intermingling his career with hers, the plans for getting that house on the Severn that they both adored.

"That's not right," he said. "I get half. Period."

She bent down close to him and mouthed each word slowly, distinctly. "Carlos. Don't you see what's happened here? We're fucked."

The commercials were over. Carlos Ibanez ignored her and threw his long arm across a plump, mauve pillow to retrieve the remote. His eyes turned cold as they locked back onto the flat TV screen. "You're wrong."

"Oh, Jesus," Joanne whispered. She fell, rather than sat, down onto the bench by the dresser. She tried to speak, but was only able to stare at the dark haired stranger in boxer shorts that she suddenly found sprawled on her bed in the afternoon sun. "Oh, Jesus."

*

It was 2:15 when Agnes Vitro bustled across the room to wipe off the window table for Michelle and Judge Spanno. Michelle marveled at the irony of it. It was the same table she had shared with Vance Berg eight months before. "Karma," she said quietly.

"Hmm?"

"Nothing, Judge. Good choice, the blueberry muffin. They're wonderful."

Trudy Spanno broke off a bite-sized piece from the top of the muffin and popped it into her mouth. "The City Council seat for the fifteenth district will be wide open in the fall," she said.

"City Council seat?"

"Oh, please, girl. Like you didn't know." Michelle's eyes crinkled into the beginnings of a sad smile, but she didn't answer. "A little footwork this summer, and it's pretty much yours." The judge took off the entire top of the muffin and pushed away the paper pastry cup before she went on. "Let's be honest, I was pulling for you through this whole thing. But, being real, I didn't think you had the proverbial snowball's chance in hell of surviving that hearing."

"I sensed you felt that way, ever since the day you came up to Canton. I still feel bad about that."

"Come on. Remember who you're talking to. I'm on the Roads Commission. If I didn't get called an old bitch at least once a day I'd figure I'm not doing my job." Judge Spanno had begun to gesture with the muffin top as she spoke. "You didn't just survive that hearing, you killed in there. And it was all you, Michelle, all charisma and chutzpah." She took another bite of the muffin and continued to wave what was left of it. "By the way, that thing about commute times in the various cities—that was genius."

Michelle kept picturing her husband's face, how it must have looked on that last morning, the anger in his eyes. She saw again the crumpled envelope on the table. *Where was all my charisma then?* "Thanks, Trudy."

"City Council and then the legislature. A year or two, and that could lead to a Senate seat."

Michele shook her head and took a sip from the blue china cup. "I was sort of with you at the beginning there. But come on—Senate seat?"

"I've seen what you can do. Everybody, I mean *everybody* in the State House knows your name now. And Schnee, let's just say I know about some world class shit in His Majesty's portfolio. I don't see another term in his future. That's all I'm saying."

You've got the world by the ass. Michelle was remembering her father's words from her graduation day, a decade ago, several lifetimes ago. *You've got the world by the ass, Michelle,* he'd said. *You just don't know it yet.*

She was looking out the window at a young couple passing on the sidewalk. They looked like college kids. The young man had his arm around the girl's shoulders. He was pulling her as tightly to him as he could and still keep walking. The girl smiled a Mona Lisa smile and put her hand in the back pocket of the man's faded jeans. Michelle kept watching them through the window. She watched them slow stepping and holding each other in that dance that only young lovers can do well. She watched the couple until they turned the corner and disappeared out of her sight.

Then she asked the question. "So, where do I go now, Trudy—from here?"

"From here, Michelle Miller Ibanez, I'd say you can go pretty much anywhere you want."